Forsaken

Realm of The Forsaken Book 1

This book is part of The Codes Of Creation Multi-verse

Arlie Sheelin

FORSAKEN

ISBN: 978-1-7777564-5-1

Edited by Dennis Doty

http://www.dennisdotywebsite.com/editing.html

Cover by: Steven Novak

http://novakillustration.com

FIRST EDITION: April/2022

https://www.arliesheelin.com[1]

---

1.   https://www.arliesheelin.com/

To Mary and Brandy

Here's to our friendship:

Deeper than the ocean, beautiful as the stars, fiercely loyal, and filled with soul-healing laughter

Author's Note

CURRAN'S JOURNEY IS about survival, strength, determination, resilience, forgiveness, and hope. Please be aware that this story deals with war, genocide, torture, betrayal, abduction, slavery, sexual abuse, violence, and sexual situations. If you are sensitive to this kind of subject matter, please be mindful of your mental health. I wish you well in your own journey of survival, strength, determination, resilience, forgiveness, and hope.

You can find content warnings for all my books on my website. www.arliesheelin.com[2]

---

2.   http://www.arliesheelin.com

Dear Reader

WELCOME TO THE SECOND series in The Codes of Creation Multiverse. Forsaken is the first book in the Realm of The Forsaken Series, which takes place in Dimensions Five, with journey's to Dimensions Twenty-one, and Thirty-seven of this multiverse.

Dimension Three is the home of the Mystic Havyn Dimensions series. The first book for this series —The Ways Of Light— will be released next.

Dimension Two is the home of The Zemyneah Experiment Series. You can find links on my website to The Way Maker, book 1 of this series, published in July 2021

These three books —The Way Maker, Forsaken, and The Ways of Light— happen simultaneously in this multiverse series.

Please note that The Way Maker, book 1 of The Zemyneah Experiment Series, contains a prologue that is important to all the books.

The three series are the beginnings of a vast multiverse of sci-fi/fantasy stories. I hope you enjoy the adventures, and misadventures of my heroes and heroines. Just watch out for the dragons.

One more thing. I'm Canadian, therefore you will find that I use Canadian spelling and grammar. Thank you for your understanding and kindness.

~Arlie

https://www.arliesheelin.com[1]

---

1. https://www.arliesheelin.com/

Part One

SAREHIRI WAS A WORLD of sunshine, deep green forests, roses, and brave warriors. The Dark Elves were born of integrity and joy and with souls steeped in adventure. Their lives were lived with principles and honor and courage— even in the face of the most callous betrayal.

Chapter One

STAR DATE: 20573.05.23

Dimension Five

Sarehiri

The Dark Elven home world

CURRAN WALKED INTO the War Room in the Spirit Warrior's compound after his briefing. The Spirit Warriors were a specialized unit of the Dark Elf Military. They were the ones that took the riskiest assignments, the ones that put their lives on the line attempting the impossible.

He planted his feet apart, dark eyes hard as he looked at his men. His hands fisted as he thought about the news he had to give them. Tonight was supposed to be a night of celebration. He and his team of Spirit Warriors were to be decorated for their bravery by the King, and they'd wear those metals with pride, if they survived to receive them.

He knew his men, knew that they'd accepted the honors with good natured discomfort. They would enjoy the accolades that came with their newfound fame though they had never asked for any kind of recognition.

But, just minutes ago, the bastards in charge of the military informed him that his team had one last mission to complete before they could hang up their laser swords.

His second in command, Falcon Keyon, stood by his twin brother Flint. They were tall, muscular men with long brown hair, blue-grey eyes, and so alike that they were often confused for one another until you got to know them. They stood in silence, as was their way, their arms crossed over their chests, waiting for his orders. And by the gods, he hated to give these orders.

"I've just come from a meeting with Commander Rav'nor." Falcon turned to look at him, and he could see the questions in his eyes. Fuck, he'd had questions too. "We've been assigned a final mission. I've been told they expect us back in time for tonight's award ceremony."

Falcon shook his head. "Do they have any idea what goes into planning a mission?"

Curran shrugged. "They should. I don't know what the fuck they thought we could do with this short of a notice. I argued that this was a mission for the new team, but fuck if they would listen to me."

"Give me the details," Falcon growled, his expression tight.

"It's a simple retrieval mission."

Flint joined into the discussion at that point. "Simple? Since when do they send Spirit Warriors to do simple retrievals?"

Curran shook his head and shoved a hand through his close-cropped curly hair, a flush of anger touching his brown skin. "From what they said, King Quilar is desperate to get the last of his debt paid off."

Falcon's jaw clenched. "As if we haven't risked life and limb enough with the fucking mercenary missions he's hired us out on. It's not our fault that the bastard borrowed heavily from the Suzerain, during the downturn. He should be paying that fucking debt back from his own coffers. And what the fuck was he thinking borrowing from those power-hungry bastards in the first place. The whole fucking galaxy is preparing for war against them."

Flint's eyes were stormy as he glared at Curran. "What in the Dimension of Shadows is so important that he is sending us to retrieve it."

Curran looked at Flint for a moment. Gods, he understood their rage. He was just as pissed. Unfortunately, there was only one way to resolve this, if he wanted his men to finally get the recognition they deserved. He turned to face the rest of his team. "Listen up, Warriors. We've been ordered on a last mission." Curses broke out across the room.

"What about the awards ceremony tonight? I have a date." Zyaire WildSky grumbled, shoving his dark tumbled curls back off his forehead.

"You've always got a date, WildSky," Talia Wyndove said as she tossed her blade into the air. Her long dark brown hair was braided into a thick tail that trailed down her back. Her blue eyes glinted with amusement. She caught the blade. It was a dangerous habit, but Talia never missed. "The ladies love your golden skin and pretty brown eyes."

Zyaire grinned. "I have room in my bed for you."

Talia sent her blade spinning, and it thudded into the wall beside Zyaire's head.

"I guess that's a no." Zyaire growled.

"If you guys quit your bitching, we can get this planned out and be back before the ceremony begins." Falcon crossed his arms and glared at Zyaire.

Rickon Dawnrunner, Trey Killian, and Imaris Sunsear looked at each other, and began to pull up star maps on the large holographic screen. "Where are we going?" Rickon asked as he drew up more information. Of them all, he was the most easily recognized as a Dark Elf. He had long ago shaved off his hair, which in turn brought attention to the distinctive pointed ears, characteristic of his race. He also had the classical warrior build of the Dark Elven male — and he owned it all — making it his with the sleeve of dark tattoos that ran up his right arm.

"The ancient city of Varl on the planet Kalyria. We have some collector who is claiming that the Priests of the Stardust Chalice temple stole his chalice. We've been ordered to retrieve the chalice and return it to the rightful owner," Curran replied.

"Rightful owner?" Imaris asked as she began to braid her long winter-grey hair. "How do we know this guy is the rightful owner? It seems highly unlikely that a bunch of priests would steal a chalice." Her tone was cool, and her silver-grey eyes were frosty"

Curran tossed a holo-cube down on the table. "Here's the documentation I was given and the history of the Chalice. Have a look at it if you want. It looks authentic from what I could tell."

The three instantly grabbed the information. Falcon walked over and leaned in to watch as they began to tap the symbols on the holo-screen. "It looks legit alright," Trey said as he brought up data from their most trusted sources. He rubbed his dark scruff covered jaw and shoved his hand through his brown hair. "But I agree with Imaris. It's fucking odd." They began to go over the maps, arguing, as usual, about the best weapons for this job, and tossing out backup plans.

"I wanted to tell them to fucking shove this mission up their asses, but the amount of money the collector is offering is enough to repay the Suzerain and get our young warriors back."

Talia caught her knife and looked at Curran. "I'm in. Maybe we can get them back before this whole galaxy erupts in war. I don't want my brother caught up in that shit. Did you see the last bunch of young warriors they returned to us? They were shells. I don't know what the Suzerain has them doing on the outer frontier, but I know it's sure as fuck not scouting missions."

Zyaire nodded. "If we can stop this nightmare for our young warriors, we need to do it. They haven't even come into their full power yet."

"All or None!" Echoed around the room as the Spirit Warriors agreed to this last mission. Curran swore to himself that he would personally end the Dark Elf King, Aeson Quilar, if any of his men were lost. The bastard should have known better than to borrow from the Suzerain, especially since they were working hard to forge friendships and allies who would stand with them against the Suzerain.

Chapter Two

STAR DATE: 20573.05.23

Dimension Five

Suzerain Star Destroyer

GENERAL ZEAGN, THE most feared Suzerain military leader, regarded the Fallen Angel who stood before him. He was irritated that Ash Morana saw fit to involve himself with Suzerain affairs. Why was the most dangerous being in the universe lowering himself to meddle in Suzerain business? "Are you sure your contact on Sarehiri is reliable?"

Ash tilted his head back and looked up at the ceiling before scowling at the man in front of him. *Mortals were so arrogant.* "My contact would not dare to be unreliable. Have you secured the ships we need?"

The General nodded sharply. "We are ready on our end. The question is if you can actually do what you have promised us."

Ash smiled coldly, his eyes meeting Zegans. He saw the other man flinch. Few could actually hold his gaze, and he was not surprised when Zegan looked away after a second. "The most important part of this plan, General, is that your men are prepared to do what I have instructed them. Even a small error and they will not survive their encounter with the Spirit Warriors. The whole plan will unravel if you have not brought in your most," he paused, and a hint of a sneer touched his tips. "hardened bloodthirsty soldiers. Tell me when you receive the signal."

Chapter Three

STAR DATE: 20573.05.23
Dimension Five
Ancient city of Varl, Kalyria

THE SPIRIT WARRIORS landed in the ancient city of Varl on the planet Kalyria with no trouble. After all, the Kalyrians were a peaceful race conquered early on in the Suzerain's relentless campaigns to overthrow the galaxy. They approached the temple as a group of tourists wearing normal everyday clothes and with their deadly weapons secreted away. With their plan firmly fixed in their minds, they sought out the High Priest of the Stardust Temple. He was happy to show them the chalice and claimed it was a vessel of great power to heal the mind. A sip from that chalice would do miracles for them.

Curran exchanged a jaded look with Falcon. As if drinking from any cup would heal their minds from the horrors they'd experienced as mercenaries trying to make enough money to help pay off their King's debt.

Curran agreed to sip from the chalice. He was hoping they would at least use a decent wine. At that point, Imaris would release an odorless gas that would put anyone to sleep who hadn't been inoculated against it. It was a specialized inoculation which, of course, Curran and his men had been injected with years ago. But a temple full of priests? There wasn't a chance they would even know such an injection existed. The Spirit Warrior's walked into their last mission full of confidence and a little swagger, eager to be home in time for the night's celebrations.

The temple was eerily quiet as they walked with the High Priest to the inner sanctuary. Curran shrugged off his suspicions as being a bit too paranoid. He was glad this was their last mission. His Spirit Warriors had been through the fucking Dimension of shadows and fought their back over the last few years. They deserved a life where they could finally relax and enjoy all the things they'd given up in order to help their people. Barring an imminent war of course.

The inner sanctuary of the Sacred Stardust Chalice was dimly lit by the glowing chalice sitting on a table in the center of the vast sanctum. It seemed odd to him that there were no other priests here, where the holy relic they'd stolen was displayed, but shadows, this was Kalyria, a world of peace.

They gathered around the chalice, and as Curran reached for the mystical cup, the lights came on. They turned as one, hands reaching for their weapons, but it was far too late. They were surrounded by soldiers from the Suzerain's army, half of whom held captive young Dark Elven warriors. Razor sharp daggers held to their throats.

"Whoa!" Curran held out his hands. "We're just here to try the healing properties of the chalice."

A dark laugh fell from the lips of a rough looking light-haired man. "The Dark Elf Spirit Warriors seek healing? I don't think so. You're here to steal the sacred chalice."

Curran felt more than saw Talia tense, and knew she was about to throw her dagger.

"You will command your warriors to stand down, Curran Nadiir, or we will be forced to slaughter these young elves. That would be a terrible shame. They have not lived enough yet." There was something in that soldier's voice that Curran did not trust. He exchanged a look with Falcon, but they both knew they had no way to win. Not yet. Not with the young elves lives on the line. Curran nodded to his men. They surrendered their weapons. Their hands cuffed behind them, they were forced to their knees.

The light-haired Commander strode around the Spirit Warriors. "I expected more of a fight. Not that it would have done you any good. Your ship has been confiscated, and we have secured your plans to steal this sacred relic. Your greed has been your downfall."

Curran raised his eyebrow. "You expected us to disregard the lives of our younglings? We are the protectors of our people, not the slayers."

"And that is your fatal weakness, Dark Elf. We are not so squeamish."

"So, you're going to send us to prison on trumped up charges?" *As if any prison could hold his Spirit Warriors.* "Who are you?"

The man laughed, and Curran stiffened at the malicious light that entered his eyes. "I'm Special Lieutenant Reddix.

My men have reported the discovery and confiscation of detailed plans for an insurrection against the Suzerain."

Curran shook his head. "There were no plans of that nature on our ship."

Special Lt. Reddix shrugged. "Be that as it may, I have my orders." He reached over and picked up the chalice, then walked over to the soldier nearest him with a young Dark Elf hostage. "Kill them." And he held the chalice out as the young Dark Elves throat was slit, catching the bright red blood in the cup.

A roar went up from his team, and they surged to their feet. The Dark Elven people had the ability to travel through space and dimensions, but it was a closely guarded secret, and it was their only hope. "Shift!" Curran screamed at the young warriors struggling against their captors. "Shift!"

Reddix laughed. "We have a little device that we installed in the temple last night. You cannot shift into another dimension." He turned to his men with a snarl. "Finish this!"

How the fuck had the Suzerain found out about their ability to shift through dimensions? Curran slammed into the fucking bastard. His shoulder ramming deep into the man's gut. The impact knocked them both to the floor. "Stop them or die!"

Reddix gasping for air, slammed a punch into Curran's jaw.

A wild roar filled the room. Curran saw Falcon snap the metal cuffs that bound his wrists. He grabbed the Suzerain soldier nearest to him and slammed him down onto his knee. A loud snap. The soldier screamed. Falcon tossed him aside and reached for the next one.

"Stop him!" Reddix screamed. And Curran headbutted the bastard. He strained against the cuffs but could not break them. Cursing, he struggled to his feet, as Reddix rolled away from him and rose. He drew a phase pistol and aimed it at Curran. Talia kicked out. Her foot smashed into his hand. The pistol went flying.

Trey slammed into two soldiers, his weight carrying them to the floor. A shout from the door. Rickon saw a group of priest's rush in. Kicking out, he slammed his foot into the throat of one of the Suzerain bastards. The man went down choking and gagging. "Die you bastard."

"I said stop them!" Reddix screamed again, and laser fire filled the air.

The Spirit Warriors continued to fight, savage warriors who refused to simply kneel, and watch their young people being slaughtered before their very eyes, even at the cost of their own lives.

In the end the battle was no battle. There was no way for them to win. Those who were not brought down by laser fire, were smashed back down with the butts of blasters and fists.

Curran could hear the screams, the pleas of their young warriors. He could see the terror on their faces. The Suzerain were working systematically, mercilessly slaughtering the young warriors. The stench of death filled the air, colored with the sounds of the Suzerain's laughter. He would never forget the sight of their dead bodies falling to the floor. The High priest and the priests that rushed to defend them lay where they had fallen. Their holy place desecrated by violence and death. Their holy relic used for the most unholy of rites. He clenched his cuffed fists and bared his teeth. A dangerous growl leaving his throat as he lifted hate filled eyes to Reddix.

Lt. Reddix walked over and studied the Spirit Warriors. "Him." He pointed at Falcon. In the next instant portals began opening all through the massive room, dark holes that pulsated with black energy and seeped the scent of evil. Curran had no idea how the Suzerain opened those dimensional gateways, but he knew that nothing good would come of it.

Falcon fought against the bastards who dragged him before Reddix. Loud curses filled the air and he managed to take more than a few of the bastards down before they forced him to his knees. Horrified realization filled his eyes as they brought the blood-filled chalice over. Curran watched helplessly as Falcon lost control, struggling wildly. The butt end of a blaster slammed into his head, and he went down barely conscious. They dragged him back up to his knees, and the cup was put to his mouth. His nose was pinched shut and the foul fluid poured into his mouth. He swallowed, gagging, and gasping for air. Blinding pain flashed behind his eyes, and they let him drop as they grabbed the next Spirit Warrior.

Curran heard the screams of his warriors, watched them drop, writhing in agony. Lt. Reddix began to question them. Curran's eyes widened as his warriors agonizingly answered. Clenching his jaw, he looked away, understanding they had no control. The foul fluid in that cursed chalice was brutally ripping information from their minds. Information that endangered many worlds, not just their own.

Chapter Four

STAR DATE: 20573.05.23
　Dimension Five
　Helix Nebula

WHEN THE SIGNAL CAME, Ash Morana, Fallen Angel, past lover of a mighty Creator, and former friend to the mightiest Creator to ever exist, began to open portals. Small portals on a peaceful world and massive portals in the deep reaches of space.

Chapter Five

STAR DATE: 20573.05.23

Dimension Five

Ancient city of Varl, Kalyria

TWO SUZERAIN DRAGGED Falcon over to the first portal, blood seeping from his ears, cursing and swearing, his face a mask of agony as he fought against the effects of the chalice. The portal seemed to reach for him, and the second its black energy touched him, he dropped to his knees, a scream tearing from his throat. The Suzerain holding his arms, jumped back, as the black energy closed around him. Falcon disappeared as the portal winked out of existence.

Curran saw the horror growing in his warriors' eyes, and knew they saw his own shock. *Falcon! My gods. Falcon.* Anguish welled up in his chest, even as some part of his still functioning brain scrambled to understand the level of pain it would take to force that terrible scream from his friend and second in command.

One by one the Suzerain threw each of the Spirit Warriors, still screaming, fighting desperately to get away from their captors, through the dark portals. Until there was only Curran left.

Reddix turned to him. "Hold him."

The bloody chalice was forced against his lips. He clenched his teeth and twisted his head. Cursing the men who held him. He tried to gain his feet. A brutal kick to his knee brought him back down. They pinned him to the floor as he struggled against their hold and poured the blood into his mouth. He sputtered and gasped. And they let him go. Excruciating pain ripped through his brain. It was as if invisible claws were tearing apart his mind. Rolling to his side, desperate for air, he sucked in a hard breath. Another. Holding back his screams until he thought he would choke from them, he managed to make it to his knees. Reddix crouched down in front of him. "The price for treason is the total annihilation of your race. Your world is forfeit. We will mine it of all its resources and reduce it to a barren shell. Curran Nadiir, you are the man solely responsible for the destruction of your race and your world. For your crimes you will bear the mark of a betrayer and be given over to the Dark Elves' worst enemy, just as your men were."

He heard the sizzle as a red-hot branding iron was pressed into his cheek. The smell of charred flesh filled the air, and he choked off a scream, as a mark was seared into his face. Teeth bared in a vicious grimace, his rage burned through his eyes as he faced his captors. "I will come for you."

Reddix laughed. "Curran Nadiir, mighty hero of the Dark Elves. Leader of the famed Spirit Warriors. Your name shall become synonymous with traitor."

The black energy surrounded him, snapped through him, tore him into atoms, and in a rush of fire reformed him. What followed was torture beyond anything he'd ever endured, as he was given into the hands of the worst enemy of the Dark Elven home world, an enemy that had once been their closest ally.

Chapter Six

STAR DATE: 20573.05.24
>Dimension Five
>Suzerain Star Destroyer

GENERAL ZEAGN TOUCHED his communications panel. "Now!"

And legions of ships that bore a striking resemblance to the Dark Elves space fleet poured into those deep space portals and out into the solar systems that were home to the allies of the Dark Elven people, weapons blazing.

Part Two

THEY ARE THE REMNANTS of an ancient race. Their history merely whispered legends now, lies and more lies that twisted their proud heritage into a thing of nightmares. They are Dark Elves.

Chapter Seven

STAR DATE: 20573.06.25
Dimension Twenty-One
Anassoi Star System
Zosuna

WHEN CURRAN AWOKE, he was lying on cold cement in a dank little prison cell whose only light came from high up windows with heavy metal bars crisscrossing their openings. The metal cuffs were no longer around his wrists. There was a small foul-smelling hole in one corner. He grimaced and struggled to his knees, everything aching. He had a feeling that sewage hole was his only luxury. Rising to his feet he staggered to the wall and leaned there, his head hanging as he tried to get his bearings. Gods, everything hurt. He swallowed against the rawness of his throat and turned so he could lean against the rough cement wall. He tried to shift out, but nothing happened.

A small amount of food and water sat on a tray in front of the door. He stumbled over to it. Desperate to remove the foul taste from his mouth he grabbed the cup and drained it. He banged on the door, but no one came.

It was a month before the door to his cell opened. A month before he saw another living being. And when he did, he simply could not comprehend who he was seeing. "Dak'ar?"

"Hello, Betrayer."

"I don't understand." Curran searched the eyes of the man he had called a friend for the last couple years. There was only hatred and contempt in those eyes now.

Dak'ar laughed, the sound bitter. "Eh, of course you do not understand. You thought your people were so mighty. You thought you could conquer my world. You almost succeeded. If it were not for the Suzerain that you so maligned, we would be slaves of the Dark Elves even now."

Curran stared at the man. "I don't know what you are talking about. We are allies."

"Allies." Dak'ar spat on the floor. "You betrayed us!"

Curran shook his head. "No. Dak'ar there has to be some kind of mistake."

"Mistake? Is that what it is called when the Dark Elves show up in a fleet of their warships? Was it a mistake when they fired unprovoked upon my world? Was it a mistake when they ignored our pleas to stop? Was it a mistake when they killed millions of my people?"

Curran could feel his heart pounding in his chest. "Dak'ar... is your family alright?"

"My family? Do you know that my wife thought we should find you a woman from my people? She wanted to introduce you to her sister." He walked closer to Curran. "My wife, and my children are dead." His fist shot out and slammed into Curran's face. Curran reeled back and smashed into the wall. Dak'ar was on him, punching and kicking until Curran blacked out. The next morning the torture began. Torture that left Curran bloody and broken. And Dak'ar visited often, showing him pictures and news stories of the destruction of Sarehiriri.

One thought kept Curran alive. One thought made him choose survival. His warriors. The Spirit Warriors. All or None. He knew his team. Knew them right down to their stubborn warriors' hearts. They would endure. They knew he would come for them. And by all that was holy, they would find a way to clear the Dark Elves name. Their vengeance would be a terrible thing.

Chapter Eight

STAR DATE: 20574.05.20
    Dimension Twenty-One
    Anassoi Star System
    Zosuna

CURRAN WATCHED AND waited. It was almost a year before an unwise guard thought him too broken to be a threat. He tore out the guard's throat with the rough blade he'd managed to fashion. And he began to hunt. The swift deaths of every person who dared to torture him had been too merciful, but he had to get to his people. He had to rally a force strong enough to rescue his men. There was no doubt in his mind that the Dark Elven people had survived the Suzerain.

Several hard dimensional jumps, and a stolen spaceship, and he was heading home to Sarehiri, the Dark Elven home world.

Chapter Nine

Dimension Five

Sarehiri

The Dark Elven home world

WHAT HE FOUND, BROKE him. His planet was a virtual wasteland. A once thriving civilization, annihilated. He landed the ship unable to believe the computer readings. It was worse than he'd imagined. Only dry dust, rocks and the decimated ruins of their cities remained. He collapsed against a boulder, sliding down to sit on the ground, unable to comprehend what he was seeing. How had the Suzerain taken Sarehiri? The might of the Dark Elves was legendary, and yet, they were gone.

Lost. Sick at heart, his whole body shaking, he remained where he was as the sun set. As the stars began to appear on their blanket of midnight black, he became aware of the complete silence. There were no sounds of the thriving civilization that had joyously lived here. There was no sound of water running, or even leaves fluttering in the breeze. So, this night, Curran Nadiir, Leader of the Spirit Warriors, with only the silence of death to keep him company, mourned and remembered the Dark Elf people.

It was deep into the third hour of darkness that he heard the noise. At first, he wondered if a Zeakseon had somehow escaped the mass slaughter. Zeakseon's were mid-sized herbivores with twisted blue horns and soft curly black fur. And hardy as the Shadow beings that inhabited the bowels of the Dimension of Shadows.

Curran stood up and moved silently behind the boulder as he listened. He could hear the sound of running and harsh gasps as whatever it was drew closer. He heard the clear sounds of a scuffle. What the fuck? He moved from his crouched position and in the moonlight of the twin moons, Ankian and Elrian, he saw two men grappling with a woman. The blue light of Elrian glinted on the unmistakable emblem of the Suzerain on the men's uniforms. Bounty hunters. Suzerain bounty hunters. He launched himself from behind the boulder, the Spirit Warriors war cry bursting from his lips. He would never forget the startled look on the faces of the two men. A startled look that quickly changed to horror. They must have thought him a night specter, a ghost come to life to save possibly the last Dark Elf on this forsaken planet. His fist slammed into the throat of one man, while he fired a plasma gun at point blank range into the heart of the second man. They both fell. The one dead before he hit the ground, the other dead within a minute, his trachea crushed, and his throat slit by the crude blade that Curran had fashioned in that filthy hole of a prison.

He turned and caught a glimpse of the woman disappearing into the night. Sinking down onto the boulder he shoved his hand through his hair. Had he imagined her? He looked over at the dead Suzerain bounty hunters. No. She'd been real. In the morning, he would track her.

Chapter Ten

STAR DATE: 20574.05.24

Dimension Five

Sarehiriri

THE NEXT MORNING, TO his utter disbelief, a tattered, dirty, and broken group of Elves stood before him. Their leader, a man who was clearly a warrior, big, tough and scarred. Curran knew, just from looking at him, that he would be a difficult man to defeat in a fight. And just behind him stood the woman he'd saved. "Curran Nadiir." The man's voice was a low rumble, "Spirit Warrior. I'm Garrett Wyatt. Come to save us, have you?"

Curran eyed the big man, his deep mahogany colored hair long and wild. A red beard covered his jaw, and his amber eyes almost glowed in the sunlight. "Do you need saving?" He lifted his eyebrow. "I thought everyone was dead. If it wasn't daylight, I would think you were all night spectres. However," he gestured towards the two dead bodies. "I took issue with those bastards daring to think they could collect bounty on a Dark Elf." His eyes met the eyes of the woman standing behind Garrett, and she gave him a curt nod.

The big warrior nodded. "Marina was going to lead them to us. We were going to force them to take us on their ship, to a safe harbour. Where are your men, Spirit Warrior?"

Curran looked over the group before turning his eyes back to Garrett. "Captured. We were all captured and imprisoned in separate locations. I escaped."

Garrett walked over to him, taking in his rough appearance, the beard that didn't cover the brand on his face. "Looks like the bastards tried to break you."

"They tried. They failed."

Garrett nodded.

"How many more of you are there? I knew they could not have killed our people."

Garrett shook his head. "They tried. They failed. Here we are, all that remains. The last survivors of a once glorious empire. One hundred and seven including you, Spirit Warrior. If the Suzerain find out that we live, they will hunt us to extinction."

"There must be thousands who shifted dimensions and escaped."

Garrett exchanged a look with Marina. "They had several ships in orbit around us. Positioned so they were spread out evenly. They lowered some kind of devices into the atmosphere. We couldn't shift." Looking around, Garrett nodded at a silent young woman. "Zarah, can you tell Curran what happened?"

Zarah nodded, stepped forward and looked at the man who stood before them. His tight curly hair was much longer than she remembered from all the media that had surrounded this man. He looked unkempt and dangerous with his beard, the longer hair, and the brand that scarred his cheek. She swallowed. "I was eighteen, laughing with my friends over the com and dreaming about my boyfriend's return home later that day." She paused and looked away from the intense gaze of perhaps the last Spirit Warrior to exist. "Jez—" She looked down and fought the tears. "His name was Jeziah, but we called him Jez. He was in one of the troops of younglings taken by the Suzerain to fight their battles. The young warriors were allowed communication privileges, and he sent me a message. The Suzerain had ordered his troop to some temple on Kalyria—" She heard the choked sound the man made. Her eyes met his, anguish was the only word she had for the emotion shadowing his eyes, shadowing— No, it wasn't a shadow it was a storm. A raging chaos filled storm. And somehow knowing that their greatest hero, a man who had seen firsthand the betrayal of their people allowed her to forge on. "He was coming home after that mission. I-I was so excited. Jez was my whole world, even if my parents regarded our relationship with amused tolerance."

Zarah looked up into the sky, blinking away the moisture gathering in her eyes as she remembered the sexy, brash, confident young man she'd thought would be her husband someday. He'd been tall and leanly muscled, a youngling of twenty-one, his body promising to fill out into the solid hard body of a warrior. A smile crossed her lips, as memories of their love, their wild passion filled her mind. She missed him terribly and could hardly contain herself the next day as the time for his arrival drew nearer. "He never came home." Her hands trembling, she looked at Garrett and he nodded. "The skies—" a breath in before she could speak, the memories pouring into her mind. "The skies seemed to darken as fleets of Suzerain ships arrived. So many ships, so many troops.

"My parents were law enforcement, and they worked with me from the time I was small, training me in self-defense and martial arts." She shrugged. It was not uncommon in their world, they were a warrior race after all and with parents who understood the darkness that could happen, self-defense training was a natural way for them to ensure her safety.

"My parents began loading supplies into our vehicle." Zarah could see them in her mind, grimly silent as more and more ships landed. The Suzerain were their enemy, the enemy of the whole universe. A mighty army sweeping through solar systems and across galaxy after galaxy. Their King had betrayed them to the Suzerain long ago. Peace in exchange for money. A betrayal that the Dark Elven people only tolerated because their hero, the Spirit Warrior, Curran Nadiir, fought to save them from the King's betrayal.

"The emergency communications system sounded, and our communication displays went live with the scene that unfolded at the royal castle. I stood beside my parents and watched. The King was dragged from his castle along with his family." She blew out a breath and drew one in before she continued. "General Zeagn addressed us, all of us. He said the King was guilty of betraying the Suzerain, by allowing the outlawed mercenary Spirit Warriors to undertake a mission to steal the Sacred Stardust Chalice." A tear trickled down her cheek. "The Spirit Warriors had been captured and found guilty of treason. And... And then a holo vid began to play, it was dated the twenty third. Three weeks before we saw it." She remembered watching in horror as their beloved hero and his Spirit Warriors were trapped in a temple on the planet of Kalyria and a troop of youngling Dark Elf warriors were forced into the temple. She had cried out as she saw the emblem on the troops' uniforms, her eyes frantically searching for Jez. Her father reached out and set a hand on her shoulder. They knew what was coming could not be good, but none of them had been prepared for the Suzerain to brutally cut the throat of the first youngling. Blood. So much blood. The Spirit Warriors had broken from their captors. Chaos erupted. She saw Jez a mere moment before he fell. He stared into the camera as if he knew they were being filmed and had mouthed a single word. Zarah. And her youth ended as the beautiful young man she had loved with all the passion of her young life, fell under the onslaught of blaster fire as the Suzerain struggled to contain the Spirit Warriors.

She screamed and her father swept her into his arms, holding her tightly as she shook and sobbed hysterically. A great roar seemed to go up from the whole planet and her eyes snapped back to the screen. The Spirit Warriors and their leader, beloved heroes of the Dark Elven people were pronounced traitors and their world condemned to annihilation.

"There was silence. This shocked silence that fell everywhere. General Zeagn turned and fired his blaster, killing King Quilar instantly. Immediately, fighting broke out as the King's guard fought to get to the rest of the King's family.

"My father shouted to my mom as he turned us towards the door. My last glimpse of the communication screen showed a fierce battle taking place. As we rushed to our vehicle, we could hear gunfire, and I saw a huge mining drill lowering from one of the massive ships in orbit." Terror had filled her heart as she understood that their world was going to be stripped of every resource until it was a dead husk, a warning to any world foolish enough to oppose the Suzerain.

"Our small village had been built upon a hill, my father said that strategically it had the advantage." She knew that it was one of a series of villages built into hills that contained interlinking natural caves that went down far, far into their planet. It gave them an advantage, but Sarehiri had never faced such an enemy as the Suzerain.

"As we sped through the city streets heading towards the entrance to the caves, my mother helped me change into the dark armored micro thin clothing that was worn by the law enforcement officers under their uniforms. She had me put on a blast resistant vest before handing me weapons, and she helped me to fasten them into hidden pockets and holsters. She was working so fast, and I was more terrified than I'd ever been in my life. I knew my parents would fight to protect our people, and I— I also understood that any chance of survival was remote. As I began to lace up the tough combat boots my father maneuvered our vehicle through streets crowded with people evacuating to the caves. I looked out the window and saw the Dark Elven military spacecraft begin to lift off." A terrifyingly short aerial battle ensued, and she watched in shocked horror as the Dark Elves' crafts were blasted from the sky.

The sounds of blaster fire filled the air, blaster missiles began to rain down from the Suzerain fleet in orbit over their world. "It felt as if the Dimension of Shadows itself was being unleashed. Explosions rocked the vehicle as we sped through a scene of complete chaos".

A tear slid down her cheek as her eyes met her mothers. Her mother smiled gently at her and reached out to stroke her cheek. *We are Dark Elves, Zarah, we will fight until we are all gone. We will not go quietly into the darkness.*

"We all fought. Every man, woman, and child old enough to hold a weapon. I watched my parents die, my friends, family, teachers, store owners, the gentle old lady who lived down the street." Her hand lifted to cover her mouth as a broken sob burst out of her. "I learned the meaning of being a Dark Elf that day. I will never forget our people's honor, their courage, how they fought so bravely, so boldly, and determinedly, even in the face of certain defeat. I will never forget their heroic courage; their valor will remain with us forever."

Zarah wiped at the tear that slid down her cheek. "The Suzerain have not won —the Dark Elves live. You," her voice was fierce as she looked at Curran, "you live, and I believe the Spirit Warriors live still."

Curran rocked back on his heels; his eyes closed for a moment. A single nod and his eyes met hers. "All or None brave little warrior."

She nodded. "All or None, Curran Nadiir."

He looked at Garrett, struggling to find words as the images bombarded his mind. He squeezed his eyes shut, blowing a hard breath, fighting to contain the devastation that left him reeling. Finally, he looked at the man who led these survivors. "Our space fleet?"

Garrett shook his head. "They fought hard but—The Suzerain were accompanied by a massive fleet." Garrett looked over at a man who looked just as unkempt as the rest of them. "Dreven, maybe you should explain."

The man named Dreven looked at Curran for a full minute before nodding. "Lieutenant. Dreven Avanth. Space Fleet. I was part of the Star Fighter squadron assigned to the Star Destroyer Marauder. The fleet that accompanied the Suzerain were made up of ships from our allies. We didn't stand a chance."

Curran swallowed. "Survivors?"

Dreven shook his head and shrugged as he stared off into the distance, a muscle in his jaw ticking. "I'm not even sure how I survived. When I came to, Garrett was pulling me out of my fighter. I crashed on Sarehiri."

Curran clenched his teeth and nodded. *Fuck.* "Are there more children?"

Garrett shook his head. "Who you see here are all that remain."

Curran looked at the silent group. Three children under twelve and five teens. "Gods," he breathed. His heart hurting, he sank onto the boulder and shook his head fighting the rage and grief. He had to think. They couldn't stay here. Curran leaned forward frowning. "Why haven't you all shifted away to some place safe?"

Garrett sighed. "Those devices that prevent shifting. The bastards also embedded them deep into the ground, we've been working at digging one up. Haven't got to it yet, but we've been trying."

Curran immediately tried to shift, but it was as if the ability had never existed. He swore, and forcing his numb mind to work, began to consider the possibilities. Technology was their worst enemy. The Suzerain would be able to trace any of the advanced technology that they used. If they were going to survive, they would have to start over in a place free of all the high-tech electronics that they depended upon. And where could they hide that technology would not see them?

"I know of only one place, and the risks are immense." He didn't sugar coat his words. They needed to know exactly what they were getting into. "There is a hidden realm that I once passed through, in the vast reaches of the outer galaxy. In that realm is a world untouched by any modern technology. That is important because any use of tech will be like lighting up a dimensional path right to us." He turned slowly, looking over the half-starved group. "The very nature of that realm makes it impossible for any electronics to survive, but we are not even going to attempt to take any with us. We'll be starting over. From scratch."

Garrett crossed his arms. "How did you come across this place? Why were you in the outer reaches of the galaxy?"

"I was on a mission for the King, shifting through the dimensions, traveling fast and light. I saw the dimensional pathway light up. I was curious and you never know when a Dark Elf will need a bolt hole." There was a bit of laughter and many nods. "I entered the realm. The planet is vast and certainly capable of sustaining life. It's our best chance for survival.

"Our only chance, I'd wager," Garrett said and turned to the broken group he led. "I say we give the Spirit Warrior a chance."

They boarded his ship, and Curran flew it to a high orbit around the moon, Ankian. From there it was a simple matter to shift to another dimension. Though Curran tried it several times first to be sure. He would not risk all that remained of his people. The ship was left behind, set to a deteriorating orbit that would cause it to crash into the moon within the hour. They began to shift through space and dimension after dimension, until he worried that he'd failed his people once more.

Chapter Eleven

STAR DATE: 20574.05.28
> Dimension Five
> Realm of the Forsaken
> Aezorwyn

GARRETT TOUCHED CURRAN'S shoulder and he turned. There it was. The hidden realm with its shining dimensional pathway that only they could see. One shift into the realm, and onto the world, within it. They shifted onto that planet a broken, near-death group of people, and it was as if they'd found home.

In this new world, where they could be anything, they chose to build their society based on the legendary Middle Ages of a mythical planet named Earth. A legend told to all school children of a man named Arthur, only a legend, but one they desperately needed to believe in. The Dark Elves had always held to valor, honor, and integrity. Now, it became the foundation on which they would build their society.

His people began to settle in, to learn this new world that they'd named Aezorwyn, after the mighty creators of the universe. And he named the realm. Realm of the Forsaken, because he'd been brutally taught that if there were any Creators, they had turned their backs on the Dark Elves.

Together they worked, side by side. Gathering food, hunting and building a fortress that would protect them if there should be any enemy upon this foreign world. They'd always had limited telekinetic abilities but, on this world, they discovered mysterious new elemental abilities. The ability to sense water, the ability to call a small flame to their hand, the strange ability to move the air into a slight breeze and terrakinesis. Even with these new abilities it took them five years of back breaking labor to build that castle. Five years that he lived knowing that his men were suffering. Five years that every chance he had, he shifted through dimension after dimension looking in vain for his men.

Chapter Twelve

STAR DATE: 20579.06.01

Dimension Five

Realm of the Forsaken

Aezorwyn

THE DAY THE CASTLE was finished, Curran stood before them all and confessed his crimes, expecting their hatred, resolved to walk away and let them live in peace— or die if that was what they required of him.

It was right that he accepted the judgment of his people, for his failure. He would finally know justice. Kneeling down he held out his sword. Silence reigned until Garrett took the sword. He swallowed, and bowed his head, accepting death.

"Curran Nadiir," The warrior's voice rang out. "We proclaim you Leader of the Dark Elven people in every realm and dimension in the universe. We choose to willingly follow you to, and through, the very doors of the Dimension of Shadows itself, if you deem that we need to take that place by storm. You are our leader, our commander, our King."

The sword touched his right shoulder, his left, and a great shout arose as his people cheered, and he stared in shock, slowly standing to his feet. Garrett handed him back his sword and looked him in the eye. "Curran, don't you understand? We stand with you, every last person here, would face death for you. You condemn yourself, not us. We know you. We all have been to the Dimension of Shadows, together. We have seen your soul. You're wild and dark, but we'll take your darkness over the lightest Suzerain."

Chapter Thirteen

STAR DATE: 20579.06.10

Dimension Five
Realm of the Forsaken
Aezorwyn

FROM THAT DAY FORWARD, he did not look back. It was not in his nature. He knew that the only way to survive was to move forward—And it was the only path to vengeance.

The time had finally come for him to seek out his men. He would not forsake the mighty Spirit Warriors that had fought for so long to protect their people.

Over the next year, he took many trips out of the realm. His mission clear—find his men and bring them home. Those trips taught him as nothing else could have, the incredible powers the Dark Elves now possessed. This new world had gifted them with the means to ensure their survival— on and off Aezorwyn. It was as if the hidden realm they inhabited was determined to keep them hidden. He could walk down the most crowded street on an alien world and not be seen—Except by a rare few. That anomaly presented a problem that he had to solve. He could not risk their secrets being told. His people needed supplies, and he had to search for his men. He had to save his men. Hardening his heart, he decided that if anyone saw him, they would have to die. It was the only way to protect his people.

The next time he was off world on a remote planet seeking information and seeds for crops, a young woman with a child spoke to him. He'd turned, his dagger in hand. She was a beggar, dressed in rags and holding the hand of a small, undernourished child.

Do it. Just fucking do it. His heart ached as his dark eyes held hers. *You have to do this!* He swallowed hard as he saw fear starting to appear in her eyes. *Fuck. He couldn't kill her. What was he to do? What the fuck was he to do?*

In a split-second decision, he tucked the knife away and wrapped a hand around each of their arms. Calling a dimensional portal to him, he scooped them both into his arms and stepped through the portal back onto Aezorwyn. For the survival of his people, he would be a monster.

Part Three

IN ANOTHER WORLD, FAR from this one, he'd lived a life so different that he had no way to even compare who he'd once been. They'd called him a hero.

Chapter Fourteen

STAR DATE: 20580.06.17
Dimension Thirty-Seven
Perileos Star System
Xehshyhra

FALCON CLUNG TO THE rough rocks that formed the ceiling of his cell, his fingers wedged tightly in between the stones. Seven years he'd been in this Shadow trap. Seven years of torture and pain, almost a decade of the most degrading, dehumanizing, brutal treatment that he'd ever endured, and it was slowly snuffing out the tiny flicker of hope he so stubbornly held on to.

Over the years, he managed to wear away places in the stone roof where he could fit his fingers. Tiny spaces that tore skin from bone, and made his fingers ache so fucking badly, even when he was not clinging to the ceiling like a gods-damned arachnid. He wondered at times if he would ever be able to hold a weapon again. But those small crevices were all that stood between him and death, and he stubbornly refused to allow that final darkness to win this eternal game they played.

He tightened his hold, ignoring the pain in his fingers, the burn in his muscles, and the way his arms shook. He pulled his body up, a millimeter at a time, until he was close enough to press his face to the cold damp rocks and take a few precious gulps of stale air.

The icy water would recede soon, he knew. It was how this cruel game his captors played, worked. Every single night his cell was flooded to within a few centimeters of the ceiling, and every morning it was drained. The first night he'd almost drowned. Shadows, he'd lost count of how many times he'd almost drowned. Except even if he was lost in the horrors of the Dimension of Shadows, there was no way he would ever give his enemies the satisfaction of killing him. Fuck that shit.

Chapter Fifteen

STAR DATE: 20580.06.17

Dimension Five
Ancient city of Varl, Kalyria

WILLOW SOLAR SAT IN her tiny garden drinking her morning tea as she read the daily news on her com device. Pushing her long red hair back over her shoulder, she settled more comfortably in her floating chair, scrolling through the news stories. Same thing as every other day. Politicians lying. The Suzerain imposing more tax increases. And of course, wars on the frontiers of the galaxy, as the Suzerain sought to conquer all in their path. When would they learn that the bottom line was not credits, it was the people?

She finished her tea and turned off the news to open her com mail, hoping for a letter from her brother, Jericho. He rarely wrote, and since the death of her parents two cycles ago, he'd distanced himself further. He seemed determined to end his life fighting in the endless battles that the Suzerain engaged in. When she saw him on his last leave, she'd asked why he continued to fight for the Suzerain. He'd looked at her with cold, dead eyes, and simply stated that he had seen too much, committed too many acts of death to stop now. Her heart aching, she'd reached out to touch him. He'd stepped back and shaken his head. She knew why of course. He worked for the very people who, given the slightest chance, would turn her life-giving gift into a thing of nightmares.

A tiny ping sounded, and she opened the mail program, one spam mail advertising mail order brides. She chuckled, deleted it, and picked up her teacup and plate. Taking them into the tiny unit she lived in, she set them in the cleanser, wondering who on Kalyria would take such a risk. *Going to a planet you didn't know, in a distant star system, and marrying a male you'd never met? Yikes. That would take a very adventurous soul.*

She opened her eco friendly cooler for a glass of juice and realized a trip to the market was needed. *Hmmm, that will take up a good portion of the day.* But she had supplies to pick up, and she was out of fresh dazzleberry juice and her favorite sweets. And it was a beautiful day.

Walking over to the wall mounted computer she tapped a few symbols and pulled up her schedule. Biting her lip, she considered how to get in some work today. *Oh.* She could deliver that order she'd completed yesterday. It was on the way, and her client would be delighted to have it early.

She really was quite pleased with how the necklace turned out. The design she'd created could easily be used to craft bracelets and earrings as well. In fact, when she got home, she would start on a bracelet. Happy with her plans, she quickly braided her hair into a thick rope that hung down to her waist and got ready to go.

The jewelry she made provided a good income and allowed her to live a quiet, if somewhat boring, life. Not that she was complaining, she lived this way intentionally. When you had rare, and potentially dangerous abilities, you stayed under the wire. In fact, you hid.

Chapter Sixteen

STAR DATE: 20580.06.17

Dimension Five

Ancient city of Varl, Kalyria

THE SINGLE ENCOUNTER she had with the Suzerain as a naive teenager left her family in ruins. She would always remember the day the Suzerain came to their home. They'd been after her. She'd made a mistake.

In an innocent moment of compassion, she'd spoken with a homeless man at the market, and realized that he suffered from the trauma of war. Her heart ached for his struggle. No one should have to live on the streets fighting every day for their survival. She knew that even a small amount of her time would start healing him. What would it hurt if she spoke to this forgotten member of society? So, she bought him a meal and sat with him at a public table while he ate, knowing instinctively that he needed the extra time near her. Her brother had also been in the market with his friends, and when he saw her, he came over and told her that their father was looking for her. She quickly headed home, never giving another thought to why he remained behind to talk with the man.

She sighed at the memory. *If she had only known, she could have changed things, couldn't she?*

She'd reached her client's home and was invited in for tea. Knowing how lonely the elderly lady was, she accepted. Even now, compassion was the core of who she was. She could no more stop herself from reaching out to those in need than she could stop the energy of the planet from flowing through her.

Willow was the rarest of beings in the universe. A healer of souls, kind, compassionate and powerful beyond what anyone understood. But that was the way of Energy Enchanters.

The energy from Kalyria continually cycled through her. It was like the planet had found something precious that it wanted to stay in contact with. A seamless exchange from the moment of her birth. A gift that converted all that raw energy into life and released it back into the planet creating a richer, more diverse, more resilient environment and people.

Willow's very nature drew people to her, and most often, people who suffered traumatic soul wounds. The more time they spent with her, the more the energy she produced affected their neural pathways. New connections formed, the mind began to regenerate, enabling healing to naturally take place.

Surely these gentle, compassionate healers were welcomed everywhere? Every inhabited planet must want them. Surely whole armies protected these soul healers.

But as with everything there was also a dark side. Energy Enchanters had a single lethal ability. A deadly capacity to pull vast amounts of energy from an individual. No one understood why a gift that created life could be turned into death. Though some speculated that it was a natural defense system.

In the past, many eons ago, corrupt governments and criminals had discovered the dark ability of these gentle souls. The Energy Enchanters became merely a means to an end for those hungry for power. They were rounded up. Their loved ones held hostage under threat of death and they, themselves, often tortured until they broke. And the evil ones who committed such heinous acts, forced the compassionate healers to assassinate targeted individuals and, in extreme cases, whole planets.

Forced to kill, to destroy whole societies, irreparably broke these beings whose sole purpose was to heal—turning them into monsters that could not quench their thirst for energy. The perfect killing machines for an evil regime.

The family lines that produced Energy Enchanters went into hiding, with the aid of resistance fighters. And they begged those same fighters to find the shattered Enchanters—and end their suffering.

Finally, in a desperate attempt to prevent evil from forcing them to become terrible monsters that could not be stopped, they actively sought to breed out the very genetics that gave birth to their gift.

But in some families, no matter how they tried to dilute it, the gene for the gift was too strong. The Solar lineage was one such family.

Chapter Seventeen

STAR DATE: 20580.06.17

Dimension Five

Ancient city of Varl, Kalyria

LEAVING HER CLIENT'S home, with a carefully wrapped chocolate spice tea cake tucked into her bag, she started off for the market. The early afternoon sky was a soft orange, with only the occasional white fluffy cloud. She took a deep breath of the fresh air and reminded herself that it didn't do her any good to dwell on the past. But some memories could not be hidden from.

Her father, Kano Solar, was a huge bear of a man with ruby colored hair, so dark it was almost black. She smiled, remembering how the sunlight made his hair glow a shade so beautiful that it was haunting. Of course, it was her brother who had been blessed with that same color, not her.

By the time the Suzerain regime came to power, Energy Enchanters were only a carefully crafted myth. But a myth that the Suzerain were very much interested in.

The Suzerain had taken an interest in several people who had energy skills including her father when he was a young man. He had been tested several times over the years. But he only ever showed a type of energy used in the medical field to help diagnose the ill. An aura reader. And that is all he ever admitted to. It was in fact his career. He worked in hospitals alongside the doctors, reading people's energy, which helped the doctors make highly accurate diagnoses.

Her father was a man of deep convictions and strength of character. And he was an Energy Enchanter. He hid in plain sight. Defying the Suzerain and their tyrannical ways.

A loving father, he spent a lot of time with his kids, teaching them not only how to control their different gifts, but how very important compassion and kindness were in this universe.

Suzerain Commander D'miron, young, newly promoted and looking to make a name for himself, showed up at their home, insisting that her parents release Willow into his custody. A homeless man had been killed and the vids showed that Willow had been the last person to spend time with the man. Her eyes opened wide, and she'd frantically shaken her head. Her father put his arm around her and faced the man who accused his gentle daughter of murder. "Willow would never harm anyone. If she was talking to that man, she was probably giving him her lunch money."

"That doesn't change the fact that your daughter was the last person seen talking to him. We need to question her."

Her brother Jericho stepped forward, insisting that it had been him. He had been trying to see if he had his father's talent for reading auras and had accidentally killed the man.

The young Commander D'miron had been skeptical. It was Willow in the pictures not Jericho. Until Jericho demonstrated his powers.

Her brother was a brilliant strategist, even at his young age. Excelling in sports and leadership. His potential to bring good to the universe, a wonderful shiny thing. Jericho had his whole life before him, he was eighteen years old with dreams of joining the academy and becoming a space explorer.

And he could siphon energy from the very core of a planet as long as he could find a way to release that energy. It was considered to be a martial ability that sometimes occurred in Kalyrian families and was known to turn up in their mother's lineage. And it had nothing to do with the genetics that produced Energy Enchanters.

For the Suzerain Commander this was almost as good. It meant that they had a being who could feed raw energy into their weapons. Raw energy derived from the very planets they were fighting. His gamble in killing the informant had paid off.

Horrified, Willow opened her mouth to admit her gift, to save her big brother who she knew could not have killed that man. Jericho met her eyes, gave her a hard look, and shook his head. And her father gently pushed her into her mother's arms. Her gift could never be revealed.

Two years later the Suzerain came back. This time they tried to take her mother. Her father's love for his wife had been legendary and, in the end, he died attempting to save her from the Suzerain who decided to use her to control their son. They'd died together when their spacecraft was destroyed as they attempted to escape. Her heart ached with the memory, and she rubbed her chest. "I miss you, Papa and Mama."

Blinking away the tears and memories, she forced herself to focus on the things she needed to get done. Walking down the street intent on picking up some supplies for her new design, the credits from the finished order tucked securely into her bag. Willow had no way of knowing her future was about to be changed irrevocably.

Chapter Eighteen

STAR DATE: 20580.06.17

Dimension Five
Ancient city of Varl, Kalyria

A GENTLE BREEZE CARRIED the scents of freshly baked bread and spiced tea as Willow entered the open-air market. She decided to pick up both and maybe a little pot of dazzleberry spread too. The market was busy today, a sea of people shopping and browsing. The haunting music of a woodwind instrument danced in the air, and she hummed along as she browsed through a stall containing silk scarfs. Finding one in a rich shade of deep purple that she couldn't resist, she paid the credits for it and tucked it into her bag, then wandered over to the stall with the bread. She chose her loaf, savoring the aroma, and put it carefully into her shopping bag.

It was as she was on her way to the preserves and jams stall, that she noticed him. He was tall, with hair so black it shone blue in the sunlight. Even from here she could sense the air of danger that surrounded him. He stood in front of the temple of the Sacred Chalice, and as she drew closer, she became aware of the massive trauma injury that scarred his psyche. Turning without thinking, she walked over to him. She couldn't let such an injury go unattended, not when she had the power to help.

He was even taller and more muscular when she drew closer, with hard, dangerous eyes. It gave her a nervous feeling in the pit of her stomach when his dark eyes met hers briefly. Her gaze moved over the golden brown of his face, her eyes widening as she realized that his ears were pointed. Dark Elf. How could this be? The Dark Elves had all been killed, and goddess forgive them, but her people had been partly responsible for that terrible genocide. In their sorrow, they held a planet-wide memorial service every year in remembrance of the Dark Elf people.

At that point she should've run. Instead, she approached him with a half-formed thought in her mind that she needed to warn him.

Curran's eyes swept over the crowd of shoppers, lingering for a moment on a petite redhead with hair down to her waist. She was all lush curves and big bright blue eyes. His body reacted, and he knew that, once upon a time, he would have tried to seduce her. Forcing his gaze away he turned towards the temple. He had a mission to complete. Today he was going to speak to the priests of the Stardust Chalice and find out about those dark dimensional portals. How had they been opened? Where did they lead? His jaw hardened. They would tell him what he wanted to know or, creator help them, they would die. He glanced back around once more, and realized the small woman was heading right for him. He almost groaned. This was not the time for his invisibility to fail.

Stopping in front of the man, Willow glanced around quickly and whispered. "Why are you here? You are in danger! Grave danger. You must leave, at once. If they catch you, it will be very bad. You must leave!"

"You can see me?" His voice was flat, and he wanted to curse.

She frowned. "Of course, I can see you. You're not a night specter." She reached out and touched his shoulder as if to prove it. "Did you hear me?"

He stared at her pretty face, a muscle jumping in his jaw as he felt the zing of her touch, a small electrical shock that went directly to his cock. He considered the danger if he were to ignore her and continue with his mission. Ah Fuck, there was no way he could risk it. He would have to return another day. Glancing around at all the shoppers, he growled. Too many people who might notice if this woman suddenly disappeared into thin air. He circled her, and she turned as he did. Her eyes widened, and he wondered if she was realizing that she should have been more careful. He took a step forward, and she stepped back. Step by step he moved her around the corner of the temple into a shaded alley, and before she could dash around him, he reached out and tossed her over his shoulder.

Dismayed when he reached for her, she twisted to evade him, but he simply grabbed her and threw her unceremoniously over his shoulder. With an angry shriek she struggled, hitting him with the loaf of bread, realizing the bread was not going to cut it with this... this barbarian, she dropped the loaf and started kicking and punching. No way in the Dimension of Shadows was this man taking her anywhere! He ignored her, so she did what any sane woman being carried off by a stranger would do. She bit him. Hard. "Ass! Let me go! Help! Someone help me!" But no one seemed to hear her, or even notice her desperate fight. In the darkness of the alley a dimly glowing shape appeared, and the man stepped into it.

Chapter Nineteen

STAR DATE: 20580.06.17

Dimension Five

Ancient city of Varl, Kalyria

ELIANA AND HER BROTHER Rune appeared in the inner sanctuary of the Sacred Stardust Chalice. It was dimly lit by the glowing chalice sitting on a table in the center of the vast sanctum. Four warrior priests surrounded the energy shielded chalice, and two warrior priests stood guard at each entrance point in the room. They drew their swords. Rune smiled and both of them stepped into the stream of light he created. "May we speak with the High Priest of the Stardust Temple?"

The High Priest entered the inner sanctuary with one of the warrior priests a short time later. He took one look at Rune and Eliana and his ancient face, marked by a million wrinkles lit up. He laughed and stepped forward, his hand held out in greeting. "Rune and Eliana Aezorwyn. We are honored."

Eliana touched his hand in the greeting of the Kalyrian people. "We are honored, Guardians of the Sacred Stardust

Chalice. We wish to examine the Chalice and have a demonstration of its powers."

The High Priest hesitated, his eyes narrowing. "You do not know it's powers?" He crossed his arms and stood with his legs apart as he studied them.

A slight smile touched Rune's lips. "I am glad to see that you are a careful man."

"Careful?" The man tilted his head. "I am a deeply suspicious man. Trusting cost us gravely and resulted in the death of a whole species of people. I will not allow that to happen again."

Eliana nodded. "We know the cost that you paid. All the priests at the temple that day died. Along with sixty young Dark Elf soldiers in service to the Suzerain and a specialized Dark Elf Military team."

"What we do not understand is the role the Sacred Chalice played," Rune said. "Since the Chalice was placed in your keeping, millennia ago, it has been used to help people. To heal people. We need to know what changed the Chalice."

"Should you not have come seven years ago? When this temple became a place of horror and death. Should you not have stepped in to protect the priests and the Dark Elves? Where were you when we needed you?" The ancient priest set his jaw and stared at them.

Eliana sighed and looked at her brother. "We were embroiled in another war, in another dimension, fighting to save the multiverse from a being so evil that to have ignored him would have resulted in the destruction of the multiverse. We were not aware of what was happening here until far too late."

"A distraction?"

Rune nodded. "We believe so. We were not aware of the role the Chalice played in this tragedy until recently."

The High Priest looked at the two Creators and considered their words. "All I can tell you is that when the Council of priests was informed of the battle, they dispatched Warrior priests immediately. We were too late. We entered a scene of mass slaughter, though of course the Suzerain did not see it as a crime. Our temple had been violated, our priest murdered, and young men and women who were following Suzerain orders were dead. We found no specialized unit of Dark Elves. The Chalice was here, and it contained blood. We had it analyzed and it was from the young Dark Elves." The man's eyes were shadowed as with the darkness of his memories. "We will never know exactly what went on here, but I will tell you the temple had a stench that took us many days to get rid of. There are massive scorch marks on the walls and floors that remain a mystery to this day."

Eliana looked at Rune, then back at the High Priest. "Can we look at the Chalice? May I hold it?"

The priest nodded once. "I will permit it."

"Thank you," Rune said with a respectful inclination of his head to the man.

The priest brought a slender device from a pocket hidden in his voluminous robes. A few touches to the screen and the energy shield that surrounded the chalice disappeared. He tucked his device away, walked over to the table, and lifted the chalice, handing it to Eliana.

Eliana turned the chalice in her hands as she analyzed the composition of the relic. "This chalice was created from an ancient meteorite. It's incredibly old. I would say from the start of the multiverse." She paused and her head tilted, her brows furrowing. "Rune. There is more than just stardust embedded in this chalice." Her breath caught and she looked at her brother. "There is a fragment of coded stardust. It calls to me."

Rune walked over to her and touched the chalice. "Hmm, there is indeed." He turned to look at the priest. "What did you use to activate the chalice? We have only heard of this chalice being used to bring healing."

The priest nodded. "We only ever used the finest wine from grapes grown on this world."

Rune and Eliana looked at each other. Eliana held up her hand and a second Chalice appeared, identical to the original. She handed both Chalices to the priest. "Guardian of the Sacred Stardust Chalice, this is a second Chalice made of the same meteorite that the first was made of. The only difference is the one fragment that made the chalice vulnerable to the perversion of its powers, is not present. The original Chalice needs to be taken to a place where it can never be found by any with evil intent. Will you trust us to do that?"

The ancient priest studied both cups and handed the original back to Eliana. "I have felt the evil that was committed every time I have touched the chalice since that terrible day. We have not dared to use it for healing since. I will gladly trade so that we might continue our service of healing hurting people."

"Thank you." Eliana smiled and gently touched the wise leader of the priests of this temple. Stepping back, she and Rune disappeared.

Chapter Twenty

STAR DATE: 20580.06.17
  Dimension Five
  Realm of the Forsaken
  Aezorwyn

WILLOW FELT DISORIENTED, for a moment, as the energy from her home world slipped away, dizziness sweeping over her, and she couldn't catch her breath. Trying desperately to pull air into her lungs, she began to shake as an icy coldness crept through her veins. She shook so badly that she wondered if she was going to die. Until the foreign energy of an alien world rushed into her, flooding her system. She gasped as heated air, pure and sweet, pulsating with erotic life, came rushing back into her aching lungs. Heat swept over her, through her, and she became shockingly aware of her body. Her nipples were tight, and she could feel silky dampness between her thighs. She gasped in another breath, everything happening too fast, and she struggled to shove aside the physical reactions she experienced. What was happening to her? Fury began to race through her blood, and she swore at the man and bit him a second time, not letting go until she tasted blood. That got his attention. "Let me go! Put me down!"

Curran growled and yanked the woman off his shoulder. One hand grabbed her arm, and the other wiped blood from his shoulder. He looked at the red smeared on his fingers. His eyes met hers. "If you bite me again, I'll take it as an invitation to fuck you. Are we clear?" His eyes staring into hers were hard as obsidian, his voice was a dark rumble. Willow swallowed hard, fully convinced that this man meant what he said.

Jerking out of his grip, she turned around. Stone walls? Stone floor? Where had he brought her? How had they gotten here? She was frightened, terrified. Too many things happening too fast, made it hard to process everything, let alone control the raging arousal flooding her system. *How could she be aroused? She didn't have a kidnapping fetish. Did she?* A searing pain burned the skin over her breast, and she gasped, her hand pressing over the area.

Curran swore as she jerked away from him, but his attention was on fiery pain burning into his chest. *What in the Dimension of Shadows?*

Willow scrambled back from him as he swore and tore at his clothing, yanking his shirt over his head. She stared with huge eyes as a dark red and silver crescent moon appeared on his chest. But it wasn't just the strange mark that held her attention. The man was built like a warrior, rippled abs, and sleek muscles under his brown skin. She snapped her gaze forward, a blush heating her cheeks as she took a step away and bumped into a wall. Trying to gain her bearings, she flattened one hand against the cool stone, the other still pressed to her chest. She took a deep breath, hoping that the mark she saw appearing on the man was not appearing on her as well.

Curran reached out and grabbed the woman's arm, jerking her around, fury riding him, what the shadows had she done? His eyes fell to where she was pressing her hand over her breast, and he fisted his hand into her shirt and tore it from her body. His fingers closed over her wrist, and he pulled her hand away from the area she was holding. A silver and red crescent moon, exactly the same as the one that now marked him.

His fingers brushed over that burning spot on her chest and she gasped, looking down to see the same mark that had appeared on him. She struggled furiously, trying to push his hands off her. The man stepped back, his face unreadable. "Who are you? Why have you brought me here?" She spat, her arms crossing over her chest.

Curran eyed the woman, turned, picked up his shirt from the floor and handed it to her. He wasn't a saint, of course he'd seen her breasts, and now he was struggling with a rock-hard cock, but he also was not an asshole. There was no reason for her to know that the sight of her breasts had caused an unusually strong reaction in him. He waited patiently as she struggled into his shirt and fuck if that didn't cause an even stranger feeling deep inside him. He wanted to growl but instead kept his face expressionless, until she had smoothed the much too big garment down over her hips.

"Curran Nadiir. Spirit Warrior." He identified himself. "You are on the planet of Aezorwyn, home of the Dark Elves."

"Dark Elves." She shook her head slowly, confused and more than a little afraid. "They are gone."

He shrugged. "And yet, here we are, on the planet of my people. We are not as easy to kill as the Suzerain would like you to believe."

Ushering her farther into the room, he closed the heavy door and she glanced around. The room was warm with a fireplace burning, and glowing stones acting like lights sat on a few surfaces. She frowned, feeling like she had traveled back in time.

"Curran?" A feminine voice spoke, and she glanced over at the bed. A very naked woman with pale blue skin knelt, watching them, and Willow gasped.

Curran turned, a frown on his face, to see Keanna kneeling naked on his bed. He'd told her to be ready for him when he got back, but his entanglement with the little redhead had completely driven the beautiful Keanna from his mind. He gave Keanna a cursory glance. With her long black hair and slender body, she was beautiful, but his eyes lifted back to the redhead. Keanna didn't hold a candle to this stranger. And the hard on he was currently sporting had nothing to do with the sensual Keanna. He looked back into the bright blue eyes of the stranger as he breathed in her sunshine and cinnamon scent. "Who are you?"

She stared at him with huge eyes as he cast a brief glance at the naked woman then looked back at her. Those dangerous hard eyes now lit with a powerful inner fire. No, no this was bad. Every feminine instinct she possessed was screaming at her to get away from this dangerous male. He stepped in, inhaling deeply, and she pressed back against the wall, her heart racing.

He leaned down, nudging her head to the side so he had access to her neck. He took another breath, savoring the unique scent of the woman, but there had been fear in her eyes. He'd never hurt a woman in his life, and he did not intend to change that now. He stepped away from her and looked back over to Keanna. "Leave. I'll speak with you tomorrow."

Keanna arched an eyebrow and rose from the bed. "Well, that is a shame," she said softly, her golden eyes moving over the woman that Curran had brought to his suite. "I will need to make other arrangements for this evening." Curran gave a curt nod as he watched her shrug into her robe.

After belting her wrap, Keanna walked over to Curran. "What is this?" She trailed her fingers lightly over the mark on his bare chest. Curran hissed, and took a step back, a feeling of unsettledness sweeping over him at her touch.

"Interesting," Keanna said and turned to the woman standing against the wall. "What is your name?"

"Willow Solar."

"Hello, Willow, I'm Keanna Starsong." She ignored Curran's low growl as she tilted her head. "Do you have one of those marks too?" She touched Willow's sleeve, well aware that it was Curran's shirt.

Willow automatically put her hand over the mark on her chest. "Can you help me? He brought me here against my will."

Keanna slanted an enigmatic look at Curran and shook her head. "I'm sorry Willow, there is no way to take you back. Did he hurt you?"

Curran glared at his dark-haired meddling friend. She fucking knew he would never hurt a woman.

Willow shook her head. "No. I mean he brought me here against my will, but he never..." She trailed off, her eyes huge.

"Why are you wearing his shirt?"

Willow shrugged, and Keanna turned to Curran, arching an eyebrow. Curran swore, "I do not know what magic this is, but when I realized she was in pain, and it was most likely the same reason I was, I tore her shirt from her to see if she had the same mark."

"And does she?"

Curran crossed his arms over his chest and narrowed his eyes, but he nodded.

"In my world," Keanna explained, "When a Dragon Warrior finds his mate, a mark appears on both of them."

Chapter Twenty-One

STAR DATE: 20580.06.17
Dimension Five
Realm of the Forsaken
Aezorwyn

CURRAN WATCHED KEANNA leave, her words hanging in the air. What the fuck? He walked over to lean against the stone arch of the window and watched Willow moodily. "I've never heard of a Kalyrian mating mark."

Willow stared at the man. "There is no such thing."

"As a Kalyrian mating mark?" Curran asked curiously, he had a feeling she was not going to simply accept that her life had changed.

"As a mating mark of any kind." Her tone was scathing. "Nice try though. Now take me home."

Curran crossed his arms and studied her face. "Keanna already told you that there is no way back."

"I don't believe that. You obviously come and go from wherever this is. And if you try to 'mate' with me, I'll remove your balls." Her tone was fierce, but in her head, she was struggling with panic and terror. This couldn't be happening.

She glanced towards the door, wondering if she was fast enough to make it before he caught her.

Curran shook his head, "I wouldn't. You'd never make it." Her bright blue eyes met his, and he could read the fear. "I don't know anything about any kind of mating mark. It's not something that has ever occurred in the Dark Elf population. But" He shrugged. "Since coming to this new world, anything is possible."

"If you—"

"I know." He interrupted. "You will cut off my balls." He reached out and she saw that he was holding out a dagger. Handle first. "Take it."

When she cautiously reached out to take the dagger, he let her have it, but twisted his hand at the last moment and caught her wrist. "Willow, we are the last of the Dark Elves. I cannot risk anyone finding out that we survived. Most people cannot see me when I am off world. But every so often, someone does. I am faced with a choice. Do I kill them, or do I bring them here?" His eyes hardened. "I will do whatever is necessary to protect my people. Do you understand?"

Willow nodded, her throat dry as the last of her hope disappeared. He would never let her go.

Curran stared at her for a moment, nodding towards the door. "You are free in this world. You can stay here in the castle, or you can leave. My people will treat you fairly. The choice is yours."

His words infuriated her, he was an arrogant bastard who'd stolen her from her home, when she'd tried to help him. She whirled around to glare at him, "You had no right to take me, you bastard! I want nothing to do with you! I will find a way off this planet. You can't keep me here!" Turning before he could see the tears she was fighting, she bolted as if all the hounds of the Dimension of Shadows were after her, terrified he would change his mind.

She almost fell down the first set of stairs in her panicked flight away from the crazy man who had taken her captive. Grabbing the handrail when she stumbled, she forced herself to slow down, glancing back over her shoulder in case he pursued her. The man was nowhere to be seen and that was all she cared about.

She hurried down another flight of stairs and another, ignoring the people she saw, hurrying, and dodging to avoid them. She bumped into a man as she finally spied a huge door, and they both crashed to the floor. Scrambling to her feet, she evaded the mans helping hand, ignored his concerned words and dashed out through the huge door— and she ran.

She would never know how long she ran in that headlong flight. Survival instincts drove her, pushing her as far from danger as it was possible to get. Finally, when she could no longer see the castle, she slowed to a stop. Gasping desperately for air, she leaned against an enormous, towering tree and looked around. She was surrounded by forest, as far as the eye could see. Massive trees of all kinds surrounded her, their colorful leaves dancing against a darkening purple sky. This was not her world.

She swallowed as she began to realize her new predicament. The sun was setting, and three moons hovered in the skies above her. One of them, the largest, was in its crescent phase, and was a deep red color that she'd never seen in a moon before. Night was coming, and she had no idea where she was, if she was safe, or what kind of creatures inhabited these woods. She began to shake as an eerie howl filled the air and a new kind of fear filled her. Oh gods, would she die out here? Alone and so far from everything she'd ever known? Would her brother miss her? Would anyone?

Dashing away the tears that trembled on her eyelashes, she became aware of a sound that she knew. Water. Rushing water, and where there was water, there were often people. She turned toward the sound, and began to walk, knowing she had to find the source of the sound. She walked for quite a while before she got a glimpse of water through the trees in the darkening light. It was a large stream, with no signs of people.

Stumbling over to it, she knelt at its bank to drink. The water was ice cold and refreshing, and the purest she'd ever tasted. Standing up, she wiped her hands on her pants and saw a waterfall just a short distance down the path, some unknown instinct nudging her to get closer. As she approached the falls, hidden deep in the beautiful woodland, she noticed a slight trail. Hoping the meandering path meant a village was close by, she followed it along the edge of the pool formed by the falls. She wondered if the sun would warm it enough that a person could swim in it. It was a thought that had her sigh with longing, her body aching, but this was neither the time nor the place for such things. Glancing back the way she came, she frowned, noticing that the path she was following disappeared as if the grass had already grown up over it. She hesitated, but there was nothing back there for her, so she forged on. The trail seemed to end at the base of the waterfall, and she frowned, but as she drew closer, in the rapidly dimming light, she saw that the way continued on, leading directly to the waterfalls. It was only as she stood right at the cascading waters that she realized the trail did not end there.

Following the path, scrambling over damp rocks and around huge boulders with some kind of pink moss, she stared around in wonder as she found herself in a small hidden cave behind the waterfall. The waters veiled the entryway so effectively that she couldn't see past them. The cave was darkening as the remaining rays of the setting sun receded, but the stone wall closest to her had an unusual glow in one spot. She walked over to examine the sight curiously.

A stone about the size of her fist glowed a pale yellow that cast a shallow circle of light. She reached out to touch it, and it tumbled from the wall in a small avalanche of stones to land at her feet. She crouched down and brushed some of the smaller stones away and drew her hand back in surprise as every stone she touched lit up. Realizing she had a source of light, she moved around the cave carefully touching the stones in the walls. A few lit up and cast the room in a soft glow. She could see that the only way in and out of the cave was through the path she'd taken to get here.

Feeling a bit safer, she decided she would stay here for the night and in the morning, hopefully, she could find her way to civilization where she would find the first ship going off-world. Easing down to the floor, she leaned back against the stone wall. Wrapping her arms around her knees, as she tried to push away the dark arousal that had plagued her from the moment she stepped onto this planet. Goddess, she burned. Lifting a trembling hand, she pushed it through her heavy hair, and dashed away the tears that refused to quit falling. She fell asleep on the cold, damp stone floor in that dark little cave behind the waterfall, shivering, cold, and yet, burning with dark unfulfilled needs.

Chapter Twenty-Two

STAR DATE: 20580.06.17
Dimension Five
Realm of the Forsaken
Aezorwyn

WILLOW AWOKE TO SOMEONE calling her name. A low, masculine voice that sent shivers down her spine. Opening her eyes, she blinked against the golden light flooding the cave. Sitting up, she put a hand up to shield her eyes.

"Willow Solar."

The bright light dimmed, and she blinked as her vision adjusted. A man stood in the cave, surrounded by a pale glow. Tall with a muscular build and a strikingly male beauty, his long silvery white hair flowed down his back and chest. He stood with his legs apart, all arrogant assurance and bold sexuality. His arresting, dark gaze made her think of ancient things. She'd never seen eyes like that before. Purest black yet filled with the unearthly colors of nebulas and galaxies.

"Willow Solar"

"Who—" She swallowed against the sudden dryness in her throat. "Who are you?"

"Rune. Creator. Protector. Charming Rogue." He said with a quirk of his lips, counting the titles off with his fingers. When she slowly stood, his eyes tracked over her. He made a low masculine sound of appreciation that sent a flicker of awareness through her blood. Then he lifted one eyebrow. "You are a brave one. Most would be kneeling right now."

"I'm not most."

He chuckled again. "As Curran found out, I believe."

She watched him warily. Curran. The man who'd kidnapped her. "Did he send you to bring me back?"

Rune seemed to find that even more amusing. "Ah, Willow Solar, I believe I shall enjoy knowing you. Come sit with me. We need to talk."

With a flick of his hand, soft pillows appeared along with a low table spread with delicious food. Food from her home world. Tears filled her eyes, even as the aroma caused her stomach to growl. She cautiously sat at the table, filled with astonishment. How had he done this? The man handed her a plate piled high with all her favorite foods and she took it, her hands shaking badly.

"I mean you no harm, Willow Solar. Eat and be at peace while I tell you a story."

As Willow ate, Rune began to tell her of the creation of the Dark Elf people in a world and dimension far from this one. The story was beautiful, filled with so much richness and life that she felt as if she was there watching it happen. When he came to the destruction of the Dark Elves, she cried. Her heart broken by the knowledge of the role her people played in the decimation of another species.

He paused and considered her for a long moment. "Willow Solar, I have seen the sorrow of your people, the guilt and the shame." He shook his head, "They were not to blame for what happened, and they have redeemed themselves beyond measure with the yearly tribute they pay to the memory of the Dark Elves." He reached out and touched her face, and she froze as his energy surged through her— foreign, heated, pulsating with erotic life. She lifted stunned eyes to him, for his energy was the energy of this planet.

"Ah, finally you notice, Willow Solar, Energy Enchanter. This planet is called Aezorwyn. The realm it's hidden in has no name, though my people, these wild Dark Elves, call it The Realm of The Forsaken." He gave a low chuckle. "If only they understood."

She hugged her knees and considered his words. She was confused. She thought him to be a native to this planet, but he was clearly telling her that he was a Creator. She took a deep breath. "How did they survive?"

"So very few made it here." His voice was heavy with grief, the sort of grief only a parent could feel. "I did not foresee the destruction of Sarehiri." He sighed heavily. "Though I should have. My attention was elsewhere. Another battle. Which I now believe was meant to be a distraction. That cursed Ash Morana almost succeeded!" Rune clenched his jaw and turned away from her for a minute as he battled his emotions. "I, their creator and the one sworn to protect them, did not see until it was almost too late." He turned back to Willow, his eyes filled with lightning and storms. "And then I saw them all dying. Their life breath taken from them like mist in the wind." His gaze hardened, his fists clenched, he stared at the gentle soul before him. "I could not allow it. I would not allow it. They deserved life! So, I created this realm." He gestured with a wave of his hand. "It's a mystery. Invisible, undetectable, a place of safety for my people."

He looked at her for a long moment as if studying the very core of her being, analyzing her right down to her DNA. He continued when she began to squirm under the weight of his gaze, his mouth almost curving in amusement. "I was certain I thought of everything, but after they arrived a new future came into being. A future that must be stopped— and, Willow Solar, you, will help me. I cannot bear for my people to suffer again, Energy Enchanter."

His eyes burned with his rage, with his fury that such a fate again awaited the ones he sought to protect. "There is much you do not know. The Suzerain are a vile people who have become corrupt and bloated in their power. They have built a kingdom on the blood and bones of countless civilizations. So many lives lost to their butchery and greed. They must be stopped, and the only ones powerful enough, brave enough are my Dark Elves."

With a burst of energy, he stood up and began to pace. "They are not ready yet. They have not recovered. They have not healed. You, Energy Enchanter, you are needed here. Your skills will bring the healing they need to save the universe."

With a wave of his hand, he cleared the table and dropped to the floor kneeling in front of Willow. "Unfortunately, the future is bleaker than what I have spoken of. You see, my power is enriched from sexual energy." He winked and continued as if he hadn't noticed her shocked blush. "I created this world, this realm, in such a manner that the natural sexual desires of everyone who enters have increased. This realm is a storehouse of such energy." He shrugged, "It's a unique phenomenon. The very atmosphere, the air in this world changes with the crescent phase of the crimson moon. That night, the men and women of Aezorwyn burn with a fever of unimaginable lust, their normal inhibitions cast aside. The extraordinary sexual energy from that dark night will, with the help of an energy enchanter, soon begin to overflow the planet and fill the entire realm."

He reached out, and stroked her cheek, and she froze, leery of what this being wanted from her. His chuckle was dark as he rose to his feet. "It's not enough, Willow Solar. All of this glorious sexual energy that they release with all their frenzied fucking, is not enough to give me the strength to protect this realm. I must ensure that it remains undetectable to the Suzerain. I must stop the blind destruction caused by a race too foolish to see the consequences of their actions—Before they find this realm and my people again."

Reaching down, he plucked the silent woman off the floor and set her on her feet, looping her arm through his with a debonaire flare. "I have a plan." His eyes filled with light and power, and far too much humour. She could not look away as he poured hot, burning erotic energy into her.

The mark on her chest began to heat up, and she gasped as ribbons of light filled the cave, their beauty binding together to create a vision of shapes and mists, couples appearing all around them. Couples enacting all of the sensuality and passion that he spoke of the Creator at her side slowly began to turn with her. The images shifted, darkness giving way to the light, and with each passing figure she recognized the silver and red mark they all bore.

"Mates." He said softly in her ear as they watched. "Couples whose hearts and souls are bonded in unheard of passion. Lives tied together in explosive ecstasy, in undying love. The energy they release will pour unprecedented raw sexual energy into the atmosphere of the planet." *And straight into me.* He did not speak of the most important ingredient in that empowering energy. He did not speak of the unending power of love. Without love, sexual energy was just a vitamin, but when it was colored and shaped by love it became a source of infinite undefined power.

She was stunned by the depth of his plan, with the sheer beauty of it. And it was beautiful. Love and passion and souls bound forever. It would take boldness and courage and fierce determination. Curran. His name whispered across her mind and Rune poured the heart of Curran Nadiir into her. She saw his courage in the face of terrible danger. His determination to save his people. To find his men. His valor in spite of the impossible odds. And she felt the greatness of the love that Rune felt for this man who had endured the unimaginable to save his people— to save Rune's people. She lifted tear filled eyes to the being who was touching her soul and he stepped back from her. "So now you know, Willow Solar. You know that you are key to saving the Dark Elves. That it must all start with Curran and you. What the two of you achieve as mates will set the precedents. Can you— No. *Will* you, set aside your fears, your preconceived ideas, and save my people?"

Chapter Twenty-Three

STAR DATE: 20580.06.17

Dimension Five
Realm of the Forsaken
Aezorwyn

CURRAN STARED OUT THE window of his tower suite, the slender crescent of the crimson moon rode high in the sky, and he burned. His cock had been hard since he'd returned with his captive, and he was resisting the intense urge to hunt her down. To hunt her down and— He cut off the thought. Shadows no. He was not going there. He shouldn't have sent Keanna away. She knew how to handle the darkness of his needs.

Keanna had been with him since he'd gone with the Sarisian, Thorne Feral, on a rescue mission. He never could stand the thought of slavery. They'd taken the Althanian women they saved from the cruel bonds of the Zemyneah slave trade to Sarisia, a world in a far-off dimension, where they were freed from the technology that forced them into sexual slavery. Keanna, and several others had opted to come with him back to Aezorwyn. Just as she had chosen to call herself his pet. His, to do with as he pleased. He had argued against that, insisted she take time to heal and start a new life. In the end, six months after she came to Aezorwyn, he found her kneeling naked in his bed.

He'd thoroughly enjoyed her brand of sexuality. Submissive, and willing to do anything he wanted. And she had never been shy about bringing her friends to his bed for some more adventurous games. He smirked at the memory, and contemplated seeking Keanna out. She would probably be in her suite on the next floor with at least one of her friends. Probably, Nia. They would be more than happy if he showed up. He pictured Keanna with her slender body, her high firm breasts with their dark blue tips, and her friend Nia spread out naked on Keanna's bed. He was certain that Keanna would have tied her hands and feet so she could do all kinds of wicked things to Nia. Things he wouldn't mind helping with.

His hand found his cock and he stroked, his tongue sliding over his bottom lip as he pictured the scene more fully in his head. The soft red curls between Nia's thighs, her rose colored nipples, the crimson and silver moon mark above her right breast.

Ah fuck. He turned from the window. He wasn't imagining Nia and Keanna, he was imagining Willow. His fucking captive. And the idea of Keanna touching Willow pissed him right the fuck off. Just as the thought of Keanna's hand on him did. Growling, he stomped into the bathing chamber and poured cold water into the basin. Splashing his face, he looked into the mirror. "Curran, you have a long night of jerking off ahead of you. Fucking Crimson Moon Fever."

Chapter Twenty-Four

STAR DATE: 20580.06.17

Dimension Five
Realm of the Forsaken
Aezorwyn

ONE MINUTE WILLOW HAD been standing in the cave agreeing to help Rune Aezorwyn, Creator of the universe, the next she was standing in Curran's castle bedroom. She gasped, and turned, but Rune was not there. She swallowed, and hearing a noise, looked up to see Curran coming out of a side room. He was still not wearing a shirt, and his pants clearly outlined the condition of his cock. Her eyes widened, her nipples grew hard, and she whirled around to stare out the window. The dark sky was sprinkled with stars and three moons hung in all their splendor. The largest was a slender crescent of crimson red. She blinked. *That bastard, Rune!* She could feel her woman parts growing damp.

"How the shadows did you get back into my room?"

Willow turned slowly, licking suddenly dry lips. "I... Uhm... Rune. Rune brought me here."

"Rune?" He raised a brow. "I know every person on this planet, Willow. There is no one named Rune here."

She stared at him in confusion. "Rune Aezorwyn. Creator."

Curran crossed his arms, irritated beyond measure. "The Creators forsook us long ago. My people insisted on naming this world after that bastard. I believe they thought it would return his favor to us." He shrugged, "There is no favor to be had from a being who does not exist."

Willow stared at the man before her and had no idea what to say. "I—"

"You decided my bed was warmer and safer than a night in the wilds?" His eyes glinted in the soft glow cast by the fire in the fireplace, as she shook her head.

"No! I... Rune really did bring me here."

"Do you need a Creator's permission to fuck, Willow?"

She blinked, her mouth falling open. "What? No. What?"

"So, you are saying that Rune has finally heard my people's cries and brought you as a..." He stared at her, his eyes hard and unreadable. "As a gift? For me."

Willow shook her head. *What the shadows?* She opened her mouth, but nothing came out, even her thoughts stuttered.

"Take off your clothes."

"What?"

"Either take off your clothes or leave. Those are the only choices you have." Curran crossed his arms and waited.

"Can we slow this down. Please."

"You see that big red moon outside?"

She nodded, her heart racing in her chest.

"Did someone," he waved a hand at the door, "Out there, explain it to you?"

"Y... Yes." She nodded hesitantly.

"You know that tonight is only going to end in one way, either you will choose to fuck me, or you will choose to fuck someone else. So, choose."

Willow shook her head. "I'm not going to... "

Curran wanted to growl. Standing here arguing with the little red-haired spitfire was not even close to what he wanted to do with her. If she could read his mind, she would probably be running for the hills. His eyes narrowed. Shit. Knowing his luck... "Are you saying the crimson moon fever is not affecting you?"

Willow licked her lips and froze as his eyes drifted over her body, her nipples hardened further, and she grew warm just from the fire in his eyes. His mouth kicked up on one side, and he looked at her with a crooked grin. "Just based on the power of observation, I would say that you are not resistant to the crimson moon. So here is the deal, you have a choice. You can leave or you can stay. If you leave, no one will force you to do anything you don't want to do. But you should be aware that the arousal you are already feeling is only going to get stronger as the night progresses. Eventually you will end up in someone's bed."

She wanted to stand on her principals. He had kidnapped her! But Rune had kind of ruined that for her. *If you can hear me, Rune, you are a bastard!* She thought she heard laughter and she wanted to throw something, but maybe not as much as she wanted to touch Curran. This was the closest she'd ever been to such a gloriously fit male body. She fully understood why Keanna had been disappointed to be sent away. She frowned. "Ground rules. I don't share. Ever." *Oh. My. Gosh. What had she just said?*

"I will agree to that." Curran stepped right up to her, and his scent washed over her. Her lady parts responded enthusiastically. "My turn." His eyes drifted over her, his nostrils flaring as he breathed her in. "You have to be open to what I do. Are you brave enough, Willow"?

Willow stared into his eyes, some part of her terrified, but she nodded. Rune had shown her this man's heart, she knew he would never harm her. "I am."

"Take off your clothes, Willow." His eyes held her gaze and she couldn't look away. Swallowing, she kicked off her soft boots and socks, pushed her pants down, and stepped out of them. His shirt was long enough that it more than adequately covered her.

Curran let his eyes drift over her. She was still covered more than some people at a market. His shirt was like a dress on her. His eyes moved over her bare legs, noting her trim ankles and small feet, before moving back up. She would barely reach his shoulder. And she lifted off her shirt. Fuck! She was tiny but she was curvy in all the right places. Soft red curls covered her mound, her waist was slender, and her tummy gently rounded. Her breasts were full and crowned with pink nipples. He wanted a taste. His eyes lifted to her face, big blue eyes, a scattering of freckles across her nose, and her mouth was lush enough that he wanted to feast on it. He leaned down and his mouth covered hers. A gentle first kiss, another, and another each one getting more demanding, hungrier. Finally with a harsh groan, he picked her up and strode over to the bed.

She felt the softness of the bed beneath her, and he was coming down beside her, taking her mouth in a hot hard kiss that shook the foundations of her safe little world. He took charge completely, controlling the kiss in a way that made her stomach flutter nervously and heat bloom between her legs. When he finally lifted his head, she was breathless and clinging to him. Did he like what he saw? She lifted her chin, she might not be the most beautiful woman in the universe, but she was who she was and had no wish to change. His mouth settled on hers again, and he took the kiss deep. His tongue parted her lips, and he plundered her mouth, shifting his body to cover hers. Her hands settled on his shoulders and stroked, slid down over his back. He felt amazing, hot and hard muscled. Her breath caught when he cupped her breast, his thumb brushing lightly across her nipple. Oh. She arched into him, shocked by the intensity of the pleasure that he was drawing from her with that one simple touch.

His head dipped down, and he took a nipple in his mouth, his teeth closing gently around the sensitive tip before he tugged. She gasped, the sound shooting straight to his groin, and he did it again.

Reluctantly, he let go and stood up, stripping off his pants. His cock rose to rest against his belly, and when his eyes met hers, he couldn't help the grin at her shy glance and the way she bit her lip. He lay down beside her, catching her hands and lifted them up beside her head. He moved between her legs and slid his hands under her knees drawing them up so her feet were planted on the mattress. "How pretty." He murmured as he stared down at her pussy. He eased her folds open and leaned in to lick.

She clutched at the sheets in shocked ecstasy as his tongue slid over her hard little clit, sending fire rocketing through her veins and she writhed under the onslaught. "Oh gods! Oh gods! Oh gods!" His teeth closed over her clit, and she cried out, her hips pushing up. He bit down carefully, testing to see how she would respond. She jerked, a soft crying leaving her mouth, and he felt her get wetter. Her hands slid into his hair, clenched. And he decided that next time he was going to tie her hands to the headboard. Pushing her legs further apart, he began to lick again, alternating with thrusting his tongue deep inside her.

Goddess, she was going to die from pleasure. Her heart raced, she panted, and helplessly squirmed against him. He pushed her thighs further apart, and she cried out, jerking as he sucked her clit into his mouth. Lost in the sensations, she could only ride out the storm he brought. His tongue drove her crazy and she arched when he thrust it deep inside her. She could feel her inner walls clenching, and she bucked again. Too much, she thought, dazed. Too much. But he wasn't backing off. She whimpered and tried to move away, but he followed her, his nose bumping against her clit. She whimpered again, moaned. She was rising fast towards an orgasm.

"Not yet," he said and backed off. She moaned in disappointment, and he smiled understanding what she wanted but he wasn't done yet. He wanted more. He brought his hand down in a sharp little spank on her open pussy and she gasped. The tap to her clit jolted her and she gasped at the slight sting, he thrust a finger deep inside of her. Tight. So tight. She moved her hips, and he added a second finger. He began to thrust them and with his other hand, he plucked at her clit. Pinching lightly, she moaned, her eyes closing. "Open your eyes, Willow." She blinked open her eyes and he smiled at the confused look he saw in them. "Keep your eyes on mine." She cried out as he thrust in and out of her tight pussy with his fingers while he circled her clit. She tossed her head on the pillows, her hips rising and falling, beautiful panting cries filling the air. Her body started to tighten, and he eased his fingers from her sheath, bringing them up to paint her lips. "Open your mouth." She blinked at him, startled, but opened, he eased his fingers inside. "Taste."

She closed her mouth over his fingers, licking as her own flavor burst over her senses and she moaned. He rose up on his knees and the look in his eyes, made her stomach clench. His face was shiny from her juices, and she licked her lips, when he eased his fingers from between them, and bit her lip as a shiver slid over her.

Kneeling between her spread legs, he grasped her hips and lifted, bringing her into his lap. He grasped his cock and eased it into her, clenching his jaw so he didn't go off like an untried youthling.

Gasping, she could feel herself stretching to accommodate him. She squirmed helplessly. She felt so full, stretched to the point of madness, and with each thrust she felt her slickness increasing.

He took her nipple into his mouth and his teeth caught it in a firm hold. Every thrust of his hips, drove his cock deeper and harder inside of her, and tugged on her nipple.

She gasped and met him stroke for stroke. *She was perfect. Everything he needed.*

She was caught up in the fire, burning for him, in a way she had never burned before. She could feel the energy coursing through her body, feel its power and she shuddered, as it seemed to spark her lust higher and higher. A shiver traveled over her body; her nipples tightened impossibly. And he bit harder. Fire and pain seared through her, and she cried out, arching up and shockingly felt more moisture pooling. Every slick thrust of his cock, slid wetly through her swollen flesh, sparking nerve endings she had never known about. Pleasure, intense and driving, rode through her body with every thrust of his cock over her inner walls. She gasped when he reached down and rolled her clit between his thumb and forefinger, circled it, squeezed. She cried out, tossing her head against the sheets and arched helplessly. Whatever he wanted. He could have whatever he wanted, because he was doing things to her, wicked, wicked things and she would do anything for him not to stop. Not yet, not while she was so close to toppling over this abyss into a sea of pleasure.

He could not believe how responsive she was, how perfect she was for his brand of fucking. Reluctantly letting her nipple slide from his mouth, he looked deeply into her eyes, and pinched her clit. Growling, "Come!" And she shattered, her body convulsing, her pussy clenching so tight that she dragged him over the edge with her. He shouted as his balls tightened and a shiver of ecstasy shot down his spine.

She gasped as she felt him jerk inside her, felt the first spurt of his hot cum landing against the wall of her pussy, gasped again as he pulled out and hot liquid splashed over her sensitized clit and a smaller second orgasm swept through her. He plunged back inside her, and she arched helplessly as his hot seed filled her. Panting, she rested against the bed, totally limp. He slumped over her, a heavy weight that grounded her. His breaths panted in her ear for a couple of minutes, before his arms closed around her and he rolled to the side, still inside her, and just held her tightly against him. After a few minutes, he pulled away just enough to see her face. "Rest, it won't be long before the crimson moon fever starts again."

He woke her a bare hour later and took her from behind. His hands gentler but no less demanding. She lost track of the number of times she came, but in the end, he'd bitten her shoulder as he flooded her with his seed. The third time, she'd woken him. He'd been very accommodating as she climbed on top and ridden them both to a powerful climax. The night continued, snapshot after snapshot forever imprinted on her memory. Forever imprinted on her soul. Bent over the bed, against the wall, on her hands and knees, on her back with her legs over his shoulders, she'd never made love that many times in her whole life. She'd never known it was possible to have that many orgasms in one night.

Chapter Twenty-Five

STAR DATE: 20580.06.18

Dimension Thirty-Seven

Perileos Star System

Xehshyhra

HOW MANY TIMES HAD he gone over the whole clus-terfuck in his mind? How many times had he tried to figure out what had gone wrong, who had betrayed them and why? His gut had warned him to be careful from the moment he'd heard of their new mission, and he'd paid attention. They'd checked every fact. Shadows, he'd triple-checked that fuck-ing information that they'd been given. He'd sent the info to sources so remote that no one should have been able to pay them off. No one should have even known about the sources he had. In the end his mind came back to the same fact over and over again. They'd been set up.

His arms trembling in agony, he took a deep breath be-fore allowing his muscles to relax, as he slipped back under the water. *Ah, Curran,* he thought of his commander, his best friend, the man he had dedicated his life to protecting. *I failed you, my friend. I failed us all.*

Chapter Twenty-Six

STAR DATE: 20580.06.18
Dimension Five
Farport City, Tryria

COMMANDER D'MIRON WAS tall, dark haired, and considered handsome, until you looked into the shadowed iron grey of his eyes. He turned the page of the report he was reading, frowning at the holo-image that appeared. "When was the last time we tested this woman?"

His assistant, Tamika Firemyst looked up, her lush red lips dipping in a frown of confusion. "Why would we test her, sir? She's a jewelry maker. The real power in that family is her brother, Jericho Solar. He's an Energy Manipulator, one of the most powerful ones we've ever found." Ok, so she had a thing for Jericho Solar. Who wouldn't? The man was 'be still my heart' and 'I need to change my panties', hot. He was also dangerous. The last time he'd been in the office, he'd looked at her with such intensity that she'd almost gone up in smoke, even though she knew she should stay as far away from him as she could possibly get. Sexy? Oh, yes please. Dangerous? No. Shadows No. Her mother had not raised a senseless girl.

But... On his way out, he'd paused by her desk and leaned down to whisper that he loved the three small dots above her eyebrows that spoke of her Alraran heritage. It was so not politically correct, but he'd given her that look. The one that said he'd like nothing more than to see her naked. To see if the rumors about those dots being on other places was true. She'd given him a quelling look, all to aware that the Commander could walk in at any moment. But she had felt the slickness between her thighs long after he'd gone. And she'd called herself all kinds of a fool for it.

A thick silence permeated the air as Commander D'miron stared at her, and Tamika cleared her throat, pressing her suddenly damp hands against her skirt, then hurried on, "His father, Kano Solar, was a medical energy reader, and at one time, we thought he was an Energy Enchanter, but after testing him repeatedly." She shrugged. "It was apparent that he was just a reader. Disappointing, but, to my knowledge, it looks like the Enchanter genetics have failed to appear in several generations of this family."

She watched the man she worked for, taking a careful step back at the look in his eyes. She was not foolish enough to trust him. No, she had seen far too much for that. If she hadn't so desperately needed an income, there was no way in the galaxy that she would have voluntarily brought herself to the attention of this high-ranking member of the Suzerain.

Commander D'miron let his frosty gaze settle on the perfectly attired blonde woman until she shifted uncomfortably and ceased her prattle. Fool. "The Solar family has had an Energy Enchanter born into every generation for the last millennium. Somehow, I fail to believe that their DNA has suddenly changed. Bring her in. I want to meet with Willow Solar."

Chapter Twenty-Seven

STAR DATE: 20580.06.18

Dimension Five
Realm of the Forsaken
Aezorwyn

THE SUN WAS HIGH IN the sky, flooding the room with light when Curran woke her the next day. "I've run you a bath. A soak will probably do you good. When you are done, come down to the library, and we'll eat and talk."

She answered in a sleepy voice, and the corner of his mouth quirked up. She was gorgeous. Her hair was tangled, her eyes that stunning bright blue when she opened them, and her lush mouth swollen from his kisses. He could see a bite mark on her shoulder and more than one red mark from the scruff on his face. The cover slipped when she turned and he feasted his eyes on her beautiful breasts with their rose-colored nipples, before she blushed and pulled the cover back up. *A shame that.* Leaning down, he placed a hand on the pillow beside her head and took her mouth in a long slow kiss. A slide of lips and mingled breath, his tongue sweeping into her mouth with a lazy stroke that drew a soft moan from her. "Good rising, Willow Solar." He spoke against her lips.

"Good rising," She whispered, and he smiled, straightening.

"Enjoy your soak, then come downstairs to the library. No need to rush, unless you're starving of course." He winked at her, turned and headed out of his bedroom and down the stairs to his meeting. He was more than a little puzzled by how good he felt this morning. Especially since it was the morning after the Crimson Moon.

Walking into the library, he found that breakfast and coffee were already set up on a side table. Garrett Wyatt, Marina Anluan, and Dreven Avanth were sitting at a round table at one end of the big room, and they all looked like shadows. He strode over and got himself a plate of food and a cup of morning brew.

He nodded at the team he had put in place to help him with the madness of building a society. "You three look like shadows. Did you try to fuck everyone on the planet last night?"

Dreven looked disgusted. Marina almost choked on her morning brew, and Garrett laughed, his amber eyes amused. "I was too busy with Nia and Keanna to consider taking on the whole female population, but I did try to tempt Maya into joining in."

"Did she?"

"Nope. She was quite frosty actually."

Marina, a slender, fit woman with long dark hair and hazel green eyes, shook her head. "Garrett, have you considered trying to talk to her when you're not caught in the middle of the crimson moon fever?"

Curran took a sip of his coffee to hide his grin.

"How come you're so full of energy this morning?" Dreven asked, his voice surly. His brown hair was cut brutally short and combed to within an inch of its life.

Curran shrugged as he swallowed. "Maybe I'm just a morning soul."

Marina burst out laughing, and he eyed her. "You? A morning soul on the morning after the crimson moon?" She laughed again, ignoring his raised brow. "Not likely."

Garrett grinned, took a drink of his brew, and stretched. He yawned, set his drink down and rubbed his scruff covered jaw. "What was so damn important that we needed to meet this morning anyways?"

Curran leaned back in his chair. "When I went off-world yesterday, my hope was to find information about how the Suzerain had opened those fucked up dimensional gates and where they led too. Unfortunately, I got sidetracked." He rubbed his neck and looked at the others. "I was seen."

Marina sighed and shook her head. "Damn it to shadows and back. Man or woman?"

"A woman," he hesitated. "This was different."

Garrett leaned forward a frown on his face. "How was it different?"

Curran reached down, and pulled off his shirt, revealing the mark on his chest.

"What the shadows is that?" Dreven demanded.

"It's been suggested that it might be some kind of mating mark."

Marina looked blankly at him, then at Garrett. Dreven snorted. And Garrett cocked his head. "Nia told me that there are some races in her dimension that mark the people they are joined with. 'Soul joinings, she said."

Curran nodded slowly. "The woman I brought here has the same marking, in the same place as mine."

"What witchcraft is this?" Dreven looked disgusted. "We should kill her."

"Overreact much?" Marina said and gave Dreven a hard look.

"I'm not killing her." Curran frowned. "Why would you even say that?"

"She obviously marked you. We have no idea why or how. For all we know she could've planted some kind of tracking device on you. And if that isn't enough, we're Dark Elves, we don't need mates or any mark that implies owner-ship." He looked at the mark of a betrayer branded into Curran's cheek.

Curran took a sip of his brew, while he contemplated how good it would feel to beat Dreven to a bloody pulp. "Dark Elves have married their lovers since the beginning of time. As for ownership, you fucking well know my stand on that." His voice harsh, he glared at Dreven until the other man looked away.

Garrett shook his head and glanced at the small red head who was hesitating at the doorway. "Come on in, little one. I promise we don't bite unless you ask nicely."

Curran snorted. "She's the one who bites." He looked at Willow and grinned at her outraged gasp. "But I did warn her that it would get her fucked."

Garrett laughed, a loud booming sound, that filled the room with the feeling of camaraderie and acceptance. "Did she bite you again?"

Marina rolled her eyes, "I think that it's more than obvious what Curran got up to last night with this pretty redhead." She looked at the redhead and winked. "Don't worry, all the women have a thing for Curran."

Curran groaned and looked at Willow. "Please ignore my people." He pulled his shirt back on and walked over to the small woman. Taking her arm, he led her over to the side table and handed her a plate. "Please help yourself to anything you wish to eat and come and join us at the table. Do you like brew?"

Willow nibbled her lip and began to put some of the delicious smelling food onto her plate. When Curran mentioned brew, she shook her head. "No, I drink tea, do you have any?"

Marina rose from her chair and approached the woman. "There is tea. It's a kind of spiced tea that we brew here on Aezorwyn." She picked up a small, rounded pottery jug with a spout and poured Willow a cup.

Once they were seated again, Curran introduced Willow to the people around the table. "Everyone, this is Willow Solar. She is from Kalyria. And she is... my mate" He glanced over at the blue-eyed redhead whose eyes were huge, and at his friends whose mouths were hanging open. "This is Marina and Garrett and Dreven. They help me to look after my people." He reached over and tugged aside the edge of Willow's shirt revealing the mating mark on her upper right shoulder just above her breast. Willow slapped his hand away and glared at him. Marina chuckled. "Don't let him get away with anything, Willow."

"Does that make her our new Queen?" Garrett asked, a teasing light in his eyes. Willow's eyes got even bigger, and she started to shake her head.

Dreven interrupted. "No. She's simply his latest fuck. Isn't that right Curran?" He stared at their leader, his jaw clenched.

Curran stood up fast, his chair crashing to the floor. "Willow is mine. You will treat her with respect, or I'll kick your fucking ass. Do you understand?" His eyes, cold and hard, held Dreven's until the man finally looked away. He put his hand on Willow's shoulder, and his eyes met hers. He could see her fury and feel it in the fine tremor of the shoulder beneath his hand.

Willow took a deep breath, the last time she had been this angry was when her brother had been taken by the Suzerain. She fought for control while she looked at each person in the room, studying them. Curran was red hot with fury, a seething cauldron ready to erupt at any moment. She put her hand on his leg, breathed in calmness, and gently sent it to him. Her eyes moved over Garrett, anger, alertness, and regret all swirled through him along with a terrible trauma that held the faintest beginnings of healing blue. She knew he had not intended harm to her with his words. Marina was interesting in a different way. She moved with the controlled grace of a dangerous predator. Yet, Willow could see the energy scars that spoke of harrowing trauma. Last she looked at Dreven. The same trauma, but here was a man who had chosen to let his rage and hatred consume him.

"Curran." Marina said, giving Dreven a look of disgust, and turned her back on him. "Perhaps I can show Willow around the castle and help her to get some clothing and other supplies."

Curran nodded, his eyes back on Dreven. "Thank you, Marina."

"Do you want me to assign her a suite?"

Curran shook his head, turning to Willow. "No. Willow will share my suite." Willow blinked and looked at Curran. She hadn't even thought about where she would live. She frowned, and stared down at her hands, feeling a deep sense of surrealness. This whole situation was insane.

"Willow."

She looked up and met Curran's eyes. He gave her a faint smile and she nodded. "Thank you, Marina, I would like a tour, and I really do need some things."

Curran watched them leave and turned slowly. "I think we should go and help the men train." His eyes remained on Dreven. "A hard workout is in order."

Chapter Twenty-Eight

STAR DATE: 20580.06.18

   Dimension Five
   Realm of the Forsaken
   Aezorwyn

"I THOUGHT YOU WERE going to slap Dreven. Or yell at Curran," Marina said as she led Willow down the hall.

Willow looked at Marina with a faint smile. "I was angry."

"You either have remarkable control, or you were afraid."

"I wasn't afraid. I probably should've been, but I wasn't." She stared at Marina for a second. "I don't think that Curran would allow anyone to harm me."

Marina nodded. "Curran wouldn't, but aren't you afraid of him?"

"Of Curran? I was. He's a dangerous man, and he took me from my home world."

"And yet you fucked him."

Willow looked at Marina, "But first I bit him hard enough to draw blood, and I ran away."

The other woman looked at her with serious eyes, "Did he hurt you? Did he force you?"

Willow shook her head, her eyes grave. "Of course, he didn't force me, nor did he hurt me. Do you think Curran is that kind of man?"

Marina paused, and really looked at Willow. "No. Curran would never hurt a woman. I know that, but how do you know that?"

Willow smiled faintly. "I'm a good judge of character."

Marina watched the red-haired female for a moment, assessing her silently. "So, you had the hots for our King, huh?"

Willow laughed and looked aghast all in the same moment. "Oh heavens, he really is a King?"

Marina nodded amused. "He really is."

Willow winced. "This is not what it looks like."

Marina burst into laughter. "Oh, Willow if you could only see your face right now. Look, we all know that there is no way you could have known that. Garrett was teasing you, and Dreven is a complete asshole. Stay away from him. Come on, let's get this tour done and go and find you some clothes."

Chapter Twenty-Nine

STAR DATE: 20580.06.18

Dimension Five
Realm of the Forsaken
Aezorwyn

STANDING ON THE EDGE of the training field, Curran grimaced and looked over at Garrett and Dreven. Five bloody years they'd been doing this, and yet every single time he walked out onto the training field, he felt like he was transported back into an ancient past. The weapons they used were crude at best compared to the blasters, phase pistols, and laser swords of the current time. Bow and arrows, Jeiria staffs, spears, daggers, and metal swords were long forgotten, obsolete, instruments of war.

Dreven argued that they'd found paradise, and they had no need to train for war. They were safe. No Suzerain battleship could ever get to them. Curran understood. He would like nothing more than to promise his people that they were safe for all eternity here. That there was no need for every person to be trained as a warrior. He would give a lot, to be able to do that. But he was no fool. To underestimate the

Suzerain was to invite death to his people. He would not do that. He had learned that lesson and paid a bitter price for it.

The field was divided into different arena's: archery, sword practice, staff and spear training, hand to hand combat, both armed and unarmed. Every adult on this planet put in time, every week, on these training fields. It did not matter if they were Dark Elves or one of the people that had been brought here by him or Garrett. Another thing that had been argued against. How could they trust captives?

Curran turned to watch the hand-to-hand combat training. How could they not trust the people they had brought here? These people had been torn from their lives. They were survivors just as the Dark Elves were. *Were they not his people too? Was he not responsible for their being here?* He did not take that matter lightly.

His soul was stained with the sins he willingly committed to keep his people alive. Someday he would wander the Dimension of Shadows. His soul was already damned. But until that day arrived, he would do everything in his power to restore what had been stolen from *all* his people.

Trust was a precious commodity, and one he was not going to squander. Everyone here understood that, if the Suzerain found them, they would not be on a rescue mission. They would be coming to destroy. So, everyone trained to defend their home.

"Curran," Garrett said, "what are you in the mood for today? A little hand-to-hand?"

Curran shook his head, "I'm thinking we should practice with the Jeiria staff today." He walked over and picked up a hardwood staff that was easily as tall as him and had a good solid weight to it. He waited while the two men picked out their staffs, and the next few minutes were spent going through a series of warm up movements. Garrett called out when he judged the warm-up was complete. Without pausing they flowed from warm up to combat, their staffs crashing together with heavy thunks. Time seemed to slow as Curran focused on defeating his opponents. Dreven was the first down, falling onto his back with Curran's staff at his throat. Garrett was harder to take down, and they fought back and forth for several minutes, sweat dripping down their bodies, before Garrett swiped Curran's feet out from under him. Grinning, Garrett held out his hand to Curran and helped him up. They joined an irritated Dreven, who leaned against a fence watching them. Curran rested his forearms on the top of the fence and stared out at the forest. "We need to find my spirit warriors."

"We'll find them, Curran," Garrett said, reaching out to put his hand on his friend's shoulder.

"Every bit of information we have found has been useless."

"It's just a matter of time, Curran," Garrett spoke with the calmness that seemed so much a part of him. "We will find them"

"We're going to need to go to the shadow region."

"What? The shadow region?" Dreven asked. "We can't go to the shadow region. It's too risky."

"There is no risk too big when it comes to saving my Spirit Warriors."

"How can you say that, Curran?" Dreven looked disgusted. "Look around you. This is your first responsibility. Our people must be the priority. We do not have the resources or the time to waste on the hopeless pursuit of warriors who are more than likely long dead, or far worse, insane. Would you unleash killers on us, Curran?"

Curran shifted, his staff snapping up to press hard against Dreven's windpipe. "My warriors live. I will not give up on them. They are depending on me to save them."

Garrett looked at Dreven with hard eyes. "That's twice today, Dreven. Do you want Curran to kill you?" Shaking his head Garrett looked at Curran, "I agree we need to go to the shadow region. The information traders there should be able to give us some kind of info on your warriors. Nothing is ever hidden forever. And while we are there, I think it would be a good idea, if we check out the slave markets. There were Dark Elves on many planets besides Sarehiri. The Suzerain would not have left them in peace. Perhaps they were all killed, but..." He raised haunted eyes to Curran. "What if the Suzerain decided to profit off our undefended people?"

Dreven glared at them both and shoved Curran's staff away from his throat. "You are both fools." Turning, he stormed off.

Curran shoved away from the fence and stalked a short distance away before turning and stalking back. He wanted to destroy something. Anything. He stopped in front of Garrett, his right hand gripping his left wrist, squeezing until the pain drove all other thoughts from his mind. "I have considered this too, Garrett. Figure out what we need to make this excursion work."

Chapter Thirty

STAR DATE: 20580.06.31
Dimension Thirty-Seven
Perileos Star System
Xehshyhra

DAYS AND NIGHTS PASSED in a blur of pain, and nightmares. The pitch blackness of the icy water brought his mental demons to life, fueled his darkest dreams, even as he fought to stay alive. Images of the massacre tormented him. The faces of the dead and dying haunting him in a horrific cascade of blood. The screams of his team as they were tortured and handed over to their enemies. There were nights when he wanted to just lay on the floor and let the water pour over him. Let peace finally find him. But his survival instincts were just too fucking honed for that kind of bullshit.

Chapter Thirty-One

STAR DATE: 20580.06.31

Dimension Five
Realm of the Forsaken
Aezorwyn

WILLOW WOKE UP ALONE, for the first time in a couple weeks, in the huge bed that was Curran's. She paused,
Curran's and hers now. She bit her lip and smiled, stretching
slowly, feeling aches in places that had never ached before in
her life. The room was dark but for a glow on a small wooden
table beside the bed. Glancing up, she saw a large moon hov-
ering in a dark purple sky, a second, smaller moon floated on
a higher orbit and then she noticed a third.

Standing, she pulled the sheet from the bed and
wrapped it around herself. Stepping out onto the balcony,
she inhaled and tilted her head to stare at the purple night
sky. The three moons lit up the sky, and she could see stars
sprinkled across the expanse. This was definitely not Kalyria,
and it was breathtaking. Her hands clenched the stone rail-
ing, and she couldn't tear her eyes from the beauty spread before her. "Willow Solar, you are standing on an alien world."

The night was so clear she could hear every sound. The faint song of the light breeze, the chirping of a small creature. She inhaled the fresh air not wanting this magical moment to end. She'd never dared dream that she would ever leave Kalyria. Opening her eyes, she stared at the alien sky, shifted a bit to look in another direction, and those aching parts of her protested, reminding her that this was no vacation. Deep inside, she understood that this was where she was supposed to be. This was a place of safety for her. No one here knew that she was an Energy Enchanter. No one here ever needed to know. On this planet, in this hidden realm, her enemies would never find her.

Her whole life had never been hers, not from the moment of her birth when her family recognized her unique gift and began to teach her to hide. To be invisible. Her coming here hadn't been her choice either. To stay, to risk being with a man like Curran Nadiir, to accept everything he was, and everything he demanded of her. That— that had been all her choice. And she did not regret it. Not even a little bit.

Some hidden part of her had woken up at his touch. Some part of her gloried in his wild taking. She did not understand that unexplored part of herself, but she understood that she'd been truly living at that moment. That she had finally been true to herself. Whatever that part of her was, it was real. Not invisible, not hiding, but demanding that she take notice of it. So, Willow Solar was about to have an adventure. The first one of her life. And it was glorious.

A gleam of light caught her eye, and she looked to the east, the sun was starting to rise. She sat down on a bench and watched as the sun rose higher, painting the deep purple sky with oranges, yellows, pinks, and soft blues. It was beautiful.

She'd been so caught up in her life back on Kalyria that she'd rarely stopped to watch a sunrise or a sunset. Which was a pity, she thought, as ideas for new jewelry inspired by the sunrise began to form in her mind. When the sun finished its glorious show, she returned to their bedroom and opened a wardrobe to look for something to wear.

Curran's clothes were simple but good quality. Soft cotton shirts, and leather pants. The clothes that Marina found for her were simple as well, a blue cotton shirt and a pair of loose pants, and a dress in a deep turquoise that she loved. She put it on, the skirt settling around her ankles, the top with its low square neckline, fitting snugly with long sleeves that came to a point over the backs of her hands. She also added the pretty gold chain girdle that rested low on her hips, her fingers trailed over the long chain. She felt like a princess. Or a Queen? She swallowed and pushed the thought away, and her stomach chose that moment to growl. She pressed a hand to her stomach and hurried into the bathroom. It took just a few minutes to take care of her needs and brush her hair and teeth. Heading out of the room, she hoped she would not get lost on her way to the kitchen.

The aroma of fresh baked bread reminded her of the markets at home, so she followed the warm scent and ended up in the large castle kitchen. She stood in the doorway, watching in amazement as the bustling kitchen staff pulled trays of bread and pastries from huge stone ovens. Other people sliced some kind of fruit that she'd never seen before, cooked what looked like pots of porridge, fried eggs and meat, and sliced up the fresh bread.

Her eyes met those of a pretty, dark haired woman in a long dress, who paused, and approached her. "So, you're the one that Curran has been secreting away in his rooms these last few days."

Willow blinked and felt her cheeks heat. The woman laughed. "Oh, you are interesting. I'm betting that Curran has never had anyone who blushes. Where in the universe did he find you? What's your name? I'm Annora."

Willow was completely unsure of what to say. "I'm Willow." She paused. "I'm from Kalyria."

Annora smiled, her green eyes twinkling with amusement. "Welcome to Aezorwyn, Willow. What are you going to be doing here? Besides joining the throngs of women that warm Curran's bed?"

Willow's eyes got large, and she nibbled her lip. "I only know about Keanna. But things are going to be different now." Annora raised her eyebrow. And Willow swallowed. Things would be different, but she understood that it was something she would have to prove. Words were just words until actions proved them out. She felt the mark on her chest heat up at her thoughts, and she absentmindedly put her hand on it before meeting Annora's gaze. "I'm a jewelry designer."

Her stomach growled again and Annora chuckled. "Let's get you something to eat."

Willow started to nod, paused. "Is it possible to make me a tray for two, and point me to Keanna's room?" She saw the surprise on Annora's face, but the woman just nodded and set about making her a tray.

A few minutes later Willow found herself standing in front of a large wooden door, she knocked as she balanced the tray carefully. The door opened, and Keanna stood before her, surprise showing in her golden eyes. She was dressed in a long gown of rich rose, her dark hair secured in an intricate braid.

Willow hesitated. What in the Dimension of Shadows did you say to the woman who was your new mate's former lover? She swallowed and gathered her courage. "Hello, Keanna. Could we talk? I brought breakfast and tea."

"Did Curran send you?" Keanna asked, tilting her head slightly to the side as she stepped back to allow Willow to enter.

"No." Willow shook her head. "I came on my own. I wanted to talk."

Keanna took the tray and led the way to a table stationed by a sunny window. As Keanna set the tray down, Willow looked out the window. A garden filled to the brim with colorful flowers that spilled over the pathways that wound through it. A small pond sat to one side surrounded by blue grass. "It's beautiful," she said, as Keanna came to stand beside her.

"I find gardening relaxing," Keanna said with a smile and indicated that they should sit. They both sipped their tea. "What do you wish to speak of Willow?"

Willow gazed at the woman and bit her lip, uncertain where to even begin. "Do you... Do you love Curran?"

"Do I love Curran?" Keanna's accented voice was low, her tone thoughtful as she looked directly at Willow. "I do love Curran, but I'm not in love with Curran. Do you understand?"

Willow nodded slowly. "But you were his lover."

"Were?" Keanna set down her tea. "So, the rumors are true. He has kept you in his bed for the last weeks."

"I... yes."

"If I hadn't seen the mating marks you both have, I would try to seduce you right now."

Willow paused with her tea halfway to her mouth. "I... What?"

Keanna laughed. "Oh, Willow, you are very innocent, aren't you? I did not want to leave last week when he arrived with you in tow. I knew as soon as I saw those marks that Curran and I were over. I was tempted to offer to help him seduce you, but..." she shrugged her slender shoulders. "I know Curran, and I knew that look in his eyes. He would not have welcomed me into whatever was going on between the two of you."

Willow opened her mouth and closed it. She swallowed and took a sip of her tea. "I would not have..." She shook her head.

"You might have, Willow, it was the crimson moon that night. If Curran and I had worked together, you would have had great pleasure."

Willow could feel her cheeks heating. She shook her head, bit her lip, and took a deep breath trying to find the words she needed.

Keanna took a sip of tea, watching as Willow's cheeks flushed with colour. "Even though I saw the marks, that doesn't mean that Curran must give me up, and it doesn't mean that you can't join us when we play our games. I'm his pet, his playmate, and I like that role in his life. It's no threat to you." Setting her cup down, she rose as gracefully as a dancer. "In fact, I would go so far as to say that those marks guarantee that no one can take Curran from you. We can be friends, Willow. Plus, I think you're going to need some help with him, at least at first, and especially during the crimson moon fever. I'm happy to help you. I can teach you many things."

Willow blinked slowly, her brows furrowed as her thoughts swirled in a chaotic storm. Shaking her head, she lifted her eyes to meet the gaze of Curran's former lover. "No, Keanna, you misunderstand. This is not just about what Curran wants. This is about what I want too. And yes, I understand that it will take a woman of courage, strength, passion, and loyalty to hold Curran's interest. I intend to be that woman. I will not share my mate with anyone. Not even you."

"Do you believe you are enough for a man like Curran?" Keanna asked, her head tilted to the side.

Willow met Keanna's eyes. "I'm more than enough. As for the Crimson Moon Fever," she smiled, "Curran and I were rather spectacular together."

The dark-haired woman watched Willow for a long moment, then smiled. "Curran saved my life," she said calmly, her demeanour open and honest. She knew Curran was a hard man. She also knew their ways were hard to understand. Hoping to give the younger woman some clarity, she explained herself. "I was born in another dimension on a planet called Althanea. I was born with a birthmark which meant I wasn't perfect, and I was taken from my family and sent to the Zemyneah ranks. The Zemyneah are... females who have been designated as sex slaves." She nodded to confirm what she said when Willow stared at her in horror, and she once again was reminded of how innocent the woman was. "I was eighteen when I was sold at the Zemyneah Auction, the first time. I was sold five times in the next few years and the last was to a pleasure house. Fortunately for me, I was rescued by Curran and a man named Thorne."

Willow pressed trembling fingers to her lips, deeply horrified for the woman. She could not imagine the nightmare this woman had survived. "I... I'm sorry you had to endure such a terrible thing, Keanna. You did not deserve what they did to you. No woman deserves that." Reaching out she touched Keanna's hand, focusing to see the trauma injury that would naturally be present from such a terrible violation. Instead, she saw the steady blue aura of a person who had peace with their life. "I don't understand why, after all you've endured, you would want a sexual relationship with Curran or with any man?"

Keanna smiled. This time, the answer was simple. "I had the freedom to choose. I could be anyone, go anywhere, do anything. For the first time in my life, I was totally free. I wanted to put the past behind me. I wanted to start over. I wanted to build my life, on my terms.

Curran is not from my galaxy or even my dimension. If I went with him, I would be safe from the bounty hunters that might return me to my world, where I would be enslaved again. I felt safe with Curran. He had treated all of the Zemyneah slaves with respect and kindness during our rescue and during the time when our bonds were broken. I and several others chose to come to Aezorwyn with Curran. He explained his world to us. He explained the Crimson Moon Fever." Keanna leaned forward. "Do you understand, Willow? We were given a chance for a new life where we would have control of our own destinies. I own a clothing shop. Can you imagine it? A woman who had no future, a woman only valued for the pleasure she could give to a man. And here I am now, a business owner, and a friend of the King. I am a respected and valued member of our community. I even own a house in the village. I only stayed at the castle because it was more convenient for Curran." She smiled at the red-haired woman sitting across from her. "One of the consequences of the Zemyneah bond, even after it has been broken, is a higher sex drive." Keanna shrugged, "I like sex, Willow. I like a lot of sex, and for the first time in my life, I could choose my lover. I chose Curran knowing exactly what kind of man he is. I was happy to submit to any need that Curran had. It's not something I've ever regretted. And neither will you."

Willow studied Keanna. No one should ever have to endure such a terrible disregard for their personhood. She didn't know if she could have survived such a thing. Everything was such a tangle in her mind, and that was when Willow understood that she had in some small way been judging this woman who deserved nothing but her profound respect for what she'd endured.

The words that Keanna spoke echoed the thoughts she'd had when she stood on the balcony watching the sun rise on an alien planet. They rang through her mind with such clarity. *I have the freedom to choose. I can be anyone, do anything. For the first time in my life, I'm totally free. I can build my life, on my terms.*

And Willow knew, in that moment, that she was going to make a choice, she might not have normally made. She was going to take another risk. "I think you are a strong woman, Keanna. I'm glad that Curran rescued you. I'm even glad that he has been there for you. And I would like us to be friends, but you need to understand that I will not share him."

Chapter Thirty-Two

STAR DATE: 20580.07.07

Dimension Five
Realm of the Forsaken
Aezorwyn

KEANNA WAS SUPERVISING a couple of men who were helping her to move her furniture from the castle to her home in the village, when Curran walked into her suite at the castle. He looked around at the chaos of her normally neat and tidy surroundings, and frowning walked over to her. "Keanna."

"Hello, Curran." She tucked the blanket she'd been folding into a large chest. "What can I do for you?"

"Are you moving?"

Keanna looked at him and arched her eyebrow. "Yes, as you can see."

"Why?"

"I had a conversation with your mate. She is a lovely woman, Curran. Just what you need. And she is not open to the idea of sharing you."

Curran crossed his arms and raised his brow. *The fuck?* "She did mention that."

Keanna nodded, "I suspected with those mating marks that you might become exclusive. And when time passed without an invitation to join you with your new mate, I realized that our time together had ended. Of course, when your lovely mate showed up here a few days ago, I did try to convince her that we could all have a very exciting time together."

Curran winced and cleared his throat. "I doubt that went over well."

"Actually, Curran, Willow was very gracious, but she left me with no doubt that she is your mate, and she will not share." She smiled at the gorgeous man standing in front of her. "I shall miss our times together, but I think I shall enjoy my new friendship with your mate, more."

Curran gave a bark of laughter and shook his head. "Seems like my mate is a bit of a handful."

"Oh yes, Curran." Keanna grinned, her eyes sparkling with amusement. "I believe she is. And I am going to enjoy the fireworks."

"If you need anything, Keanna—" Curran began.

"I shall ask Willow for it."

Chapter Thirty-Three

STAR DATE: 20580.07.07

Dimension Thirty-Seven
Perileos Star System
Xehshyhra

FIVE SECONDS, FOUR seconds, three, two, one, his oxygen starved lungs screamed for just a single breath of air. He set his jaw, his muscles tight, and forced himself to wait another second. Lifting himself back up on arms that shook with cold and fatigue, he pressed his face to the icy wet rocks. His first breath a ragged gasp that left him coughing and clinging to his only means of survival. Regaining control he breathed deep, filling his lungs over and over until his fingers could no longer bear the pain of holding his weight. Teeth clenched, he lowered himself back into the icy black water.

The sons of bitches were taking their sweet time this morning. He wondered if this might be the day. No. He cut the thought off. All or None.

He fucking refused to believe that the men he considered his family were gone. They lived. Curran would find them. They would all survive, because Gods help the uni-

127

verse if he got out of his prison and found that even one of their men was dead.

There would be no place to hide from the desolation he would wreak upon those responsible. And if Curran was gone. A cold rage filled what was left of his heart. Every person ever connected to those sons of bitches Suzerain would die. He would rage across the universe annihilating them all.

Chapter Thirty-Four

STAR DATE: 20580.07.07

Dimension Five
Realm of the Forsaken
Aezorwyn

CURRAN HEADED UP THE stairs to his room, intent on finding his new mate, and having a discussion with her. How the shadows had he ended up with a Sh'arie? A mischievous sprite, in the language of his people. A defiant, rebellious being that would bite if provoked. Gods, the name suited Willow. He shook his head. He chose women who were naturally submissive for his lovers. Women who enjoyed his roughness and dominance in the bedroom. He told them the rules from the start, so they had the freedom to choose. And why the fuck was the thought of a woman who would not easily obey every command, turning his cock rock hard? He pushed the condition of his cock to the back of his mind and considered the discussion he wished to have with Willow.

First, she should have talked to him about his former lover, not just gone to Keanna and staked her claim. What was that? Second, how the shadows had she gotten into his room that night they sealed their bargain. How the shadows had she done that? She claimed someone named Rune had helped her, but there was no one named Rune on his planet. But what if someone was here that he was unaware of? What if someone had found them? It was time for him to get some answers. Walking into their suite, he locked the door behind him and turned looking for Willow. She stood on the balcony, the sunlight glinting in her hair. He steeled himself against the instant lust that roared through him, hardened his jaw, and watched her with narrowed eyes. "Willow."

Hearing her name, she turned and saw Curran standing by the bed. Stepping back into the room, she closed the glass doors that led to the balcony and walked closer, unaware that the sunlight was shining on her through the glass. Concern began to fill her as she saw his face. Something was wrong. "Curran? What's wrong?"

"We have some rules we need to discuss."

"Rules?" Willow tilted her head.

"Between us. Rules I have for all my lovers."

Willow grimaced and shook her head slightly. Oh no, she had no intention of being a stand in for Keanna. "Hm-mm."

Curran eyed the woman before him, his jaw tightening, then continued. "But before we discuss that, I would like you to tell me about this *Rune* you say helped you into my room on the night of the crimson moon.

"No." She crossed her arms and looked at the man calmly. She'd tried to talk to him before, and all she had got for her effort was disbelief.

Curran frowned. Maybe he should have started with the rules. Or maybe a demonstration would make things clear. "You have a choice, Willow. You can tell me what I want to know, or I can spank you, every time you choose to disobey me."

Willow glared at the man. He wouldn't dare. Would he? She took a step back from him, and glanced around the room, wondering if she could make it to the door before he caught her.

Curran shook his head as he easily read her intentions. "I told you the night I brought you here. You'll never make it."

"And I tried to tell you about Rune already. All I got was disbelief. He's your god. You can ask him yourself and leave me out of it." She was irritated at his demands, cross that he was threatening her. She glanced at the door again and ran as fast as she could.

Gods, a fucking Sh'arie. He growled and went after her. His hands closing on her shoulders before she even reached the locked door. Turning her, he tossed her over his shoulder, and strode over to his favorite chair by the fireplace.

Willow shrieked in frustration and pounded her fists against his back. "Put me down! Put me down, right now!" She twisted trying to escape and reached up and pulled his hair. "Put me down! Curran Nadiir, put me down! This is not funny!"

"Ouch." He winced. "Sh'arie, you are only making things worse for yourself." Sitting down he set her on his lap, flipping her over so that she was draped over his knees.

"Don't you dare, Curran!" She screeched, struggling against the hard arm holding her over his lap. She could feel her face heating up and wasn't sure if it was because she was embarrassed or furious.

"I would dare more than you would ever believe, Sh'arie. I am a man fighting to save my people." He gathered up the turquoise skirt of her dress until her ass was bare to his eyes. He really did need to arrange for her to get a full wardrobe but, maybe he would instruct Keanna to not include undergarments. He liked that she was available to him whenever he wanted. He rubbed his hand over her soft flesh, and she stiffened. His hand came down hard on her ass.

She bit him. Hard. Consequences be damned. The beast wasn't going to get away from this encounter unscathed.

He brought his hand down twice more, hard enough that the soft skin of her ass began to turn a rosy pink. "Tell me, Willow. Tell me who this Rune is."

"You son of a bitch!"

"Talk, Willow. Who was that man and what did he tell you? Did you know him from before?"

Willow blinked. "What?"

Curran's hand descended again. Harder this time, and she shrieked and began to struggle furiously, her nails digging into his leg through his pants. He shifted her, upright and caught her hands bringing them behind her back. "You will tell me everything, Sh'arie, or you will pay a price. Do I make myself clear?"

"I tried to tell you!" She snapped, wiggling a bit trying to find a better position for her stinging bottom.

"You told me some nonsensical story about a fictional character. A being that does not exist. I am not a child, Willow. I do not believe in fairy tales." His voice was hard, and the look in his eyes worried her. Grabbing the neckline of her dress he ripped it right in half. She gasped and jerked back, but his hand on her arm stopped her from escaping. He tore the dress from her leaving only the golden chain hanging low on her hips, the long end trailing down over her mound. Another tearing sound as he tore a strip from her dress and began to wind it around her wrists, effectively tying them behind her.

"Untie me." She struggled against the bindings, against his hold on her.

"I don't think so, Willow. I like you like this. I can do anything I want to you." His thumb rubbed over her nipple, and he smirked. She narrowed her eyes and jerked forward to bite his lip—hard.

A hard half smile tilted up the corner of his mouth. "You just have to answer my questions, Willow. It's your choice."

Her bottom stung. She was naked with her arms bound behind her, and the bastard was threatening to spank her again. He could go straight to the Dimension of Shadows, she thought furiously. Willow glared at him. That was the only answer he was going to get.

"Willow, Sh'arie, this is your choice. If you tell me what I need to know, I will stop... if you want me too."

She gasped. "If I want you to? You... You ass!"

He laughed, and it was a deep rich sound that sent shivers down her body, her nipples hardening even further.

"We are definitely going to need to speak about my rules."

She'd never heard anything so arrogant in her life. "You can shove those rules right up your—" His hand covered her mouth, and she could feel the hard callus on his palm against her lips. *Why was she tempted to lick that hard flesh?*

"I wouldn't." His voice was conversational. "You are already in way over your head, Sh'arie." His other hand slid down over her mound and his fingers parted her flesh. She swallowed hard, and his fingers glided through the silky wet evidence of her arousal, stroking around her clitoris.

She stayed very still, struggling not to show how much his touch affected her. He would get tired of his game once he understood she was not affected by it, and that she wasn't going to tell him anything. She was sure of it.

She worked on keeping her breathing even as she focused on ignoring the sensitivity in her nipples and the heat rushing to her pussy. She was not going to respond. She was not going to respond. The sharp smack to her ass took her by surprise and she gasped. Shocked, she jerked, attempted to move backwards away from him. "Bastard!"

He grinned, "I should just gag you."

She raised her eyebrow. "That seems counterproductive."

"Sassy." He pinched her nipple.

She gasped and a soft moan almost escaped her when she felt his finger pressing against her opening.

"Willow, who helped you get into my room?" He gripped her clit between his fingers and looked into her eyes.

She shook her head, and he brought his hand down on her ass in another hard slap.

The force of the slap to her ass pushed her hips forward and as she swayed back, the grip he had on her clit pulled. She gasped, a tiny whimper following her indrawn breath at the pleasure-pain that seared through her clit. Frozen in place and panting, the awareness of her burgeoning desire made her resolve to not give in even stronger.

He gripped her chin, "Look at me."

Her eyes met his, watching him warily, her breasts heaving as she tried to bring her breathing back under control. She was not going to give in to this sensual coercion. She was stronger than this. Right? Right.

Ignoring the uncertainty lurking in the back of her mind, her eyes held his, defiant. "I'm not telling you anything. Go ask Rune."

He leaned in, milking her clit gently, his voice whispering over her ear. "Tell me where to find him, and I'll ask him." *Or kill him.* An intruder in this safe haven for his people would not be tolerated. He had to know where the man was and how he had gotten here. He slid two fingers into that tight sheath that took him to heaven every night and began to thrust them gently. She moaned. Just a whisper of sound, but it was enough. "Tell me, Willow."

She closed her eyes, fighting her body's betrayal. She would not give in. She would not give in.

She pictured herself diving into an ice-cold lake, pictured any mundane, boring task she could think of. Her ass stung, her nipples ached, her clit throbbed, but she was not going to give in.

Her breath hitched and she fought against the urge to rock her hips against his hardness. Her eyes opened at his words. She stared at him and shook her head. "No."

He continued to play her body, withdrawing his fingers from her tight pussy, he painted her nipples with her juices, and leaned down to suck them clean one at a time. His tongue stroking over them, his teeth grazing the sensitive flesh. Sliding his fingers between her swollen folds again he rubbed over her clit before he gently pushed two back into her.

She made an inarticulate sound and rose up higher on her knees as his fingers slid inside her, and when he ground his hand against her clit, she shook with the surge of pleasure that flooded her body. Her hands clenched behind her, and she fought her soaring arousal, panting as she tried desperately to regain her control.

"Curran." She clenched her hands again, fought her need to ask for more. *No giving power to the enemy.* She sternly told herself. *You can do this, Willow. Remember how boring sex was before you met Curran? It's just sex. Nothing but a thing.*

So, she tried to ignore what he was doing. He leaned in and nipped her neck, and as she gasped, her eyes flying open, he withdrew his fingers and brought his hand down on her pussy in a stinging slap.

A shocked sound burst from her lips, her clit stinging. Her eyes flared wide, arousal and anger almost glowing from their depths.

She rose up, some half-formed thought of moving away from him in her mind, but he was already filling her again and this time she could not control the arch of her hips. Her breath rasped from her throat as he took her closer and closer to the edge.

Clenching her teeth, she fought against the rush of desire, the moan that wanted to spill from her lips, but a second later, a startled cry burst from her throat as her clit burned and throbbed, from the second smack he'd given that ultra sensitive bundle of nerves. Another gasp as his fingers filled her again and rubbed against that spot. That terrible, wonderful spot. "Oh god. Curran." Trembling, she arched against his fingers, her body tensing as an orgasm began to build. "Never said no to sex." she panted.

"Not yet." Curran's voice was hard as he withdrew his fingers. "You have some things to tell me before we can fuck."

"Bastard!" She hissed as the orgasm that had been building suddenly winked out of her reach. Her whole body seemed to ache in protest, and she took several deep breaths trying to calm her rioting nerve endings.

"Are you ready to talk to me now?" He set his hands on her hips and pressed her down against his hard cock. "I'd rather fuck you than tease you, Willow, but if you are still too stubborn to tell me what I want to know about Rune, I'll keep right on teasing. Are you ready for round two?"

Her eyes went wide at his words, and she tried to scramble backwards. No way was she doing round two. No way. If he thought he was going to do this to her again, he had another think coming. She gave him a dirty look, letting him see her fury. "I've had more than enough of your games for today."

She struggled futility with her bonds for a moment, glaring daggers at the big man whose lap she perched on. "Untie me! And you can sleep on the couch tonight, because you are not sharing my bed!"

He almost laughed, the corner of one side of his mouth tipping up in an enigmatic half smile. "You are a Sh'arie.

There is no doubt in my mind. Unfortunately, Willow, I know exactly what to do with a defiant woman. His fingers moved through her swollen folds, sliding easily with the wetness of her arousal. He circled her clit, and gently tugged on her hard nipple with his other hand.

Her body betrayed her with its lust for this man and what he could do to her. She was past being able to hide her arousal from him, long past pretending that what he was doing wasn't working. Her arousal had returned so fast that she was shocked, and she leaned forward to rest her head against his shoulder for a minute, trying to remember why she was resisting him. "I already told you everything." She closed her eyes and whimpered as her body moved against his hand.

"Tell me again, Sh'arie. Tell me, and I will make you feel so good. He pinched her clit, his eyes dark as he fought his own lust. Gods, this woman was more than a match for him.

She inhaled sharply, her breath hissing out at the sharp pain that somehow only accentuated the arousal she was feeling. She needed to come.

She clenched her hands behind her back and knew that, if she didn't give him something, this was going to keep going on. She couldn't handle more of this exquisite torture. "I met Rune in the caves. When you let me go. The first day." She shifted against him and forced herself to straighten up from his shoulder and look him in the eye.

"What did he tell you?" He kept his voice firm, stroking her swollen clit gently.

She closed her eyes, her hips moving with the strokes of his finger. She was a mass of confused emotions and lust. Taking a breath, she tried to resist what he was doing to her, tried to force her mind to focus. He was so stubborn. "You are being an asshole." She said clearly. "Rune..." She pressed more fully into his hand, a tiny whimper leaving her throat. "He... told me... about you. Curran. Please."

"What about me?"

Fury filled her and she struggled trying to move her legs. In frustration, she leaned forward, and bit his shoulder, hard. "Let me go!"

I can do this all day, Willow."

A trickle of sweat rolled down her neck and she felt every inch of its path, her skin hypersensitive. Her hips bucked as he ground his palm against her clit. He leaned in and licked her nipple, his fingers easing from her, to gently stroke around her clit barely touching it.

She moaned at the light touch to her aching clit, arching, trying to get closer, to press herself against his hand for a firmer touch. "I—" She swallowed and panted trying to remember what he wanted to know. "He told me—" She panted. "What happened to your world." Goddess, if her hands were free, she could touch herself. "What happened to your men. Please Curran! I need to come."

Fury filled him at her words. Fury at a Creator that would let his people suffer so much. Fury at himself for failing his men, for failing his people. Forcing the anger down, he eased his pants open and set his aching cock free. "Talk to me Willow, and I'll end the game. I'll fill you up with my cock and fuck you until you come apart in my arms." His fingers entered her again, and he began to fuck her with them.

She moaned and rocked her hips. His cock was so close that she groaned and forced her eyes from that hard piece of flesh. "He—" She swallowed and licked her bottom lip. "Rune told me about what your people survived, about this place." The wet sound of his fingers fucking into her made her need all the more pronounced. "Curran. I— Please."

His fingers stilled, and she moaned brokenly. "Shh. Tell me all of it, Willow." He eased his fingers from her to stroke his cock, almost groaning at the sharp pleasure.

"No!" a shocked protest was torn from her throat when he withdrew his fingers. Breasts heaving, nipples hard and aching for his touch, she forced her mind to remember the rest of the information. "Rune. He made that moon. The red one. He needs sexual energy. It strengthens him." She frowned, trying to find the words to explain about the moon. "He did something so that we are all affected by the crimson moon." The images that Rune had shown her when he told her about the crimson moon filled her mind and her arousal ratcheted up again.

"If you don't let me come soon, I might do bad things to you!" Her voice was fierce as she struggled with her bonds again, wanting nothing so much as to be able to touch herself and end this game. Growling in frustration she finally stopped long enough to tell him the rest. "Rune has a plan. To defeat the Suzerain. To save your men. To keep your people safe."

Curran laughed a brief hard sound that drew Willow's eyes to him. "I can see that you believe what you are telling me." He slid his hand into her hair and wound it around his fist. "I will never believe in a Creator who let his people die." He lifted, and she rose up on her knees, grabbing his cock he nudged it against her slick entrance. "Take me."

He wasn't gentle and she didn't care. His cock nestled against her entrance, and she eased herself down, her eyes closing as a moan of sheer pleasure escaped her. Goddess, that was exactly... what. she. needed. She was breathless by the time he was fully seated inside her. Why hadn't he untied her? She needed more. She rose up on her knees and sank down again. So good. Panting, she opened her eyes. "Curran."

His hand settled on her hip, reaching out with his other hand he lifted her chin, his dark eyes met hers. The intensity in his gaze made her eyes widen. "You are mine." He began to pound into her, her breasts bouncing at the hard fucking. The slap of wet skin against wet skin filled the room, and she moaned, her eyes closing. "Eyes. Open your eyes, Willow. Look into mine. I want to see your pleasure." He leaned in and nipped her lip, moving one hand so that he could touch her clit. "Come all over my cock, Willow."

It was a rough ride, a hard ride, but she was past caring about the niceties. Her body tightened and she convulsed over and over, swept up in a violent blend of color and sensation that seemed to last forever.

He roared his own pleasure as her sweet pussy clenched hard on his cock, drew every drop of come from his balls, and turned him inside out. Fuck. Fuck. Fuck. Breathing hard, he pressed his forehead to hers.

If Rune existed. If he had a plan. Curran growled. If. What the fuck was he supposed to do with this information? He had no doubt that Willow had told him the truth. That she fully believed she'd met this Creator. Where did that leave him? Standing he carried his mate over to the bed and laid her on it, gently releasing her wrists before laying down beside her and drawing her into his arms.

Chapter Thirty-Five

STAR DATE: 20580.07.07
> Outside of the Multiverse
> The In-Between

RUNE GRINNED AND STRETCHED as he stood up. That had been… invigorating. Nothing like a rousing bout of sexual torment to get your energy flowing. Well, unless he had actually been there playing the game. That would have made things much more interesting.

He smirked at the thought and disappeared from the room in the in-between, reappearing a few seconds later with a piece of parchment in his hands. He was standing by the table reading the old document when his sister appeared.

Today, her long, silvery white hair was heavily streaked with purple and dark blue, glowing sparkles scattered throughout so only fine strands of her natural colour peeked out. He raised his eyebrow at her. "What did you do to your hair, Eliana?"

"Don't you just love it?" She twirled in front of him, her hair swirling around her in a cosmic explosion of colour and sparkles. "There's this little shop on Earth. The woman who owns it is a miracle worker. I'm going to keep this look for a while. It's very... celestial." She noticed the document in her brother's hand and cocked her head curiously. "What is that?"

"This?" Rune glanced up from the aged paper. "This is temptation." He disappeared and returned in the next instant, the parchment gone and a large glass of purple ale in his hand. "What are you doing here, sister?"

Eliana raised a brow. "Don't you think the cloak is a bit dramatic, brother?"

Rune pushed back the hood of the cloak he'd acquired a moment ago. "It was rather necessary in that dive. I think it's a dress code or something. Anyways..." He shrugged out of the cloak and tossed it on a large white couch. "What does the way I dress have to do with why you're here?" He took a drink of the purple ale and frowned. "That is not what I expected. It's... good." He finished the ale and looked at his sister again. "Eliana? Is something wrong?"

Eliana sat down on the sofa, a wild looking young woman with eyes so ancient that few people could look into their star filled depths. Few beings could even begin to fathom the depths of pain and grief that she and her brother endured. They were the last of a once flourishing species known as The Creators. Beings so powerful that they existed outside of time and space, which made perfect sense if you knew that they were, in fact, the creators of time and space.

The story of the beginning of their race had never been written, their history unrecorded. They'd simply always been and had, with great arrogance, thought they would always be. The day of the unimaginable came to pass without fanfare or battles. The Creators simply stopped existing. One by one they vanished, until only the siblings stood by the side of the most ancient of their kind. Their grandfather. His beginning was unknown, shrouded in mystery and magics of a kind they had no knowledge of.

"Rune, Eliana, we are the last of The Creators, soon there will only be the two of you." He raised his hand when they began to protest. "I have seen the future. I cannot change it. You, though, you both have the ability to change what is happening, to create a future. It will be hard. It will take time. With time will come grief, but you must embark on this journey no matter the cost. If you two cease to exist, all that remains is nothingness." He looked at them gravely, his ageless eyes filled with sparkling lights and swirling colors. "What a great tragedy if all that we are is lost.

We had the ability to create wondrous things from nothingness, and yet, as a species we did nothing. We created nothing. We talked. We discussed. We argued, and we did nothing. All our powerful creative gifts lay silent and unused until the day came that we became the nothing that we created. One by one, we ceased to exist and all that was within us ceased to exist as well.

I have seen the future and it belongs to you. Do not waste the gifts inside of you. Create amazing things. Breathe life into the nothing. Do not fear failure or mistakes, but learn from them. It is only by using our gifts that we become what we were destined to be.

Create, find love, have children and some spark of what we are will always remain."

Eliana looked at Rune and a gentle smile crossed her face. "It's been a long time since I thought of our grandfather. You remind me of him. It's your eyes, I think."

Rune laughed. "Your eyes are the same as mine and as his were. I think perhaps that is what created that memory for us both. Tell me what brings you to my side, Eliana."

"The third dimension of Earth." Eliana waved a hand and two cups of tea, in fragile China cups hand painted with delicate blue flowers, appeared on the low coffee table. She picked up the one closest to her.

Rune eyed the teacups for a minute then sprawled on the sofa across from her, picking up the delicate cup gingerly. "Earth. Earth is always in trouble for one reason or another. You would think that a small planet deep in the Milky Way Galaxy would rarely come to our attention. But no. In every dimension, the beings on Earth are always getting up to shenanigans. Do you think it's something in the air?" He took a sip of the brew and smiled. "Earl Grey. Hot."

Eliana laughed and took another sip of her tea as well. "That was an inspired moment, Rune. A moment when some of our youngest creations glowed with creative energy and created a story of hope for their future. If only they understood the power of that hope." She looked pensive for a moment before continuing. "But my concern is not for the first dimension today. My concern is for the third dimension. Ash is acting most peculiar. Something is amiss with him"

"Amiss?" Rune raised his eyebrow. "Really? What time were you just in?" Not that he needed her answer. That archaic word was a dead give away. His sister had a thing for knights and dragon shifters. He sometimes wondered if he shouldn't have created the human who would become King Author. Ah, well, what would be would be. "Ash has always been a problem, Sis. I told you that eons ago."

Eliana felt her cheeks warm but refused to rise to the bait. Her brother was a notorious tease, and she was his favorite target. She knew full well that is why he created that damned legend that led to such a fascinating time in Earth's history. A mysterious smile curved her lips, and she changed the subject. "But we did not always know that Ash would be a problem. He was the most beautiful of the angels."

Rune snorted. "You let his beauty get to you. And when he decided to seduce you, you were quite happy." Rune saw the pain in his sister's eyes and paused. "Ah Eliana, I'm sorry. I know that you loved him. He was my friend too. We both failed to see his true nature. With as much power as we gave him, the flip side of his nature held great temptation for him. We both know that."

Eliana took another sip of her tea and set her cup back on the table. "Charming. He was charming, and fun, and I thought he loved me." She gave her brother a defiant look.

"You wanted him to be like us, but he is a creation not a Creator. And you did not take into account the first law of creation. Every creation has flaws. Perfection has never existed, Sister. Not even in us." Rune watched her, knowing that she knew all this. His reminder was unnecessary, but even Creators needed to consider consequences at times.

"I know, Rune." She closed her eyes briefly. "I wonder if Grandfather understood how very many mistakes we would make?" Opening her eyes, she gave her brother a sadly wistful look, the weight of her failures weighing heavy on her slight shoulders. "Many times, I have longed for perfection. I have longed to go back and undo so many things. But to undo time and events would change everything."

"It's the flaws that make our multiverse so wondrous, Eliana." He appeared beside her and put his arm around her shoulders. "It is the flaws, breathed into the very fabric of time and space that keep the multiverse expanding eternally. And it's those same flaws that keep all living beings growing and learning. We cannot change the past, we must do what we can in the now, to create a better future."

Sighing softly, she laid her head against her brother's shoulder. "It's the future that I'm worried about."

Chapter Thirty-Six

STAR DATE: 20580.08.27
    Dimension Thirty-Seven
    Perileos Star System
    Xehshyhra

HE'D MANAGED TO SCRATCH another mark on the wall of his prison today, though he wondered if it was only another form of torture. To count the days, weeks, months, years that he had been a prisoner, was soul destroying at times. Seven years, two months, two days. Fuck.

Chapter Thirty-Seven

STAR DATE: 20580.08.27
    Dimension Five
    Realm of the Forsaken
    Aezorwyn

CURRAN CLOSED THE DOOR of the library and walked over to sit down with Garrett, Marina, and Dreven. "This is the latest map of the Shadow Region." Curran began as he set a rolled-up map on the table and began to unroll it.

"How did you get this?" Marina asked as she stood up and helped to spread out the map, setting a heavy book on one corner.

"I can tell you it wasn't easy." Curran grinned, "But I'm not a man who enjoys easy anyway." The others burst into laughter, and he scowled. "What?"

"I call Fargon shit." Marina smirked. "You know, because of Keanna, and the throngs of women who throw themselves at you on a daily basis."

"You mean, used to throw themselves at our intrepid leader." Garrett said with a chuckle. "I've heard that Willow put an end to the Keanna saga. Tossed her right out of the castle."

Curran shook his head, as Dreven scowled. "First," Curran began, "Willow did not throw Keanna out of the castle. Keanna wanted to move back into her own house."

"And why is that Curran?" Garrett asked with a smirk.

Curran raised his eyebrow. "Willow might have... uhh—"

"Staked her claim?" Marina asked with a grin. "I like this woman, Curran. She has fire. I would say your easy days are over." Garrett and Dreven roared with laughter as Curran scowled.

"Okay, okay, knock it off." Curran grumbled as he set another heavy book on the other side of the star map. "I got this map from Dayan Covaire."

"He went off-world?" Marina asked quietly.

Curran nodded. "The last time I was talking to him about how the mapping of Aezorwyn was going I mentioned that we needed a star map of the shadow region and asked him if he remembered anything from the old star maps on Sarehiri. He said he would think about it. But you know Dayan, he is a force to be reckoned with. When I didn't see him last week, I thought he was starting on the planet survey. Instead, he'd gone to the shadow region."

"Fuck." Garrett swore quietly. "Do you think anyone saw him?"

"I asked him that very question, he laughed and told me that no one sees him unless he wants to be seen." Curran shook his head. "The guy has always been independent, Dimension of Shadows, on Sarehiri he was one of the best woodsmen we had. I always suspected that is why he chose to become a cartographer rather than a warrior. I was not surprised he survived the attack on Sarehiri. We got very lucky with that. He has been a huge help. We would not have made it the first year on Aezorwyn without him."

"We wouldn't have survived the nightmare that Sarehiri became without him either." Garrett said quietly.

Marina looked at the map, "At least we know this map is accurate. Dayan is a perfectionist when it comes to his maps."

"I need to speak to the manager of the glow stone mine after we are done here, so can we get back to business?" Dreven asked as he surveyed the star chart. "How do you propose that we get intel about our lost warriors from the information brokers without giving ourselves away?"

"I was planning to shift to the Lore syst—"

"No."

"Uhuh."

"You can't do that, Curran."

Curran eyed his team. "Why not?"

Marina shook her head. "You have a new mate, Curran. You can't just leave her. She doesn't know anything about our world or our people."

"I'll go." Garrett said. "I want to have a look at all three of the outposts in the shadow region."

Dreven snorted. "You just want to check out the brothels."

Garrett laughed, and Marina grinned. "Maybe I'll go with you, Garrett. I hear the brothels are excellent."

Dreven chuckled. "Shadows, maybe I'll go too."

Curran shook his head and smirked. "I should have known. You bunch of reprobates. Alright, the three of you can go, and I'll stay home and enjoy my mate." He paused and looked at them all seriously. "Don't take any unnecessary risks. Go to the Lore Star System first and get the holo emitters. Be damned careful, the shadow region is a bloody nest of vipers. They would love nothing more than to get their hands on some Dark Elves. The Suzerain would pay handsomely for even one of you. If it's possible, get some supplies. But" Curran looked at each one of them, "the most important part of this mission is to get intel on the Spirit Warriors. Do you understand?"

The three nodded, and they all began to discuss how they could find that critical information without giving themselves away.

Chapter Thirty-Eight

STAR DATE: 20580.08.26

Dimension Five

Realm of the Forsaken

Aezorwyn

WILLOW STOOD ON A LARGE balcony looking out over the castle grounds. It was a hive of activity, but what held her attention, at the moment, was the small village she could see just a few kilometers away. Tiny well-kept cottages lined the streets, and she could see that each home had a large garden behind it. She could also see a well laid out town center with shops and other places of business. To the east of the village, farms nestled along the fertile banks of a river. She was amazed at how much Curran had accomplished in the time since he'd brought his people here.

Her mind went to the terrible massacre that had happened in the ancient temple on her world. A massacre that had begun the annihilation of the Dark Elves. She'd been twenty-one at the time. Seven years. It had been only seven years since that terrible day. In that time Curran had not only escaped his captors, but he'd rescued the surviving remnant of his people and brought them here. And they'd built all of this. She looked around again in amazement. It was even more astonishing because she knew that they'd done it all by hand. No computerized technology to assist them.

She thought about all she knew of this man she'd found herself mated to and realized once again that she didn't know much. She had so many questions, so much to learn about him, and this kingdom he was carving out with his bare hands.

She heard the door to their room open then close and turned. Curran gave her a distracted half smile, as he walked out to join her. She smiled back at him. "I love the view from this balcony. I can see so far. What you have accomplished here is amazing, Curran."

He looked out over the vista spread before them and nodded. "What my people have accomplished is amazing. We worked hard. It hasn't been easy, but it has been worth every bit of effort."

"Could you take me to see the village?"

Curran turned and looked at the woman beside him. She seemed genuinely interested. He probably should have expected that, but he'd been too busy fucking her, and she'd been a very eager participant. "Of course. Do you want to go now?"

Willow smiled into those dark eyes and nodded. "Yes, please. And I want to know how you did all of this." She waved her hand to indicate the village, farmland, and castle. "All of it."

He laughed. "All of it hmm? I can do that." He took her hand and led her from their suite noticing that the dress she wore today was a little long for her. "We can stop at some shops, too, if you want."

The castle was a busy hub of people rushing around doing their business, and they were stopped more than once on their way out. Curran, without fail, spoke to each and every person who stopped them and introduced her as his mate. More than one person seemed surprised, but they were all friendly to her and she began to relax. When they finally made it out of the castle, Curran directed her to a cobblestone path, and they turned towards the village. "You introduced me as your mate."

He looked at her and smiled, taking her hand in his. "We are mates, Willow."

"That simply? That easily?"

Curran laughed, a deep rich sound that sent a warm feeling through her. "You are the one who gave my lover her marching orders. I figured out quickly that you were taking this mating seriously."

Willow paused and looked at him, her eyebrows rising. "I don't share."

He nodded. "I understand that, and I'm not willing to share either. So that means I need to make people aware of this mating business."

Willow nodded, "It's weird isn't it."

"Weird?" He laughed again. "The Dark Elves have always believed in commitment and loyalty to the people they love. We did not, however, have mystical marks appear on our bodies proclaiming us bound to another, without love being part of the equation. I'm not sure how they will react to that. So far, it is just you and I who have this mark, so maybe it's not something that we need to concern ourselves with." They walked a little further, each caught up in their own thoughts. "No. I don't believe that." Curran said. "Usually when something weird happens on this planet it happens to all of us. Take that invisibility thing. Any of us who have gone off planet have the ability to become invisible until we wish to be seen."

"I saw you." Willow said dryly. "And I don't think you wished me too."

"I did not. But that is a rare anomaly that we have seen before. We can't risk being discovered."

Willow nodded gravely, her eyes troubled. "I do not agree with this, Curran."

"I know." His words were curt. "As the leader of the Dark Elves, I alone bear the responsibility for this decision. It is one of the reasons that I have restricted my people from leaving our world at this time. Only a few of my most trusted warriors have gone off-world. And even that is a rare thing. Normally I undertake those missions myself."

"You're only one man, Curran. You can't do everything." Willow said, turning towards him, and reaching out to touch his shoulder.

He looked down into her bright blue eyes and nodded slowly. "So, my advisers tell me. In fact, just this morning, three of them undertook a dangerous mission on my behalf." She could see his frustration, his worry, the energy that surrounded him slowly changing color. He turned, and they started walking again.

"Who went?"

"Garrett, Marina, and Dreven. They'll look out for each other and get done what needs to be done. Maybe stop in a brothel or ten."

Willow choked, her mouth falling open. "A brothel or ten? Aren't they worried about getting caught?"

Curran shook his head. "Apparently not."

Their arrival at the village prevented any more discussion on that particular subject, and Willow soon stared around in amazement. "This has to be one of the prettiest villages I've ever been in. How many villages do you have? I saw the farmland from the balcony. Do you have other farms too?"

Curran gave her a sideways glance. "This is our only village at this time. Our population is about 399 people, give or take." He shrugged, and his voice became amused. "We seem to have had a bit of a population explosion over the last six years."

Willow nodded. *So few, so very few.* Her heart hurt.

"We started out with 107 including me." He gave her a crooked smile that hid his agony, but she saw it in his eyes. "This crimson moon fever seems to be helpful with population growth."

She paused, "Do... Do you have any children?"

"No." Curran shook his head. "I've been careful about that." He frowned and looked at Willow. *Shit. He had not been careful at all with her. Where the shadows was his brain?*

Willow raised her eyebrow. "Good thing I had a birth control shot at my last check up, Mr. Careful."

He cleared his throat. "Yep, it is. What are you doing to my brain, woman?"

Willow laughed, "Not a damn thing." Except she was. That was the nature of her gift. Her natural energy was slowly healing his trauma.

Chapter Thirty-Nine

STAR DATE: 20580.08.26

> Dimension Five
> Secret Cache
> Moon orbiting Venia, Lore Star System

AFTER A QUICK DIMENSIONAL shift to the Lore system, they stepped into a deep cave on a small moon, one of dozens that orbited the planet Venia that Curran had converted into a secure cache. The high-tech security system scanned them, and a female computer voice welcomed them. "Warehouse secure. Last accessed 3 weeks ago by Curran Nadiir."

Here was all the tech that they could not have on Aezorwyn. Garrett decided he would be taking advantage of the amenities on the small space jet they would take to the Shadow Region. "Hello, computer." Marina said, "Prepare the CS Star Opal for launch." Marina immediately went to inspect the small cargo ship. She wanted to be sure the hold was ready for any cargo they might want to return with. Dreven accompanied her, and headed to the bridge, while Garrett went to the safe to retrieve the small ear jewels, they would all wear on this mission. The computerized safe scanned his retina and his hand and verified his voice print. "Authorization granted." The door to the safe slid open and a shelf containing several sets of the holo imagers rose in front of him. He selected two and shut the safe, waiting for the brief seconds it took to secure it. Once he was on the ship, he headed directly to the bridge. Dreven sat in the pilot's seat going over the controls and inputting their destination. Garrett took the captain's chair and Marina moved to the communications/security station. She would monitor all channels and be able to report to Curran any new information that she heard. She was also deadly with the phase cannons this small space jet was equipped with.

The first day in the Shadow Region they spent on the planet Tranquility. There was a lot of irony in the names of the three worlds that made up the Shadow Region. Tranquility, Hope, and Prosperity. The whole area was riddled with criminals and outcasts. It was a dangerous place, but the best place to get black market items, information, or even pleasure.

Tranquility was a water world, and that meant the outpost was deep under the oceans that covered the surface of the small world. Garrett hated being under all that water, but he'd known that would be the situation so he put it as the first of the three worlds they would visit. Get it over and done with.

They landed on the large floating space dock after being Okayed for landing by the 'authorities. Garrett was amused by the use of that title on a world that in no way was under any official Authority. They secured the craft, and disguised as Laenus bounty hunters, complete with red eyes and fangs, they went to the high-speed lift that would take them five miles under the sea to Tranquility's single outpost, Grimway.

The outpost dealt in black market trade and was a thief or mercenary's paradise. It was also their best bet at finding intel on the missing Spirit Warriors. They all knew the chances were slim. It had been over seven years since any of the legendary warriors had been seen.

They wandered the streets of the underwater bubble encased outpost, stopping in at markets and purchasing a few items here and there that would be useful on Aezorwyn, and keeping their ears and eyes open for any indication of trouble. They made a deal for an entire shipment of Drion archery equipment and blades. It was shockingly expensive, but such a rare find meant others were bidding too. Not many would go up against a Laenus bounty hunter though. In the end Garrett nodded his agreement to the sale and wiped the blood of his opponent off his knife on his black leather vest. It was the way of the Laenus and no one would go against it.

From there, they walked over to the local bounty hunter drinking hole and took a table that enabled them to watch all who entered. As they sipped their second ale, a man approached, and Marina's eyes narrowed. "Suzerain scum," she hissed to the others. The man dressed as roughly as any thief, his hair tied back with a leather strip, and he had a few days' growth of beard. He looked the part, but Garrett trusted Marina's assessment. The man requested to join them and Dreven snarled but pushed out a chair with his foot. The man ordered a drink and leaned in to speak quietly to them. "My boss is looking for any of the exterminated Dark Elves."

Garrett growled, his red eyes glowing. "Do you take us for fools? Why would you search for that which is no more?"

The man glanced around and spoke quietly. "My boss wants to make sure they stay 'no more'. There is a persistent rumor that the betrayer escaped his jailers."

"That rumor is old and false. The betrayer was killed along with his men when they tried to steal some old cup. Fools." Garrett's voice held nothing but low growled contempt. "Are you testing us, dog?"

The man shook his head and slid a Suzerain credit onto the table. "The betrayer and his men were not killed. That would have been too easy a death for the treacherous bastards. They were given to their enemies to endure a lifetime of torture for their crimes."

"What has that to do with us?" Garrett's voice was cold, his eyes hard. "No, Dark Elf has been seen in years. This is a fool's mission that you speak of. You are lucky I don't kill you where you sit."

The man drew back, narrowed his eyes. "I have proof. There is a small private auction taking place on Prosperity at fifteen hundred hours, two days from now. Five Dark Elven women will be auctioned off to the highest bidder. They are exotic and make good pets. And they bring a high enough price that it has been worthwhile for the Suzerain to keep a few to sell every once in a while."

Marina grinned, her eyes glowing red, her fangs showing. "You should kill him Gar. He is diseased. He believes his own lies."

The man looked panicked for a moment and held up his hand. "I will get you an invitation to the auction."

Garrett shifted his look from Marina back to the man. "And if I wanted to purchase a pet of my own?"

The man nodded eagerly. "If you have enough credits there is no reason why you cannot participate in the auction."

Garrett nodded slowly and looked at his two companions. "We will attend this auction, but what has this to do with this betrayer you speak of, or his men?"

The man slid a holo vid chip across the table to Garrett. And activated it. A small image appeared. Curran. A map appeared. "This map shows you how to reach the Xehshyhra home world. I can equip your ship to jump dimensions."

Garrett drew back, his face taking on an insulted look. As he fought to hide his shock. *They can jump dimensions with their ships?* His eyes met Marina's and Dreven's. "You would send us to those shit smelling genocidists? They killed their own females. Those dakens have no care even for their own survival. Find other fools to take on this mission. Perhaps they will take you with them." He shoved back his chair and started to rise.

The man was shaking his head and speaking urgently. "We will pay you five million credits. What we want in return is proof that a Dark Elf is held prisoner there."

"The man in the holo vid?"

"No. This man." He reached over and touched the holo vid chip again. Another picture appeared. A Dark Elf with long dark hair. "Falcon Keyon, second in command to the Betrayer. We plan to use him to lure the Betrayer out of hiding."

Garrett shook his head. "Foolishness. But if you wish to waste your credits, we will undertake this mission. But first," He looked at the man and narrowed his eyes. "Why do the Suzerain need a lowly Laenus Bounty Hunter to find you proof that this misfortunate creature lives."

"Have you ever had dealings with the Xehshyhrain?"

Garrett shook his head.

"They are impossible. Their reports are always late, they always want more credits, and they always demand women. Dark Elf women specifically but they are willing to settle for other compatible species. They are walking a thin line with the Suzerain. We simply require proof of life. Get that for us and we will reward you with the five million credits."

Garrett paused. "And one of those Dark Elf women, with the option to buy more if we choose. We will take the woman with us, and you can deliver the credits upon receipt of this 'proof of life' you require."

The man looked as if he was going to argue, but finally nodded. "Alright."

"Do it now. Send us the invitations and put reserves on the women. I want to see it before we go any further with this fool's mission." Garrett picked up the holo vid chip and pocketed it.

The man glared at them and slid out his device. He punched in a series of codes and when he nodded, Garrett slid the device he'd brought from the ship onto the table. Seconds later his device lit up indicating he had a communication. He opened the message and nodded his head when it showed the invitation and a first-choice reservation put on the five women in the name of Gar, Laenus Bounty Hunter.

Garrett grinned slowly and shouted for the server to bring them a round of ale. "Let us celebrate the victory that awaits us comrades." After they had drunk their ale, Garrett stood up and insisted the man join them on the pleasure planet Hope. They were going to hit all the brothels they could find, and they wanted their new friend and business partner to join them.

Chapter Forty

STAR DATE: 20580.08.27
Dimension Five
Farport City, Tryria

"WHAT DO YOU MEAN, YOU can't find her?" Commander D'miron's voice was as icy as his gaze as he waited impatiently, staring at his assistant.

"She's gone. Her apartment has been empty for days." A shiver of warning tried to slither down her spine, forcing her to put more steel into her stance as she stood under the weight of his gaze. She had learned many years ago not to shrink in front of the top players in the Suzerain world. The weak were not tolerated. "Law Enforcers on Kalyria have been looking for her. It's like she disappeared into thin air."

She cleared her throat, breaking eye contact with the Commander to look down at her thin tablet. "Our agents are investigating. It seems she had a bad habit of talking to known undesirables. Our agents think one of them killed her and we will eventually find her body, or that she was sold to slavers. I'm sending you the file now."

His frigid gaze narrowed on the woman standing before his desk, and he wondered how he had come to be surrounded by such incompetence. "Do you know the powers of an Energy Enchanter? Of course, she talked to the undesirables, and if your agents were competent, they would know that to be the most basic sign of an Energy Enchanter. Her death is highly unlikely, but yours is becoming more likely by the second. I want her found."

Steel spine, Tamika, she thought. "Commander, we've looked everywhere. We searched her apartment, all the places she was known to frequent, and her last reported destination which was the market by the Stardust Temple in Varl. We even searched the temple, Commander. We found no trace of her." Tamika said in a calm tone, proud that she hadn't stuttered it out as she stood stiffly in front of the man who had risen to the highest ranks of the Suzerain in a re-markably short time.

"The Stardust Temple? Interesting." He sat back in his chair and considered what he knew of Willow Solar. He didn't believe in coincidence. "What day did Miss Solar at-tend the market?"

Tamika looked through the notes on her tablet, her brow furrowed. "That was her last known sighting. Star date: 20580.06.23"

What would an Energy Enchanter have done if she came face to face with a dead man? He frowned, considering what he knew of Energy Enchanters. "Does Miss Solar attend the Kalyria Day of Mourning for the Dark Elves."

"Yes, she has consistently attended The Mourning. So does the vast majority of Kalyrians. I don't see how that helps us."

"Have you told her brother that she's missing?"

"He was informed by the Law Enforcers of Kalyria shortly after her disappearance." *A lie, she had told him herself, he'd been in the office when she received the news and she'd seen his shock, his worry, and the fury that filled him. She'd instinctively gone to him. Had touched his arm. He'd turned into her and wrapped his arms around her. His face burying into the crook of her neck as he fought the tremors wracking his big body. And somehow what she intended as comfort had turned to something else instead. When he'd lifted his head, his eyes meeting hers she'd been shocked by the glow. She could feel the energy surging through his body. His mouth on hers, his tongue surging into her mouth as he backed her up to her desk. She'd moaned, and her hands had risen to tangle in his hair. The kiss grew hotter and hotter, and his hands began to move over her body. His thumb brushing against her hardened nipple. She gasped, and he lifted his head, his eyes blazing down into hers. His hands found the fastening to her dress, and he paused waiting for her response. She'd licked her lips. What was she thinking? This was crazy. This was dangerous. If they were caught... But she nodded and he slid down the zipper before pushing the top down over her shoulders to her waist. Her wrists caught in the sleeves and when she attempted to free them, he shook his head. Her breath caught, but she stopped. He'd yanked the straps of her bra down, baring her breasts and she caught her breath when he groaned at the sight. His eyes moved over the light purple of her aureola with the dark spots that circled her nipple, and he leaned down and took the nipple into his mouth, sucking hard. She gasped and felt the heat of arousal pulsing between her legs. Oh gods, oh gods, oh gods!*

Jericho's hands clasped her hips, slid down over her thighs until he grasped the edge of her tight skirt and pushed it up to her waist. He bit down on her nipple just as he ripped her panties from her. She gasped, and he turned her and bent her over her desk. The brief sound of clothes rustling, and his fingers slid through her wetness, circled her clit and his cock surged into her. What followed was the most frantic coupling of her life. Her nipples rubbing against the cold metal of her desk, the heat of his cock slamming into her over and over, his fingers playing over her clit, pinching, tugging, rubbing and she could do nothing, her hands still caught in her dress. The helplessness, the knowledge that someone could walk in at any moment, the rough frantic way he was touching her as if he were out of control, her body responding in the most intense ecstasy she'd ever felt. She stiffened feeling her orgasm sweeping over her, and her body convulsed, her pussy tightening on his cock. He bit down on her shoulder, and she felt him go over the edge, his jetting hot seed splashed inside her. His breaths were harsh, gasping for air as his heavy body crushed her against the desk.

"Bring him in. Let's see what he knows."

"Jericho?" She forced her mind away from the illicit memory and ordered her mind to focus on what her boss was saying.

Commander D'miron fixed his cold stare on the incompetent assistant.

Fear welled inside of her, but she forced herself to meet his gaze and speak calmly even as her fingers clenched around her tablet. "Commander, he's a loyal soldier to the Suzerain. I'm sure if he knew anything he would have told you." Her heart cringed at the idea, but if she was honest, she had no idea if Jericho Solar was a good guy or a bad guy. He worked for the Suzerain, had for many years. She should never have let her compassion lead her into fucking the man.

"Loyalty is not what I am concerned with. Bring him in."

Chapter Forty-One

STAR DATE: 20580.08.27

Dimension Five
Realm of the Forsaken
Aezorwyn

SHE FINALLY GAVE UP trying to sleep while it was still dark outside. How many hours had she spent tossing and turning in this giant bed by herself? How many strange noises had jolted her awake? How many times had she rolled over to curl up against Curran, only to find herself alone? He'd been called out shortly after they'd gone to bed. Something about a man who'd been injured.

She sat up, pushed her braid back over her shoulder and sat on the edge of the bed for a minute. She had no idea what time it was, and that only added to her frustration. She wasn't like the Dark Elves. She couldn't tell the time just from looking at the damn moons.

Grumpily, she padded out to the balcony and curled up on the chair she had dragged out there yesterday. The sky was a star encrusted backdrop of lush black, lit softly by the three moons that guarded it. If she had her tools, she'd make a necklace that represented this glorious scene. A sigh escaped her as she realized that she didn't even have her personal communication device to record what she was seeing.

She missed being able to lose herself in her work, she missed designing and creating the beautiful pieces of jewelry that had been so sought after by her small number of clients. Her work had often been her escape from the stress and worry of her life, the place she could go to focus her mind on something that had nothing to do with the powerful abilities she was forced to hide. It was in this world of gems, precious metals and beautiful creations that her dangerous secrets could be forgotten, and she could simply be a woman who created jewelry.

She guessed that it was still at least an hour from dawn, though it could have been two or three hours even. What did a person, on this planet, do at this time of the night when she couldn't sleep? And did it make a difference if you were mated to a King? A real queen would probably send for tea and sit down to draw up a plan for an important function for interplanetary dignitaries that would entail delicate negotiations and a chance to meet with her top intelligent officer. while she spoke with her advisors about political difficulties and arranged for aid to be sent to a part of her world that had just been struck by a natural disaster. Her eyes widened at the thought, and she laughed, happy to be just Willow, a woman who made jewelry and kept her own secrets. She had to get her own tea in the dark hours of the night. With a sigh she got up from the chair and made her way to the castle kitchen.

The night staff in the kitchen stared when she walked in, and she glanced down at herself wondering why they were looking at her like that. Nope, perfectly presentable, the hem of Curran's shirt reached her mid thigh. She looked back up at the woman closest to her. "I would just like a cup of tea and something to nibble on."

The lady bobbed into a curtsey and Willow's eyes widened. That was interesting. The lady hurried over to the counter and poured a pot of tea and set it, along with a delicate cup and saucer, on a tray. Cream, honey and a plate of cookies were all added, a bowl of fresh berries and another plate with several slices of fresh bread and a pot of butter. Willow hurriedly stepped forward. "That is enough. Thank you, it looks lovely."

The woman picked up the tray and handed it to a young man. "Take this to the queen's chambers and be quick about it."

Wait. What? Willow started to reach for the tray shaking her head, but the woman stopped her. "You are the queen. This is a small courtesy. Let the boy take the tray. He will have it in your room before you are even there."

Eyes wide, she opened her mouth to firmly refute the outlandish comment, and the youth picked up the tray and hurried from the kitchen. Willow looked at the woman again. This was something she was going to have to discuss with Curran. What a mix-up. She was horrified, and it took her a moment to realize the woman was waiting for her to speak. *Bluff*, she told herself sternly. "What is your name? I've met Annora."

The woman nodded. "Annora runs the kitchens, but she works the day shift. I am Lake, I run the night shift. I'm from the planet Zaytis. My people are nocturnal, so this job is a good fit for me. I've been on Aezorwyn for five years. It is a good place to call home."

"Thank you, Lake, for your help and the tea. I hope the rest of your night goes well."

"Thank you, ma'am. If you could remind Curran that we are low on salt and sugar and canning season is coming up, that would be a big help. He is very busy with all the things it takes to provide for our safety, of course. I just don't want him to forget these small but important details."

After promising to remind Curran, she walked back to her chambers through the dimly lit castle halls and staircases, her mind busy with a growing understanding that there were things these people needed. There were things that Curran needed, things that she might be able to help with. When you were focused solely on survival, many things got set to the side. Many things *had* to be set to the side.

She knew that these people had endured the worst kinds of trauma. They had been broken, suffered unimaginable loss, and they had survived. This world and everything in it was a testament to their incredible resilience, courage and determination. The Dark Elf people were survivors, but she wanted so much more for them than to simply survive. She wanted them to thrive. And... weren't they her people too? After all, she was mated to their King.

As she walked, she began to make a mental list. She needed to know about their health care system, their education system, how they were producing enough food to feed everyone and the plans in place if there was an emergency.

The tea tray was waiting in her chambers when she got back, just as had been promised. She poured herself a cup, frowned, and began searching the room for paper and some kind of writing implement, which led to some fascinating discoveries and a few that she was entirely uncertain of. Finally, she located some blank paper and took it and one of the pens back to the small table to sit down and start her list.

After the sun came up, she dressed in the beautiful green gown that Curran had bought for her when they went to the village. Determination filled her and she headed out the door.

Item one— clothes.

The walk to the village was refreshing in the cool morning air, and she decided that she must make this part of her morning routine. Well, maybe after she bought a coat or something, it was a little brisk. Arriving at the clothing shop, she realized how early it was and went around back to the pretty little cottage located behind the store. After knocking on the door, she straightened her skirt, and pushed her long braid back over her shoulder as she let out a breath. The door opened and she launched into her speech. "I need your help. I really need your help. I don't have any clothes. Just this dress..." She looked down at the beautiful green gown and back up into Keanna's bemused golden eyes. "And I have so many things to do. There are things I can help with here. But I need clothes first. I don't think I can wear this dress all the time and Curran's shirts just won't do."

Keanna's soft laughter filled the air. "I'm sure that Curran wouldn't mind at all if you wear his shirts, but I doubt either of you will get anything done." She reached out, taking Willow's hand and drawing her into her home. "I'm honoured to help you, Willow. Have a seat while I change. Maya and

Nia should be in the shop by then, they are both remarkable seamstresses"

"Nia? Maya? I think Curran might have mentioned Nia to me once."

Keanna nodded as she began to walk to her bedroom, untying her robe as she went. "She's a lovely person."

"I didn't know she was a seamstress. Curran said she was your— uhmm"

Completely comfortable in her nudity, Keanna turned back to face Willow, the navy silk robe she wore hanging open displaying her firm breasts and slender body. "Nia is my lover. Maya occasionally too." She watched as Willow's cheeks turned pink. "Please, don't be embarrassed. I am not shy about that part of my life at all. I'll only be a moment."

Willow nodded and tried to ignore the warmth of her cheeks as Keanna casually went into her room to change. The people here were so different from those of her home world.

A few minutes later, Keanna walked back into the living room wearing a long lavender dress. The sleeves ended in points, and she wore a golden chain low over her hips and hanging down one side. Her black hair was worn in a braid but woven in a way that Willow had never seen before. "Oh, I love your braid. How did you do that?"

Keanna smiled. "I can braid yours if you'd like. It's the way we do it in my world. Come and sit here and I'll do yours. It will only take a few minutes." Keanna returned to her room for her comb and came back to her main living area, to stand by a chair.

Willow moved to the chair and sat still as Keanna undid her braid and gently combed through her waist length red hair. It had been a long time since anyone had done her hair for her, and it felt... calming? She wasn't sure that was the right word, but it was all she had right now.

Keanna wove the silky strands of Willow's hair together and asked Willow how she had slept. She could almost feel how anxious Willow was and that was something she want-ed to change. It would probably take some time, but she was determined that she and Willow would be friends. Close friends. She tied off the braid with some soft leather ties and squeezed her shoulder. "There, all done. Shall we go?"

It only took a minute to walk to the shop. A bell tinkled as they opened the door and Maya came out from the back. She was a small woman, her black hair fell in a straight sheet down her back, her uptilted green eyes warm as she took one look at Willow and Keanna and hurried over to hug them both. "What are you doing here so early, Keanna? Is every-thing ok?"

Keanna hugged Maya back and laughed. "Yes, every-thing is fine. This is Willow, Curran's mate. She has a little dilemma."

"Curran's mate? But..." Maya trailed off her eyes wide.

Keanna chuckled. "Curran is a law unto himself, but he has more than met his match in Willow. Willow needs some clothing, as she came to Aezorwyn rather unexpectedly."

Maya nodded, understanding in her eyes.

"Just a couple dresses will do." Willow said with a smile.

"No, no. That will not do. She has nothing." Keanna said in her exotically accented voice.

"Nothing?" Maya looked at Willow for confirmation.

Willow shifted uncomfortably. "Uhmm. I would really love some undergarments."

Keanna rubbed her hands together suddenly all business. "Don't worry, I'm just the person you need."

Turning, she called out and Nia came out of the back to stand beside Maya. "Maya and Nia are my assistants. Maya is from Parthena. Nia is, of course, from Althanea like me." Maya with her light rich amber skin, like the finest of silk, had faint stripes and large, catlike green eyes, whereas Nia was pale blue like Keanna, with long silvery blonde hair and deep purple eyes.

Willow smiled and briefly touched hands with each of the women, as was the custom on her planet.

"You are from Kalyria." Maya said with a smile. "I was there once. That was long before I was captured and brought here, of course."

Willow paused in surprise. "You were captured? You have a Dark Elf mate?" A pregnant pause followed her questions and she looked at Keanna questioningly.

Keanna hesitated as she looked at the younger woman and took a deep breath. Willow had a lot to learn about their world, they all knew that she just hadn't thought she would've been the one to teach her. "We have never had a situation like you and Curran." She reached out, and gently brushed a strand of Willow's hair back from her cheek. "Curran and his team have an unusual ability. Maybe all Dark Elves have this capability now, I don't know. What Curran told us is that when they're off planet, they have the ability to become invisible to others."

She recognized the look of dawning understanding on Willow's face, mentally winced, and moved forward. "We don't fully understand it at this point. The medical team has tried to figure it out, but they couldn't find the answers." She gave a short laugh that was somehow filled with frustration and wry humor in the same moment. "We need trained people. Scientists and others who can help us to understand everything that has happened, that *is* happening to us in this world." She looked at Willow earnestly. "The most we know at this time is that, *maybe*, it's the atmosphere on the planet that's affecting the Dark Elves. There have been other changes, too." She shrugged but her gaze grew fierce. "I just know I'm grateful. It protects them. It protects us."

Willow sighed quietly, deeply concerned with the information she was receiving.

Keanna looked at Maya. "Could you tell Willow how you met Curran and Garrett?"

Maya nodded. "I was on my way home from work and decided to take a short cut through the park. As I rounded the bend by a big cherris tree, a man suddenly appeared. I was so shocked, I just stood there and stared. There were many people in the park that day, they never even noticed this alien standing right there. It was so odd. He noticed me staring, and he walked over. It was Garrett. He has amazing eyes, yes?"

"Among other things." Nia said with a husky laugh.

Maya blushed and continued. "He asked me some questions about Zresa, that is the city I lived in, and introduced Curran to me. I thought they were going to play tourist. We had many alien species vacation on Parthena. Curran sent

Garrett back with me. I was terrified and angry. I..." She hesitated and glanced at Keanna before continuing. "I scratched his face. It left a scar." She looked down at her hands then up at Willow. "I do regret scarring Garrett. He was protecting his people. I know that now."

Keanna smiled at Maya. "Things are different here, Willow. Yes, we have people who have been brought here against their will, but they are few. And they are part of our society. They are not mistreated in any way. We help them to build a life here." She sighed. "I can see on your face that you don't agree with what has happened. None of us want this, Willow, but Curran can't let anyone who has seen him, or his team go. We can't risk being found. The Suzerain would kill us all."

"How many people has he taken?" Willow whispered, horrified understanding in her eyes.

"Willow." Keanna began.

"No. Tell me. You cannot keep this information from me."

Keanna shook her head, and Maya stepped forward. "If I could go home," she gave Willow an earnest look, "I honestly don't know if I would. I have come to love Aezorwyn. I have many friends here. I have built a good life for myself."

Willow stared at the feline woman. "Maya, no one should ever be taken against their will. It's not right."

"What in this situation is right, Willow?" Keanna's voice was bitter. "Was it right for the Suzerain to destroy Sarehiri? Billions died, Willow. Billions. None of us would be safe if they knew we were here." Her voice was fierce. "Curran has no choice in this. We must remain a secret from the rest of the universe."

Willow looked around at the women. She could clearly see their energy. The deep contented blue of Keanna and Nia, who had both come here of their own free will. Maya's was a lighter blue but marked with the scattered reds and blacks that spoke of past trauma.

Willow looked down at the floor, considering all that she had heard and seen. So many wounded people in this world. So many who hurt. She had no idea how to heal them all, but she knew it was imperative that they begin to heal.

Keanna stepped forward. "I believe we all need some tea." She smiled kindly at Maya and reached out to take Willow's hand, giving it a gentle squeeze. "Come on, ladies, let's proceed. We have a lot of clothes to make, and we all get to see Willow blush when she has to strip so she can be measured." Willow blinked, and the two shop assistants laughed. The tension broke, and they all moved into the back, where there was a beautiful sitting area and a large changing area, which they ushered Willow into. Maya gave her a beautiful deep red robe and Nia brought tea while they discussed designs and tested fabric against her. Willow grew worried about the sheer number of dresses being ordered and finally protested that she could not possibly use that many clothes.

"You're Curran's mate." Keanna said quietly. "You'll need all of them and more. But I think that you also have a practical side." She set Willow's list on the table. "Pardon me, Willow, but you dropped this when you were changing. You're going to be very good for Aezorwyn. We should also get you some practical clothes because you're going to need them if you are going to accomplish all the things on that list."

And that brought out a whole new set of designs to be discussed. As they finished up that discussion Keanna led them over to some tall wooden drawers and several wardrobes. She opened them and Willow was surprised to discover a treasure trove of lingerie. She picked a few items before Keanna tsked and started adding to the small pile. "Trust me, a girl has to have a few surprises up her sleeve."

Chapter Forty-Two

STAR DATE: 20580.08.27
Dimension Thirty-Seven
Perileos Star System
Xehshyhra

FIVE SECONDS, FOUR seconds, three, two, one. Gasping, he lifted himself again. A few deep breaths of air and back into the icy brackish waters. *Ah Curran, I've waited a long time my brother. Where are you?* Despair welled up. *Where are you?* His hand slipped. *No! No!* He tried to adjust his hand hold, but it was too late. He lost his grip. Clinging with just his right hand, his muscles screaming as pain tore through him. He flailed, trying desperately to reach the ceiling again. His body felt heavy, he was so tired. He kicked his legs, gasping as the numbness disappeared. Agony robbed him of his breath, and he inhaled. Icy foul water flooded his lungs. *Gods, he'd forgotten!* The bastards last sadist torture session had left damage. Desperate, he lunged upward using his one-handed grip on the ceiling and managed to catch the rock above his head. He tilted his head back, dragging air frantically into his lungs, coughing and coughing as his lungs fought to expel the dirty water that had invaded them.

Shaking, fighting the terror that had him in its icy grip, he forced his muscles to relax, and took several deep breaths. His lungs felt as if they were on fire and he was still coughing, his stomach threatening to revolt on him. *You're ok. You're ok. You can do this.* He took another deep breath. Then another, before he forced himself to slip back under the water again. Knowing, even as he battled the fear flooding his system, he would drown, if he did not space out the times when he used all his strength to cling to the ceiling.

Chapter Forty-Three

STAR DATE: 20580.08.28

Dimension Five
Realm of the Forsaken
Aezorwyn

"COME FOR A WALK WITH me, Willow." Curran smiled at her, and she saw the mischievous glint in his eyes. "I'll even behave."

You rascal. Willow laughed. She couldn't help it. From the stories she'd heard, that was an impossibility. "It's not nice to tell tall tales to your mate," she said and laughed again at the look on his face, the narrowed gaze he fixed on her. She heard the muffled chuckles of the kitchen staff and tilted her head, a smile on her lips as she regarded this man who she was forever bound to.

And there she was, his Sh'arie. His mischievous sprite, defiant and rebellious when it suited her, and sweetly submissive when she chose. A grin curved his lips and he leaned in close. "I don't *have* to behave, Sh'arie. Remember that."

Willow blinked and arched her eyebrow. He'd called her that before when he was playing the big bad Dark Elf and seducing information out of her. "What is Sh'arie?"

"My new pet name for you." He stood and held out his hand.

"Pet? I don't think so." But she put her hand in his much larger one and let him help her to her feet.

Sweet temptation. Her defiant reply and the way she'd obediently taken his hand were exactly why the nickname suited her. He dipped his head and took her lips in a lush, sweet kiss that ended with the cleared throat of the head cook. Slowly lifting his head, he grinned at the blush of heat that bloomed on Willow's face, turned and accepted the basket of food that the cook had packed for them. "Thank you, Annora."

"Don't waste my cooking, Curran," Annora said with an affectionate look in her eyes. "And don't forget that your mate needs to eat to keep up with you."

"Maybe he needs to keep up with me." Willow muttered under her breath as she allowed Curran to lead her from the kitchen. He heard that muttered little bit of sass and rubbed his mouth to hide his grin. Sh'arie.

The sun shone brightly as they walked along the small path that led away from the village. She was enjoying the warmth and the beauty of this world that was her new home. Part of her wondered why Curran had sought her out, but some part of her didn't care. It just felt good to be with him like a normal couple — Walking, talking about inconsequential things, his hand holding hers. People called out greetings to them or nodded as they passed. It all felt so normal. So wonderfully normal.

After a while, they left the path and turned into the forest. It was dimmer and cooler in the heavily wooded land with bright spots of golden sun rays shining through the colorful leaves of the trees. They traveled through mystical glens that filled her mind with images of fae and unicorns. He lifted her over tiny, trickling streams, and they made their way up rolling hills.

The beauty of Aezorwyn settled over her like a gentle refreshing mist, and she breathed deep as she realized how tense she'd been. Out here, the only energy bombarding her was the energy of the planet and her mate. She drew deeply of the life force of this world and let it flow into her. It's purity, the heated spice of its erotic current, the immense power of this planet cascaded through her, flooded her senses, and flowed back out of her. She closed her eyes, caught up in the sensual bliss of allowing her gift to fully open, unhindered by the shields she was always maintaining to prevent overload.

Curran turned when he realized that Willow had fallen behind and he froze, staring in wonder. She was standing in a shining sunbeam, her eyes closed, her face reflecting pure sensual enjoyment. Her beauty struck him, and he wished for a holo camera to capture this moment.

The look on her face was one he was deeply familiar with. It was the expression of erotic pleasure, one that often lured him to even more erotic actions when they were in their bed. He wondered what she was thinking even as some part of him understood it was an innate reaction to the beauty that surrounded them, to the sunshine she was basking in.

He resisted the temptation to strip her naked and tie her to the tree that the sunbeam was streaming over. Taking her naked in the forest, her bright hair lit by the beam of light played through his mind. His cock was rock hard with the thought of her pink nipples, and the soft curls that guarded her sex. The sheer ecstasy of her expression was allurement itself. He had a strip of leather in his pocket that would work to bind her hands. Gods, he was tempted.

Willow opened her eyes, still caught up in the sensual enjoyment that had flooded her senses and her eyes met Curran's. His gaze was intense, and she shivered as a curl of feminine anticipation flowed through her body. She swallowed and her eyes lifted to meet his again, her tongue peeking out to slick moisture over her lower lip. He took a step toward her, and her nipples hardened, liquid heat slicking over her feminine folds as her heart rate sped up. He pulled a strip of leather from his pocket and once again started toward her, hot sexual determination in his eyes.

He was going to tie her up, she realized, her eyes briefly flaring. In the next instant her facial features relaxed into a blend of anticipation, need, and her own desire as she came to another conclusion— there was nothing she wanted more at this moment. That didn't mean she wasn't going to make him work for it though. Flashing him a mischievous smile, she grasped the folds of her dress and bolted into the trees.

His mouth dropped open, and he chased her. Trees flashed by. They found themselves in an open meadow with one tree holding court in the middle, a small stream running nearby. The tree was massive, it's leaves a shimmering lilac color. And this spot was perfect. A wicked glint entered his eyes and he reached out, his hand catching her shoulder, turning her. They both tumbled to the ground laughing.

"I thought you were going to behave yourself?"

He grinned. "You were the one who ran."

She swallowed, heat surging through her. "What does that have to do with you behaving yourself." She met his eyes and bit her lip, anticipation working its way through her body. Her nipples were hard, and she could feel the heat of arousal coating her feminine folds. What was he going to do?

He stood up and reached out to help her to her feet. "Running fuels the fire, Willow. Don't you know that?" He slid his hands around her wrists and took a step forward forcing her to back up.

"Trust, Willow. I want your trust. I need your trust." His eyes were dark with desire and Willow tilted her head as she considered his words. "I'm a dominant man, Willow, and I'm not going to pretend to be anything else. I admit to having a kinky as shadows side, which means that trust between us is imperative. But I need you to know that I will never hurt you, and I will always respect your no. This is not about pain, or humiliation, or abusive control. What it comes down to for me, is trust. I need you to trust me. Trust me to give you pleasure. Trust me to meet your needs."

Willow watched him and thought about what she knew of him. It was not shocking to her that he needed his mate to trust him deeply.

"I'm going to ask you to do some things today that might be outside of your comfort zone. I promise, if you want me to stop, I will. Will you trust me today, right now, to give you pleasure?

Willow bit her lip and considered his words, before nodding. "I'll trust you."

Curran gave her a slow grin, his eyes almost sparking with mischief.

He took another step forward, and she stepped back again. Her back bumped into the tree, and she raised an eyebrow.

"Take off your dress, Willow."

Flutterbys soared in her stomach, and she hesitated. What if someone came by? Curran narrowed his eyes, and swallowing, she reached down to gather her skirts so she could lift it over her head. Trust. She had agreed to trust him, and there were times when obedience was wise. She didn't relish the idea of walking back to the castle in Curran's shirt and having everyone smirking, nor did she want Marina to be exasperated with her again like when Curran had torn the pretty turquoise dress from her body.

"Hmmm, obedience from my Sh'arie. How interesting. Perhaps I shall reward you." Curran watched as Willow pulled the dress off and started to fold it. He reached out and took it from her, dropping it where it would not get stepped on. His hand cupped her breast. He squeezed gently before gripping her nipple and tugged. She gasped as pleasure zinged through the sensitive tips, and he smiled. "Hands in front of you, wrists crossed." When she hesitated, he pinched her nipple and she jumped, though it had only been a little sting. "Ouch."

"Hands in front of you, wrists crossed."

Willow wanted to rub her nipple, but she held out her hands, wrists crossed and watched as he tied them firmly together. Not too tight, but she couldn't pull them apart either. He lifted her bound wrists and tied them to a thick branch overhead, pulling her up until she was on her toes. "Aren't you pretty," he murmured walking around her, his hands lightly smoothing over her bare skin. "Did you know the sun makes your hair look like fire? You look like a mythical magic princess caught by a wicked warrior."

Willow tilted her head, a smile curving her lips at the imagery her warrior mate's words painted for her. She would never have expected those words to come from his lips.

"A few rules Willow. No means no. If you say no, I stop. No matter where we are in this game. Do you understand?"

"Yes." Willow said, biting her bottom lip and glancing around the empty meadow. She'd never been naked outside in her life. Never mind, naked and tied to a tree. Trust. She was trusting Curran.

He stepped a little closer, "Does it make you feel vulnerable to be naked and tied to this tree, knowing anyone could find us at any moment?"

"Yes." Willow's eyes widened at his words. "That is what you want isn't it? For me to feel vulnerable."

Curran nodded and gave her a roguish half smile. "Trust me, Willow."

She took a deep breath, her hands clinging to the leather strip that bound her to the tree branch above her head. A gentle breeze sprang up, stirring her hair, the cool kiss of the wind tightening her nipples. "I do, Curran."

Heat rose in her mates' eyes, and he nodded. "Instant obedience results in a reward, Willow. Hesitation or defiance results in punishment. Understand?"

Willow's eyes widened. "What kind of punishment?"

"The kind I choose, Sh'arie."

This was probably the kind of thing she should have discussed with him after the last time he'd played his dominance games with her. She swallowed, but she could feel her arousal building. She squeezed her legs together and watched him warily. A spiral of feminine arousal heated her veins as Curran, fully dressed, watched her with that look in his eyes.

"Are you wet, Willow?"

A light blush touched her cheeks as she stared at him. Did he really expect her to answer that question?

His fingers closed around her nipple again and he twisted, not too hard, just enough that she gasped and tried to step back. "Uh Uh, Willow. You take your punishment like a good Sh'arie, or I'll add to it. Do you understand?" He tugged on her nipple, pinched down. "Are you wet?"

"Yes." She answered with a gasp, trying to hold still. He reached down and slid a finger between her folds. Looking into her eyes, he smiled. "You're very wet, Willow. I'm pleased." Only then did he release her nipple, leaning down to suck it into his mouth, gently laving it with his tongue.

She moaned softly, and he straightened. "Willow, I don't want you to be quiet."

"What if someone hears us?"

"If someone hears us and comes to investigate, they will see me playing with my mate, and they will leave."

Willow's eyes got huge. Curran circled her clit and slid his finger back to press it deep inside of her. She gasped.

"Better." He said, adding a second finger and began to move them in and out. She could hear the wet sounds and her cheeks heated again. He eased his fingers from her, painting her nipples, and her lips. "Suck them clean."

She could taste herself on his fingers and swept her tongue over his digits before sucking. "Have you ever given a man head?"

Willow shook her head. Curran smiled. "You will today. After I'm done playing." His fingers tangled in her hair, and he took her mouth in a wild deep kiss, enjoying the taste of her sweet pussy as he ravished her mouth. "You don't come until I tell you to. Understand?

Willow blinked, her chest heaving as she caught her breath, "I understand. But what if I can't stop it?"

"Try Willow. Try hard. I will spank you if you come before you are told, and I will go right back to playing with your sweet body. Over and over again until you learn control. Do I make myself clear?"

Eye's wide, Willow nodded. "Curran I... I don't know if I can do what you want."

"Trust me, Willow. The goal is trust and pleasure." He stepped away and turned, walking away from her over to the small stream. He knelt down and cupping his hands dipped them into the icy cold water then lifted them to his mouth drinking the refreshing water as he stared out into the forest.

Willow watched him walk away, puzzled. Her eyes lifted to take in the forest, and she nervously licked her lips. Anyone could be out there in the forest watching them. Flutterbys in her stomach again, her gaze shifted to where Curran was kneeling by the stream drinking from his cupped hands. He wanted her to trust him. She took a deep calming breath as he took a small square of cloth out of his pocket and dipped it into the water. Rising, he came back to her. A smile curving his lips. And before she understood his intent, the soaked cloth, icily cold was pressed against her pussy. One hand worked it between her folds as the other hand closed over her breast. She gasped and writhed trying to escape the shocking cold. Somehow, he'd managed to get the freezing cloth directly over her clit and he was rubbing her with it.

She arched, "Cold!" His fingers were just as icy as they plucked at her nipples. Oh gods! She gasped again and tried to pull away, but the solid bulk of the tree was at her back. He dropped to his knees, the cloth disappearing, and the heat of his mouth settled on her pussy. He sucked her cold clit into his mouth, his tongue circling the sensitive bud of nerves. She cried out, and she felt his mouth curl into a smile against her. He sucked and rubbed her clit until she was teetering on the precipice of her orgasm. "Do not come, Willow."

Her chest heaving, her body on fire, it took her a few seconds to understand his words. "Curran!" She cried out in dismay.

He lifted his head and met her eyes. "Do not come." His voice was hard, and she swallowed. He licked her again, sucking on her swollen clit. She moaned and her fingers clung hard to the leather strap. Breathing harshly, she forced her body to relax, and his fingers began to tug on her nipples. She bit her lip and closed her eyes, panting, trying to slow the fire spreading through her. "Curran! I can't—" She panted, going up on the very tips of her toes as her body began to tighten.

He lifted his head, and she shuddered, pushing two fingers into her, pumping in a steady rhythm. "Do not come, Willow."

"I- please."

"No. Obey me."

She moaned softly, fighting her body's need for release. Tipping her head back she stared up at the lavender leaves above her. Sunlight streamed down on her. She could see flutterbys dancing through the beams and hear the sweet notes of avian song. The heat of Curran's mouth covered her pussy again and she arched, crying out. His tongue lashed her clit, and she lost the small grip she'd had on her control, her body bowing with the force of the orgasm that swept through her. Panting, she turned shocked eyes on Curran as he rose to his feet. "I didn't mean to!"

"I know, Willow, but that doesn't change the fact that you came before I said you could." He caught her shoulders and turned her, so she was facing the tree, her nipples brushing against the rough bark. He brought his hand down on her ass three times. The sharp slaps resounding through the peaceful meadow. Each slap pushing her against the tree, her nipples rubbing against the hard wood. Willow cried out, shocked. Turning her back around he ducked his head down between her legs again. His tongue moved between her swollen folds, back and forth over her sensitized clit. She cried out. "Too much! It's too much!"

He paused and lifted his head to look at her. "Do you want me to stop?" She stared at him, her breath heaving and swallowed as she saw the glittering wildness in his eyes. Biting her lip, she shook her head. She had to trust him. "Don't stop."

"This time, don't come until I tell you to." His voice was firm, harsh, his eyes holding hers. "Every time you disobey, I'll increase the punishment. Understand?"

Willow swallowed but nodded.

"Say the words, Willow."

"I understand, Curran."

His head dipped and his tongue found her sensitive flesh again. She cried out, clinging to the strap above her head, and he began to circle around her clit, gentle licks, soft kisses, murmured praises for her trust. Arousal began to build again, her nipples tightening and the cool breeze teasing over her heated skin. Her hips arched into his mouth, and he leaned back, rose to his feet, his eyes dark, he took her mouth in a heated kiss. By the time he ended the kiss, both of their chests were heaving. Reaching into his pocket again he pulled out a second thin leather strap and began to wrap it tightly around her nipple. She gasped. "Ouch!" And stared down at what he was doing. He smirked and tightened the leather cord again, before tying it securely around the strain-ing tip.

"Curran!"

"Shhh, it will add to your pleasure." He leaned down and sucked her other nipple into his mouth, his tongue rubbed over it, and he bit down gently, pulling back, stretching the tender tip. She whimpered even as his fingers found her clit and began to stroke it. She was overwhelmed with sensa-tion. One nipple aching, the other sending shards of plea-sure straight through to her clit. He pinched her clit lightly, and she gasped as he pinched a little harder. "You're so beautiful, Willow. I love to watch the pleasure crossing your face." He leaned down and kissed her clit. She whimpered and struggled to maintain her balance. His tongue on her clit tore away the little control she had, and she arched into his mouth, devastated by the pleasure he was wringing from her.

"Oh gods. Oh gods. Oh gods."

"Do not come, Willow." The hard voice that she was beginning to understand meant she must obey.

She twisted and writhed, her toes pushing down on the soft grass. Her breath sawing in and out. "Curran!" She wailed.

"Do not come, Willow." His voice, harsh.

She whimpered and forced her body to relax, to endure the pleasure that was overwhelming her. The tie around her nipple released and she cried out sharply. His fingers brushed the over-sensitive tip, squeezed gently and she cried out. She didn't want him to stop, she never wanted him to stop, she wanted this to go on for all eternity. "Don't stop!"

"Good. Sh'arie." His voice a heavy whisper over her clit. She shuddered and stared blindly up into the purple leaf-covered sky.

"Just a little more, Sh'arie. Just a little more." His fingers driving her to madness, his tongue tearing away her control little by little. She could hear the wet slap of his fingers thrusting into her. His tongue played over her clit, and his other hand tormented her nipples. She had become a creature bound to pleasure, her body overwhelmed with the exquisite feelings he was wringing from it. She writhed, she trembled, she arched, and her voice carried the cries of her pleasure on the wind. And just when she knew she couldn't take it anymore, his voice rose in a sharp hard command. "Come, Sh'arie." And she shattered, her body convulsing over and over with every stroke of his tongue, every pinch of his fingers. Until she was a limp boneless mass.

Curran rose to his feet, lifting his mate and reaching up to release her from her bonds. He set her on her dress, and lay down beside her, his cock so hard, he wondered if it would be permanently damaged. His own needs raged at him, but he waited until she recovered. "Beautiful, Sh'arie." His dark eyes locked to her bright blue gaze. "Thank you for trusting me." His fingers gently stroked back sweat soaked long red strands of hair from her face. She smiled and lifted her hand to touch his face. He gave her a few more minutes before drawing her to her knees between his legs. Leaning back against the tree, he undid his pants, letting his cock spring free. One hand closed over the aching rod of flesh, and he stroked. A growling groan tore from his chest and he reached out. Lifting her chin, he stared into her eyes. "My turn, Sh'arie. Take me into that beautiful mouth." He took her hand and wrapped it around his cock. "This is for control. You control how much you take." His hand fisted her hair, and he nudged her head down.

Willow swallowed and licked her lips. She glanced up into his eyes, saw the flare of heat and felt a corresponding heat surge through her. Why did being on her knees before him do that to her?

Licking her lips again, she stroked her hand up and down his shaft. He was all velvety heat and hardness. She trailed her fingers over his length, stroked a finger over the head, felt him shudder and glanced up. He'd closed his eyes.

She leaned in and licked him. Her tongue stroking over the broad purplish head of his cock. He inhaled sharply and she smiled a tiny thrill of something she had never felt before curling through her stomach. He'd liked that. So, she tried it again. A slow lick across the head of his cock, she caught a drop of precome on her tongue and his taste flooded her senses. Salty. Male.

Mmmm, she hummed and slowly licked him a third time, enjoying his reactions to that lingering caress. Leaning in closer, her hand clasped his shaft, and she took him into her mouth, gently sucking. His hips rocked and his cock moved a little deeper, she could hear his breaths getting harsher. She peeked up at him and his face was contorted in pleasure, his breathing as harsh as hers had been. She was giving him pleasure. Something unfurled inside her, and she began to suck harder, delighted with the understanding that she was doing to him what he had done to her. The hand in her hair tightened and she hummed against his cock. "Goddess!" His voice was harsh, his hips jerked, and his seed began to flood her mouth. She swallowed and swallowed again and again until he collapsed back against the tree, his fingers relaxing in her hair. She sat back on her legs and grinned at him. Curran opened one eye and raised an eyebrow. "Have I created a monster?"

Willow laughed with delight and crawled up to curl against him. "Possibly."

His hand curved over her ass. "Sh'arie, remember who is in control here."

A sassy smirk covered her rosy swollen lips. "I believe that was me at the end."

Chapter Forty-Four

STAR DATE: 20580.08.28
  Dimension Five
  Prosperity, Shadow Region

GARRETT LOOKED GRIMLY at Dreven and Marina. This was the third day of their mission and they needed to return. They had important information, but before they could return to Aezorwyn, they had to secure the women that they had been told about. It had not been hard to deal with the fool who had hired the Laenus Bounty Hunters. A quiet word with the brothel owner and a transfer of credits. Something slipped into the man's drink, and when he collapsed on the pleasure worker, he had been taken out through a secret entrance, and his body disposed of in one of the millions of tar pits that dotted this world. Life was expensive on Hope. Death was cheap.

They walked into the private auction, beautiful deadly ghosts and every one of the fancily dressed people gave them room. Marina casually asked if she could buy a pretty woman who held an auction card. The woman motioned her bodyguards forward in outrage. Dreven laughed, the sound rough and hard, and they walked over to examine the merchandise.

Garrett braced and turned to see the women. He swept his eyes coldly over them, taking in their pointed ears, even as his stomach roiled. "They will do." His voice was a growl, and his hand twitched by the phase pistol holstered on his hip. The situation was dangerous, and the plan they had was simple to the extreme. He turned and glared at the Auction Master. "I want a closer look."

The man gave a long-suffering sigh and nodded. "Of course. We will allow everyone to examine the merchandise."

Garrett growled again. "No. These ones belong to us. I reserved them, and no one else will go near them. Dre, Rina keep those feckmergs back."

Marina and Dreven turned and drew their weapons. Their eyes glowing red and warning growls rumbling from their chests. The crowd of eager buyers took a step back. Their gasped breaths and outrage filling the room. Dreven growled again and several of the buyers jumped. Garrett nodded to the Auction Master. "Show me."

His gut tightening, he forced himself to breath normally as they approached the women. His eyes traveled over the small group. They were underweight, and several were badly bruised. One cradled her arm to her chest. They shrank back from him, and his heart ached, but he forced himself to continue in his role. "They are damaged."

"Minor damages. Nothing that can't be fixed," the Auction Master replied.

"We were given one in payment. What is the price for the remaining four?"

The Auction Mastered named an outrageous price and Garrett growled, turning to stare down at the man. "They are damaged."

"Such minor damage does not affect the asking price. If it is too steep," His lip curled, "I am sure there are others here who are willing to pay the full price."

Garrett stared at the man until he looked away. "These are mine. Transfer the ownership papers." He pulled out a slender device and tapped it a few times. "Credits transferred."

Garrett could feel the sweat trickling down his neck. He swallowed and forced his fists to unclench. The chains were cold in his hands when he took them. His jaw locked as he fought to control his need to rip the cold metal from the necks of these women. His eyes hard, he nodded at Dreven and Marina to take the others. Dreven nodded back, as he clenched and unclenched his hands, his neck corded as he struggled to maintain an uncaring visage. Marina, her face white, reached out and took the last chain. Straightening, she resolutely tightened her muscles and let the ice flow through her. With a jerk of the chain, she walked out of the building, Dreven and Garrett at her sides. Trailing behind them, weeping softly were the five Dark Elf women they purchased.

They were ushered out of the building so fast that it was almost amusing. Almost. Garrett made sure to record each person at this foul place of business. There would be a price to pay for their part in the decimation of his people.

They quickly boarded their ship, and as Dreven piloted them away from this dark area of space, Garrett and Marina took off their holo imager's. "You're safe now. We're taking you home."

CURRAN STOOD LOOKING out the window of the library when Garrett, Dreven, and Marina appeared. He turned, having sensed the energy of their dimension shift. His eyes widened when he saw the women. *How?* He swallowed the sudden lump in his throat. "You are Dark Elves." His voice was flat, hard but his hand was shaking as he shoved it through his dark curls. He took a deep breath, his eyes meeting Garretts, and he let the edge of a smile turn up the corner of his mouth. "Welcome home."

Chapter Forty-Five

STAR DATE: 20580.08.29

Dimension Five
Realm of the Forsaken
Aezorwyn

IT WAS THE NEXT DAY before they could meet to discuss the information regarding his men. The rescued women needed medical attention. When no living relatives were found, several different individuals came forward and offered to 'sponsor' them and help them to settle into Aezorwyn. Willow insisted that she meet them and spend some time with each of them. He had to admit that they all seemed calmer after meeting his mate.

He paused as a thought occurred to him. *Oh. They had met their queen, and of course they felt better. Accepted. The King and Queen had accepted them. And the queen was much gentler than the King.* What followed was an impromptu welcome party that had gone long into the night.

The next morning, he met with Garrett, Dreven and Marina in the war room. He'd never really used this room for much but with all the changes and new people it was time. "Tell me what you found out about my Spirit Warriors."

Garrett set some papers on the table. "The information is sparse. We were given a holo vid chip. We printed the images at the Venia cache and destroyed the chip."

Dreven crossed his arms. "The Suzerain have probably confiscated everything in the cache by now."

Marina shook her head. "Any tracking devices in that holo chip were nullified the moment we took it on board the Star Opal. You know that Dreven. Quit being a dick."

Curran leaned forward and picked up the papers. Frowning as he saw an image of himself, he set it on the table and looked at the second paper, a map. The third image was of— Falcon. His throat sized up, and his muscles froze. Movement was out of the question. His hands gripped the paper so hard they shook. He blinked when Garretts huge hand came down on his shoulder and squeezed. Turning his head to stare at the man who'd once declared he would follow him into the Dimension of Shadows itself, Curran swallowed. "Falcon."

Garrett nodded. "I figured. The man who gave us the chip, said he was your second in command."

Curran shoved away from the table and strode over to the window and stared out for a long moment. His fists clenched as he fought against the lump in his throat and the moisture gathering in his eyes. Finally, swallowing hard, he turned to face his team. "Of all of the Spirit Warriors, I was not sure that I would ever see Falcon again. He was in so much agony..." Curran swallowed. "Ah, fuck." He swiped his hand across his face wiping away the dampness.

"We can't guarantee he is alive, Curran." Garrett shook his head. "The man who gave us the chip was a Suzerain agent. He hired us to find proof of life. There is a lot of tension between the Suzerain and the Xehshyhrain."

Marina nodded. "The agent also said that the Suzerain are planning to use Falcon to flush you out, Curran"

Curran paused and nodded once, sharply. "I was hoping they believed I died when we crashed my ship into Sarehiri."

Dreven shook his head and leaned forward. "You have to see this is a trap, Curran. They must have made us somehow."

"If they had made you, Dreven, you would be dead." Curran's voice was a harsh bitter laugh.

"They know something, Curran. This *is* a trap. We cannot take this risk."

Curran stared at the man for a moment, before turning to Garrett. "Let's go over this map. We have plans to make."

Dreven stood up. "I'm not going to be part of this. You are risking all our lives with your obsession. Even if your second in command is alive, he has survived seven years of torture. Do you really think he is the same man? Do you really think he is even sane? Your responsibility is to your people. What will we do if something happens to you? You think your little fuck toy Queen is going to rule in your place?"

The only thing that stopped Curran from killing Dreven was Garrett's hand on his shoulder. "Get out."

Dreven turned and stormed out of the room, slamming the door behind him.

They all took their seats again, and Marina spoke up. "I don't like how he talks about Willow, Curran."

Curran nodded. "I hope this is just tension from a dangerous mission, but...." He looked over at the door again. "Marina, can you teach Willow some self-defense moves?"

Marina nodded. "I can do that. What about a bodyguard?"

"Do you really think that is necessary?" Curran looked at his two friends.

Garrett nodded. "I think it's better if we err on the side of safety. Marina would make a kickass bodyguard, and Dreven knows better than to challenge her."

Marina laughed. "Dreven learned fast to watch himself with me."

"So, it's decided." Curran took a breath and nodded at the map. "Let's figure out how to get Falcon home.

Chapter Forty-Six

STAR DATE: 20580.08.29
Dimension Thirty-Seven
Perileos Star System
Xehshyhra

FIVE SECONDS, *almost time.* Four seconds, *he could do this.* Three seconds, *why the fuck was this going so fucking slow?* Two seconds. One. He shot up out of the water, gasping desperately for air, his arms cramping badly as they struggled to hold up the weight of his body. *Where the fuck were the sons of bitches. They were late for their torture date.* Gods, he hated these slimy, reptilian, alien motherfuckers. *They called themselves the Xehshyhraen. He called them shit heads. To their faces.* He had a nice collection of scars to prove it too. He figured he was going to collect another one or two today, because he got fucking pissy if they were late. He had been looking forward to the few minutes of sleep he got on the cold, wet floor of his cell after they drained it. Before they came and got him for his torture game of the day. *Where the fuck were they? Fuck, Curran, you better be fucking looking for me. If I have to break out of here again, I am going to be fucking pissed.*

The last time they recaptured him, they broke both his legs. *How many times had he escaped? Five? No, it was seven, he was certain it was seven times now, but they always managed to catch him.* Although, the last time he'd almost made it. Almost was not good enough.

He figured he had one shot left. One last attempt, but he was waiting, because he knew, when he did, he was not coming back. The next time was do or die, and that meant that Curran was not coming. That none of them were. That he was the last and he'd rather be dead than the last. All or None.

Chapter Forty-Seven

STAR DATE: 20580.08.30
>Dimension Five
>Realm of the Forsaken
>Aezorwyn

THIS MORNING BROUGHT the beginning of grueling self-defense training sessions with Marina, and Willow was not sure what she thought of that. But Curran had been insistent, and after an intense discussion she had agreed. What she discovered was that she was not in any kind of shape to take on Marina. With grumpy humor after being slammed to the floor way too many times, she acknowledged to Marina that she probably did need some self-defense training.

After showering and dressing, she headed out to find a woman named Kailene O'Rinn who Marina insisted she needed to meet. Marina of course felt that she should introduce them.

Willow narrowed her eyes, and they had a stare down which Marina won after she threatened to lock Willow in her room. Willow had no desire to be locked in her room until Curran got back from overseeing a meeting with the hunters. She had too much to do, and she didn't think she could climb down the castle wall.

The house they went to was at the edge of the village and had a massive greenhouse attached to it. There was a large field behind the house and many squares of different grains growing along with rows and rows of vegetables, and bordering one side, several rows of flowering trees. She knocked on the door. There was no answer, and she turned to look at Marina when they heard the sounds of voices raised in anger.

With a frown, she hurried around the house, Marina right behind her. A woman with long dark hair was arguing with a tall, muscular, golden god of a man, with stunning good looks. The woman was fierce and not about to back down, and the man looked furious as he argued with her.

Willow looked at Marina with wide eyes and turned back. This was awkward. She cleared her throat, trying to politely break their argument. When that didn't work, she cleared her throat again, this time loudly, and both people swung around to look at her.

"What?" They yelled in unison, and upon recognizing her, their expressions changed. Twin looks of shock and horror spread over their faces.

Marina stepped forward. "Doc." She nodded to the man. "Doc." She nodded to the woman. "Willow, Curran's mate, wants to speak to both of you today, so this is kind of fortuitous."

Willow stepped forward, "You're both doctors?"

The woman nodded. "Yes."

The male shook his head. "No."

Willow looked at Marina, who growled in irritation, which seemed to stop the imminent argument and the man stepped forward. "I'm a medical doctor. Jase Aries. She's a biologist."

The woman glared at Jase and turned to Willow. "Hello, your highness. I'm Doctor," she said with emphasis as she shot another scathing look at Jase. "Kailene O'Rinn, biologist. Since you're at my home, I presume you were looking for me and not him."

Willow was taken aback at the 'your highness' business, but her amusement overrode that, and she almost smirked at the glares those two were exchanging. "I did come to find you, Doctor O'Rinn, but I was going to find Doctor Aries next, so this makes things much easier for me. Is there somewhere we can sit and talk? I have questions for both of you."

Chapter Forty-Eight

STAR DATE: 20580.08.30
Dimension Thirty-Seven
Perileos Star System
Xehshyhra

THEY WEREN'T COMING. They'd never been this late before, and if there was one thing he knew about the Xehshyhraens, it was that they were creatures of habit. They must have decided they were finally tired of the torture games. *Fucking assholes. Shit heads.* He was going to kill every fucking one of them. The only good Xehshyhraen was a dead one. He couldn't even fucking remember why they'd declared themselves enemies of the Dark Elves. He racked his brain trying to remember. *The failed alliance. They'd wanted the Dark Elves to provide them with brides. Fuck that shit. As if they would ever send their women into the hands of walking lizards who had treated their own women so harshly that they had become extinct. Not a fucking chance, the sick motherfuckers. They deserved to die. Every last fucking one of them.* His brain pushed another memory to the surface. When he'd first awoken here, confused and hurting like he dwelt in the Dimension of Shadows, *those fucking bastards had beaten the fucking shit out of him. They'd almost succeeded in killing him that day. He remembered their hatred as they screamed that his people had attacked them. And he remembered the sounds of bombs dropping.*

Five seconds, five fucking never ending seconds, Four. *Shit. Fuck.* Three. His lungs burned and he fought not to take a breath. Two. He tightened cramping burning muscles. One. *Focus. Focus.* He lifted up, his arms shaking, teeth chattering, trying to ignore the cramping, and just concentrate on breathing, on surviving.

Chapter Forty-Nine

STAR DATE: 20580.09.05

Dimension Five

Realm of the Forsaken

Aezorwyn

SEVERAL DIFFICULT EXHAUSTING sessions with Marina later, she once more walked along the lane that led to the village. Marina was with her and so was Keanna, Maya, and Nia. They were all armed with notebooks and pens. Their mission today seemed simple. Mingle. Ask the people what they missed most. What they would like brought to Aezorwyn if it was safe to do so. What they needed.

She worried all the way to the village. Would people accept her? Would they talk to her?

And it was here, in the village, that she learned so much about the kind of man she was mated to. It was here that she saw the incredible impossible feat he'd accomplished in just seven years. It was here that she saw the honorable heart that he had. The heart that had put his broken people before the men, that were the brothers he loved, and desperately wanted to rescue. His choices must have been agonizing. What kind of strength did it take to sacrifice everything for a shattered people? How it must haunt him, to know his men were out there suffering, maybe dying and not be able to do anything. The impossible choices facing this man had burned away all the polite civilized facades. To some he might seem hard, and dark, a dangerous man who would do anything to protect his people, a man who walked the edge of lawlessness, but to her his heart had been revealed. The heart of a man who sacrificed everything for his people. The heart of a man who loved deeply. The heart of a King.

The village was small, but every home was lovingly crafted. These were homes, not just houses. Brightly colored, many with elaborate woodwork and beautiful windows, there were plants hanging by doors, window boxes, small gardens in the front yards and bigger gardens in the back yards. Cold running water into each house, a waste system that was efficient and must have been extremely difficult to construct. They had a windmill system that provided a basic electrical system to power the pumps.

As she walked back to the castle that evening, she thought about all that she had heard and seen. She'd gained a whole new understanding of the man she was mated to, and for a brief moment, she wistfully wished for a love that powerful in her own life, but she had secrets. Secrets she could never share— with anyone. She was mated to this man, and they had an incredible physical connection, but she knew deep inside that if her secret was ever revealed he would send her away. The risks she represented were too big.

Chapter Fifty

STAR DATE: 20580.09.07

Dimension Five
Farport City, Tryria

"SO, YOU'RE TELLING me that an Energy Enchanter, a collective of beings known for their gentle nature and non-violent tendencies, has defeated the might of the Suzerain? A simple quiet woman has managed to do what no civilization has ever accomplished? She has bested the most powerful ruling species found in every star system, every galaxy and every dimension of the known Universe? Is this what you want me to believe?" His stare was filled with ice and disdain. Why he had tolerated this assistant for this long, he had no idea. Incompetent fool.

"Not defeated, Commander." Tamika corrected. "Eluded. Temporarily. But I have a plan." She set a stack of papers on the Commander's desk and smoothed her dress. "I've had these distributed to every law enforcement agency across the galaxy. We will find her." She infused her voice with confidence, but secretly she hoped that Jericho's sister would be the one to bring this monster to his knees.

Commander D'miron picked up one of the papers and studied it. The woman was beautiful. "A wanted poster? You do have holo vid posters as well, I hope." He glanced coldly at the woman on the other side of the desk. "Make sure these are sent to the Shadow Region, and every backwards world in the galaxy. In fact...." He paused to consider what he knew about Curran Nadiir. "Get them sent to every outpost and dive throughout the known universe."

From Kalyria to the outer reaches of the known universe, Law Enforcement Agents combed every record pertaining to the missing Energy Enchanter, following up every lead no matter how unlikely.

The reward for information leading to the capture of Willow Solar rose higher and higher and still none of the leads panned out. Dead end after dead end blocked the might of the Suzerain, and with each one, the price of failure grew.

Holo Vids that overlooked the busy market were studied, screen by screen, and the mystery only deepened. They tracked her from the street by her home heading to the market. There was clear vid from several cameras at the market. They knew who she had talked to and what she had bought.

The Suzerain wielded terror as easily as an artist wielded his brush, and they ruled with a ruthless hand. All of Willow's clientele were interrogated extensively, the stall owners where she'd made purchases in the Kalyria Market were grilled endlessly. No one had any information that would help.

They went back to the holo vids, pouring over them for any missed details. The final holo vid showed Willow Solar's last known minutes. She looked at the temple, an expression of shock appearing on her face. Immediately she started towards The Stardust Temple and moved out of the camera's range. That was the last that anyone had seen of her.

And Commander D'miron was not pleased.

Chapter Fifty-One

STAR DATE: 20580.09.15
  Dimension Thirty-Seven
  Perileos Star System
  Xehshyhra

YESTERDAY'S FUCKING torture session involved red hot metal bars being stabbed through his right leg. With every fucking bar the sons of bitches shoved through skin, muscle and tendon they proclaimed a name. Six names that held great importance to him.

"Rickon Dawnrunner – Dead."

What the fuck? Bullshit. All or None, he told himself as that first bar was forced into his body, the searing pain making him arch off the table.

"Trey Killian – Dead."

All or None, he reiterated in his mind as the second bolt of metal pierced his thigh, the scent of scorched flesh and blood making his stomach turn.

"Zyaire WildSky –*Dead.*"

All or None. Godsdamnit!

"Talia Windove – Dead."

No! No, No, No! He fought the gruesome images the coldly spoken words tried to paint in his mind. Refused with everything in him to allow himself to think of her broken and dead. *All or None!*

"Imaris Sunsear- Dead."

All or None! Don't react! Don't you give these fuckers the satisfaction!

"Flint Keyan – Dead."

No! I would know. I would know if he was gone. I would feel it. We're twins, godsdamnit. Flint. Flint. The thought of his brother's lifeless body thrown away like common trash, broke his hard fought for silence. "You Sons of Bitches! You fucking liars! Aaaarrrrgggggggggg!" His scream echoed off the cement walls, but they weren't done.

"Curran Nadiir – Dead."

No! By the gods no! All or None! Godsdamit! He refused to believe it. He knew. By the Gods, he knew they lived. He would've felt if they'd died. He would've known!

With a rage fueled by pain and grief, he called his tormentors every foul name he knew, and a few he made up. They would *not* defeat him. And it was fucking worth the brutal whipping that came next. "All or None!" He yelled in a harsh broken rasp through clenched teeth right before he passed out.

Chapter Fifty-Two

STAR DATE: 20580.09.17

Dimension Five
Realm of the Forsaken
Aezorwyn

WILLOW SAT IN CURRAN'S study writing carefully in a notebook. Food, clothing and shelter are the three basic necessities for survival. Curran had more than met those needs but, from what she understood, while they were learning to live on the natural resources of this world, they had not fully transitioned.

Curran and his men were making supply runs to other worlds, and that meant they were at risk. All it would take was one person seeing them and the secret of the Dark Elves' existence would be revealed. Which of course was why there were captives here. Like her.

She'd learned so much about Aezorwyn and its people in the last few days. And she had so much to talk to Curran about when he got back from the hunting expedition, he had gone on to help supply the village with meat.

She turned the page on the notebook she'd made her rough notes in. Reading the next page, she began to write her notes in the one she was going to show Curran.

Carefully, she wrote down the names that Kailene had given her. Skylar Starcrest, an inventor, and Gracen Allfire, a scientist. The biologist was insistent that Curran needed to find them. She was absolutely determined that these two women, friends that Kailene had gone to university with, would make an important difference in their world. Kailene had also requested a huge list of seeds that she hoped would be compatible with this world.

On the next page, she wrote down Jase's requests. Medicines, medical supplies, and he wanted Kittehs brought here to help control the rodents that could potentially carry disease. Kittehs.

She'd almost laughed at his request until she saw the serious look in his eyes. Kittehs were small fierce felines found on almost every planet of the galaxy, but she did not know of any that had been tamed. Jase insisted that the Dark Elves were one of the few races that had domesticated the animal. So, she'd added it to her growing list.

She ended her notes with all the things they had written down when they'd talked with the villagers. That list surprised her the most.

People missed books, simple games, and musical instruments. Yes, they'd crafted their own games and musical instruments, but it wasn't quite the same. They'd asked for domesticated animals that produced wool they could weave, several sets of the metal sticks that were used for the ancient knotting skill of Cynttan Knytia, and the plans to make an ancient handloom and spinning wheel. It had been quite an intense discussion, but finally she had persuaded them that it was highly unlikely that Curran would find an actual hand-loom or spinning wheel outside of a museum.

Cloth, thread and needles were also commonly asked for items, as well as assorted foodstuffs, small toys for children, and many other common things that most people took for granted until they didn't have them.

The list was long, but she was careful to add everything because, if there was a safe way to get it, it would bring some measure of comfort to these people whom she had come to admire.

Sitting back in her chair, she thought again about how important it was for them to become totally self-sufficient. The risks were just too high to make countless supply runs. And someone had to be noticing the missing people. On top of that, everyone they took showed signs of mental trau-ma injuries. She paused. Honestly, this was a planet full of mentally traumatized people. There were only a few hundred here currently, but it was imperative that they heal. A society only ever thrived if its people were mentally, emotionally and physically healthy. She would be spending a lot of time with Curran's people. She had a gift that would start the healing process and she fully intended to use it.

The captive situation deeply concerned her. She under-stood why Curran was making the choices he was, she also understood that the risks were mounting and that she couldn't condone the capture of innocent people. They had to find another way to do this. And that was going to be the hardest conversation to have with Curran.

It was late when she finally finished her notes and stood up. She stretched and decided that more than anything she wanted a hot bath, and she wouldn't have minded a good book to read, too. If only they had romance novels, she thought with a sigh as she gathered up the notebooks and walked out of the office. She'd even searched the 'library' for reading material, but all that room contained was mostly empty shelves, and a few old tomes of history and engineering.

Marina had given her strict orders to wait for her, but Willow thought she must've been tied up with whatever the urgent business was that had drawn her away. Honestly, Marina really was taking this protection thing much too seriously. This was the castle. Her home. She should be perfectly safe here. It was only a couple floors up to her chambers anyway.

Chapter Fifty-Three

STAR DATE: 20580.09.17

Dimension Five
Realm of the Forsaken
Aezorwyn

BROWS FURROWED IN CONSTERNATION Marina strode back to the castle. Her soft leather boots made no sound, but people were giving her leery looks. She ignored them, angry that she had fallen for the ploy that was clearly intended to get her away from the castle and Willow. She nodded at one of the guards as she entered the castle heading directly for the rooms shared by Curran and Willow. Her footsteps echoed in the hallway as her steps quickened. Something about all of this did not sit right with her and deep down she knew she had been set up. For what reason, she did not know yet, but she would find out. And when she found out there would be shadows to pay.

Lost in her thoughts and the dimness of the castle, Willow didn't see the bench sticking crookedly out of the alcove she was walking by. She hit her knee hard and stumbled, would have fallen if she hadn't managed to grab the crooked bench.

"Careful, your majesty." It was spoken with scorn and Willow jerked around in surprise. A man stepped from the shadows and Willow took a step back. Dreven.

He moved with the grace his race was known for, a tall, lithe, handsome Dark Elf male, his hair cut short to reveal his pointed ears and the sneer on his lips. "Does Curran know you have taken over his study?"

Willow frowned. "He won't mind if I use his study."

"You should ask Keanna about that. He caught her coming out of his study once," The male laughed, and it was not a pleasant sound. "She couldn't sit down for a week once he was done with her. But maybe you are like her. A whore that likes it rough."

Willow's eyes widened, and her chin lifted. "What went on with Curran and Keanna is none of your business! And neither am I. You are dismissed!"

He moved so fast that Willow didn't have time to evade his hand as it shot out and grasped her arm. "You are not my Queen, Bitch. Don't try to order me around, you won't like the consequences."

Hearing raised voices, Marina quickened her steps until she rounded the corner and stopped upon seeing Dreven and Willow having a heated discussion. Now she understood. It was all a ruse. A ruse for Dreven to corner Curran's mate.

"Dreven." Marina stepped out of the shadow and in between Dreven and Willow, forcing him to let her go. "I do not recall our King giving you permission to touch *his mate*."

With a curse he stepped back, glaring at Marina Anluan. "Permission?" Dreven laughed an ugly bitter sound. "Not you too, Anluan. She's not even a Dark Elf for the gods' sake. Has everyone gone mad?" With another vicious curse, he spun on his heel and stalked off down the corridor.

Marina watched his retreating back to make sure he kept going. "Dreven." He stopped but did not turn around. "It does not matter if she is a Dark Elf or not. Curran is mated to her. She is our Queen, and you will treat her as such." She stood there, eyes watchful and ready.

He stiffened but continued down the hall.

As Dreven disappeared down the stairs, Willow looked at Marina with huge eyes. "I should have waited for you."

Once she knew Dreven was gone, she turned to face Willow and nodded. "Yes, you should've. Are you hurt?" Her eyes traveled over Willow's slender frame making her own assessment even though Willow was shaking her head. "Come on, I'll walk you to your rooms." She needed to talk to Curran about this incident. Dreven was pushing his limits.

Willow shook her head as she rubbed her arms. "I'm fine Marina. Why is Dreven like that? I've never even spoken to him before. Everyone else I have met has been wonderful. Even the people who are not Dark Elves." She sighed. "I haven't taken the protection things seriously enough. I'll be more careful in the future."

Stepping into Willow and Curran's suite, she turned to her. "I don't have the answer for that. I suggest avoiding Dreven if you can until Curran gets back" She scanned the room to make sure it was safe and contained no hidden surprises. "If you need to go anywhere, my room is across the hall. Lock the door behind me." She went to the door, opening it before turning back to Willow.

"Don't pay any mind to what Dreven says about Curran. If there is something that troubles you, ask Curran. "Do not pay attention to the words and actions of a bitter, jealous man." Nodding she stepped out into the hallway closing the door behind her.

Willow sighed and turned the lock, leaning against the door for a moment. What she wouldn't do for a cup of tea. With a soft sigh she walked over and set her notebooks down on the table, opened one and wrote a note about finding a way to communicate with the kitchen from her rooms. Carefully she closed the notebook, set down the pen, turned and looked around her room. Their room. His room.

Chapter Fifty-Four

STAR DATE: 20580.09.17

Dimension Five
Realm of the Forsaken
Aezorwyn

THERE WAS REALLY NOTHING here that was hers. Not even her clothes. The new clothes didn't count. Not yet. She didn't have her comfy tunic, her leggings, her favorite jacket. She missed her stuff. Not that it was important in the long run, she could live without it. She sighed, and looked around the room again, the familiar comfort that she found in her little home was missing from this large stone room. And right now, she missed the feminine warmth of her home desperately.

There's nothing soft or feminine here. Nothing warm or welcoming, she thought as she shivered and rubbed her arms, wincing as her hand moved over the place where Dreven had grabbed her. She would have bruises. With a sigh she walked over to look out the window at the gardens.

After a moment she turned away and stared around the room again. Her eyes seemed drawn to the door that led down to a room that Curran said he would show to her when he had time. And his eyes had been filled with wicked mischief at the time. Which made her leery. She'd never gone into that room, even though, over time, she'd become more and more curious. She knew why, of course she did. She was terribly aware of her lack of experience, her secret fear that she would not be able to please her mate. His sexuality was far beyond anything she'd ever experienced, far beyond anything she had ever known about.

Swallowing against the sudden dryness in her throat she found herself walking toward that door, turmoil roiling in her stomach. She hesitated with her hand on the doorknob. Taking a breath, she opened it, and descended the spiral stairs.

The room was lit by the soft light of many small glow stones embedded in the walls, their light casting dark shadows that played along the floor and walls. She turned slowly, as she looked around, her gaze landing on every feature. A huge bed dominated one wall, its rich gold linens a sharp contrast in the darkened room. Steel rings and shackles were embedded into the elaborate headboard and footboard, and her stomach tightened at the sight before she glanced away. But looking across the room at the shackles hanging from the wall was no better.

Her mind skittered away from the thought of what all those restraints were for, and she once again saw the beautiful exotic Keanna kneeling naked on the bed waiting for Curran.

Why did Curran even want her? She was not exotic or trained to give pleasure. She was a quiet woman who'd made herself invisible out of necessity. She was a woman who'd tried her hardest to make herself as ordinary as possible so she could stay out of the probing light of the Suzerain. She was someone who, while looking at herself in a mirror, didn't see an overtly desirable woman. She was just ... herself.

Adjacent to the wall with the shackles was a tall wooden wardrobe and, puzzled by its presence, she walked over to look into it. She opened the wooden doors, staring in shock at the contents that lined the shelves— Dildos of every shape and size. Some of those were... excessive.

She swallowed and dragged her gaze away from the toys and opened a drawer. Jeweled clamps and rings filled velvet lined cubbies, jars and tubes filled with heaven knew what sat organized in a strangely neat way. She opened another drawer and found wooden paddles, a leather belt, and a coiled whip. She shook her head and backed away.

Turning, she ran back up the stairs and slammed the door closed, her breath sawing in and out like she had run a marathon as she stared wildly around his bedroom. She did not belong here.

Hands trembling, she looked blankly down at the floor, and rubbed her arms again. She wanted tea so badly, but she didn't dare go down to get one from the kitchen. It wasn't safe. Shouldn't your home be safe?

She walked over and sat on the edge of the bed. Instantly she jerked back to her feet, and after a wary look at the bed, walked over to look out the window again.

She missed her books, the soft throw her mother had made for her many years ago. This was not her home. She took a deep breath and decided a hot bath would help her to relax. At least there was hot water here, she thought with a weak laugh as she tried to ignore the burning in her eyes. She ran the water, and after stripping down, she got into the tub. Closing her eyes, as the heat seeped into her, she felt her muscles begin to relax. Reaching for the bar of soap that a young woman named Zarah had given to her days earlier, she rubbed it on the soft washing cloth, the scent of rosas drifted up in the air. Instantly she was reminded of her mother's rosa garden and tears filled her eyes. "Mama." She whispered as a tear slid down her cheek.

Memories surged through her mind, bombarded her, as the weight of her secret bore down on her. The constant struggle to never let her powers be seen, the day she made the mistake that had resulted in her brother being taken by the Suzerain. The grief in her parents' eyes as he was taken from their home— because of her.

Guilt and shame pressed down on her until she felt as if she was drowning in it. Tears rolled down her cheeks as she was filled with the terrible certainty that she would fail these people as she had failed her own family.

By the time she got out of the tub, the water was cold, and she was shivering. She dried off and swiped at the tears still running down her cheeks. She had to pull herself together. Normally that involved a hot cup of tea, a torrid romance novel, or a holovid. Not an option here. She could go for a walk in the gardens. No, she couldn't. Not with that man around.

She swept up one of the glow stones from a nearby table and hurled it as hard as she could. The stone shattered as it slammed into the wall with a bright flare of light, the pieces clattering to the floor in a shower of sparks.

The energy from the stone flowed into her. She gasped, inhaling sharply at the heat of the foreign energy surging through her. What was that? She swallowed and took a deep calming breath. Oh gods. She'd never flown into a rage so consuming that she'd thrown something. —That she had broken something. This world was affecting her in strange ways. She rubbed her arms, turning slowly and the violent rage that had filled her, settled into a slow simmer. This was her room, too. She would put her stamp all over it, just see if she didn't. She hadn't asked to be brought to Aezorwyn. She hadn't asked to be mated to a sex maniac, but by the gods, she would damn well rise to this challenge, even if she was not the best person for the job.

Her mama had not raised any fools, she thought. She had a chance for something completely different to happen in her life. She had spent her whole life hiding, terrified of being found by the Suzerain and forced to become a monster. Now, life offered her a uniquely safe place. The Suzerain had no idea where she was. No one here knew what she was. *I'm Safe.* She paused at the thought. *I'm safe.*

For the first time in her life, she could live without fear, and, by the gods, she was not going to let that, that... slimy Quana, Dreven take it from her.

Swiping at the tears that continued to slide down her cheeks, she headed for the tall wardrobe that held their clothes. Opening the door, she ignored the small avalanche of cloth and dragged one of Curran's shirts over her head. Searching through the piles of new clothes she found a pair of dark leather pants. She wiggled into them and found a pair of soft suede boots and tugged them on.

Considering what to do next, she glanced around the room and, as her eyes landed on the door to Curran's playroom, the anger running through her veins spiked hot again. She turned back to the wardrobe, rummaging until she found the large cloth bag she'd noticed hanging on the back wall.

Turning on her heel she marched over to the door to *that* room and jerked it open. She hurried down the stairs and over to that damned cupboard that held all kinds of things she didn't know what to do with. Sweeping the phallic shaped toys into her arms, she dumped them into the bag. She emptied all the drawers, grabbed that whip, and stormed back up the stairs. She picked up the dagger that Curran had given her and stuck it into the waistband of her pants. Coiling the whip, she looped it crosswise over her shoulder and neck. Just let that son of a bitch Dreven try to touch her now, she thought mutinously.

Opening her bedroom door, she stepped into the dim hallway and slammed the door behind her. Marching across the hall, she banged on Marina's door.

It opened a bare second later and Marina stood there regarding her silently. "Are you alright?"

"No, I'm not!" She snapped and swiped at the tears that were still rolling down her cheeks. "I'm going to see Keanna, and I want tea. You can escort me, or I can go myself, but I will not be terrified to even go to the kitchen in my own home."

Marina nodded, her head tilting slightly to the side, and stepped out of her room, fighting the urge to grin at the sight of Curran's fierce little mate. A woman who was destined to be a queen. A queen who, at this moment, was fighting tears and looked like she was going to tumble over from the very full bag she was carrying. *Was that a wooden dick sticking out of the top?* The tears concerned her. The sex toy she shrugged off, women had needs too. "I'll escort you to Keanna's home. She will have tea." They walked a few steps down the hall. "Do you know how to use that dagger?"

Willow shook her head.

"I'll start teaching you tomorrow."

Willow glanced up at Marina and saw the seriousness in her gaze. "Thank you."

Marina nodded and they continued to their destination in silence.

Knocking on Keanna's door, Willow waited, and for the hundredth time told the scared part of herself to calm down. The door opened and Keanna stood there in her robe, looking sleepily puzzled as she looked from Willow to Marina.

"Willow has come for tea. She is not to leave here without me, under any circumstances. Even though she looks like a bloody space pirate with those weapons, I doubt very much she knows how to use them. I'm holding you responsible for her well being, Keanna."

Willow turned to glare at Marina. "Are you done?"

Marina met her gaze calmly. "I'll wait outside."

Keanna stared after the warrior, before looking at Willow, an eyebrow raised. She could see Willow had been crying. Reaching out she took her hand, and pulled her into her home, closing and locking the door behind her. "Are we under attack, your majesty?"

Willow glared and put her hands on her hips, which was a bit difficult with the damn bag in the way. "Are you my friend, Keanna? Do you really care about me, or do you just want to keep fucking my mate?"

Keanna arched an eyebrow. "I am your friend, and I don't know a sane woman who wouldn't want to keep fucking your mate... but, I have given up on that particular sin."

Willow regarded her for a long moment as she considered Keanna's words. At least she'd been honest. "You can help me with something." Spying the open door to Keanna's bedroom, she stalked into it, and upended her bag into the middle of Keanna's bed.

Keanna made a funny noise, and Willow glanced at her sharply. The woman's eyes were huge as she stared at the pile on her bed, shocked laughter lurking in her eyes. "I... am at a total loss for words. Where did you get this stuff, Willow?" A large wooden phallus rolled off the bed and landed at Keanna's feet. She stooped and picked up the wooden cock and stared at it for a moment before silently setting it on the top of the pile, her lips twitching in amusement.

Willow looked at Keanna and felt her lip tremble as all the feelings of insecurity rushed back over her. "Curran's secret room."

Keanna sighed at the look on Willow's face, her levity disappearing in an instant at her friend's distress. She looked terrified and confused all at once. "Why bring it here?"

Willow looked down at the floor for a minute. "I don't even know what some of those things are for. I don't know if I can be what he wants." A tear slid down her cheek.

"Oh, Willow." She reached out to brush the tear from Willow's cheek, her voice gentle. "Curran is quite taken with you. You don't have to be anything except yourself."

Willow shook her head. "I'm not like you, Keanna, I don't know what to do with a man like him."

Keanna contemplated her for a moment, and chuckled. "You are handling him just fine from what I've seen. Take off your boots and weapons and climb up on my bed. We'll go through this pile, and I'll explain what each thing is used for. One thing you need to know is that every single thing here is designed for sexual pleasure of one kind or another." Keanna paused momentarily. "I'll make a tea tray and bring it in here. We'll have a girl's night."

Keanna came back into the room with a large tray filled to overflowing with sandwiches, pastries, fruit, and tea. She set the overloaded tray down on a low table at the end of the bed. "Just out of curiosity," she said as she poured steaming hot tea into delicate cups. "Why on Aezorwyn are you dressed like a space pirate?"

Willow glanced down at herself. "Dreven."

"Dreven? What does that bastard have to do with anything?"

Willow shrugged. "I ran into him when I was leaving Curran's study and he said I shouldn't be in there ..." She took off her boots as she went through the scene with Dreven, but she kept the dagger in her hands as she sat down. The jewels on the dagger and its sheath glittered in the light as she subconsciously rubbed her arm. "He tried to intimidate me. And damn it, it worked. Until it made me mad."

Keanna nodded her eyes concerned. "Did he hurt you?"

Willow shook her head.

"You need to tell Curran about this."

Willow shook her head, and Keanna raised an eyebrow, "If you don't tell Curran, I'm certain that Marina will. It's better if he finds out from you."

Willow made a noise of disgust. "I am not used to this mate business. I have no clue why I need to tell him everything. He is way too bossy as it is."

Keanna laughed and handed Willow her tea. "Oh, you are going to be so good for Curran. Whenever you have had enough of his controlling ways, just come here and we can bitch together about the male species."

Willow laughed, "Why do I think I will be here often?" Taking a sip of her tea, she closed her eyes for a moment. That was exactly what she needed. She took a second sip and reached for the top item on the pile and tossed it to Keanna. "Can you tell me why a male with his stamina has any need for a whole lot of fake cocks?"

Chapter Fifty-Five

STAR DATE: 20580.09.18

> Dimension Five
> Realm of the Forsaken
> Aezorwyn

"SHE'S GOING TO BE OK, Curran." Garrett said, watching his friend's furious face. "You sent Dreven out with the hunting party, and they won't be back for a couple days. Besides, with the fucking beating you gave him, I doubt he'll show his face for a long time."

"I wanted to kill him," Curran said, shoving a hand through his hair.

Garrett shrugged. "I get that. His attitude has changed a lot in the last few months, and Willow coming here seems to have aggravated it. We are going to have to deal with him eventually."

Curran nodded. "Marina was right about him."

"I don't know if that is feminine intuition or her warrior side, but she is rarely wrong about people," Garrett said, as Curran paced. "You know, Curran, I think you need to make it official with Willow. Our people need to see that this is not temporary. They need to understand that she is your mate and our Queen."

Curran's dark eyes met Garrett's. "I was planning on doing that after this mission."

"Well, let's get this mission over with then. Your warrior is waiting for you and so is your mate."

A knock sounded at the door and Marina and Willow walked in. Curran immediately went to his mate. His hands cupping her head as he looked down into her eyes. "Garrett and I have to go on a mission. We believe we have found one of my men."

Willow nodded. This was something that Curran had discussed with her shortly after he'd brought her here. His nightmares had woken her several times, but her abilities had told her even more. She was well aware of his anguish, his torment. "Who?"

"Falcon."

Willow heard the pain in his voice. "Your second in command."

"My friend."

Willow reached out and set her hand on his chest. "Bring Falcon home, Curran."

Curran knew in that moment that Willow was his fucking destiny. He leaned down and took her mouth, in a far to brief, wild, hard kiss. Stepping back, his eyes locked to hers. He and Garrett shifted into another dimension.

Chapter Fifty-Six

STAR DATE: 20580.09.18
  Dimension Thirty-Seven
  Perileos Star System
  Xehshyhra

HE AWOKE TO ICY COLD water rushing into his cell. Barely able to keep his pain-filled body afloat as the water rose to its full height, he spent a miserable night clinging desperately to the rocks on the ceiling of his cell with grim determination, planning his final escape attempt.

Five seconds. Four seconds. Three seconds. Two. One. Late again, the fucking lazy bastards, this was becoming a bad habit for them. He started to lift up, barely able to contain his agony, his back screaming as his muscles contracted and he fought a wave of dizziness.

Chapter Fifty-Seven

STAR DATE: 20580.09.18

Dimension Five

Secret Cache

Moon orbiting Venia, Lore Star System

THE HIGH-TECH SECURITY system scanned them as soon as Curran and Garrett shifted into the hidden secure cache. The female computer voice welcomed them. "Warehouse secure. Last accessed by Garrett Wyatt, Marina Anluan, and Dreven Avanth."

"Computer, open the weapons storage."

"Voice print identified. Weapons storage unlocked, Curran Nadiir."

They strode into the compartment and Garrett opened a locker, pulling out body armour while Curran got out the weapons they would need, phase pistols, blasters and several small explosive devices.

"Shit. Curran, with all the excitement of rescuing our women from the slavers, I forgot to mention that the Suzerain have technology to jump dimensions now." He nodded his head towards another locker. "They kindly provided the technology to the bounty hunters to complete their mission."

Curran turned to look at him with a frown but nodded. "We'll have a better look at it after we complete this mission."

They suited up as they went over their plans. "If Falcon is in bad shape, we are going to need to do some rapid shifts. Long distance shifts. Ending up on Aezorwyn. It won't be easy." Curran's voice was curt as he did up straps and holstered weapons.

"Agreed." Garrett said. "Computer please display the holo vid map I input the last time I was here." A holographic map appeared in front of them. "I think if we shift here." Garrett said, "We have the best chance of not being discovered right away."

Curran nodded. "Computer can you securely access any information on the highest security Xehshyhraen prison."

"The Xehshyhraen have only one functioning prison. It is located deep beneath the ground in the province of Mitrian."

Garrett nodded. "That confirms the map. Computer, how many guards are assigned to that prison."

"The last time their reports were updated was Star date: 20571.03.01, at that time the reported number of guards was forty-eight. There are no updates."

Curran swore. Two years with no updates. "Computer what is the total population of Xehshyhra at this point in time?"

"Total acknowledged population on Xehshyhra is 15,941 males, 5,321 of which are clones."

"Clones." Garrett shook his head.

Curran nodded grimly. "They are doomed."

"Computer, are there any reports that list the name of Falcon Keyon?" Garrett asked.

"Report Star date: 20573.06.25. Keyon, Falcon incarcerated on Star date: 20573.06.25. Cell UC8-5."

"Well, that was lucky," Garrett said.

Curran frowned. "Their record keeping is shit. If that was true it meant that Falcon was in the portal for a gods-damned month." Strapping on his final knife, Curran straightened and looked Garrett in the eye. "All or None!"

"They shifted directly into the prison. Appearing in a rarely used storeroom, they shifted immediately into corridor 8, and that is where their luck ran out. A guard yelled and two more opened fire on them. Cursing Garrett launched himself at the first guard, his knife sinking deep into the lizard-like creature's neck. Dark blood arched and splashed onto the wall as Garrett yanked the knife out and slammed it back into the guard's throat. Firing his blaster, Curran shifted behind a pillar, and shot again. Both guards dropped. An alarm began to sound, and Curran swore. "Down here!"

They ran down the corridor checking the numbers until they came to the steel door marked UC8-5. "What the fuck? Is that a handwheel?" Garrett muttered.

"Shit that door is watertight. What the shadows? Is this the right cell?" Curran looked at the number plate again.

"Hurry up, Curran! I can hear them coming."

Growling, Curran began to spin the wheel. "We might have to shift outta here if he's not in there."

Garrett lifted his blaster and fired down the corridor as a guard appeared, then another.

Chapter Fifty-Eight

STAR DATE: 20580.09.18

Dimension Thirty-Seven
Perileos Star System
Xehshyhra

THE SUDDEN RELEASE of pressure in his cell hit him with a renewed shock of agony, and he choked off the yell that tried to force itself from his throat as the water began to pour out. Who the fuck had opened that door without draining the water first?

Grinding his teeth together, he forced his fingers to let go of the rocks he'd been clinging to and dropped, trying to control the pain ripping through his body as he crashed into the water. *Fuck!*

Holding his breath as he was pulled under, he fought his way to the surface again, every kick of his mutilated leg, every twist of his raw back, threatened to drown him. He was going to fucking punch whoever had been so fucking stupid.

He found his footing abruptly as the water level rapidly dropped, for a second anyway, before his knees gave out. He cursed and surged to his feet. He didn't kneel to anyone. And no fucking way were those fucking aliens going to find him on his knees. He'd seen one too many prisoners ass fucked when the aliens got them on their knees. No fucking way was he going to be ass fucked by some slimy lizard.

He staggered to his feet, his teeth clamped shut to prevent the screams that wanted to tear out of his throat as he shifted to lean against a wall, soaking wet, shaking violently, hands fisted, ready to battle whoever the fuck came through that door. He was fucking tired of being a model prisoner. Time for these reptiles to learn some respect. They would never be late for a torture date again by the time he was through with them.

Cursing at the flood of water that poured out of the cell, slamming him back into the wall opposite the door, Curran fought to retain his footing. He could hear the shooting and Garrett's loud cursing. He looked to his left and saw Garrett down on one knee shooting rapidly. The fucking Xehshyhraen guards were shooting back but at least they were not coming down that corridor. Yet. Ducking into the cell, Curran saw Falcon right away. He was leaning against the wall and looked like he'd been vacationing in the Dimension of Shadows. Fuck.

Falcon didn't even blink. Was this some kind of trick? "About fucking time, you got here. You're about three hundred years late, you bastard. If I find out you were fucking some pretty little piece of fluff, I am going to kick your ass."

Curran shouldered his blaster and strode over to Falcon. "No time for nasty gossip, Falcon. We gotta go. I'll trade fuck stories with you later." Sliding his arm around Falcon's waist. "Time for us to blow smoke."

And that was when he knew this was real. Blowing smoke was a code that he and Curran had come up with long ago when they were wild, trouble making teenagers. Something only the two of them knew about, and they'd usually used it when they were about to pull a fast one on their parents and disappear like smoke.

He swallowed the sudden lump in his throat, gritting his teeth against the pain as Curran took a step, dragging him along. "Fuck!" *Mother fucking lizards, he hated those sonsofbitches.* He glared at his friend and at the man who appeared in the doorway. "It's just the two of you? Has the universe gone mad? Where's Talia and Flint? Are they waiting in the hallway? What the fuck are we waiting here for, a fucking invitation?"

They headed out of the shadow trap he'd existed in for the past seven years and he was not sorry to see the last of this version of the Dimension of Shadows. Being helped along like a godsdamned invalid made him growl furiously, but he was smart enough not to reject their help. He was a fucking mess, and he knew it. *Son of a bitch. Those metal rods hurt like a motherfucker.*

He was listening as Curran quickly explained how they were getting out of there when they heard the fucking lizards coming. Cursing a blue streak, he ignored the other man's amusement, he had no intentions of being taken alive by those fucking monsters again. "Less talk, more running. You're not fucking seducing me. You're breaking me out of fucking jail! And someone give me a godsforsaken weapon!"

Garrett chuckled and handed over his phase pistol. "Garrett Wyatt." And threw an IED down the corridor as hard as he could. "Move it! Around the corner!"

"Hang on, Falcon, we'll be outta here soon." Curran said as he and Garrett practically carried Falcon down the corridor and around the corner just as an explosion rocked the building.

Falcon stared at the guy helping Curran, searching his face for something, anything, familiar. He didn't recognize the name and he sure as fuck did not know him. He looked at Curran and searched his eyes. A cold icy feeling slid through him, and he closed his eyes for a minute. "Where are Flint and Talia?"

"Not here, Falcon. You're the first we've found."

He stared at Curran out of old, old eyes. He was the first? Something inside of him coiled tight, and he had to look away. He couldn't break here. Gods. He'd thought that Talia and Flint would already be free. Especially Talia.

He'd fought every freaking day to survive and part of that had been by convincing himself that she must be out by now. Instead, she was still suffering somewhere, if she was still alive. "Curran. It's been over seven years." He said hoarsely as he stared at his friend. "How—" He choked off the words and fought to hold on to some form of sanity. "We have to find them." He said quietly, a desperate edge to his grief-stricken voice.

"Shift!" Curran shouted as more guards raced towards them from another corridor. Nothing happened. *What the fuck?*

"It's the collar." Falcon said hoarsely. 'After my last escape attempt, they figured out I could shift."

Curran grabbed his knife. "Hold fucking still! I didn't come all this way to fucking have you die." He slid the whisper thin blade of his knife between the thick leather collar and Falcon's neck. A twist of his wrist and the blade sliced through that collar like a hot knife through butter. "Shift!"

Falcon hung on through the disorientation of the shift and blinked, blinded by the sunlight. He squinted against the brightness and drew in a deep breath of fresh air.

"Ready?" Garrett shouted as the guards burst out of the main gates of the prison. Laser blasts filled the air.

"Shift!" Curran shouted.

They reappeared in the small secure cache.

"Fuck!" Falcon snarled through the pain and the blackness encroaching on his vision, as he fought to understand where they were now. "Curran." He waited for his friend and leader to look at him. "All or None?"

"All or None!" Curran and the man Garrett replied. "Shift!"

Chapter Fifty-Nine

STAR DATE: 20580.09.18

Dimension Five
Realm of the Forsaken
Aezorwyn

A LOUD BOOM SOUNDED in the air, and even from the garden Willow saw the castle windows rattle. She looked at the castle gardener Zarah, and dropping their spades, they ran for the gate.

Marina swore, knowing damned well that Willow wouldn't return to the castle. If she was learning anything about her Queen, it was that the woman was always rushing to help. Shouting to the castle guards she raced past Willow, determined to find out what had happened and put herself between any danger and the Queen.

As Willow and Zarah reached the gate, Zarah grabbed her arm and pulled her over to the huge stone walls that protected the palace. "We have to be careful. We don't know what's out there."

Willow frowned and started to pull away when she saw the slight tremble in the gardener's hands as she pushed her heavy, brown hair back behind her pointed ears. Zarah Bishop was a Dark Elf, and that meant she had survived the destruction of her world. Understanding filled Willow and she nodded her agreement. Zarah crouched down by the gate and motioned for Willow to do the same, they peered cautiously around the massive stone pillars that supported the huge metal gate.

Two men stood there wearing military style dark body armour, a third man held in the arms of one of them. Their realm had been discovered! Willow gasped and Zarah lifted a finger to her lips, as they watched, the castle guard surrounded the men, clearly following Marina's shouted orders.

"Put those fucking guns down." Garrett yanked off his helmet and shouted for someone to get the doctor.

"What the shadows was that noise?" Marina snapped as she glared at Garrett.

"I think it was from doing three extremely long shifts back-to-back. The distance was beyond what we should have risked. It took a tremendous amount of energy." Curran said just as Jase sprinted from the castle, followed by his medical team carrying bags of supplies and a stretcher.

As Garrett stepped back, Willow's heart slammed against her chest at the sight of her mate, the limp figure of an obviously malnourished man in his arms. She dodged around Zarah and out the massive gate, ignoring Marina's shouts for her to get back.

Curran set Falcon on the stretcher and watched as the medical team swarmed him, answering as many of the urgently shouted questions as he could.

"Is that…"

Curran looked over and there was Willow, he nodded grimly. "Falcon." He stepped back, looping his arm around Willow's waist to pull her out of the way.

"Are you hurt?" Willow asked quietly.

Curran shook his head, focused on the doctor who was snapping out orders to the team around him. A second man immediately went to work on getting an IV started, his swift movements conveying a sense of urgency.

Jase Aries looked up from the man he was working on, and his eyes met those of Journey Themis. "We need to operate, and we need to do it fast."

Journey nodded, a huge bear of a man with intelligent cyan colored eyes.

The next second the whole medical team had disappeared, and Willow was turning shocked eyes to Curran. "How?"

"Journey Themis comes from a race of beings capable of instant teleportation. Come on, they will be in the medical wing operating room." Curran looked over at his Garrett, and Marina as she joined them. "I've got this Curran, go to medical."

"We have the first one, we're going to count this as a success." Curran said. Noticing the people gathering, he turned to face the growing crowd. "Today, we have brought Falcon Keyan home. All or None!"

An answering roar went up from his people and he saw tears in the eyes of some. A voice called out. "How is he?"

"He's in rough shape. Doctor Aries is operating. Remember Falcon in your thoughts today."

Chapter Sixty

STAR DATE: 20580.09.18

Dimension Five

Farport City, Tryria

COMMANDER D'MIRON STOOD up, his hover chair slamming into the wall behind him, his eyes blazing with a fury that somehow was all the more dangerous for its very coldness. "What do you mean the Xehshyhraen lost Falcon Keyan? How do you lose a prisoner that has been in your keeping for seven years?" He glared impatiently at his assistant, waiting for an explanation.

Staring back at Commander D'miron, Tamika swallowed and tried to come up with an answer that would not get her killed. "We just received the report from Xehshyhra. They claim that someone landed a small craft on their planet and infiltrated their underworld prison system. Keyan was snatched, and several guards slaughtered."

Commander D'miron turned and stalked over to look out at the city below him. His office was high up in a tower, with what was supposed to be impenetrable security. "Didn't the Xehshyhraen promise us that their prisons were impenetrable?"

"Yes, sir"

"I want a full report on Keyan from the moment he was sent to their prison." He turned and looked at Tamika. "A complete report. Am I clear?"

"Yes, sir. Perfectly clear."

"Send a team of agents, and have this situation investigated. Thoroughly. I think it's time we tested Xehshyhra's security. Launch a strike team as soon as the investigation is complete. It's time to remind the Xehshyhraen what happens when you fail the Suzerain."

"Yes, sir." She turned to leave, her hands trembling, her mind racing. *She? She was supposed to order a strike against another planet?* The Commander's icily controlled voice stopped her.

"One more thing. I want reports on all the Dark Elf Spirit Warrior prisoners. Thorough reports, including holo vids on my desk by the end of the week. I'm sending you the contact information for the five remaining penal institutes that have incarcerated those criminals on our behalf. Do not fail me."

She couldn't have replied even if she'd wanted too. She quietly left the Commander's office knowing that she was now walking a very dangerous line. Her horror filled mind was screaming at her to get out. To run. But she had to be smart about this, her hand settled low on her stomach. Because there was now more than just her.

Commander D'miron watched the low flying traffic below. Another coincidence. Another Dark Elf missing. How had Curran Nadiir managed to find one of his men in a completely different dimension, and actually rescue him? Who

had helped him? Perhaps it was also time for a reminder of
the might of the Suzerain to the universe.

Chapter Sixty-One

STAR DATE: 20580.09.18
   Dimension Five
   Realm of the Forsaken
   Aezorwyn

JASE SWORE QUIETLY in his native language as he worked on the man that Curran had brought in and, fuck, as much as he tried to disassociate, he could not think of this man as simply a nameless person. He was Falcon Keyan, a man that Jase thought of as a friend. A good man, and one who didn't deserve what had been done to him.

He carefully extracted the fifth metal bar and passed it to Axel, who set it on a small table off to the side. He hoped that Curran had killed the bastards who'd done this to Falcon. It had been a chilling moment when he had seen the names scribed on all those titanium bars and realized grimly the head games those sons of bitches had played with Falcon as they tortured his body.

"What's his blood pressure?" He snapped, as he flushed out the exit wound. Those bars were way too close to main arteries and important tendons. In fact, they had spent the first half hour repairing damaged arteries, working fast to try to prevent the loss of any more blood even as they had pumped IV bags of blood into him. If he wasn't careful, Falcon would bleed out or never walk normally again. And they were battling infection, terrible infections.

They had him on his side, he was working on saving Falcon's leg and Journey was working on the mess that was Falcon's back. Axel called out the numbers on Falcon's blood pressure and Jase nodded once. Thank the Creators, that at least his blood pressure was holding steady at this point.

The door to the surgical room opened and Breccan walked in, two clear IV bags in his hands. One was filled with a pale amber liquid, the other with a pale aqua liquid, both were powerful plant based antibiotic medications. Untested medications that Kailene O'Rinn swore would help to save Falcon. Everything inside of him rebelled at the idea of using an untested medication, but they had nothing powerful enough in their medical supplies to combat the massive infections that Falcon was fighting. Falcon would die without antibiotics.

He was being forced to trust in that wacky biologist's work. Grimly he began the delicate work of extracting the sixth bar. He glanced at Axel and the blue haired man called out the numbers to Falcon's respirations. "11 BPM. We are at three hours".

Fuck. This was taking too long. Times like this he wished desperately for a cutting-edge medical facility, but that wasn't going to happen anytime soon. They worked with what they had. Old fashioned surgical steel instruments, primitive blood pressure cuffs, stethoscopes, archaic needles, and gravity fed IV's.

Breccan attached the IV bags to the stand where a synthetic blood/plasma was being pumped into Falcon, they had precious little stores of the lifesaving synthetic blood/plasma, but he was immensely grateful that it was something that Curran always tried to find for them. He knew how high the risks were for Curran's team to acquire the lifesaving liquid. Today, those risks were paying off. "Let's get him through the surgery before we start adding in those concoctions."

Breccan nodded and walked over to watch Journey working, where they had a quiet intense discussion before Breccan disappeared and Jase knew Journey had sent him back to talk to O'Rinn. She was also supplying them with the saline wash that they were using to clear the wounds. He inched the bar a bare millimeter, easing it carefully past the deep femoral artery. How those bastards had managed to get this bar in without decimating this major artery was beyond him.

He continued to ease the bar slowly out, cursing at the damage left from the red-hot bar as it had entered. He worked it out of the tendon it was embedded in and knew he would need to do some fine needle work to repair the damage. That was one thing about that wash they were using, it seemed to have some kind of regenerative properties. He could see the seared pathways left from the bars slowly changing as he worked.

"Jase."

He glanced at Axel.

"Blood pressure is falling, heart rate slowing."

He swore and his eyes met Journey's. "Do you have a bleeder?"

"No." Journey shook his head. "I think it's the infection. His body has just been through too much."

"Get the IV's going"

Axel instantly moved to the IV stand and removed the clamps holding the medications back. "His lungs don't sound normal either. From what Curran said he was subject to some kind of drowning torture."

Jase nodded grimly. "Keep calling the numbers. Journey, we gotta speed this up."

Chapter Sixty-Two

STAR DATE: 20580.09.18

Dimension Five
Realm of the Forsaken
Aezorwyn

"CURRAN." WILLOW SLIPPED her fingers through his and tugged gently on his hand. "You need to have a shower and something to eat. Falcon has stabilized and Jase and his team will keep him safe. You won't be any good to him if you are passed out on the floor from exhaustion. It won't take us long." She could see how torn he was, but she also knew he needed to look after himself if he was going to be able to deal with the hard things to come with Falcon.

Grudgingly, Curran agreed, and they headed up to their chambers. Turning on the shower, while he stripped off, she adjusted the temperature of the water and stepped back, unable to prevent the appreciative glance at his hard body.

While Curran showered, she set out clean clothes for him and sent a maid to tell the kitchen to prepare a tray for them so they could eat in the waiting room of the medical ward. She also sent instructions for coffee and snacks to be set up in the waiting room and for the kitchen staff to keep them replenished. It seemed that every Dark Elf on the planet was drifting in and out of the waiting room checking on one of their beloved heroes.

Curran walked out of the bathing room rubbing his hair with a towel, a second towel hanging low on his hips. He paused hearing his mate speaking to the maid and his lips quirked up a bit. Marina was right, she was a natural for this Queen business. He needed to speak to her about that. "Willow."

She turned smiling at him. "I put some clothes for you on the bed. By the time we get down to the waiting room, we should have a meal waiting for us."

"It can wait a few minutes." He took her hand and tugged her over to the bed. "Lay with me for a few minutes."

She laughed as she lay down beside him. "I've never known you to only take a 'few minutes' when you are naked in a bed with me"

Curran laughed and shook his head. "I just need to rest for a few minutes."

She rolled to her side and regarded him with concern. She could feel his ragged emotions and the exhaustion riding him hard. Reaching out she stroked his chest, knowing that her touch would at least send her energy into him to help with his emotions. "I had more than one daydream about punishing you this week." She gave him a cheeky little grin. "Luckily for you, things have gotten better. In fact, if you were not so exhausted, I'd consider a little reward was in order. Ah, well. Such is life for a King."

When he growled, she chuckled and tugged her skirts up so she could get to her knees. Running her hands up his chest, she could feel the tension in his muscles, and began to knead his shoulders. "This is entirely the wrong position for a massage." She said with a playful grimace.

She was hoping he would let her touch him for a few more minutes but didn't want to push it. Just a few more minutes and he would have much better control. If he wasn't so exhausted, she would have crawled on top of him and suggested a quicky. Nothing like the total body contact of sex to let her healing energy do its work. Blushing and shocked at her own thoughts, she was careful not to make eye contact and kept rubbing his shoulders. Not the right time for such thoughts, she silently scolded herself. "You've known Falcon a long time, tell me about him. How did you meet him? What's he like?"

Curran closed his eyes, liking the feelings of her hands on him. Gods he was exhausted. "First day at the academy, we were five years old and the smallest boys in the class. This kid came up to me, and he was at least six inches taller and twice as wide. Saros Tierce. That kid was pure muscle and attitude. He had me up against the wall, his hand pulled back to punch me. Suddenly this kid with long hair grabbed me and yanked me away just as Saros struck. His hand hit the wall." a smirk flashed across Curran's face. "Shit, did he howl."

"The instructor and another boy who looked exactly like the one who'd just saved me, stepped back into the room and, while the instructor was busy helping Saros, I met Falcon and his twin brother, Flint. They'd figured out what Saros was up to right away, and Flint distracted the instructor while Falcon saved my ass." He smiled at the memory and looked at Willow again. "We've been friends ever since.

"I wish I could've known you all as kids. I like Falcon just from what you told me about him. Curran, I know you'll get all your men back." She reached up and gently brushed a lock of hair back from his face, her eyes meeting his.

"I wish you could've seen those two as kids, too. They were all attitude. I couldn't believe my father never objected to our friendship." But he did now. His father had been a warrior, and he knew the value of people who had your back.

His throat had grown tight at the confidence of her statement, the gentle stare of her eyes feeling more intimate than if they'd been having sex. "Such belief," he murmured, his head turning into her touch.

"By the time we were twelve," he continued, "we'd shot up in height and filled out until we were the biggest in our class. Saros ended up being one of the shortest. It's strange how that works." He grew silent, sadness washing over him. "Saros became a great pilot and a good man. Garrett told me he died trying to defend our world from the Suzerain."

Standing, Curran stretched wearily and dressed. Taking Willow's hand in his, they headed back to the Medical Bay.

The hours passed slowly in the waiting room as the medical team worked on Falcon. There was a constant movement of people in and out of the waiting room, and Willow understood that they were showing support for their beloved King, and at the same time, desperately needed to hear updates. Falcon represented a victory for the Dark Elves.

Finally, Doctor Aries stepped into the waiting room. Curran and Willow hurried over to him. "Falcon is in our recovery ward. We are expecting him to wake up soon. He did well through the rest of the surgery. We were able to repair the damage done to his leg." He fixed them both with a serious look. "Falcon is severely malnourished. It is going to take time for him to recover. He needs nutritious food and rest while that leg heals. He is also going to need extensive physiotherapy for both his legs, and his hands." He gave Curran a serious look. "Both his legs appear to have been broken sometime in the past and his hands...." The doctor shook his head. "It's going to take time for him to heal but physio should help him to regain most of his dexterity. I know what he is like, Curran. He isn't going to want to rest, and he will try to push himself to get back to his former strength. Let's try to keep an eye on him so he doesn't over do it."

Curran nodded. "I doubt we can stop him, but we'll try. Thank you, Jase."

Turning to the people gathered in the room, Curran said. "Falcon is out of surgery, he's in recovery and doing as well as can be expected."

The relief that filled the room was instantaneous, and everyone seemed to take a deep breath. Willow's eyes met Rune's in the back corner of the room, he nodded once and disappeared.

They'd been sitting in the recovery room for about twenty minutes when Falcon opened his eyes. "Did you get the number of the ship that hit me?" he rasped.

"I got the number and destroyed it, Falcon."

Falcon swallowed, and his eyes met Currans before drifting around the room, until they lit upon a pretty redhead. He looked back at Curran puzzled. Curran was not the kind of man to have a woman with him. "Who's the pretty fluff?" He heard the woman gasp and glanced over at her again. She was glaring at him.

Curran coughed and held his hand out for the redhead. "Falcon, you don't want to upset a redhead. They're fierce." He looked over as the woman joined him, her small hand settling into his much larger one. Falcon was stunned by the look that passed between them.

"This is Willow, my mate and..." Curran looked at Willow. "Your Queen." The redhead gasped and glared daggers at Curran. "We are going to talk."

While Falcon lay in stunned silence, the tiny woman leaned in and pressed a soft kiss to his cheek. "Welcome home, Falcon. I'm glad you're finally here. Curran has missed you terribly." A mischievous gleam appeared in her eyes. "Most people call me Willow, but you can call me Queen Fluff."

Chapter Sixty-Three

STAR DATE: 20580.09.19

Dimension Five
Realm of the Forsaken
Aezorwyn

THEY'D STEPPED OUTSIDE for a breath of fresh air on their way from the Medical Bay, when Dreven found them. Willow instinctively moved slightly behind Curran, her hands suddenly clammy. She clenched them in her skirts as Dreven spoke. "Willow, I owe you an apology. I was totally out of line, and the only excuse I can offer was that we had just returned from an upsetting mission. I hope you can forgive me."

Willow watched the man. He spoke the right words but the energy that surrounded him did not lie. She nodded, and he turned to Curran.

"Curran, I was just speaking with Jase Aries. We need to restock the medical supplies ASAP. They used a lot of emergency supplies to save Keyan. We can't afford to be low on that stuff."

Willow watched the man, heard the way he said Falcon's name, the almost accusatory tone of his voice, as if those supplies had been wasted. She felt a low burning anger rise up in her. What an ass.

Curran nodded at Dreven's words. "A supply run would be wise. I'll get a team together and—"

"With all due respect Curran, you and Garrett just returned. It would be wiser if I went. A quick trip in and out, and hopefully the Suzerain will not be looking for a single Dark Elf."

Curran frowned, but shadows he was struggling to even think clearly, he was so tired. Finally, he nodded. "When do you want to leave?"

"Now, we can't afford to wait for these supplies."

"Go to the Specter Expanse cache, the Firebrand will get you to the Bythian galaxy in a week, get as many supplies as you can fit into the ship, then get the shadows back here. We need to stay under the radar for a while. Falcon's rescue is going to have the Suzerain stirred up. Don't take any chances, Dreven."

Chapter Sixty-Four

STAR DATE: 20580.09.21
Dimension Five
Farport City, Tryria

TAMIKA STARED AT THE computer screen, her eyes wide, trying to make sense of what she was seeing. She swallowed, her trembling fingers raising to cover her mouth. *Oh gods. How could— No! Oh gods.* She took a deep breath and swallowed hard, tears filling her eyes. Slapping her hand down on the pause symbol she jerked to her feet and walked away. *Oh gods. Those poor men and women.* She had to get this to someone. Someone who could stop it. She glanced around the office, her eyes coming to rest on Commander D'miron's closed door. He would kill her if she— She walked back over to her desk and sat down, closing the holo vid that had come in with the reports. Picking up her water container she took a sip. The door to D'miron's office opened and he stepped through, his iron-grey eye's cold. "Have you received the reports yet?"

Tamika shook her head. "I'm expecting them this afternoon."

Commander D'miron watched her silently. "You will remain at the office until they come in."

"Of course, Sir."

"I have a meeting with headquarters. I won't be back until tomorrow. I expect those reports to be on my desk when I get here. I spoke with the head investigator in the Xehshyhraen matter. They report that there is no evidence that a ship landed or left Xehshyhra during the escape." His voice was coldly emotionless.

Tamika stared at him in surprise. "There had to have been, Sir. How else would Keyon have escaped?"

"How indeed." Her boss closed his office door with a sharp bang and engaged the lock. "You need to study the Dark Elves. There is no excuse for your lack of knowledge in this matter. I expect my assistant to be fully versed on every species we deal with." He paused by her desk. "You've lasted longer than my last assistant." His cold hard eyes met hers. "My patience is not endless."

Tamika nodded, and D'miron walked out the door.

She waited fifteen minutes, before getting out the tiny but powerful drive that contained the novels, she read on her lunch break. She slid it into the slot on her computer as she always did and began dragging the reports with the holo vids into it. It made the copy in seconds. She removed the drive and put it back into her purse. Working swiftly, she transferred the original reports, and the accompanying holo vids to a slender tablet. Signing off on the finished reports, she secured the tablet so that only Commander D'miron could open it. Standing, she walked over to the Commander's office, and the computer scanned her and disengaged the locks. She set the tablet on his desk and exited, pausing to make sure the locks engaged. Returning to her desk she began to go through several other cases they were looking into. *There.* The Hunter. Leader of the resistance and a man, D'miron, was keenly interested in speaking too. She read a report that Commander D'miron had already rejected as being too ridiculous to believe. She hoped that this time he was wrong. It was her only chance. She completed the rest of her work in that file and sent it to the data storage system. When her day ended, she tidied up and made sure to engage all the security protocols. She walked out of her office knowing she would never return.

Chapter Sixty-Five

STAR DATE: 20580.09.27

Dimension Five
Realm of the Forsaken
Aezorwyn

HE HAD BEEN WAITING for over a week to talk to Curran about what the shadows was going on, and he'd had enough of the serious topics being pussyfooted around as Curran waited for him to heal enough. It was time for him to go and find his friend.

Yes, he'd spoken with that very luscious redhead a few times. She seemed to come by a lot to just see how he was doing, which he found incredibly suspicious. The woman was his friends 'mate,' whatever the shadows that meant, so why was she hanging around him? And Curran said she was the Queen, so shouldn't she have some kind of royal teas to attend?

He looked out the window again and growled low. Fucking purple sky. Where the fuck were they? Every time he saw that sky he got pissed. He needed answers and he needed them yesterday.

He flipped back the blanket covering him and sat up, carefully. He grimaced at the sight of the bandages wrapped around his thigh, shrugged and slowly stood up, cautious about putting any weight on that leg. He was bare ass naked. Why the fuck they hadn't left even a robe here he had no clue.

He glared around the room. Stone. Fucking stone. The bathroom was primitive at best. A stone shower stall with actual water. A basic toilet and a small sink. No auto shavers. No auto soap dispensers. He wasn't a man who needed a million luxuries but was it too much to expect the smallest basics?

He used the bathroom and limped out to stare at that godsforsaken sky. He braced his hands on the window frame and stared out at the alien landscape. And it was incredibly alien. Three moons hung low in the sky, a massive forest stretched as far as he could see, majestic trees with leaves of every color fluttering in the breeze.

A feminine gasp sounded behind him, and he stiffened. Fuck. Casually he turned around and settled his ass on the window frame, his arms crossing over his chest. "Hello, Queen Fluff." He'd known Curran was fucking some piece of fluff. "I could use a pair of pants. I plan to go and find your mate, and honest to fucking gods I really don't want to shock all the maids in this pile of rock, but I will if I need to." He grinned when she turned and hurried out of the room, calling over her shoulder. "I'll get Curran for you."

Curran walked into the room not five minutes later. "My mate tells me that you're well enough to take up stripping?" He picked up a blanket from the end of the bed and tossed it to his friend. "And that you want to speak to me. I've seen enough of your scary ass body to last me a lifetime so I'm going to take a hard pass on the stripping."

Falcon snorted and caught the blanket. "First question. Is there a law about giving a man some pants? Second question. Why is your Queen coming to see me so much? My loyalty is to you first." He gave his friend a hard look. "Third question," He wrapped the blanket around himself and sat down in the chair. "How did you end up mated to a woman from the planet where we were betrayed?"

He sat back and watched Curran. He was his fucking best friend. They had known each other since they were small boys, and shadows if he would simply toe the line.

"I knew I should have brought my last fucking bottle of Devil's Fire with me." Curran leaned against the windowsill and studied his friend for a moment. "There is no law against pants, obviously. Dr. Aries thought they might cause you pain until your thigh healed up a little more." He shrugged. "I told Willow to bring some of mine down for you. Willow is from Kylaria, I'm surprised you recognized that."

Falcon simply stared at him. Curran shook his head. *Fucker.* Falcon was the one who checked everything out before the missions. He would know exactly what the people of Kylaria looked like. "This is a long story so get comfortable."

Falcon wondered if Curran had lost his ever-loving mind. "You captured your mate? Hold it there a minute. You captured your mate? As in abducted? You stole her? What the fuck, man?"

He held up his hand, shaking his head. Shoving a hand through his hair he thought about everything that Curran had just told him. "Our world is gone? You kidnap people? And we have no technology?"

Curran shrugged uneasily and nodded. "We're starting over, Falcon. Rebuilding our society, and this planet is like nothing you've ever seen. And I don't run around kidnapping every person I meet. What do you take me for?"

Falcon listened, nodding slowly, and wondered if he even knew Curran anymore. His friend had always been one of the most honorable men he knew. If he was kidnapping people now, what did that say? What the shadows had Curran gone through?

He considered his own honor and knew that he would do everything in his power to help Curran find their team. The Suzerain had bought their own ticket to the Dimension of Shadows. "All or None, Curran. I'm with you, and I'll even be sweet to that pretty little mate of yours. How many of our men have you found, and what's the plan for the rest of them?"

Curran swallowed and turned to stare out the window. "You're the first Falcon." He turned slowly back to face his friend and found a chair, suddenly feeling old and tired.

So, it was true, he hadn't imagined it. He was the first one who had been found. He rubbed his chest with a clenched fist and tore his eyes from Curran's to stare up at the stone roof, blinking away the burn. He was the first, he told himself, not the last. He fought the lump in his throat and the moisture gathering in his eyes, as the full understanding of everything that had happened slammed into him like a rogue comet. All that remained of his family was his twin brother if they could find him. He'd lost everyone.

Everyone. His gentle mother, his wild little sisters and his fierce warrior father. Images of his family poured through his mind, and in all of his life he had never felt so alone as he did in that moment. He pressed his clenched fist hard into his chest struggling mightily to find some handhold so he wouldn't drown in the grief that consumed him. Desperately, he looked to Curran, his despair branded on his very soul, an agony he couldn't contain contorting his face. The first tear fell.

Curran rose so fast his chair fell over. He wrapped his arms around Falcon. This was his best friend, his brother in arms. They were closer than blood in some ways, their bond forged through blood and shadows, and by the gods he would not lose him now. Not after he had fought so hard to save him. He closed his eyes and for the first time since this nightmare had begun, he didn't try to hide his own agony as his tears joined Falcon's.

Chapter Sixty-Six

STAR DATE: 20580.09.28

Dimension Five

Farport City, Tryria

THIS WAS HER LAST HOPE, Tamika knew as she entered the dive. Commander D'miron's forces had almost caught her last night. She'd ended up spending the night in the alley behind this seedy bar. She hadn't eaten in two days, and the only thing she had with her was that damned drive with the information that she was trying desperately to get into the right hands. The hands of someone who could stop the horror. She rubbed dirty hands over her arms, shivering in spite of the warmth of this building and looked around. The bartender looked over at her and scowled, throwing down his cloth and starting towards her. A big disreputable looking man with dark scruff and messy dark blue hair stepped forward. "She's with me."

Tamika swallowed as she stared up into his scarred face. He met her eyes and stepped close, leaning down to pull her into a hug. She went stiff and he whispered. "I'm The Hunter, and you better have a damned good reason for mentioning my name at every fucking dive in this city." Tamika swallowed, as the man stood up. "I've reserved a room for us." He frowned. "With a bath." He turned hard eyes on the bartender. "Send a meal back." His arm settled around her waist, and he led her into the dark corridor where the pleasure rooms were located.

Her heart pounding in her chest, she went with the man and prayed to whatever supreme being existed that he was the man she was looking for. The second they entered the room, the door barely having time to swing shut behind them, he shoved her up against the wall and his hands were moving over her body as he searched for a weapon. She gritted her teeth and shoved at him, stomping on his foot when he ignored her struggles. "Get off me!" She hissed.

He let her go and stepped back. "Betray me and you won't leave this place alive."

"I have in—"

His hand covered her mouth and he growled. She blinked at him, her eyes huge. "Go take a shower, you stink." His voice was deliberately loud.

She gasped and started to jerk away from him. *Asshole.* His hand closed over her arm, and he marched her into the cleaning chamber. Letting her go, he watched as she scrambled away from him. He took a tightly wrapped package out of the pack she hadn't noticed and set it on the counter. Turning on the shower, he stepped close to her again, crowding her back against the wall. Leaning down he whispered. "There are clothes in the bundle, and two tabs of soap. Use the green one on yourself, if you have any kind of tracker, it will be destroyed. It won't hurt you. After you are done throw your clothes and the blue tab into the shower and turn it on. The blue tab will dissolve your clothing and any trackers there." He gave her a hard look. "You better have a fucking good reason for this. My people have been hunting for you since you started spreading my name, putting us all at risk. And I'd say you managed to piss off some pretty big fish, because the Suzerain are on your trail too. D'miron is no one to play games with."

He left the room and she stood there shaking, more terrified than she'd ever been.

She followed his instructions to the letter. After a hot shower that left her feeling somewhat better, she dressed in the dark leggings, tank top, jacket and boots that were in the pack. Straightening her shoulders, she took a deep breath before stepping out of the bathroom. The smell of food made her stomach growl, and she was relieved when he motioned her to sit and eat. She had to trust someone with this information. "I was Commander D'miron's assistant. I have some information... you— you need to save them! But... I need to disappear. D'miron will kill me for this. I'll give the information to you, but you have to get me to safety."

The Hunter watched her for a long moment. "If your information is good, I'll get you to someplace safe. If it's not, you won't have to worry about the Suzerain taking you, because you'll be dead."

Hands shaking, Tamika passed him the small drive. He sat back and motioned her to eat while he looked at the information. She ate quickly and kept her eye on him. She saw the exact moment when he stilled, he looked up at her. "Safe passage."

Chapter Sixty-Seven

STAR DATE: 20580.09.30

Dimension Five

Realm of the Forsaken

Aezorwyn

HE FINALLY FOUND HER in his study of all places, her head bent as she pored over a couple notebooks and made notes. He eyed the books and how full they were, debating if he should throw her over his shoulder and take her to his playroom. He'd set aside today to be with her. Not that she'd known that. He hadn't expected her to be awake before the ass crack of dawn, though.

She looked up when Curran entered his study and smiled. "Hi. I'm just going over the information I gathered. I have a lot of things to talk to you about."

"Good thing I sent the maid to bring us a breakfast tray. Good morning, Willow." He placed one hand on the desk and one on the back of her chair and leaned in to kiss her. Slow and lazy, the kind of kiss that would have ended up with her under him... if she'd still been in bed when he woke. Her hand settled on his chest, and he shivered, surprised by how cold it was. Damn. Moving away from her, he lit a fire in the fireplace and walked back to scoop his mate up into his arms and carry her over to the two overstuffed chairs by the fireplace. "The fire will warm you up soon enough." He crouched down in front of her and took her bare foot into his hands, rubbing to bring some warmth to it. "Slippers or shoes are important when you live in a stone castle, Willow."

She laughed and pointed at the desk. "My notes are over there."

Curran shook his head just as a tap sounded at the door. Walking over, he took the loaded tray from the maid and brought it back to set on the low round table between the two chairs. Retrieving her notebook from the desk, he handed it to her. "Looks like you've been very busy. Why don't you tell me about this while we eat?"

She licked her lips, and glanced at her notebooks, wondering where to start. She wiped her hands on her robe and glanced up at him. "I've spent a lot of time in the village while you have been busy doing King stuff."

"King stuff?"

Fiddling with her pen, she wished that he would sit down. She also desperately wished she had tea. Tea was good. She could hold it in her hands and sip it when she needed a few seconds to think. "Doctor Aries wants you to go on a Kitteh expedition. I need some tea."

"Tea it is, milady." Curran chuckled and sat down across from her. He poured her a cup of tea and added the honey he knew she liked. Handing her the cup filled with the steaming liquid, he poured himself a cup of brew. "Aries wants a Kitteh?" That was a strange request he thought. "Who else wants things?"

"Doctor O'Rinn wants an inventor and a scientist." She carefully ripped a piece of her page off and handed it to him. "That's their names... I told her no." Her eyes met his. "Because you would have to kidnap them."

He almost choked on the brew he'd just drank. "First. I don't kidnap on demand. Second. It's not kidnapping. I'm not holding them for ransom. I'm protecting my people. And Willow, you don't have a say in this."

She watched him in silence for a minute, fully aware of his strength and the power that filled him, and she remembered her mother telling her that, when it came to relationships, you had to begin as you meant to go on. She could work with the submission he demanded in the bedroom but not here. Not about this. "It's not right, Curran. They have families and lives." She frowned fiercely at this man who had captured and mated her. "And it's dangerous. You can't just go around kidnapping people. You are not a space pirate or a slaver. You are a King. They will come looking for you, Curran." Her voice was quiet with her last words.

"I said that it's not your business."

She hmmmed and shook her head at him, her long braid sliding over her shoulder. Taking a sip of her tea, she raised her eyebrow at him. "I'm your mate. That gives me just as much say over you as you have over me."

His mouth dropped open. Growling under his breath, he took another drink of his brew.

Willow smiled sweetly and tapped her pen on the notebook as she curled up on the chair, tucking her chilled feet under her robe. "If the Suzerain discover that Curran Nadiir is capturing people, they will investigate. It's one thing for them to know you are out there in the Galaxy, I'm sure they're hunting you, but it's another thing entirely when you do things that will get their attention. On top of that is the morality of the situation. How can we just steal people from their lives? What if they are married, or have children? If someone were to steal one of us from Aezorwyn, you'd hunt them down and kill them. I know you would. I've seen how you are with your people.

"I'm protecting my people, Willow. This is not a game. I can't just turn a blind eye when someone sees us. If the Suzerain find out about us, there is nothing in the multiverse that will stop them from coming for us. You have no idea what they did to us. You weren't there, Willow. My people have suffered enough."

Curran's words were stark, and she could feel his pain, see his aura changing color with his guilt. He was not as un-affected by what he did to protect his people as he let on. Her heart ached for him, and it became all the more impor-tant to her to make him understand that a different way was possible. "Curran, the more self-sufficient we become the less those trips to the outside universe are necessary."

She picked up her notebook with its lists and a couple pages dropped out onto the floor. Frowning, she replied as she picked up some of the scattered pages. "I know you don't take these trips for fun. I'm just thinking we need to look at what we can do to minimize your exposure to outside eyes." She shuffled the pages trying to find the list she had been looking at as Curran reached for a stray page that had landed by his chair. He scanned the note, reading her words and in-sights on what his people felt they needed. What she'd written was insightful and showed that she had a clear under-standing of their situation. He handed the paper back to her and ran a hand through his hair. "I'll make arrangements for the Kitteh expedition, and I'll talk to Garrett and Marina about the supplies our people are asking for. That's all I can promise you, Willow."

Chapter Sixty-Eight

STAR DATE: 20580.10.02
Dimension Five
Realm of the Forsaken
Aezorwyn

CURRAN HAD SPENT WAY too much time looking for Falcon. He finally found him out in the training field. The man was fucking stubborn. He walked over to where Falcon was examining a bow. "I didn't know that Jase was releasing you today."

"Two weeks is more than enough of any hospital room."

"You had surgery and almost died from pneumonia."

Falcon shrugged. "I need to get back in shape."

Curran studied his friend. His long black hair was free of matts, and he was putting on weight. Not nearly enough but it was coming. "Physio not enough for you?"

Falcon shrugged and looked at Curran. "I needed to be outside. Needed to see my new home. And I wanted to check out our weapons situation. These bows are hand-made?"

Curran nodded. "Dayan Corvaire survived, and he taught us how to make them."

Falcon studied the bow, drew back on its string. "They're good, but we should consider acquiring some Drion bows and blades."

Curran smiled. "We actually lucked out the last time Garrett, Marina and Dreven went on a mission. They were able to secure a whole crate of Drion archery equipment. I'm glad to see that you are still looking out for us."

"Has my job description changed?" Falcon asked, shooting him a penetrating look.

Curran shook his head. "You are my second. That's never going to change Falcon. In fact, it's why I was looking for you. We have a mission to plan. I was coming to get you. Garrett, Marina and Dreven are already in the War room."

"A mission? Are we going after the fucking Suzerain?"

Curran shook his head. "Kitteh's"

"Kitteh's?" Falcon looked at Curran as if he was crazy.

"Kitteh's." Curran grinned and slung his arm over Falcon's shoulders as they started back to the castle. "You can even come on this mission."

"Fuck you." Falcon growled.

Chapter Sixty-Nine

STAR DATE: 20580.10.05
Dimension Five
Realm of the Forsaken
Aezorwyn

CURRAN LOOKED DOWN once more at his sexy little mate and wondered how the fuck he was supposed to concentrate on this mission, when she was dressed like that? A leather vest that showed a hint of cleavage, Tight leather pants, his dagger strapped to her thigh, boots that came to her knees and her long red hair braided in a thick rope hanging down her back. He could wrap that braid around his fist. She looked like a wild space pirate and his dick was hard as a fucking rock. He longed to drag her off to a private place and order her to her knees to suck him off. She chose that moment to look over at him and he saw the instant her eyes traveled down his body and lingered on the fucking evidence of his lust. Her eyes lifted to meet his, and the damned Sh'arie grinned and winked at him.

Willow was excited and nervous to be part of this expedition. And she knew more than she was supposed to. She'd overheard Curran, Garret and Falcon planning this undertaking, she knew they planned to grab the scientist and the inventor after they caught enough Kitteh's and sent them and her back to Aezorwyn. She wasn't having it. She'd thought long and hard about this, how to prevent another kidnapping. Curran refused to see reason when she spoke to him, and to a point she understood. The vast majority of the people he had taken were those who had the ability to see through the invisibility that cloaked him and his men when they were off world. That invisibility protected all of them. She understood that. The Dark Elf people had to remain a secret from the rest of the universe. But for the Dark Elf people to survive and thrive and become the mighty civilization they were destined to be, they needed their King to lead them. So, she'd come up with her own plan to prevent an unnecessary risk.

Curran looked around at the group of people gathered for this expedition and shook his head. His original plan had been for him and a few of his men to come to this world, round up a few Kitteh's, and grab the two women that Dr. O'Rinn thought necessary. So much for his plans. Grumbling, he looked at Falcon, who was well enough to join them, and Garrett who was openly amused. They both shrugged. Fuck. Pointing to the map pinned to the wall, Curran began to give instructions. "We are going to Keleon." He pointed to a wilderness area on the map where the Kitteh's were known to thrive. "Everyone is to shift here. I mean everyone. If anyone is caught outside that area, there will be shadows to pay when we get back." Everyone nodded, relaxed and happy to make this excursion. He growled. "Wait till we give you the all-clear." He shifted through the dimension onto Keleon with the team of guards, alert for any danger. The sunny forest around them was peaceful. Pale yellow sunlight streaming through the branches of massive trees. Insects fluttered past them, avians sang their songs unconcerned by the beings who suddenly appeared. His guards spread out, disappearing as they moved to search the area.

This world was safe, with little chance of Suzerain presence. The people here had submitted gracefully to the rule of the Suzerain and cooperated fully; they were a gentle species, more concerned with learning than war. Many of the scientific community lived here where they were welcomed to continue their research in peace.

Minutes later the all-clear was given and he returned to Aezorwyn and held out his hand. Willow's dainty fingers closed around his and he shifted along with the Kitteh hunting group of his people to Keleon.

A base point was set up and the expedition split into groups. "Remember we only take Kitteh's that come to us. That has always been how the Dark Elves have tamed the Kitteh. We wait for them to choose us." Anwen Light-Tracer's words rang through the group. "In this we must follow the old ways."

"You heard Anwen. She's the expert in the old ways. Let's go, people." Curran grinned and joined Anwen and Willow. Their jobs were to go from group to group, lending a hand where necessary. Anwen had spent several days training all of them on the art of Kitteh appropriation. He'd been more than happy to make the only elder among the Dark Elf survivors, the leader of this expedition. The fierce old lady knew more than all of them combined about the Dark Elf history and shadow archives about almost any random topic you threw at her.

At first Willow stayed with Curran and Anwen, as the groups split up and disappeared into the forest. They went from group to group, helping them as needed. The Kittehs were very adept at blending in with their surroundings and it took patience and savory bits of meat to coax them out of their hiding spots. Kittehs were similar to other feline species throughout the galaxy. Small, with strong, agile, flexible bodies, they had the quick reflexes, retractable claws and sharp teeth needed for killing small prey. And a habit of always landing on their feet. They came in a variety of colors, gold, orange, pink, blue, white, purple, and assorted combinations.

As they walked through the forest of this alien world, in search of the elusive Kitteh's, Willow spoke with several different teams. They were excited to have Kitteh's on Aezorwyn. Many of them told her stories of the pets that had not survived the fall of their world. The tears that filled their eyes as they told their stories deeply touched her heart. This was another step in their healing, in the rebuilding of their society.

She looked up at Curran and his eyes met hers. In them she could see the depth of his understanding and compassion. Again, she understood the importance of this man leading the Dark Elves back to wholeness. She smiled at him and admitted to herself that she had a bit of hero worship going on for her mate. Not that she was going to let him know that, but it did make her think about submitting to whatever wicked plans he might have for her when they got home.

Heat rushed between her legs, and she bit her lip, glancing away from his too aware gaze. Turning she began talking to a woman about the characteristics of the Kitteh she hoped to find.

Kitteh hunting took time and patience, but they were slowly filling the crates at the base point. Anwen, Curran and she had eventually split up to help more people, and hopefully speed the process along. This world was safe, but they all were aware that the longer they stayed the greater the risk of being seen.

She was kneeling by a fallen log and staring into the big green eyes of a lavender Kitteh. Beside her, a young teen was engaged in the same activity with a teal blue Kitteh with a patch of white on its chest. She could feel the desperate hope of the young girl and she reluctantly took her eyes from the lavender feline to help the teen. It was far more important that this girl have her Kitteh. She smiled and added her gentle energy to the girls, hoping to make the teen irresistible to these unusual animals who chose their owners. The teal Kitteh crept closer and closer, finally deciding that the girl was safe, it rubbed up against her. The girl reached out trembling fingers and stroked the feline's silky fur and the creature purred and turned to lick the girl's hand. A tear slipped down the girl's cheek, and she gently gathered up the little animal and hugged it to her. The Kitteh responded by purring louder and rubbing its head against the girl's chin. Willow smiled. "Your Kitteh found you, Eden."

"Thank you for helping me Willow." The girl's voice was soft, filled with joy and Willow could not help but reach out and stroke her hair.

"It was my honor, Eden." And it had been. It had also been a chance to spend time with the teen and let her healing energy pour into the hurting girl. The girl hurried off to find her friends and Willow stood up, the lavender kitteh long gone, and looked around. Everyone was busy with their hunt, and she realized it was the perfect moment to put her plan into motion.

Casually she headed towards a group a little farther away but as she walked by a massive tree, she turned and headed away from the group. From the position of the sun, she knew that they would be rounding up the teams to head back through the portal in the next half an hour. It would hopefully give her the head start that she needed.

When she was far enough away, she pulled out the folded piece of paper that Kailene O'Rinn had given her and studied the hand drawn map. She was going to be hard pressed to get to her destination before Curran and his men showed up. Tucking the map safely back into her pocket, she ran towards her first stop.

Chapter Seventy

STAR DATE: 20580.10.05

Dimension Five
Realm of the Forsaken
Aezorwyn

SHE PEEKED OUT FROM behind the large boulder she was hiding behind and took another careful look around. The house on the edge of the forest preserve was quiet. With a deep breath, Willow straightened and walked up to the door, ringing the door chime.

A few moments later the door opened and a slender woman with golden skin, large pale green eyes and hair the color of mulled wine, pulled up into a messy, haphazard bun, stood there. She was dressed in black leggings and a long green tunic with large pockets, filled with all kinds of instruments and tools. The woman just stared at her, so Willow held out her hand to touch the woman's in the way of Kalyrians. "Skylar Starcrest?"

The woman nodded warily but touched Willow's hand.

"I'm Willow, Kailene sent me." She carefully transferred the tiny charm that Dr. O'Rinn had given her, into Skylar Starcrest's hand. The woman looked at the charm and her fingers closed around it. She lifted shocked eyes to meet Willow's but stepped back to allow her to enter. The woman entered a code and Willow felt a powerful energy field slide silently in place.

"This way." Skylar's voice was a soft, husky sound and Willow followed her through the house to a large work area filled with many interesting devices. "This is my workspace. It's safe to speak here. This area is impenetrable for any listening device. Who are you and how is it possible for you to have Kailene's amulet?"

Willow smiled. "I'm a friend of Kailene's. She asked me to tell you that she calls for you."

Skylar regarded her for a long moment, and Willow could almost feel her thinking. Finally, she turned and went to a closet and took out a backpack. Shrugging into it, she turned back to Willow. "My dead friend calls for me. Does she call for anyone else?"

Willow nodded. "Gracen Allfire."

Skylar watched the redhead for a moment before going over to her computer and typed out a message to her assistant. I'm heading over to Hilreon 6 to try to find a specific part I need. If I can't find it, I'll have them fabricate one. In fact, I'm going to stop at several of the industrial worlds and see if I can lay in a supply of parts for my inventions. I'm at an impasse and I need some inspiration. Go home to your family. I'll contact you when I'm ready to get back to work. She hit send and turned to Willow. "I go on my inspiration trips a lot. It's always been part of the plan with Kailene. We'll take my flyer, it's the fastest way to get to Gracen's lab."

The trip to Dr. Gracen Allfire's house took longer than Willow would have liked but it couldn't be helped. They landed the flyer on the remote island and the two of them approached the door and rang the chime. Several long minutes passed before a blonde woman opened the door. Her hair was carefully coiled into a sophisticated bun, her turquoise eyes framed by old fashioned eyeglasses. "Skylar?" She was evidently surprised and took off the eyeglasses and let them hang on the chain around her neck.

"Hello, Gracen." Skylar held out her hand and Gracen took it, squeezing gently and smiled. The smile froze for a split second, as she felt her friend press the tiny amulet into her hand. "Please come in." She left the door open and as Skylar stepped in, she hugged her tightly. Gracen shut the door behind Willow and put a finger to her lips. Silently she led them through the house into a large laboratory. Walking over to a panel on the wall, she tapped in a code. Willow again felt an energy shield slide into place. She watched as Gracen stepped back from the panel and turned to look at them. "Skylar where did you get Kailene's amulet?"

Skylar's eyes met Gracen's. "Kailene is calling for us."

Gracen blinked. "How is that possible?"

"She said you would ask that." Willow replied.

"And the answer is?" Gracen and Skylar both watched the red-haired woman carefully.

"Eliminate the impossible, whatever remains, no matter how improbable, must be the truth" Willow replied with a quote from a man long dead.

Gracen nodded slowly, walked over to a closet in her lab and took out a backpack. Returning to her computer, she sent out a message to her colleges, while Skylar and Willow watched. *My research has reached a stage where I need more hands-on information, I am joining my research team on the planet Aturna in the remote outer fringes of the galaxy.* A plan she had set in place many years ago in case the Suzerain ever tried to retain her for their own purposes. "Let's go."

Willow let out a shaky breath and nodded. "Is there a clearing in the jungle behind your house?"

Gracen raised an eyebrow and nodded.

"Good that is where we need to go. He will come there."

"Who will come there?"

"The King."

"Why does Kailene always get us into these situations?" Skylar asked.

"I don't know, but I'm going to ask her this time. And who the shadows is this King?"

Willow laughed as they went out the back door and began their hike through the jungle. "He's my mate, and he won't hurt you. I promise. Just ignore his growling, I got the jump on him."

The women looked at her warily, but before she could reply she felt the massive energy signature she was coming to recognize as a dimensional shift. Curran, Falcon, and Garrett stepped through, and guards spread through the forest.

"Hi, Curran." Willow walked up to her mate and ignoring the ticking muscle in his jaw went on her tiptoes to kiss him. "This is Skylar Starcrest and Gracen Allfire. We're ready to go."

Curran's arm banded around her, his other hand fisted in her hair and his dark eyes met hers for a split second. Long enough for her to realize that he was furious. His mouth crashed down on hers and his tongue surged into her mouth. Her heart skipped a beat, then picked up a fast rhythm as she wrapped her arms around him and kissed him back. She understood his frustration and even his fear, but she did not regret taking an action that would protect him. In the end, your life had to back up your words.

When Curran lifted his head, they were both breathing hard, and everyone was looking anywhere but at them. Humor lit her eyes, even as Curran spoke into her ear. "There are consequences for disobeying the King."

"Still worth it," she whispered back.

Chapter Seventy-One

STAR DATE: 20580.10.05

Dimension Five
Realm of the Forsaken
Aezorwyn

THE DAY HAD BEEN A success as far as Willow was concerned. Curran on the other hand seemed a bit grumpy. She shrugged, the kitteh's all had new homes and they now had a scientist and an inventor added to their numbers. Voluntarily added to their numbers. That was important. Even if she was a bit nervous about being alone with Curran right now. She glanced around the main hall where they were all gathered while they waited for the last of the Kitteh's to be claimed. It had been a disconcerting moment when they had shifted back to Aezorwyn, into the main hall of the castle, and discovered at least a dozen extra Kitteh's had joined them. A messenger had been sent to the village and those who wanted to provide homes for the remaining Kitteh's had come. She smiled. The Dark Elves were good people. "Ok," she walked over to Skylar and Gracen. "Let's get you two set up."

Curran turned and wrapped his arm around her waist. "Kailene is on her way here. Skylar and Gracen will stay with her until we can build them homes that suit their needs."

"Oh." Willow glanced up at her mate, and her eyes rounded at the look he gave her. It seemed he had not gotten past her little adventure. Darn it. She'd hoped that time spent getting everything sorted would have given him a chance to cool off. "I can help Kailene get our new friends settled."

"No." Curran said, giving a half shrug, and his hand dropped to her ass. "Willow and I have some things to discuss. We'll be by tomorrow to check on how you are settling in."

Kailene arrived just then and amid the laughter and hugs, Curran steered Willow out of the main hall. Stopping only to pick up a small crate on their way.

They walked into their room, and Willow turned to eye her mate. "Don't you think that was a little rude?"

"Nope." Curran set the crate on their bed and turned to meet her eyes. "This is for you."

Willow's eyes widened and she approached the crate, a smile lighting up her face. "For me? You got me something." She opened the small latch and gasped when a lavender Kitteh with large green eyes poked its head out. Reaching trembling hands into the crate, she picked up the creature and cuddled it to her chest. The Kitteh promptly nudged her chin with its softly furred head. "Oh." Willow turned shining eyes to Curran. "How?"

Curran shrugged. "I saw that you were enchanted with this Kitteh, but Eden needed help, so you assisted her instead of securing the Kitteh. When you went on to help the others, I persuaded the Kitteh to come home with us."

"Thank you." Her voice husky, she went up on her toes and pressed a kiss to his jaw. His arm curved around her, and he gave her a half smile. "What are you going to name him?"

"Arthur."

"Arthur?" Curran scratched his cheek. Willow laughed and set the Kitteh down to explore. "I once read this wonderful story about a mythical King named Arthur. Everything here, this castle, the village, the way everyone dresses remind me of that story. So, since we live in the castle, I think it's only right that there is an Arthur here too."

Curran smiled, and scooped Willow up into his arms. "Tomorrow, remind me to tell you about how all this came to be, but right now, I have a personal dungeon I think we should explore."

"Curran." Willow laughed.

"Oh, I mean it. I've been planning to shackle you to the wall and do bad things to you, ever since I discovered you were missing on Keleon."

Willow swallowed. "You want to shackle me to a wall?"

"And do bad things to you."

Her eyes were huge. "I... we can't leave Arthur by himself."

Curran nodded over to the bed. The lavender kitteh was curled up on the bed, sound asleep. He turned so Willow could see that over by the fireplace was a pillow and food and water dishes. "I've arranged for Annora to come by in half an hour and take Arthur for a walk. Any more reasons why I shouldn't take you to my dungeon?"

Willow bit her lip. "I... What I did was for the good of Aezorwyn."

Curran snorted and walked over to the door that led down to the room that Willow had discovered a few weeks ago. "And what I'm going to do is for your good, and the future of Aezorwyn and my heart."

Willow scowled at him as they descended the stairs. "I have seen your dungeon, Curran. There is nothing down here that is going to be for my good. Or Aezorwyn's good."

Curran smirked. "I think you should let me be the judge of that."

Willow's mouth fell open as he set her on her feet in front of the wall with the shackles. "I shall decide what is for my good."

Curran crossed his arms over his chest, a big man, with dangerous determination in his eyes. "Sh'arie, what you did today was reckless and dangerous. There are consequences."

Willow narrowed her eyes at him. "I was in no danger. I knew that Skylar and Gracen would come with me."

"How could you know that?"

"Kailene told me what to say to them."

"Did you have a plan if they refused? What would you have done if one of them had alerted the Suzerain?"

Willow nibbled her lip.

"And this is why we are here. Today is all about obedience."

"Haven't we already had this lesson. Multiple times." Willow rolled her eyes.

"Apparently we need to have it again." He turned from her and strode over to his cabinet and pulled open the doors.

He stood there silently for a full minute, before turning slowly back to face her, his eyebrow raised. "Sh'arie, do you have something to tell me?"

Willow raised an eyebrow back at him. "Actually yes, there are a few things we need to discuss." She walked over to stand beside him, peering into the large cupboard. "The pile on the right are things I am willing to try. The pile on the left is things I will not even consider. The pile in the middle is things that you need to explain. Why would you even own such things?"

Curran growled, and she reached into the cabinet and picked up the whip from the middle pile. She looked at him, mimicking his stance, feet apart, arms crossed over her chest.

"For fuck's sake." Curran shoved a hand through his hair. Growling, he stomped around the room. Willow waited with eyebrows raised.

"There are going to be consequences for this, Sh'arie," he said in a hard tone of voice.

"I'm sure there will be."

Frowning, Curran rubbed the back of his neck and walked over to stare into her eyes. He opened his mouth to say something and seemed to think better of it. Finally, he exhaled a gusty breath. "To be honest with you, I've never used that.

"Why do you have it?"

"Ambiance." Curran ran his hand through his hair and looked sheepish.

Willow blinked and started to laugh. "Believe me, Curran, you are one scary looking man. You have danger written all over you. You don't need any props." She laughed some more.

Curran narrowed his eyes. "I'll get rid of it."

"No. no. I'm going to keep this."

His eyebrow rose, a wary look entering his eyes, and he stood looking at her, his head tilted. "Why?"

A slow smile curved her lips. "Ambiance. This is going on our bedroom wall."

Curran groaned, a pained look in his eyes, and Willow laughed even harder.

The negotiations lasted the rest of the day and well into the night. By the time both parties were satisfied, they had come to a mutual understanding of consequences and respect. But obedience? Curran had a sinking feeling about that one.

Chapter Seventy-Two

STAR DATE: 20580.10.06

Dimension Five

The outer belt of the Bythian galaxy

DREVEN RAISED HIS GLASS and took a long drink of the golden ale. He needed to figure out what to do about that bitch. Didn't it just figure that Curran the King of male whores would fall for a sweet, gentle, caring, intelligent woman. He snorted and took another drink. Fucker had the luck of that fucking space pirate, Captain Alek Tempest. Willow represented the death of all his plans, and that he would not allow.

He stared around the dark gloom of this particularly disreputable establishment, taking in the dark wood walls and cement floors. There were no windows, and the owners were smart enough to keep the lights down low so that no one would realize the squalor they were drinking in. It didn't matter to him in the long run, it was simply another hole in the wall bar he was forced to patronize if he wanted to have a good ale. The brew that they made on Aezorwyn was Daji piss. Thank the gods that he was deep in the outer fringes of the shadow region, where good ale was at least buyable.

The bartender was the perfect accompaniment for this place with his rough appearance and the stone hard look in his eyes. As he started another porn holo vid, Dreven shook his head. It was a good ploy to get more credits from the rough breed of beings who frequented this establishment. The pleasure house attached to it had been another smart move.

He'd told Curran that they needed to establish a pleasure house. One on their world, but also a chain of them in the shadow realm. It would provide a steady income and they could use the credits. Curran's tastes in weaponry were expensive.

Of course, Curran refused. Self-righteous, hypocritical prick. This was not a time when they could afford to be 'moral'. It wasn't as if Curran didn't use women. He'd fucking watched the parade of women in and out of his King's playroom for far too long. And that fucked up world Curran stranded them on turned their females into sex starved whores every fucking month. Why not profit from it?

Broodingly, Dreven watched the porn vid that featured a woman on her knees sucking the dick of a green Trabanic male who held her leash. It had been a shadows eternity since he'd had a woman on her knees before him.

Abruptly he turned away from the vid. This was not the time. And the only image coming to his mind was of a certain red-haired bitch. He would not indulge that particular fantasy until his plans were in place.

His eyes drifted over the wall by the door. It was littered with handbills and posters for every kind of service or business in the area, and more than a few wanted posters. He shook his head at the stupidity of the Suzerain. As if any of the men here would give up information that would get them killed. The newest looking poster featured a red-haired woman. Bitch was probably a runaway prostitute.

He took another sip of his ale, and again pushed away thoughts of that other red-haired woman on her knees before him. Didn't it just figure that even here in a dirty tavern on the edges of the galaxy he couldn't escape her.

He drained his glass and signaled the bartender for another. He needed a plan. Pausing, his eyes went back to the wanted poster on the wall. *Well fuck me sideways.* He stood up and strode over to the wall. He ripped the poster down and stared at it. Willow Solar. His '*Queen*'. He started to laugh. Maybe he was the one with the luck of Captain Alek Tempest.

Chapter Seventy-Three

STAR DATE: 20580.10.07

Dimension Five

Prison on Otania

JERICHO STOOD UP, HIS face stoic, revealing none of the pain that had him moving carefully. He was badly bruised, but nothing was broken. Yet.

He put his hand on his ribs and moved to the door. He was not by any stretch of the imagination a weak man, but after three torture sessions he knew it was time to find his way out. Fucking bastards.

He'd been playing a deep game with the Suzerain for years, but it had nothing to do with his sister. He'd been as shocked as everyone else when she disappeared.

Shadows, he'd been looking for her when Commander D'miron decided that he must know where she was. In an instant, all his years as a loyal soldier to the Suzerain regime were suddenly forgotten.

The first time he met Commander D'miron, he'd known it was time to get out. And he began to make his plans. The man was no one's fool, but Jericho was no one to play games with either. He was a dangerously intelligent, hardened soldier and right now his instincts were going crazy.

The problem with the Suzerain was their sheer arrogance, their belief that they were the superior race. They were an astute, deadly species but they had become bloated with their success. The cruelty they used to keep their subjects in line, bred dissent and hatred. They'd been warned, but their response was to kill the messenger. They considered their intellect far above every other species, their reign almost omnipotent. The idea of failure never crossed their minds. They believed that they had been created to rule, and it was reflected in every action they took. There was no way to reason with them. They knew everything.

Except they didn't.

Jericho watched the corridor silently. He was about to teach the Suzerain that they had no concept of the monster they'd harbored these many years. It was almost laughable that they thought they knew the differences between an energy manipulator and an energy enchanter. They had no clue. They'd always misunderstood his powers, and that was going to cost them.

If they'd taken him to a space station, they might have been able to contain him. He set his hand on the computer-controlled door and drew deeply from the energy of this shadows trap of a planet he was on. The air around his hand sparked and the computer released the lock as it was met with an overload of energy. He stepped out of his cell as doors all down the narrow hall popped open. The prisoners ran from their cells and the guards rushed them, waving their stun sticks. He drained the stun sticks, drawing the energy into himself as he walked through the chaos.

He dodged a punch and kept going, pulling energy from the weapons and computer systems. More doors clicked open, and the prisoners surged forward. He felt no guilt. Every prisoner in this lock-up was here for political reasons. The dangerous prisoners were always taken to a remote mining world. The Suzerain took no risks that way.

Ignoring the fighting, he smiled grimly as the lights blinked then went out. He was going to have to release the massive amounts of energy he was pulling as he worked his way out of the building, but for now he could contain it.

If nothing else, his time with the Suzerain had given him the knowledge that had just saved his life. The layout of their most secret prison. Checking each corridor, he came to, he finally found the locked entry to the passageway he'd been looking for. It was deserted. Carefully checking to be sure that he hadn't been seen, he touched the computer controlled locking device and sent a tiny current of energy flowing into it. The lock released but he kept pouring energy into the panel forcing the foreign energy to travel back up the line to the emergency generator that was powering it. A shower of sparks told him when that power source failed. *That would worry them,* he thought as he shoved open the metal gate. It swung open silently and he stepped through.

The dark corridor he ran down was known to few, and it led to the outside. An emergency escape in case the Suzerain ever lost control of this facility. He wondered how long it would take the prison officials to understand that they no longer controlled the inmates.

The prison lay in the middle of a deeply forested tract of land. He paused at the exit and looked around before sprinting into the dark cover of the trees. He ran, unconcerned by the rumors of dangerous predators inhabiting these woods. The predators were there, but he was far more dangerous, especially filled with the energy he'd pulled from the planet and the electronics of the prison. He would need to discharge it soon, and as he weaved around the wide trunks, he began to consider the possibilities.

A raindrop hit his cheek and he glanced up. The clouds were heavy, a storm brewing. He kept running, mile after mile, putting distance between himself and the prison. The wind picked up and with it came the rain, falling in a steady downpour. He was soon soaked to the skin, but he ignored it. In the distance thunder roared and he smiled.

Scrambling his way up a steep hill, he climbed higher and higher, running when he could, hiking as fast as he dared when running was not an option on the rocky narrow game trail he was following. At the apex of the hill, he stopped and looked out over the forest, the prison was miles away, but he could see its dark squat shape and tiny airborne vehicles moving in a search pattern around the cement building. The rain was pouring down in torrents, and he knew the only hope the prison officials had of rounding up the prisoners were those flying patrols.

He raised his hand sending a bolt of lightning into the dark cloud mass above him, instantly there was a deafening roar of thunder as the energy he was pouring into the storm clashed with the natural energy it conducted. Lightning began slamming into the ground in violent bursts as the storm gained intensity. A stray bolt of lightning hit him, but he merely drained the destructive current and sent it savagely back into the storm. His hair was a nimbus around him, his eyes glowing with the white heat of the energy he was discharging. Thunder roared and white-hot light crashed to the ground as the storm grew more and more massive, lightning jumping from cloud to cloud, moving inexorably closer to the prison and the flying patrols with every second. Soon they would ground the aircrafts or risk losing them.

Many hours later he made it to a small apartment that he'd rented under an alias. A retinal scanner opened the door, and he was inside. After a shower and a simple meal, he opened a hidden compartment in the closet and took out a holo emitter and attached it to his ear. Instantly his appearance wavered as a holo mask came on. He looked into the mirror in the small bathing chamber and his eyebrow lifted in surprise. Three dots over each of his eyebrows. Alraran. Out of all the thousands of possible species combinations programmed into the holo emitter, this is the one that it chose? He stared into the glass and his thoughts went to a pretty blonde with beautiful bronze eyes. Tamika Firemist. Assistant to Commander D'miron. She was probably up to her pretty little chin in D'miron's plans. But he still smiled over the memory of that time he had fucked her over her desk. Gods, he'd planned to go back, to sink into the warmth of her tightness as often as he could convince her to let him. He'd planned a torrid affair. He'd even started looking for an apartment in her city. Fuck. He pushed the memories away. He could not afford this distraction. It was time to get off this planet and find out what had happened to his little sis-

ter. He was not a good man by any means, but gods help anyone who had harmed her.

Chapter Seventy-Four

STAR DATE: 20580.10.08

Dimension Five
Realm of the Forsaken
Aezorwyn

CURRAN, FALCON AND Garrett stood surveying the river, they'd left the group of men they'd been fishing with to explore further. Plus, this gave him, Falcon and Garrett a chance to talk away from everyone else.

"So," Garrett began, "You were showing Willow the full extent of the Crimson Fever last night." Curran scowled and waited. He knew Garrett. There was a reason he was bringing this up. "I was surprised when you showed up at Keanna's house."

"You were surprised? Shadows, I almost dropped that pretty little brunette, when I saw Queen Fluff peering around Curran. Her eyes were pretty wide, buddy and she was blushing so hard she almost glowed." Falcon laughed.

Curran shrugged and muttered something about being surprised they even noticed.

Garrett grinned. "I notice everything. That is my job as head of security. I was surprised to get the invitation from

Keanna. She had quite the sex party going on. Did you have anything to do with that?"

Falcon raised his eyebrow and shook his head. "You've been so damned possessive of Willow, I never figured you would share her. But if sharing is where you're going, I'll sign up."

"Me too," Garrett said.

Curran crossed his arms over his chest, struggling to maintain his calm and glared at his friends. "Fuck off. Willow would kill you both, and then she would kill me. And I'd have to rise from the dead, and kill you both, again."

Falcon and Garrett burst out laughing. Curran scowled all the harder.

"Why were you there?" Falcon asked

"And why did you have Keanna set up that little party?" Garrett smirked, "Not that I wasn't grateful or anything. I certainly enjoyed myself."

Curran shook his head and walked over to prop himself against a large boulder, his arms crossed over his chest. "I've talked to Willow about the Crimson Moon Fever, and of course, we experience it together, but it's different for me now. I have no desire to fuck anyone but her." He shrugged. "She was curious, and I figured it was wise for her to understand exactly what happens on that night."

"And you thought it was a good idea to start out at Keanna's house?" Garrett asked. "You know that it took both me and Falcon to distract her from her mission of initiating Willow into the, uhhh, how did she word it, Falcon?"

"Into the ecstasy of the Fever." Falcon laughed. "The woman wanted to fuck your Queen, Curran. Though I think she might have let you be a part of it, *if* you asked nicely."

Curran shook his head. "It would have never happened, but thanks for distracting her. I'm sure it was a real hardship."

"Not so much." Falcon grinned, laughter in his eyes.

"We've got your back, Curran." Garrett smirked.

He laughed and stared at the two men. "I'm so fucking glad you are both here. Look, all I did was show Willow around. We peeked in on a few parties. Watched some fucking. I answered a lot of questions from Willow. When she had seen enough, we went home, and she fucked my brains out. Honestly, I don't even know how I'm upright, right now."

Garrett and Falcon burst out laughing.

"We should add that to Queen Fluff's title."

Curran made a crude gesture at Falcon, and they all laughed harder.

"But I do have a question for you, Curran," Falcon said as he leaned against a thick tree with blue leaves. "How come you haven't married that gorgeous woman and officially made her your Queen?"

"Yeah," Garrett added. "I want to know that too. We talked about this a while ago, and I thought you were going to. What's holding you back?"

Curran looked out over the river, a muscle jumping in his jaw. "It's not a small thing for me to make her my wife and Queen. How will our people react? She would be in power whenever I'm away. We have seen how Dreven reacts. What if others feel the same way? What if someone tries to harm her?"

Falcon was shaking his head. "You know Curran, you've never been a man who trusts easily. And I can see how this whole fucked up horror story with the Suzerain would only make that harder, but Willow is good. All of us can see that she is a good person. She is kind, and she cares... for everyone. And she's in love with you."

Curran growled. "She—"

Garrett cut him off. "She's jumped right in, Curran. She talks to everyone. She asked them what they needed, and she got it for them. How many trips off-world did we do in the last few weeks? The stuff we brought back will help to make us self-sufficient, and those Kitteh's... For that alone I would marry her." Curran growled again, but Garrett ignored him. "Those Kitteh's changed everything for our children and for many of our adults. Our people's spirits have risen in noticeable ways. They're not crushed anymore, Curran. She is good for us. She is good for you. She won't betray you, Curran. Marry her."

Crossing his arms, Curran glared at his two matchmaking friends. "Gods, I should set up a place of business for you two. Matchmaking Warriors. Let us find a mate for you."

Falcon smirked. "I'd fucking rock that shit."

"Just so you two idiots know, I'm planning on asking her tonight. I've already asked the kitchen staff to make a special dinner for us and set up the stone folly."

"Look at our King, being all romantic and shit," Falcon said, and Garret nodded. "We've brought him up right."

"Fuck off." Curran laughed and glanced up at the sun. "I have to run guys. Dreven is due back with those supplies, and I want to meet him at the receiving area.

Chapter Seventy-Five

STAR DATE: 20580.10.08

Dimension Five
Realm of the Forsaken
Aezorwyn

DREVEN WATCHED AS ALL the crates of supplies he'd shifted in from the Spectre Expanse cache were taken away then walked over to Curran and handed him the clipboard. "Here's all the paperwork you need. If you can just sign everything now, I'll get you a report by the end of the week."

Curran took the clipboard from Dreven and began to sign the pages. "Looks like you had a productive trip. You have a shadow's hoard more than I thought you would get. That's really great, Dreven." He flipped the page and froze, his eyes rapidly scanning the page. *What the fuck. What the fucking fuck?* His eyes shot to Dreven's. "What is this?"

Dreven slid his hands into his pocket and looked Curran in the eye. "Important information I thought you needed to see."

"Of course, they're looking for her. She is missing from her world." Curran's voice was tight with fury. *Fucking Dreven, always stirring up shit.*

Dreven nodded. "Look at the bottom of the page. She is a bit more than what we might have expected, and her brother is a very dangerous Suzerain supporter."

Curran read down the page his heart turning to stone as he read the words on the page. The reward being offered was astronomical. His mind was racing with the implications. Gods fucking damnit! Fuck! He turned a hard gaze on Dreven. "This doesn't go any further. You understand me? I will fucking kill you if I hear one whisper of this from anyone on this planet." He pulled the page from the clipboard and slammed the clipboard into Dreven's chest. His eyes brutally cold. "Not one fucking word."

Dreven just stared at Curran for a long moment. "She is a danger to everything we have built here, Curran. A risk we can't afford."

Blood was pounding in his ears, the mark on his chest burning, and cold rage filling his heart. She'd deceived him.

Chapter Seventy-Six

STAR DATE: 20580.10.08

Dimension Five
Realm of the Forsaken
Aezorwyn

THE DOOR SLAMMED OPEN and bounced off the stone wall with a crash. Willow gasped and looked up. Curran stood framed in the door, his face a mask of fury that she'd never seen before. She set her cup of tea on the small side table and rose from her chair, deeply concerned. "Curran? What's happened?"

"You." He snarled, stalking into the room and slamming the door shut behind him. "You happened. You deceiving little bitch." He thrust a crumpled paper at her.

Fighting to control the wild angry surge of energy that erupted in her at his words, she gave him a look, and took the paper. Her eyes widened and her fingers trembled when she realized what she was looking at. She closed her eyes for a second, breathing deep before opening them to stare into the face of her mate. "Curran..." She swallowed, her mouth suddenly dry, terror choking off her words. She was found out. Her heart pounded and she looked at the door struggling against the nearly overwhelming urge to run, to run as fast and far as she could.

Curran read the fear in her eyes and grabbed her arm, shaking her. "Don't you even think about it! Explain. Explain why the fuck the Suzerain are offering that kind of reward for you! Explain how your brother is the fucking son of a bitch that is responsible for the decimation of my world! Are you a fucking spy for them?"

Willow's eyes widened, her mouth falling open, as a tear spilled over, and she shook her head. "No! I swear, Curran! I would never do that to you!"

He laughed bitterly and shook his head. "You told me you were a jewelry maker."

"I am!" She jerked away from him, rubbing her arm. "I made jewelry for a living. You've seen it. There are records of my education on Kalyria. I make jewelry here, for heaven's sake." She stared at Curran as tears pricked her eyes and an ache developed in her chest.

"And what else did you do? Your whole sweet innocent act has been a lie!"

Willow drew back as if she'd been struck. "I have been honest with you about everything." She whispered, hands shaking she tried to hand him back the wanted poster.

He stared at the poster, refusing to touch it, his eyes harder than she'd ever seen them. "You either tell me everything right now or I will make you tell me. And you fucking know I can do it." He took her arm again and started walking towards the door that led to his playroom.

She shook her head, the poster fluttering to the ground, forgotten. "Curran." swallowing, she pulled back. "Not like this. I can't..."

He opened the door and reached to grab her, but she dodged him and whirled around to run, her skirts swirling around her. He grabbed a fistful of material and jerked her to a halt. "Do you prefer torture? We have a real dungeon in the basement of the castle."

She froze at his words, a deep trembling spreading through her body, as terror lodged deep in her heart. She turned slowly, and stared at him, her eyes searching his. He meant it. She could see it in his eyes and in that moment, she knew that she must risk everything and trust that Curran would stand by her. "M... my name is Willow Soriya Solar. My parents were born on Kalyria. My mother's name was Soriya Morgandy Solar, my father was Kano Hinrik Solar." She licked her dry lips, her arms going around herself, and whispered hoarsely. "My brother is Jericho Kano Solar. He is a soldier for the Suzerain. I hadn't seen him in almost a year when you took me. I wrote to him of course, but he rarely answered. He..." She paused, and blinked against the tears stinging her eyes, struggling with the fear that kept threatening to close her throat. "He is an energy manipulator." The tears fell, and she couldn't stop the tremors shaking her slender body. "Yes, he has the ability to drain a planet of its energy as long as he can channel that energy into something else. I do not know if he is responsible for the d... death of your planet, but it is possible. And... and if he did— it's my fault. The Suzerain took him because of my mistake."

Curran leaned against the doorway to his playroom, his arms crossed over his chest, a muscle in his jaw ticking as he listened to the shaking voice of his mate. The cold hardness that filled him when he first saw that wanted poster sat like an icy fist around his heart. He could tell, he fucking knew, there was far more to this tale than she'd revealed so far.

"My family..." She swallowed, seeing the hardness in his eyes, terror rising in a fast wave that left her nauseated and shaking. She was fighting years of conditioning, years of deeply ingrained secrets that could not only cost her, her life, but could potentially destroy whole solar systems. She took a deep shuddering breath, unable to stop the tears pouring down her cheeks. "My family has produced E-Energy Enchanters in every generation for over a thousand years. My grandfather was one, my father was one—" She lifted desperate eyes to him. "I am one."

Curran frowned, clenching his hands. "And what exactly is an Energy Enchanter?"

"An Energy Enchanter cycles the energy of a planet through them, changes it and releases it back to the planet. We don't know why. It's a natural process, automatic, done without conscious thought or deliberation. Like breathing."

"You are doing something to my world?" His words were ice. "What are you doing to it?"

"The ecosystem of a planet becomes richer, more diverse, more resilient and its people become healthier, both physically and mentally." She reached out to touch him, but he stepped back.

"If it's so harmless, why the fuck did you hide it from me?"

She stared at him, her shoulders slumping. "Because I was safe here." She whispered. "Finally safe. I didn't have to hide anymore."

"Hide?" His voice was incredulous. "You didn't have to hide on a hidden planet inhabited by people who are hiding?" He stared at the bright haired woman who he'd trusted. "What the shadows kind of game are you playing? Who are you hiding from?"

"The Suzerain." Her voice broke as she struggled with her fear and despair, knowing with every beat of her aching heart that she'd lost everything. "They take all the Energy Enchanters."

"Why?"

"They force us to use our abilities to help them take over planets. Whole civilizations controlled and manipulated into surrendering or—" She swallowed. "Killed. Leaving the worlds ripe for harvesting..."

"My god. My god. Were you there? Did you kill my people?"

Willow shook her head. "No! No. I swear! To kill is against an Energy Enchanters nature. We go insane. Become monsters." Curran stared at her, and she stared back, grief filling her as the silence stretched between them. And Curran turned and walked away.

Chapter Seventy-Seven

STAR DATE: 20580.10.08

>Dimension Five
>Realm of the Forsaken
>Aezorwyn

CURRAN STORMED OUT of the castle and everyone who saw him got out of his way. He ended up in the meadow that he'd brought Willow to a few weeks ago, staring at the massive tree that he'd tied his wild little mate to. The sound of the small stream rushing along played through the air as he worked to contain his anger. A nerve jumped in his jaw, and his fists clenched. *Fuck! Fuck! Fuck! She hadn't trusted him. She'd kept secrets. Dangerous secrets.* He paced the meadow, his emotions raging. *He could take her back to Kalyria. Drop her off where he'd found her. She'd never be able to tell anyone where Aezorwyn was. But she knew too much. She knew his people had survived.* He swore bitterly, knowing he'd never do it.

"I'm glad you know that much Curran Nadiir."

Curran whirled around and came face to face with a tall powerfully built man with long white hair and black eyes swirling with color and brilliant specks of light. "Who the fuck are you and how did you get on my planet?"

The man laughed. "In fact, Curran Nadiir, this is *my* planet. My realm. My multiverse. You are the protector, not the owner. And honestly, right at this moment, you are doing a piss poor job. I gave her to you, to protect. I could give you the same spiel that I gave to your mate when I met her, but somehow I think you would be less than impressed." He smiled with irony as he recognized the hatred igniting in Curran's eyes.

"You. Bastard!" Curran growled through clenched teeth as it struck him that this being was the elusive Rune Aezowyn. Creator of the Multiverse. Revered by untold trillions upon trillion of beings. But those poor bastards did not know the lie they believed. And he swung his fist with all the power in his body.

Rune allowed the punch to hit him. Let it rock him back on his feet. His lip split and blood trickled. He lifted a hand and touched a finger to the torn flesh. His jaw hard, he met the hatred filled gaze of the man that Rune loved above all others in this Multiverse. "Don't attempt that again."

Curran growled, and took a step forward fully prepared to kill this being with his bare hands. "What are you going to do to stop me, you powerless washed up has been."

"Powerless?" Rune's eyes glinted.

There were times when words, no matter if they were spoken in all the languages of the multiverse, no matter how eloquently, would not, could not be heard— the pain was just too loud, the scars too deep. Rune understood on a level that no one else ever would. *Had not this vast multidimen-*

sional universe been created from the agony, the grief, the lone-liness, the rage that he and Eliana, the last of their kind, had faced? But he had to try.

Within the space of a microsecond Rune and Curran disappeared from the planet of Aezorwyn in its hidden realm, and reappeared in the vastness of space, trillions of parsecs, and trillions of dimensions from the planet that kept the last of the Dark Elves safe.

"It's beautiful, isn't it?" Rune asked, staring out at the un-countable galaxies, nebulas, and stars.

Curran stared around him wildly. *How the fuck?* "Take me back!"

Rune stared at Curran, his gaze hard. "We need to talk."

"Fuck that shit. I've got nothing to say to you." Curran's voice was an ugly sneer.

"Then listen."

Curran's fingers curled, the line of his jaw grew hard, and he looked at the Creator with ice cold eyes. No emotion. No response.

"The Dark Elves are not the only ones who've lost every-thing."

Curran laughed, bitterness seeping through his heart. "We were just the disposable ones."

Rune stared at the man before him. "If you think anyone is disposable there is something very wrong with you."

Curran crossed his arms, a muscle ticking in his jaw. "You let my people be massacred. That sounds pretty disposable to me. That sounds pretty fucked up to me. If it was possible to kill a Creator, I would kill you."

Rune walked away, and stood staring out into the star-studded darkness, his expression grave. "I have stared into the future and the past so many times, looking for a way to change what happened, and what is coming. I wanted to take this bitter cup from the Dark Elves, but every single possibility results in death. Your race is not the only one to have lost their home world, to face the danger of extinction, Curran. Without fail, when we look through time, we see the importance of the Dark Elves and four other races, in the time of darkness that is coming. To lose any of you would be to lose the Multiverse."

Curran stood stiff and silent. Inside he felt as if everything he believed had been torn to shreds. First by Willow, and now by this Being he'd refused to even consider might exist.

Rune turned and faced Curran. "For the Dark Elves, I created Aezorwyn in its hidden realm. There was no other way to save your people."

Curran shook his head, brutally pushing past the lump rising in his throat. "No. I don't believe that."

Rune nodded slowly, maintaining eye contact with the man who also blamed himself for the destruction of his people. And Rune wished that he could show him the future. But the King of the Dark Elves, the man who had risked everything to save his people was not ready for that, yet.

Shoving his hands into his pockets, Rune turned to stare out into space. "Everything Willow told you about me is true. Do not reject the rare gift that she is, Curran. She shines in the midst of your darkness." He pointed to a distant nebula. Purple, teal green, blue, red, the colors were stunning. Deep in the center a light glowed brightly. "So much beauty, but do you notice the blackness that surrounds it? The darkness that ribbons through it. Dark matter and Dark energy are essential for the existence of the multiverse. Without them, the stars would not shine, life would not exist." He turned slightly and pointed to a brilliant star glowing in a field of darkness. "Only in darkness can you see the stars, Curran. And you are one of the brightest stars to ever light the heavens."

Curran shook his head, his arms folded across his chest, his feet planted firmly apart as if to brace himself. "Tell your lies to someone else."

"You think I did nothing while your people were being slaughtered." Rune stared at Curran. "You're wrong."

"Fuck you, Rune Aezorwyn. I am not your puppet! And I'll never kneel before you."

Rune watched Curran silently. He knew the scars that were etched into this man's soul, he knew the depth of his pain. He took no offense to his anger. "You have the freedom to choose Curran."

"I choose to return home."

Rune nodded, the single most important thing he and Eliana had ever done was to ensure that all life had free will. They wanted no puppets, no slaves. Love was not love if it was forced.

And the fate of the multiverse hung in the balance.

Chapter Seventy-Eight

STAR DATE: 20580.10.08

> Dimension Five
> Realm of the Forsaken
> Aezorwyn

CURRAN FOUND HIMSELF back on Aezorwyn between one heartbeat and the next. He stood at the door to the castle that he and his people had built with their bare hands. It was a bitter foul-tasting pill to swallow, to know that this world and its hidden realm had not been his discovery, but Rune's leading. Willow was in there and he knew he could go to her, but fuck he was not ready for that yet. He was not ready to face the woman that Rune Fucking Aezorwyn had selected for him. He turned and walked away again. Heading to the training fields. He needed to work off his rage. He needed to find his cold determination. He needed to make his own fucking choices.

Chapter Seventy-Nine

STAR DATE: 20580.10.13

Dimension Five
Realm of the Forsaken
Aezorwyn

DREVEN KNEW THE ONLY way this would go the way he wanted, would take careful planning. Careful planning and a trap to lure Curran from this world. If he did this right, he would not only get rid of the woman, but their absurd excuse for a King as well.

Everything that had befallen their once mighty race could be directly attributed to Curran Nadiir. And he still had not learned. Even now Curran was talking about launching another rescue mission for one of his men. Dreven sneered. His men were nothing but common criminals who deserved the punishment they'd been given.

He was done trying to make Curran see the error of his ways. It was time for action. Time for Aezorwyn to have a new King who would protect his people.

Chapter Eighty

STAR DATE: 20580.10.15
Dimension Five
Realm of the Forsaken
Aezorwyn

SHE LEFT THE KITCHEN, laughing at the antics of the kitchen staff, on her way to change for dinner in the main hall. *Maybe Curran would be in their suite, and they could talk.* Her smile disappeared and she sighed. *No. She did not think he would be there. She hadn't seen him for more than a few minutes since that terrible fight they'd had a week ago.* Turning the corner in the hall, she felt the energy suddenly change and she paused looking around.

Dreven stood by the huge window that overlooked the forest. Willow became very still, her instincts alert. She was close to her chambers but turning her back on this man was not an option. She wondered why he was there. His chambers were not anywhere near her and Curran's. "Is there something I can help you with, Dreven? Has something happened to Curran?"

He walked away from the window, the look on his face making her wary and she stepped back. He laughed and moved closer. "For starters, you could service me the way you service our lord and master, King Curran." He grabbed her arm with the intent to drag her closer, growling when she slapped him hard across the face.

"Get your hands off me!" She jerked back managing to break his grip, fear and anger surging through her. She could feel her energy flowing and she set her hand on the hilt of the dagger she'd slipped into the special pocket that had been sewn into the side seam of all her outfits. The instant she wrapped her hand around the hilt of the dagger her energy flowed into the weapon. A shocked breath hissed out of her, but she kept her eyes on the furious male in front of her.

"You shouldn't have done that, Willow. I was going to make this easy on you." Dreven snarled and advanced on her again. "Do you like it rough? Is that what has Curran so bewitched?"

Willow eased the dagger from her pocket. She wasn't a warrior, would never be a warrior, but she would not be a victim to this man.

She could feel the strangeness of the energy flowing through the dagger. She took a careful step back, her eyes locked on his, terror pumping through her veins. And he was on her, his hand wrapping around her throat as he slammed her back into the stone wall. His mouth crashed down on hers. She twisted, bit down hard on his lip, her hand came up and slashed downwards, the dagger slicing a clean path down over his ear and across his face.

With a roar of fury, his arm shot out, the back of his hand striking her cheek as he leapt away. Clutching the blade, even as her head bounced against the stone wall, she saw stars but forced herself to stay upright.

He wiped at the blood dripping from his lip with the back of his hand, the cut on his face stung like a son of a bitch. She would pay. "At first I was just going to kill you." His voice was conversational, and Willow stared at him, his words so terribly at odds with the tone of his voice. "I considered the slave traders in the shadow realm, I even lined up several prospective brothel owners. I figured a little bidding war would net me a good sum of credits."

Willow pressed her hand against the cold stone wall behind her, trying to ground herself. The room spun in her vision, and she swallowed the nausea that was threatening. In her other hand she clutched the dagger, he would not take her easily. Her energy was flowing, and she understood it was the very dangerous side of her nature and it was being amplified by the dagger. There was something strange about this dagger. "Curran will kill you!"

He watched the redheaded bitch and began to think that maybe he should take her to that brothel on the planet of Hope, in the Shadow region. The Desperation Outpost would certainly change her attitude. A few months in the notorious shadow region brothels fucking criminals and other less than desirable elements would teach her a lesson as nothing else would. He could take her to the Suzerain after that. "Curran will be glad you are not his problem anymore. He told me that he regrets bringing you here. You've been nothing but problems from day one. He even told me he misses the skills of his pet."

Dreven's words were an ugly sneer of sound that arrowed right into her heart. She struggled against the pain and wondered if it were true. Curran had been so angry when he left their room. "He will kill you. I would run if I were you." She said bravely, clinging desperately to the hope that the love she felt for Curran was also the love that he felt for her.

He laughed, "I'll be the one to kill Curran, but first I'm going to deal with you." He moved fast, a warrior in his prime, his powerful fist smashed into her jaw. The dagger fell from her fingers as she lost consciousness.

Dreven picked her up and slung her over his shoulder, before making his way to the secret passage built into the walls of the castle. He pushed in the stone that triggered the door and it swung open silently. Stepping through, he waited to make sure the door closed securely behind him and headed down the dark stone stairs.

The hidden passageway led to a little used storage room that he'd already prepared. He paused at the doorway to that room and looked carefully through a tiny, well disguised peephole. The room remained undisturbed. He opened the door and stepped in, closing the hidden door behind him. A large crate sat in the middle of the room.

He set the unconscious woman in the box and crouched down to check the pulse in her neck. She was alive. Grasping the neckline of her dress, he tore it right down the middle, baring her body to his gaze. A natural redhead. He wished he had time right now to take her, but he'd arranged to meet Curran at the portal in a few minutes. He smirked at the thought of stealing Willow from right under Curran's nose.

He took a minute to open the first aid kit he'd had the foresight to stash in this storage room, though at the time, he'd been more concerned with treating the woman if she'd fought and been injured. He set up a tiny mirror from the kit. Quickly cleaning up the wounds on his face with antibiotic wipes, he taped the cut on his face with steri-strips. *Bitch.* He carefully put everything back into the first aid kit and stuffed it into his traveling bag. He yanked off his bloody shirt and switched it with the clean shirt he'd packed. Once he was ready to go, he turned back to his captive.

He flipped the unconscious woman on her stomach and quickly bound her wrists behind her back, then her ankles. He turned her back over and gagged her. And because he didn't want her to die, on the way to her new life, he turned her on her left side. Stepping back, he admired his handy work. Yeah, he was going to fuck her just like that. He reached over and closed the lid on the crate, nailing it securely in place. Whistling a happy tune, he wheeled it out of the storage room, and to the shipping/receiving area behind the castle. If he was lucky, Curran would be otherwise engaged. He almost growled when he saw Curran walk out of the forest and lift his hand in greeting. *Fuck.* He forced a smile to his lips and waited as Curran drew near.

"Hey, Curran. I've got the glow stones here, I'm sure that the natives of Beron will be happy to trade for that rare plant that Doc O'Rinn asked me to get.

"What happened to your face?" Curran asked, his voice sharp as he took in the wounds on his third-in-commands face. It had been days since his meeting with fucking Rune

Aezorwyn, and he still could not get past his hurt over Willow's secret. *Why the fuck hadn't she trusted him?*

Dreven ruefully touched his cheek. "I tripped and fell when I was collecting the glow stones. Hurts like a son of a bitch."

Curran forced a laugh and shook his head in sympathy. "You know the routine, head to the cache in the Trasiom System. There is a small space jet there. Good thing you're a pilot, Dreven. You've been making a lot of off planet runs lately. Be careful out there."

"Always." Dreven replied and paused. "Shadows, I almost forgot. Garrett asked if you would meet him in the village. There is some problem with a couple of captives. He said it can't wait."

Curran swore. He'd hoped to talk to Willow before they went to dinner in the main hall. *Not that he knew what the fuck to say to her.* "Thanks, Dreven."

Dreven gave a wave and shifted off Aezorwyn through the dimensions into the dark cache hidden in the Trasiom system. It only took him a few minutes to get his cargo into the fast little space jet, and get it fired up. He launched within ten minutes of his arrival. "Computer shut down all tracking and go dark."

"Complied. Tracking shut down, all systems dark and untraceable."

He entered new coordinates and turned the space jet, as they jumped to Hyperwarp speed.

Chapter Eighty-One

STAR DATE: 20580.10.15

Dimension Five
Realm of the Forsaken
Aezorwyn

CURRAN WAITED AT THE village for about twenty minutes before deciding enough was enough. No Garrett. No sign of any problems. He talked to one of their guards making his patrol. The man shook his head and said he hadn't seen any problems or Garrett.

Swearing, Curran headed back to the castle figuring that Garrett probably decided to talk to him there. There were days he fucking wished that at least communications technology could survive whatever the shadows was in this planet's atmosphere.

He walked into the main hall, and it was full. It looked as if a large portion of his people had turned out to share this evening meal that Willow worked hard to institute a few weeks ago. She'd kept insisting that it would bring a sense of community, that his people desperately needed. *She'd been right. Gods he was such a bastard. He needed to talk to his mate.*

He paused to help a very pregnant woman sit down and laughed with one of the stable masters. It took him ten bloody minutes to make his way to the head table. Frowning, he looked around. No Willow. Though Garrett and Falcon were sitting there eating and laughing with some of the off-duty guards. "Dreven said you wanted to talk to me in the village, Garrett." He crossed his arms, and waited for Garrett's reply, while wondering where his little mate had gone off to.

"I haven't seen Dreven today."

Curran paused, and his eyes met Falcon's and Garrett's, a bad feeling rising in him. Fuck. He and Garrett had talked a few days ago about Dreven and this growing sense of distrust Garrett had for him. "Have either of you seen Willow?"

Garrett stood up. "No."

Falcon rose to his feet and shook his head. "I haven't seen her either, usually she is here before anyone else, going over everything."

Curran ran a hand through his hair. "I don't know if this is anything, but we had a fight a week ago..." He shook his head. "I was going to try to talk to her tonight."

Garrett and Falcon looked at each other and winced. "You waited a week to try to talk to her?" Garrett asked. "You are a dumbass, Curran—King or not. She is a good woman."

"We'll help you find her." Falcon said quietly.

Without a word they headed out of the hall and up the stairs towards the chambers he shared with his mate. As they started down the corridor, Garrett grabbed his arm. "Curran." He pointed to the dagger on the floor.

His heart stopped, and resumed pounding, hard. That was the dagger he'd given to Willow. His eyes took in the scene. There was blood on the wall, a few drops on the floor. Swearing, he crouched down by the dagger, the blade had blood on it. He rose to his feet, his mind fixed on only one thing. Willow. He ran down the corridor hoping, praying that she was in their rooms, that she had simply tripped, that he wasn't too late, even though he knew, he fucking knew something was wrong. Terribly wrong.

He slammed open the door to their chambers and came to a hard stop in the empty silent room. He turned to look at Garrett and Falcon. His mind was racing. Where was she? Was she lying hurt somewhere?

Falcon noticed a crumpled piece of paper lying on the floor, under the small table beside the bed, and picked it up. His eyes widened and he turned to look at Curran. "What the fuck is this?"

Garrett took the paper and swore. "Where the shadows did this come from?"

Curran rubbed his neck. "That's what we fought about. Dreven brought this back with him when he made that supply run."

"Fucking Dreven!" Garrett gritted out between clenched teeth. "If you don't kill him, I fucking will. The man is nothing but trouble! He has had it out for Willow since he met her. If you reacted the way I suspect you did, she might have run away."

Curran swore and closed his eyes. He'd been fucking sulking since he spoke to Rune. Pissed that the Creator might have had anything to do with his mating. He'd let that get in the way of resolving their argument. Fuck. He'd let Dreven, a man he knew was a threat, come between him and Willow. His mind returned to the injuries Dreven had on his face. He'd said he'd tripped collecting glow stones. Curran clenched his fist, if he'd harmed Willow, he was going to kill him. "We need to talk to Kailene O'Rinn and the Manager in charge of our glow stone supply. Dreven met me in the receiving area with a large crate of glow stones, his face was all cut up, he said that Dr. O'Rinn asked him to pick up a rare plant from natives of Beron and that the glow stones were the trade."

Falcon's eyes hardened. "Curran, I've got a bad feeling about this."

"You're thinking that Willow cut up Dreven trying to protect herself?" Garrett asked, the quietness of his voice carrying the weight of his concern.

Curran stared at Garrett for a moment, a terrible dread filling his heart. *Would Dreven betray him? Maybe Willow merely cut herself and was in the infirmary? But why would Dreven lie about meeting Garrett? The fuck kind of game was Dreven playing?* "Garrett, arrange a search party, Falcon, we need to make sure she hasn't hurt herself, check the medical wing, talk to Jase Aries. I'll talk to Kailene O'Rinn, and the man in charge of the glow stone supplies. We meet in the war room in fifteen minutes." Gods he was so aware of time ticking past. Every second seemed to be taking his mate further and further from his reach.

Curran headed straight to the main hall again, he'd seen Dr. O'Rinn sitting at a table there. He walked in and looked around, finally seeing her sitting with her friends. He worked his way through the tables, his face grim, ignoring the greetings being called out to him. "Kailene."

She looked up at him with a smile. "Hello, Curran." She paused as she saw his face. "What's wrong?"

"Did you ask Dreven to go to Beron for a rare plant?"

"Beron?" She shook her head, surprise showing in her eyes. "No. There is nothing I would ever need from that planet; we have better specimens here."

Currans eyes hardened. "Did you speak to Dreven or Willow today?"

Kailene shook her head. "I haven't seen either of them, I spent my day in my greenhouses."

Curran turned his eyes to the women with Kailene. "Keanna, have you seen Willow at all today?"

Keanna was watching him with deep concern written all over her face. "She stopped in the store this afternoon, she seemed upset, but she never told me why. When she left, she told me she was going to stop in the kitchens then help set up the main hall."

He shoved a hand through his hair in frustration. "Fuck. We can't find her." His gut was churning, his every instinct shouting out to him that something was wrong. He turned and headed over to the table where the manager of the glow stone supplies was deep in conversation with the manager of the mines.

"Why did you give Dreven a crate of glow stones to take to Beron?"

Both men looked at him in surprise. "I did not give Dreven a crate of glow stones. I rarely see the man." The manager of supplies looked irritated. "Dreven doesn't lower himself to talk to the likes of us. However, I was just talking to Rigel about a crate of glow stones that went missing from my storage building last week. We were going to come and see you after the meal."

Curran stared at the men. "Last week?"

The manager nodded. "It was odd, people here have no need to steal. I thought that one of Rigel's men needed extra's to light up the mines better. We've been talking about doing that for a while now."

Curran turned his eyes on Rigel. "Did your men take those stones?"

"No. That's what I'd just told Elio. We were going to find you after the meal and ask for your advice.

Curran thanked the two men and headed to the War Room. Why the shadows would Dreven want a crate of glow stones? He opened the door to the war room and stepped inside, and as he looked at Falcon he was struck by a terrible thought. "The crate Dreven took was big enough to hold Willow. I need to get to the cache in the Trasiom System."

"Curran, Willow might be here." Garrett spoke up from beside Falcon. "We need to do a search here before you risk exposing yourself. This might be a trap."

Curran was already shaking his head. "He took her."

Falcon looked at Garrett, "Get that search going here. I'll go with Curran. If you don't find her here, come to the cache in the Trasiom System. There will be instructions there for you. If you find her, come anyway and use the comm from the storage lockers to send a message to us." He headed after Curran, his face hard. He'd never liked Dreven.

Chapter Eighty-Two

STAR DATE: 20580.10.15
Dimension Five
Space

SHE WOKE UP TO A POUNDING head, her jaw aching and the voice from her nightmares. Opening her eyes, she stared around in confusion, she started to sit up and groaned softly as her whole body protested her movement. Her arms were numb, and it took her a second to understand she couldn't move them. Her breathing quickened as her brain sorted out crucial information. Her hands were tied behind her back, her ankles were tied and her dress was torn down the middle.

"I hope you had a good rest, Willow."

Dreven's voice. Her heart slammed into her chest and the full horror of her memories flooded her brain. "My... my arms hurt. Please untie me." Even those hoarsely whispered words hurt to utter, the ache in her jaw intensifying with the slight movement.

Dreven crouched down in front of her. "I like you like this, Willow." He reached out and brushed her hair back off her face.

She flinched away from him, fear and revulsion filling her at his touch.

"Ssh, Ssh." He said gently, his fingers trailing over her face to brush lightly against her jaw. "That looks sore." His voice was calm, almost sympathetic, her eyes met his and her lips trembled at the look in his eyes. His fingers glided down her neck and paused over her wildly beating heart rate, his lips curling into a satisfied smile. A tear trembled on her lashes as his fingers kept moving drifting down over her collarbone skimming across the top of her breast. She closed her eyes, trembling from deep inside, fighting the terror of being in this man's control. Instinctively she reached for the energy of the planet to protect herself and her eyes flew open. "Where... where are we?" Her heart was pounding, her mouth dry, as she stared at Dreven.

"Far from Aezorwyn." He stood up and gave her a smile. "You're very pretty, Willow. I understand why Curran was so infatuated with you."

Willow stared up into his face, finally, understanding the terrible weakness in her body. He had taken her off Aezorwyn. She had no connection to any planet. No way to protect herself. She wondered how long she would survive without the planetary energy that normally flowed through her. He was watching her, waiting for a response she realized. And that was when she noticed the cut she had given him with the dagger. It was an angry red with a strange blue tinge to it that was not the normal kind of bruising that could come with an injury. But it was the lines trailing away from it like a starburst, that drew her attention. Red, blue, black.

Her eyes swept over his face again. "You don't look well, Dreven. Untie me, we can use the med unit to help you."

He laughed, a low ugly sound. "You'd like that wouldn't you? I'm not a fool, Willow."

She concentrated on forcing numb fingers to try to work the knots on the leather strips tied around her wrists, her heart thundering in her chest as his hands went to the ties on his pants. No, no, no, she had to do something! The thought of what he had in mind made bile rise in her throat. Her fingers weren't cooperating, and she began to struggle frantically with the bonds as tears slipped down her cheeks. His hand closed roughly on her shoulder, and she saw his energy signature in her mind. It was a sickly putrid green, heavily marbled with the darkness of his hatred and rage. She bared her teeth at him, and he laughed, a rough bark of sound. The shrill blare of the ship's alarm blasted through the room and Dreven jerked away from her, staggered, caught himself and straightened. "I'll be back to pick this up as soon as I deal with whatever is going on out there. Don't go anywhere." His laughter followed him out of the cabin cut off only by the door sliding shut.

A harsh sob tore through her and she shifted and shuffled around until she was kneeling on the bed, crying softly. She had to find a way to free herself. She had to.

The ship jolted and shuddered, and she almost toppled over. What was happening? She sat and brought her knees up, her feet flat on the bed and inched her way back until her back was braced against the wall. She had a small amount of give in the ties around her ankles, so she began to shift her ankles around until finally she was able to get one foot free.

Standing quickly, she scanned the room for something to cut her bonds with, but not seeing anything she rushed to the door, it opened with a woosh and there standing before her was a Suzerain soldier. She gasped and took a step back, a new kind of fear raising up inside of her. Oh gods!

The soldier reached out and grabbed her arm. "I've got her, Commander." He reached out and drew her dress closed taking a moment to free her wrists. Even as a tear fell, she whispered. "Thank you." As she held the torn material of her dress together in a tight fist.

The man nodded once and led her out to the main cabin of the ship. Dreven was sitting in the ship's pilot seat surrounded by soldiers with their weapons pointed at him. He looked furious, and almost grey with the illness she could see was consuming him. His appearance was slightly different, and she watched him puzzled for a long moment before she noticed the tiny earring he wore. Curran had once shown her one like that. They were tiny holo emitters. Designed by the resistance to create a nearly flawless holo mask that would change their appearance. The trademark ears of the Dark Elves were safely hidden. Dreven could have been from one of a million different species that inhabited their galaxy. For that one cunning trick, she was grateful. Her people must remain hidden at all costs. The Commander of the Suzerain was an older man who walked over to her. "Willow Solar, you are now in the custody of the Suzerain. You will come with us."

She nodded once, knowing with a terrible clarity that she was merely exchanging one Dimension of Shadows for the next, but at that moment, the thought of never seeing

Dreven again only brought her a sense of relief. She turned to him and wondered if he knew that he was a dead man.

"You can't take her yet! We were not supposed to meet for several weeks. I told you that in our communications! I have plans for her!"

The Commander turned to coldly survey the man in the chair. "Your plans do not interest us. For future reference, if our asset had been further damaged, we would have killed you. Count yourself lucky that we arrived early. Your credits have been transferred to your account. If you are wise, you will shut your mouth and live to spend it."

With a movement of his head, his soldiers surrounded her and escorted her off Dreven's ship.

Chapter Eighty-Three

STAR DATE: 20580.10.15

Dimension Five
Trasiom System
Helea

THEY STEPPED THROUGH the portal into the secure warehouse on Helea, the third planet orbiting in a complex arrangement with ten other planets, that all fell within the habitable zone in the Trasiom System. The high-tech security system scanned them. A female computer voice welcomed Curran. "Warehouse secure. Last accessed 5 hours ago by Dreven Avanth. Cargo scan also completed. His cargo consisted of a wooden crate containing an unknown female of Kalyrian descent. The cargo was loaded into the SJ Chimera, and he departed within ten minutes of his arrival. The ship went dark minutes after its launch."

"Is the Ghost Universal Space Tracker active?"

"Affirmative. G.U.S.T data downloading now."

"Location of the Chimera?"

"The Chimera is on a trajectory to the Shadow Region."

"Computer, prepare SC Dark Storm for launch." Curran turned to Falcon. "He's got a five-hour start on us, even with

Dark Storm's speed we are going to take several hours to catch up to him. I'd shift us but it's too unpredictable with his speed. Let's go."

They caught up with the Chimera in just under four hours, but they'd pushed the Dark Storm to its limits to do it. They dropped out of Hyperwarp almost on top of the Chimera. Curran armed their weapons and Falcon opened a channel. "Chimera, this is the Dark Storm. Prepare to be boarded."

"You're too late." Dreven's voice was an ugly sneer

Curran nodded and Falcon pulled his blaster, they shifted onto the Chimeral bridge. Dreven was sitting in the pilot's seat, sprawled in a seemingly casual position, his own blaster pointed at them. "You brought company, Curran. I was only going to kill you— for now."

Falcon watched Dreven with hard eyes. "Too bad because my plan has been to kill you from the beginning, Dreven. I'm a patient man though." He grinned, a hard cold light in his eyes. "I'm going to stand here and watch Curran beat the information he wants out of you. You should have known not to mess with a Spirit Warrior. You won't live to make that mistake again."

"You are not looking healthy, Dreven." Curran moved so fast that Dreven had no chance. He screamed as his wrist snapped, the blaster now in Curran's hard grip. "I can guarantee that I will not be the one dying today, nor will Falcon. Where is my mate?"

Dreven looked at Curran, his mouth twisted in a pain filled grimace. "You have good taste in women, Curran. Willow was... delicious."

Curran growled, a low ugly sound, and Falcon lifted his blaster. "If you've hurt her, Dreven, your death will be slow and painful."

"Pain is relative, isn't it Curran? Pain, pleasure, it's all in the eyes of the beholder."

"Trust me Dreven, you won't enjoy it. Where is Willow? I won't ask again."

"You're far too late Curran. The Suzerain have her, and I've warned them that you will attempt a rescue."

Time stood still as Curran attempted to sort out what he'd just heard Dreven say. "You gave Willow to the Suzerain?" His voice was a harsh growl of sound torn from his throat. Images of his men being thrown screaming into those dark reeking dimensional gates filled his mind. His breath stuttered at a vision of Willow being thrown into one. *Gods no. She would be tortured! How would he ever find her?*

"I didn't give her. The bounty was huge. It will help our people, and it's shadows more than you've ever done."

A ragged terrible cry torn from Curran's very soul filled the air. "No! No! You fucking stupid bastard. You've sentenced her to a lifetime of torture and abuse!" He drew a ragged breath. Rage washed over him in relentless red waves, but what was worse, what was horribly, terribly worse, was the ice-cold ocean of fear that he was floundering in. *He had to save her. He had to save her before—* He cut off the thought, swallowing hard. Falcon's hand came down on his shoulder, grounding him. He took another deep breath. The sound of the air entering his lungs was loud in his ears. He could feel his hearting pounding, slamming against his ribs. His eyes rested on Dreven. The need to destroy this pathetic excuse for a Dark Elf, to beat him to a bloody pulp rioted through him. His fist clenched, and he spoke through teeth clamped together, his fists shaking as he fought to control himself. "You have committed treason." His eyes burned into Drevens. "You have betrayed your people." *Gods. He'd trusted him.* "You are guilty of kidnapping, assault and conspiring with the enemy of the Dark Elf people. The sentence is death."

Dreven stood slowly. "I do not recognize you as my King, nor as the King of the Dark Elf people. You have no power over me."

Curran's arm shot out; his hand clamped around Dreven's throat. He lifted the man and shook him. "Why?"

Dreven clawed at the hand around his neck. "Q-Queen Sionia—" He gasped. "Was my— half-sister." Curran let go. Dreven fell to the floor and glared up at him. "She is dead!" Dreven's face was a mask of hatred. "Because of you— Betrayer!"

Curran shook his head, his stomach clenching. "The Spirit Warriors were betrayed."

Dreven sneered. "That is what you want us to believe. The Suzerain told me the truth."

Curran stared at the man. "The Suzerain massacred our younglings!"

"Lies!"

"I was fucking there! They cut their throats and made us drink their blood!" The memories were hitting him hard. Image after bloody image filling his mind and he cursed. "Those fucking bastards killed our younglings. They attacked our allies. They destroyed our world! And they fucking televised it—" Curran swallowed hard and fought the wash of red that colored his vision. Fought the nausea.

"*Your* Spirit Warriors killed those younglings. You betrayed the Suzerain, and our world paid the price." Dreven spat as he struggled to his feet. He swayed, yanked a small but deadly weapon out of his pocket, and pointed it directly at Curran's chest.

Falcon fired his blaster, watching emotionlessly as shock appeared in Dreven's eyes seconds before he fell. Curran turned and looked at Falcon. "Some people want to believe lies, Curran. They accept them as truth because they want something those lies promise. Dreven wanted revenge. How could he avenge his sister if he did not have a target?"

Curran swallowed. "It is a documented fact. We have the old holo vids stored in all our caches. Our people lived through it. They have spoken of what they witnessed."

Falcon's hand came down on his shoulder. "We know the truth, Curran. But Dreven... wanted revenge more than he wanted the truth."

Chapter Eighty-Four

STAR DATE: 20580.10.16
Dimension Five
Space

"I DON'T LIKE THIS PLAN." Falcon said to Curran. "I'll have no way to track you. What if you give yourself up to them and she's not there? This is not a good plan. For fuck's sake, Curran. What logical reason would any of us have for giving up to the Suzerain? We all have a death sentence hanging over our heads."

Curran handed Falcon a small ear jewel. "Put that on, it will change your appearance. It's a holo emitter. The plan is not for me to give myself up to them. You are going to hand me over and collect the reward."

Falcon stared at Curran, a muscle ticking in his jaw. "The fuck I am."

"Yeah, the fuck you are." Curran's voice was hard. "We detected energy signatures from the Chimera and from a Suzerain cruiser. There is no fucking reason for those ships to have been within even a parsec of each other. Especially not in this system. We fucking know that Dreven told us the truth about giving Willow to those bastards. We also fucking know what they will do to her." Curran set his jaw and looked at his best friend. "We know, Falcon."

"Curran, we can't lose you. Let me go. I promise I'll find her and bring her back to you if she is there."

Curran stubbornly shook his head and Falcon swore viciously.

"They don't want you, Falcon. They want me. Just stick with the plan. Hand me over, collect the rewards then get your ass back to our cache in the Trasiom System. From there shift home. I'll find Willow and get us to the cache and contact you."

"I hate your fucking plan! If I have to come and rescue you, I'll never let you live it down." He attached the jeweled stud to his ear and activated the unit. Seconds later he looked like a scarred Laenus bounty hunter, right down to the elongated pupils, red eyes and striped hair. He glared at Curran. "And how do you think that you will find Willow? There is no guarantee that you will even be taken to the same place as her."

Curran looked broodingly at Falcon. "I'll simply tell them the truth. I'm her mate."

"And you think they will just happily take you to her?"

"If they are trying to find a way to control her, they will. They'll know they can use me to control her."

Falcon swore. "Control her? What the fuck Curran? She is the bait. It's you they want. Gods don't you get it?"

"Falcon. She is an Energy Enchanter. They want her far more than they want me."

Falcon stared at his best friend. "An Energy Enchanter?"

Curran nodded. "Do you know what that is?"

Falcon nodded slowly. "I've heard the myths. But—" He shook his head. "Are you telling me they really exist?"

Curran nodded and walked over to stare out the view screen. "I don't think there are many. It sounds like they were hunted by corrupt governments and individuals in a bid to gain power."

Falcon swallowed. *Fuck.* "Curran if this is true, you have to see that they will stop at nothing to keep her in their grip. Do you understand that Curran? They will fucking torture you to gain control of her. Don't risk this."

"I can't leave her there, Falcon. I love her." He turned haunted eyes to his friend. "She is far too powerful to leave in their hands. They will turn her into a monster that none of us could ever defend the universe from."

Falcon stared at Curran. *Fuck. Fuck. Fuck. Gods, he would be walking back into the dimension of shadows.* Swallowing, Falcon nodded once. "All or None."

"All or None."

Chapter Eighty-Five

STAR DATE: 20580.10.17
Dimension Five
Farport City, Tryria

WILLOW PACED THE CELL and struggled to contain the fear that was threatening to consume her. Her best protection was to remain calm, but it was hard to remain calm when you knew there was little chance of anything good coming out of this. She'd spent a lot of time trying to figure out a way to escape. There was no escape from this prison they had brought her to, even though the energy from this world flowed through her in rich nourishing currents.

Her second-best option was death. That terrified her, but not as much as the thought of what would happen to the universe if the Suzerain forced her to use her powers to further their goals.

She leaned against the wall and put her arm over her eyes. Please gods no. A tear slid down her bruised face. She fought the sobs that wracked her slender frame and forced herself to think about what Curran would do. Her fierce, unstoppable mate would never give up. She knew that much. He had fought and overcame impossible odds.

She pictured his face, and a wobbly smile touched her lips briefly as she remembered his fierce gaze, and all the intensity that surrounded him. She knew without any doubt that he would come for her, just as he had come for Falcon. Just as he would for all his men. She could almost hear his fierce vow 'All or None' and somehow part of her knew that she had become part of his All. He would come for her. And she desperately needed to feel his arms around her. How she wished that their last words had not been spoken in anger. She hoped he knew that she did not blame him for any of this.

Leaning her head back against the cold stone wall, more tears spilled down her cheeks. Curran and what he was fighting for were too important to be lost. In the end, she was a tiny blip in the crucial quest to save his men and his people. What Curran did would change the universe. No matter what happened, he must continue. This was the one fact that she was absolutely sure of.

She took a breath as a deep calm settled over her. She would not be the reason that Curran faltered. When the Suzerain guards opened the door to her cell, she went with them silently, knowing what she needed to do.

The trip down the hall was silent except for the soft sound of the material of the simple grey overalls rustling as she walked. They took her into a brightly lit room, with an operating table on a pedestal that could be raised or lowered and was equipped with straps and movable components. A table of sharp metal instruments sat to one side. She paused, a deep trembling beginning inside her as the full realization of what she was facing swept through her. The guards pushed her forward and she took two steps, her eyes fastened on the dark-haired man, with cold iron-grey eyes, but she couldn't stop her gaze from returning to that table.

"Hello, Willow. My name is Commander D'miron. We met years ago. You have led us on quite a chase. Your brother has been quite worried."

Shivering, she wrapped her arms around herself. Her eyes moved from the table to meet his. "Jericho? Is he coming?"

"Unfortunately, he is not." Commander D'miron picked up a scalpel and examined it carefully before looking at the tiny woman before him. Watched as the brief flare of hope died in her eyes. "You are an Energy Enchanter, Willow Solar, a very valuable asset to the Suzerain. Cooperate with us and we will make you a rich woman.

Willow simply stared at the man. *Didn't he know anything about Energy Enchanters?*

"No? I didn't think so. Money isn't what motivates you is it? How about this? We are poised on the brink of taking the Castilian home world. The war has been devastating. Help me to end their suffering. You have the ability to calm the Castilian people, to show them how much better their lives will be with the Suzerain in control. We would much rather a peaceful resolution to this conflict. Sending in your brother is always such a tragic end to a species. You have the power to prevent this, Willow." He watched her as he spoke, his eyes never leaving hers.

Willow shivered, her heart breaking, but remained silent. Nothing she did would save the Castilian people. She would not be party to their subjugation.

Commander D'miron stepped closer. "It did not have to be this way, Willow. If you change your mind at any point, simply tell us. Remove your clothes."

Willow raised startled eyes to his.

"Blood is hard to remove, Willow. Take off your clothes."

She shook her head backing away from the man. He moved faster than what she would have ever expected, erupting into violent action. His hand sinking into her hair and yanking her head up until her eyes met his. His other hand closed hard over her throat. "Remove your clothes or I will have my men do it for you. They would enjoy that far more than you would." He released her as quickly as he had grabbed her.

Willow coughed as she struggled to catch her breath, her heart thundering in her chest. The door opened and in stepped a tall thin woman, her skin a satiny grey, her eyes large and black, a cruel smile curving her lips. "This is Farren. Her species thrive on the energy that pain produces. She has graciously agreed to help in our negotiations. Remove your clothes, Willow, I will not tell you again."

Numbness crawled through her, and Willow understood that she had run out of time. Hands trembling so bad she could hardly open the fastenings on the overalls, she slowly undressed and prayed desperately for strength to face what was to come.

"Such a shame to mar that beautiful skin," D'miron murmured.

"She will be beautiful bearing the scars of my artistry." Farren's voice was a warm husky drawl. "What is this mark, Little One?" Her fingers grazed over Willow's chest in a light caress. Willow flinched at the woman's skin-crawling touch on the crimson moon symbol that marked her as belonging to Curran.

Farren felt the flinch and smiled in triumph. "Perhaps I shall cut that mark from your flesh and keep it for a trophy. I hope you will not break easily, Enchanter. It's been long since I have tasted the energy of one of your kind, and I want to feast."

Chapter Eighty-Six

STAR DATE: 20580.10.19
Dimension Five
Space

THE PLAN WENT OFF WITHOUT a hitch. Falcon contacted the Suzerain and arranged to rendezvous with them in a typical Laenus manner. Which meant that they had three different routes out of there and every one of those routes would mean the death of anyone who betrayed them, including Suzerain scum.

The Laenus bounty hunters were dangerous warriors, and many despised them for the appearance of greed they portrayed to the universe at large. He knew differently though. They were a complex species, who had also been betrayed to the Suzerain, many years ago, and while it might appear that money was their motivator, it was far, far more complicated than that.

Curran kept his expression cold and emotionless when the Suzerain stepped onto their ship.

"Bring the prisoner, Bounty Hunter." The Commander of the Suzerain demanded as soon as they stepped out of the airlock.

Falcon folded his arms and gave the Suzerain a forbidding look. "Not until my credits have been transferred, Suzerain trash."

The Commander looked at the Laenus Bounty Hunter, irritated by his lack of respect. Unfortunately, the Laenus Bounty Hunters refused to show even the slightest amount of deference to their Suzerain Rulers. In this the Suzerain had learned to keep their silence. The Laenus were unpredictable at best, and it was not worth the loss of Suzerain soldiers to force their verbal respect. The Laenus were securely under the Suzerain thumb, there was no need to force the issue farther, but it had cost the Suzerain several thousand soldiers to figure that out.

The Commander looked over at the prisoner and lifted his communications device. "Transfer the credits"

Curran stared straight ahead in grim stillness as the credits were transferred, his wrists secured in front of him with tritanium steel restraint cuffs.

The Leanus Bounty Hunter watched silently his red eyes glinting eerily in the low light of the cabin. A computer voice spoke. "Transfer of one milllion credits complete." The Bounty Hunter growled, and the Commander felt the hair on the back of his neck stand up. "Suzerain Cur, this is Curran Nadiir. I lost seven good men, capturing him. You will pay me three times the amount, or I will sell him somewhere else." And the bastard had the fucking balls to lock his blaster on the Commanders chest. "And you will die."

The Commander glared at the man. Fucking Laenus vermin! They should have killed them all. "I'll need authorization."

The man waved his blaster, and the Commander lifted his communicator again. "The Bounty Hunter is requesting three times the award offered. There was an extended pause and finally a voice came back over the comm system. "Authorized and transferred."

The ship's computer voice came back on. "Three million credits transferred and received." The Bounty Hunter stepped behind the prisoner and nudged him forward. "Rune go with you, Curran Nadiir, last of the Dark Elves. May you die covered in the blood of your enemies." It was a Laenus warrior's way to honor warriors who had earned their highest regard. That alone earned the Laenus Bounty Hunter a look of hatred from the Suzerain Commander.

The Bounty Hunter's lips turned up in the faintest of smiles, revealing his fangs. "But do you dare, Suzerain dog?"

With a furious curse the Suzerain Commander turned. "Bring the prisoner." His words were hard and clipped. Curran was shoved forward into the airlock. He stared straight ahead. He was once again in the power of his most hated enemy, the Suzerain. He relentlessly kept his expression stoic. He would endure whatever they did to him. Finding Willow was all that mattered. Once he knew where she was, he would free them. He refused to consider any other option.

Chapter Eighty-Seven

STAR DATE: 20580.10.30
    Dimension Five
    Farport City, Tryria

SHE WALKED SILENTLY with her captors as she had done for many days now, her face carefully blank, not letting the agony that resounded through her body with every step show in any way. She forced herself to take deep even breaths and release them slowly, trying to still her instinctive panic the closer they got to that room of horrors. Every breath hurt. But she would not give them what they wanted. She had endured all they had done to her. Today would not be the day she broke. Her fingers were trembling badly, so she pressed them against her legs as they walked. Death might visit her this day, but if it did, she would meet it bravely. She had not become the monster they sought to make her.

One of her guards opened the door to the room, and she stepped in, ignoring the pounding of her heart. She would not break. Commander D'miron was waiting. Her eyes met his, impassively. This man did not have the power to destroy Willow Solar Nadiir, no matter what he thought or what he did.

"Good morning, Willow. Are you going to be reasonable today?"

She remained silent.

Commander D'miron watched the tiny redhead, for a few moments. He had to admit she was courageous. He was also positive that she was an energy enchanter. She would bow before the might of the Suzerain. He would see to that. The fact that she had withstood as much as she had, impressed him, but it changed nothing. Today he had finally found the means to break her. "Bring him in."

The door opened and six guards entered surrounding a man. Dread curled in her heart. The guards stepped away and her eyes met Currans. He'd been beaten savagely. One eye swollen closed. His face bruised, and cut, dried blood along his cheek and under his split lip. She was unable to contain a gasp.

Commander D'miron smiled at that little gasp. Today was going to be a good day. He would finally break the energy enchanter and kill the man who had eluded him for years. And he would use her to do it. He almost rubbed his hands together. "Curran Nadiir, betrayer of the Dark Elf people, claims to be your mate."

Willow's eyes turned to her captor. She remained silent, forcing herself to stand tall.

D'miron watched Willow closely, saw far too much and smiled coldly. "This is all in your hands, Willow. No one has to suffer here."

Willow looked at the man she despised with every ounce of her soul. She had no doubt that people would suffer today. There were no illusions in her mind of finding a way out of this terrible situation. She remained silent and turned back to meet Curran's grim stare. His left eye was swollen shut. He was covered in bruises and blood and her heart broke at how much pain she could see hidden in the depths of his eyes.

The energy coming off him changed as his eyes traveled over her, his pain morphing to violet fury as he saw her bruises and wounds. A roar filled the air, and Curran broke free of the soldiers holding him. He picked one up and threw him, kicked out and sent a second crashing to the floor. The remaining soldiers rushed forward smashing the butts of their blasters into him. Curran went to his knees, managed to stagger up, only to fall under the brutal blows they rained down on him.

"No!" Willow screamed.

D'miron lifted his hand. The beating stopped, and Curran was dragged back to his feet.

She could feel his tension and knew he was still struggling with the drive to protect her, to kill those who had harmed her. But there was nothing he could do. Nothing she could do.

"Do you love him, Willow? Do you love this betrayer? This man who caused the destruction of a whole civilization? This murderer of children?" Commander D'miron looked at her, and she could see the calculation in his eyes.

"With everything I am." She said clearly, her eyes locked on Curran's.

"I think that Willow needs to understand the cost Curran will pay if she doesn't give me what I want." Commander D'miron's voice was cold, "Proceed."

She flinched as a brutal fist slammed into Curran's face. Flinched again as Commander D'miron wrapped his hand around her arm. "Will you save him, Willow?"

She could feel the energy of this world flowing into her, the current gaining strength with violent turbulence of her rage. She looked into the eyes of the Suzerain Commander, her contempt a violent thing written on every line of her face.

She looked back to Curran, but the sight of the beating made her flinch, tears burning her eyes and she turned her face away. D'miron brutally grabbed her hair, turning her face so she could not look away.

Fury and hatred welled up inside of her, and she longed for the dagger she had lost. She would happily plunge it through the heart of this vile man. "I will never submit to you. Curran's enemies are my enemies." Tears slid down her cheeks, her heart breaking as she teetered on the edge of the abyss, the monster raging to be released and she prayed that Curran would someday forgive her.

"Kill him." Commander D'miron's voice was cold.

And Willow let herself fall into the abyss, let the dreaded monster rise as she inhaled— the energy of this dark world flowing into her in a powerful rush. Time seemed to slow, the sounds of the terrible beating intensifying as she consumed more and more of the energy of this hate filled planet. Her rage grew and grew. Every drop of blood that splattered on the floor, every thud and smack of fist hitting flesh adding to the insane wrath burning inside of her.

For herself she had endured, been willing to meet death. —but for Curran? She would kill to protect him. No matter the cost to herself.

Around the room, the energy of each man present suddenly lit up in her mind. Like a map, each glowing with the colors of their emotion— the blackness of the evil they participated in. Without hesitation she ripped open the shields that normally prevented her from drawing in the energy of living beings— and she drank deeply.

Screams filled the room. Commander D'miron dropped to his knees, his anguished wails joining with the others, as they writhed on the floor.

Energy signatures in the corridor popped up in her mind. More signatures throughout the complex, and Willow drew the energy to her in a powerful rushing current. *They would die. They would all die.*

Curran heard a body drop, then another. His attackers lay on the floor writhing in agony and screaming. He saw D'miron go down. His eyes turned to Willow. She was lit up like a beacon, energy pouring into her, energy from everywhere. His heart slammed into his chest and ice filled his veins. *Oh gods! No.* The screams in the room fell silent, but the eerie sounds of screams from the rest of the building echoed back into the room.

He staggered to his feet. "Willow! Stop!" He fell to his knees when he tried to take a step but grimly fought his way back up to his feet. "Willow!" He made his voice a harsh command, but still the screams continued. He stumbled over to her, and grabbed her shoulders, shaking her. "Willow! Stop!" He grabbed her chin and turned her eyes to meet his.

"Willow! It's me. Sh'arie." His voice was hard, commanding. "You will stop now!" He felt her sudden hesitation. "Sh'arie. Stop. Let them go." Willow's eyes cleared, and he saw her looking back at him.

"What's happened?" Her voice was faint, strained.

Relief flowed through him. "We've gotta get out of here. Hang onto me and don't let go, Willow." He was hurting badly, knew it would take a miracle for them to find their way out of this complex, find a ship and take off.

"What's happened?"

He heard the confusion in her voice. "Damn it, Willow, just keep hanging on. I'll get us out of here." He caught her hand and pulled her over to the door.

"What's happened? Where are we?"

He turned to her, his stomach dropping, a feeling of terrible dread flowing over him. His eyes met hers and she collapsed. He caught her, terror filling him. Without any thought of the caution, he always used to protect the knowledge of the Dark Elf dimensional shifting ability, he shifted. *Fuck the cameras. Fuck the Suzerain.*

Chapter Eighty-Eight

STAR DATE: 20580.10.30
Dimension Five
Realm of the Forsaken
Aezorwyn

CURRAN APPEARED IN the medical bay, Willow in his arms. Dr. Jase Aries and Journey Themis looked up. Shock in their eyes, they leapt to their feet and rushed over to him. Journey took Willow. Jase wrapped an arm around Curran's waist to help him over to an examination table, while he shouted for Axel, Breccan and Kace. His team rushed in, took in the situation in a glance, and like the well-organized team they were, they moved into action. Vitals were taken, the numbers called out and recorded. Dr. Aries switched places with Journey, his face grim. As bad a Curran looked, and he looked fucking bad, Willow was worse. "Someone let Garrett know."

Falcon, Garrett, and Marina burst into the med bay short minutes later.

"What the fuck, Curran. You were supposed to shift to the cache and contact us to help the second you knew where

Willow was." Falcon said as he stepped up to the gurney that Curran was giving Journey a hard time from.

"Falcon! Find out how Willow is!" Curran's voice held an edge of fear that Falcon had never heard before. He put his hand on Curran's shoulder, wincing at the evidence of the brutal beating that his friend had endured. "Jase is looking at her right now. I'll talk to him. You lay still and let Journey and Axel do their jobs. I'll be right back."

Falcon exchanged a look with Garrett and Marina and walked over to talk to Jase. "How is Willow? I need to tell Curran something, or he is going to come over here."

Dr. Aries looked at Falcon. "Not good." His voice was grim. "She's been tortured. I need to know why she lost consciousness. Find out exactly what happened."

Swearing, Falcons hands clenched, his eyes turning to ice cold flint. Muscle ticking in his jaw he reached out and gently squeezed Willow's shoulder. "Fight Willow. Curran needs you."

Taking a deep breath, he returned to Curran. "Curran, why did Willow lose consciousness? Doc needs to know exactly what happened."

Curran swore as Journey worked on his face. He looked up at Falcon's words, his eyes haunted. "Falcon." His voice broke. "She... killed— to protect... me." He shook his head. *Gods, his heart hurt.* He'd thought she'd betrayed him. He'd been a fool. "Tell Jase what I said. Tell him she is an Energy Enchanter. I'm praying that he knows what to do."

Deeply concerned by the devastation in his friends' eyes, Falcon returned to Dr. Aries to deliver the message.

"She's an Energy Enchanter? And she killed? My gods!" Dr. Aries sounded stunned, "How did I not know she was an Enchanter?" He started swearing, and scooped Willow up into his arms. "Get Curran up. Now! Our chances of saving her are growing more remote by the minute. Follow me!"

Jase led them out the patio doors of the ward, down into the lush garden that was bathed in moonlight. In the center of the garden was a beautiful stone folly with intricately carved columns and archways surrounding it. Ivy and roses twined around the marble pillars. And the light of the three moons filled the circle with light. Jase stepped into the stone circle and carried Willow to the center, while Journey and Garrett helped Curran. Marina and Falcon strode beside them, their faces grim.

Jase closed his eyes for a moment. "Curran. Right here. I need you right here." Falcon helped Curran to the place that Jase indicated, easing him to the ground when Jase motioned for him to sit down. Jase placed Willow in Curran's arms. "There is an ancient legend about the Energy Enchanters. A legend that claims the way to save a damaged enchanter is the center of all power and energy on a world. Curran, you are the center of power on this planet, and by all that is holy, this place is the center of the massive amount of energy this world puts out.

Focus on Willow. Think of the natural shields that guard the Dark Elf mind. Picture them, feel their power. Push your shield out until it's surrounding her, protecting her mind as well as yours." Jase touched Curran's shoulder. "This is the only chance we have to save her." At Currans questioning look Jase explained. "I'm from the planet Seniea. We have the ability to read light energy. Basically, it's the way energy moves in nature. The castle garden is full of potent, dynamic energy but here in this location, is the convergence of all energy on this planet. It makes total sense that she was always in this garden. And it makes sense that this garden has become a lush oasis.

Curran, I've seen the connection between the two of you from the start. I've seen her energy healing you from the moment she first set foot on this world. And I've seen times when your energy has surrounded her, like a protective shield. Do what I said Curran. Do it now, before it's too late."

Curran wondered if the doctor had lost his mind. The words Rune had spoken to him whispered through his mind, and he saw everything in a far different light.

Closing his eyes, he concentrated, and the energy of Aezorwyn swept over him. His eyes snapped open, and Rune appeared kneeling beside him. The Creator nodded gravely. Curran could see the planet's energy as Willow breathed it in. Somehow, she was part of the very planet that had saved his people. Rune put a hand on his shoulder and on Willow's, and Curran saw that her natural shields had been ripped away, her energy was bleeding out of her as fast as she breathed in the planet's energy. His heart clenched and he swallowed. *Fuck. Fuck. Fuck!* He was shaking. "Don't leave me, Willow! Don't you fucking leave me!" He lifted wild eyes to Rune. The Creator met his gaze and squeezed his shoulder.

Curran swallowed, his pulse racing as he saw how the energy from everyone in the garden was flowing into his mate, and she had no way to stop it. No way to protect herself. And he understood why an Energy Enchanter went insane if they lost their shields.

"You can do this, Curran." The confidence in Rune's eyes calmed him. Holding Willow tightly against him, he rested his forehead against hers. And pushed the golden energy around himself, outward. He felt a snap, and the air around them seemed to waver. Light flared bright. Falcon and Garrett shouted. The blinding light disappeared, and his vision returned to normal. Willow stirred in his arms, and he looked at Rune. Rune nodded once, a faint smile curving his lips and disappeared.

"It worked. I can see a Dark Elf shield around her mind. Let's get her back to the med bay. She needs medical attention." Dr. Aries helped Curran to his feet and reached to take back his patient. Curran shook his head. There was no fucking way he was letting go of Willow. The Doctor nodded and slid an arm around Curran. "Let's go."

Chapter Eighty-Nine

STAR DATE: 20580.10.30

Dimension Five
Farport City, Tryria

ASH STEPPED OUT OF the vortex that took him through dimensions, and shook out his wings, the deep obsidian color of the feathers absorbing rather than reflecting any light. He looked around the silent building and frowned. Normally, he was met by low-ranking officers who would immediately take him to whoever had made the appointment to see him. *It should not be this silent.* He drew his sword. His footsteps echoed through the corridor as he made his way to the area where he knew Commander D'miron was holding the prisoner. He'd been promised a fabled creature called an Energy Enchanter. D'miron better make good on his promise.

He turned the corner and paused. Several bodies lay scattered on the floor. He swept out his senses. They were all dead. Frowning, he crouched down by the first body. A young healthy looking male. The next body was a woman. He moved down the corridor stopping and checking each body. All had been healthy and young enough that it ruled out sudden onset medical conditions. There were no marks on the bodies so that appeared to rule out an enemy force. He cocked his head to the side as he looked back over the bodies. There were a myriad of species, which made sense. While the Suzerain were a small ambitious species, they readily brought in loyal followers to boost their numbers. And they used captured species for their ground wars. It was not uncommon for a member of a captured species to make their way up in the ranks, if they proved loyal and competent. He listened carefully for a moment then, sword in hand, continued down the corridor. By the time he got to the room he was looking for he had found thirty-six bodies and encountered no living being. Instead of opening the door he simply opened a vortex and stepped through into the room. A quick glance around showed him this was a torture chamber. A faint smile touched his lips. Crude but effective. He took a longer look around the room and scowled. Farren, one of the last of his V'ran, lay lifeless on the floor. He'd lent her to D'miron with strict orders to keep her alive. He looked around the room, his eyes hard. A group of six men lay close to each other, and his eyes lingered there as he studied them. These men were warriors in their prime, their hands bloodied as if they had been in a fight. There was blood on the floor and the wall but not enough to cause death for even one of them. He turned, and over by the door, he saw Commander D'miron. Walking over, he crouched down and heard a faint groan. "D'miron. Who did this to you?"

"En-" His voice faint, D'miron broke off and swallowed. "Energy..."

Ash frowned. "D'miron. Energy?"

"Enchanter." The man's voice was so quiet that Ash had to lean close to hear, and even then he was confused. "An Energy Enchanter did this? Killed all these people? I thought they were pacifists."

"Have to..." D'miron took a breath that seemed almost as faint as his voice. "Motivate them."

Ash stood and picked up D'miron, stepping through a vortex into the top hospital in the outer belt of the Bythian galaxy. Leaving D'miron with their top doctor, he walked out the door and soared up into the sky, going higher and higher until he was soaring among the stars. He could have opened a vortex that would take him anywhere through time and space that he wanted to go, but he needed to consider what he had seen and what D'miron had told him. He had to come up with a plan to capture as many Energy Enchanters as he could. He paused. Shit. Opening a vortex, he stepped out into the treatment room where the doctors were trying to save Commander D'miron's life. "D'miron. Where is the Energy Enchanter now?"

"Gone. But..." He took several breaths of the oxygen that he was hooked up to. "We will find her—she has killed."

Ash glared at D'miron with cold hard eyes. "So?"

"She will kill again— and again— and again."

Chapter Ninety

STAR DATE: 20580.11.02

Dimension Five
Realm of the Forsaken
Aezorwyn

WILLOW WOKE UP AND lay still feeling a difference in her energy. She wasn't on that horrible world anymore. And the memories came rushing back. Dreven, The Suzerain, Commander D'miron and the torture. A thousand images flooding her brain. Her breath seized, and she sat up bolt upright with a gasp, her hand lifting to her throat. Her body trembling, she fought the scream welling in her throat.

"Breathe." A hand clamped down on the nape of her neck. Curran. She knew that voice. Curran. More images tumbled through her mind. Each more terrifying than the last. *Oh gods, oh gods, oh gods.*

"Breathe!" Rough fingers tipping up her chin to meet his eyes. "Breathe, Willow."

The tightness in her throat eased and she rasped in a breath, then another one. "C-Curran." Tears spilled down her cheeks. "You're..." she lifted trembling fingers to touch his cheek, her wide eyes searching his face, "alive."

Curran laughed, "I am alive." His face grew serious. "Because of you." Willow tilted her head and touched gentle fingers to the bruises on his skin. "Because of me? I don't..." She frowned, drawing back as horror filled her. "I—" she swallowed, "I let the monster out. How are you alive, Curran? How am I alive?" Her voice shrill, hands shaking, she looked wildly around the room. "Where are we? Oh gods, please tell me you did not bring me back to Aezorwyn!" She snatched her hands away from Curran and scrambled to put distance between them, backing into the headboard of the bed and drawing her knees up.

Curran reached for her, shocked by her sudden panic.

"Don't touch me!"

"Willow, you're safe."

She shook her head, tears running down her cheek. "I'm not safe. I let the monster loose."

"You are safe, Willow. You are not the monster. I promise. Those bastards thought they could take advantage of your gentleness. They thought they could control you. They had no idea of the warrior you are. They underestimated you. You not only tore off their blinders and revealed what happens when the monster is awakened. You opened the Dimension of Shadows gates, and you hurled them into the middle of the fucking horror. If any of them survive, they will remember what the Dimension of Shadows looks like, and they will remember that it was a gentle Energy Enchanter who showed it to them." His hands gentle, he gathered Willow into his arms.

"I... I don't remember. I remember letting go when he ordered you to be killed."

"You're one scary assed heroine, Willow Solar-Nadiir."

"I should be dead." She swallowed. "Or worse."

Curran nodded. "You almost were. What do you think the chances are that the one person who knew how to save an Energy Enchanter, would be here, on Aezorwyn?"

Willow swiped at her tears. "Who?"

"Doctor Jase Aries. I don't believe in coincidence." Curran shook his head. "I seem to have had several encounters with Rune fucking Aezorwyn since we had our fight."

Willow gave a watery laugh. "I told you."

Curran groaned. "Don't be a smartass, Sh'arie."

Chapter Ninety-One

STAR DATE: 20580.11.21

Dimension Five
Realm of the Forsaken
Aezorwyn

WILLOW WALKED THROUGH the coolness of the forest, listening to the avians singing, and smiling as she caught an occasional glimpse of their brightly colored wings. She wondered if anyone had begun to name them yet. That was part of the challenge of settling a new world— naming all the lifeforms that inhabited it. She made a mental note to speak to Kailene and Gracen about it. There was a beautiful purple bird that sang sweetly in the castle gardens. She wouldn't mind working with them to come up with a name for it.

She stopped by a small brook and scooped some water up in her hand to drink. It was icily cold and refreshing. This was a good place to rest and have the snack she'd brought with her. She stood and walked over to sit under the broad boughs of a massive tree with delicate pink leaves. She smoothed her hand over the silvery bark and smiled at the velvety feeling. Everything was different here, from the bark of the trees to the lavender of the skies. It was exciting and astonishing but there were also times she longed for the familiarity of the coral skies of her home world, Kalyria.

She noticed a small delicate flower growing along the base of the tree and leaned forward to examine it. It's long slender stem and delicate, lacy, heart shaped, foliage was deep purple. The flower itself was a bright shade of green that glowed softly in the dim forest. This was one of the million times that she wished she had an imaging device. She reached into her pocket and pulled out a small notebook and pen, something she had learned from Curran to carry with her. Carefully, she drew the small plant, wishing with her whole heart that she had drawing skills. Finally satisfied with her sketch, she leaned in and smelled the flower. It had a spicy-fruity scent and she smelled it again, thinking it would make a wonderful perfume. She noted that along the side of the drawing, almost hearing Kailene asking what it smelled like.

Leaning back against the trunk of the tree, she took out her snack and ate it, while enjoying the view around her. A tiny rodent peered inquisitively at her from a large rock by the stream. Its big dark eyes and softly shaded blue fur ensured it would be well camouflaged in the blue grass that grew with such abundance in this world. She had heard the villagers refer to a blue rodent before. It was harmless but very curious. They called it the Sapphire Scaled Murinae, because of its blue color and its long-scaled tail. She smiled at finally having seen one for herself.

She finished her snack, and as she stood up, she noticed a bush of raspise berries. She really needed to get back to the castle, but the fruit tempted her. She walked over to the bush, plucked a berry and popped it into her mouth, humming her approval as its sweet flavour burst across her tongue. The bush was heavy with fruit, and she began to pick the berries, putting them into a pouch she created by gathering up the edges of her long skirt. Thoughts of berries and cream, and berry scones filled her mind, and she lost track of time as she worked, humming a song her mother had taught her as a child. Finally, her fingers stained from the delicate berries, she straightened her aching back, and chuckled as she saw the bulging skirt pouch. There would be lots of raspise berry treats for the castle this week.

A strange disturbance in the forest energy caught her attention and she paused. A second later, she heard a noise and she looked around. There it was again, a puff of breath and the sound of something almost metallic scraping over a rock. Her eyes widened and she turned slowly, her heart starting to hammer in her chest. Curran hadn't said anything about predators. Of course, she hadn't actually asked Curran about predators or told him about these walks she'd started taking.

There was an odd shimmer in the air about two meters in front of her and she took a step back, the thorns from the raspine bush burying themselves into her back and hips. She froze, ignoring the stinging pain as the shimmer began to solidify, she wanted to run but the only way was towards whatever was materializing in front of her, and she was not going near that. She glanced to the left, but the brook widened into a deep pool there. To the right was a huge boulder she would have to climb. She pushed back further against the bush, disregarding the pain from the thorns, clutching tightly to her skirt pouch. Between one blink and the next the creature became solid, and terror rushed up Willow's spine as her eyes traveled slowly up burnished amethyst scales, to finally meet the fierce golden gaze of a Dragon. Oh gods! oh gods! *Where was Rune when she needed him?* she thought frantically, as her brain skittered into survival mode. Time seemed to slow, and she could hear every pant of her breath, every insect buzzing around the flowers and bushes. Black horns grew back from the dragon's head, and she knew its snout was filled with deadly sharp teeth. *Did dragons eat people?*

A chuff sounded, and clear as a bell she heard a disgruntled female voice in her head. *"I'm not going to eat you. That would be a terrible example for my hatchlings."*

The air began to shimmer again and suddenly there were five little dragons sitting around the female dragon, their colors ranging from palest purple to a deep ruby red. Willow stared at the little dragons, with wide eyes, and back up at the mother. "I-" She had no idea what to say, she licked her lips and tried again. "I did not know there were Dragons on Aezorwyn. Curran didn't mention dragons."

A snort in her mind. *"Curran does not know about us."*

Willow swallowed. "He doesn't know?" Her voice was a squeak and she coughed trying to clear it.

"We have been watching."

"Watching? Watching who? Why are you watching?"

"Your mate has honor, as do the people he leads. You have honor." The dragon inclined her head in a gesture of respect. *"We have been the guardians of this world since its creation, and we have waited for the promised ones to arrive."*

"The promised ones? Do you mean the Dark Elves?"

The dragon inclined her head. *Dark Elves. Aezorwyn's promise. The bringers of light. A new era will arise, the darkness will end. But there will be much trouble first. We come to align ourselves with you. Bring your mate here, on the rising of the second moon. We would enter into an alliance with the King of the Dark Elves.*

The air shimmered again, and the dragons disappeared. A rush of wind and energy blew through the forest and Willow knew they were gone. A single amethyst scale lay gleaming on the ground. She picked it up consideringly and began her walk home, her heart slowly returning to its normal pace, even if she could not stop trembling.

Chapter Ninety-Two

STAR DATE: 20580.11.21
  Dimension Five
  Realm of the Forsaken
  Aezorwyn

HE FOUND HER ABOUT fifteen minutes after he'd started looking, and it was a fucking relief. The woman was going to be the death of him. He honestly needed to break her habit of disappearing without a word, and he needed her to talk to him more. Did she really not understand that he was fully aware of all her nightmares? Did she think that he did not understand that she was struggling and easily overwhelmed right now? He watched her walking deep in thought, her skirt held in a pouch to hold whatever she had collected on her walk. As he stepped into her path, he decided that a session in his playroom was in order. "Hello, Willow."

Willow jumped and gasped when Curran stepped out in front of her, almost losing her tight grip on her skirt full of berries. "Curran!"

He would have been amused, but she was frightened. Not surprised, frightened. Her hands were shaking, her color was pale, and her eyes had that look that spoke of something very wrong. "What's wrong, Willow?" He wrapped an arm around her waist and pulled her to him, even as he turned, his eyes seeking any danger. The woods were filled with Avian song and the chatter of an ice-blue bushy tailed Sciuridae as it ran up and down the trees searching for nuts and berries. No danger there. He glanced down at his mate. "What's frightened you so much?"

Willow blinked away the sudden rush of tears and held up the dragon scale, with a trembling hand. "I-" She swallowed. How did she begin to explain this? "There is something big in your forest." she finally whispered as he took the scale. "Do you believe in Dragons?"

Curran glanced at Willow sharply. "Dragons? Plural? As in more than one?"

Willow nodded, her eyes huge. "A mother and five hatchlings."

Curran rubbed his hand on her back, attempting to help her relax. She winced and he frowned, He'd felt something catch when he'd rubbed her back. He looked down at her back and frowned. "You seem to have encountered thorns, spitfire."

She nodded and looked a bit forlorn.

Curran smirked just the tiniest bit. "Is the Dragon gone?"

Willow nodded. "The scale is all that's left."

Curran tucked the scale into a pocket and turned his mate, so her back was to him. He quickly started unbuttoning the long dress she wore, and she gasped as her dress slipped down catching on her breasts for a moment before slipping down, her hands holding her skirt full of berries, she could do nothing. "Curran!"

He laughed at the shock in her voice. "I've got to get those thorns out, Sh'arie."

Willow paused at that name, and glanced over her shoulder at him, her eyes wide. Curran laughed again at the look on her face. "Thorns first."

Chapter Ninety-Three

STAR DATE: 20580.11.21
> Dimension Five
> Realm of the Forsaken
> Aezorwyn

REMOVING THE THORNS turned out to be much more complicated than either of them expected. Curran lost all his playfulness and got growly because he could not carry her without making things worse. Gripping her hand, they went directly to the med bay. In the end it took several of the medical staff working with tweezers to get all the thorns out and an antibiotic injection. By the time they were done all Willow wanted was a hot bath and a soft bed.

As Curran walked Willow upstairs, they stopped by the kitchen and Curran asked the staff to send up something to eat. In their room, Curran went directly into the washroom and started the large tub filling with water. When it was full, Willow was more than happy to soak. She heard the knock when the tray was brought up and heard Curran speaking to the maid. She finished washing her hair, climbed from the tub, and put on a soft nightgown that she'd brought into the bathroom with her. Walking out of the bathroom braiding her wet hair, she smiled seeing Curran had set up the table in front of the fireplace.

"We need an astronomer." Willow curled up on Curran's lap after their meal and they were looking out the window at the stars, as she pointed out different groupings.

Curran groaned. "Gods, Willow. Don't you dare tell me you know someone."

Willow laughed and snuggled into his embrace. "Ok. I won't tell you that. Tonight."

Curran growled. "I don't think you are up to a session in my playroom, Sh'arie."

"I've been thinking about this playroom business"

"Oh, you have, have you, Sh'arie."

Willow nodded. "Our playroom is not the solution to everything that comes up between us."

Curran looked down into Willow's upturned face. *What the shadows had just happened here?* "Our?"

Willow nodded. "Our playroom. I don't think you would have fun playing in it alone."

Curran's eyebrow rose. *What the fuck?* "Are you threatening me?"

Willow laughed and shook her head. "I'm having a conversation with you."

"Conversation." Curran narrowed his eyes. "And this conversation involves you deciding you have half ownership of my playroom, and you get to dictate if you will play with me?"

Willow fought to hide the smile trying to curve her lips. "Don't get me wrong, I happen to love it when you get all growly and carry me off to your lair of darkness. You have an amazing talent for giving me mind shattering orgasms."

Curran smirked and glared at her.

Nice touch, Willow thought, but shrugged and shook her head. "You know you do that dark intense thing really well. No wonder the ladies of Aezorwyn were falling all over themselves for you."

Scowling Curran said. "Not just the ladies of Aezorwyn."

Willow's bright laughter filled the room. "Poor Curran, now you just have me to use it on."

"I can see a spanking in your future."

"Not tonight, my bottom is already sore enough. Look Curran, I'm always going to do things to encourage you to carry me off and do bad things to me. But sex is not the answer to everything. Take today for example. When I first saw you, you looked like you wanted to talk to me about something." She looked at him. "I know we had the whole dragon thing come up, and the thorns." She ruefully rubbed her bottom. "But you never said you wanted to talk to me, instead you announced we were going to your playroom. Why?"

Curran frowned. "I need you to trust me."

"I do trust you, Curran. You know that."

"You haven't been talking to me about what is really going on with you since—" He cut his words off and stared at her. "I guess, I thought I could force you to talk to me." He met her eyes and noted her raised eyebrow. "Which is bullshit, isn't it?"

"Utter bullshit." She said solemnly. Sighing, she shook her head. "But you are correct, I've been avoiding talking to you about what's going on with me. So, let's start here."

She took a deep breath. "Since you rescued me from the Suzerain. You can say it. We can't avoid the subject no matter how much I want too."

"Since we rescued each other," Curran said quietly.

Willow smiled through the shadows that wanted to steal her soul. "Yes. Since we saved each other." She took a deep breath. "I know that I keep waking you up with my nightmares. I'm struggling right now, Curran. I killed people."

"You killed people who were trying to kill me. You saved me. You went against your own nature. You sacrificed yourself to save me." Curran's hand trembled when he stroked it through her hair. "Don't you ever do that again. I couldn't survive without you."

Willow blinked, her suddenly damp eyes. "Curran..."

"Willow, killing people is never easy. You can't shut me out. I know what that feels like. I know what it's like to believe that you're a monster. It's fucked up shit."

"I'm a healer, Curran. Me. With all this healing energy." Tears started to trail down her cheeks. "And I can't get it outta my head. I can't heal myself."

Curran wrapped his arms around her and pulled her into his chest. "It takes time to heal. You get your soul back by leaning on the people you love. This is not something you can heal by yourself. That's something you taught me. And maybe we never fully heal, Willow."

She pulled back and looked into his face.

"Maybe we always have scars on our souls." His dark brown eyes held hers. "But I do know that you are no monster. And I'm here for you."

Chapter Ninety-Four

STAR DATE: 20580.12.08

Dimension Five
Realm of the Forsaken
Aezorwyn

IT WAS THE NIGHT OF the rising of the second moon, and Willow, Curran, Falcon, Garrett and Marina were at the meeting place the female dragon had designated.

"Leave it to Curran to find a fucking real dragon," Falcon said as they took up their positions. "You know, Curran, I've been meaning to ask you a question. Where in the shadows did you find those wild blue women?"

Willow blinked. "They are Althanean's, Falcon." She scolded. "From another dimension."

Curran raised an eyebrow. "Willow is the dragon finder. As for Keanna and Nia, I was on a mission to seek out new allies and shifted into a dimension I'd never seen before. I was on a rough trader's world in a seedy bar, and this huge man with blue hair and pointed ears came in. There weren't many open tables so when he asked if he could join me. I agreed. Shadows, I was curious if there were some kind of Elves in that dimension as soon as I saw his ears. But nope.

The pointy ears and blue hair are a trait of a species from a planet called Sarisea. His name is Thorne Feral, and we got along well. The man is pure rebel." Curran laughed and shook his head. "He travels a dangerous path, skirting the edges of the law, and I'm not sure where he will fall in the end. He convinced me to go on a mission with him to save some slaves. Which is how I met Keanna and Nia. As for the Dragons. I've known of the existence of dragons since I met Keanna and Nia. They have both spoken about dragon warriors and the dragons on Althanea." I'm surprised there are any here on Aezorwyn, but we can chalk that up to our interfering Creator.

"Which Creator?" Marina asked.

"Rune Aezorwyn."

Marina hmmphed. "I wish it had been Eliana."

Curran, Garrett, and Falcon all turned to look at her. "Why?"

Marina shrugged, "Women are always more reasonable."

The men burst out laughing, and Marina shrugged again and exchanged a wry look with Willow.

"Here they come." Willow said as she sensed a disturbance in the energy of the forest. The air wavered, and dragons began to appear.

Curran decided that being surrounded by massive, dangerous beasts was one of his least favorite things. He stepped in front of Willow, crossed his arms, and set his feet apart eyeing the creatures. Seven. Seven Fucking dragons.

"*To be honest,*" the biggest dragon spoke easily into their minds, his black scales gleaming in the moonlight, "*Eliana is the one who brought us here, and she did it without telling her brother. She seemed a little irritated at the time and kept muttering about arrogant males and how they thought they could save the multiverse on their own."* The beast shrugged.

Willow laughed and stepped out from behind Curran. "Hi, I'm Willow Solar."

Curran scowled as his little red-haired mate. "Willow Solar-Nadiir." He looked at the dragons. "I'm Curran Nadiir, King of the Dark Elves, Willow is my mate. Falcon Keyan is my second in command, Garett Wyatt and Marina Anluan are the leaders of my Spirit Warrior teams." He ignored Garrett's raised eyebrow and Marina's growl. No, he hadn't had time to talk to them about their new titles yet. "Willow told me you wanted an alliance."

A green dragon chuffed his amusement with a rich joy that they all felt in their minds. *"Eliana is correct about the arrogance of men. Surprise Garrett and Marina. You know, I think I will enjoy this alliance."*

The amethyst dragon beside the green one snorted. *"As if you do not have your fair share of arrogance, Tythayn. I'm Ledyssa. I was the one who met with Willow. Thank you for meeting with us. Allow me to introduce The Aezorwyn Ruling Council of Dragons."* She nodded her head respectfully at the huge black dragon who had spoken first. *"Chy'zir. Guardian of the High Dragon."* She turned her head and nodded to the red dragon to Chy'zir's right. *"Eve'anah, Chy'zir's Lady, and Second to the High Dragon."* Her eyes settled on the green dragon again. *"Tythayn, Council member."* She nodded at a cerulean blue dragon, *"Sha'reynoryth, Council member."* Ledyssa nodded to a coral orange colored dragon. *"Mi'azia, is a council member as well.'* Finally, she nodded at the final remaining dragon, a massive bronze dragon. *"This is Khe'harys, he is the seventh member of the council."* She paused, and Chy'zir spoke up. *"Ledyssa is the High Dragon."*

Ledyssa stepped forward. *"Curran, King of the Dark Elves. We desire to align ourselves with you. The dragons on Aezorwyn number over a thousand. We have much knowledge of this planet and would be happy to share it with you. Our territory is in the high mountains far to the west of your village. We have much to speak of, would you join us for a feast?"*

Curran studied the group of dragons, before turning to his people. Willow met his eyes. "I read their energy. They mean us no harm. Falcon was studying the creatures, and finally he said. "I agree with Willow." Curran saw the surprise on her face, and he laughed. "Falcon has the best instincts about people that I've ever seen."

"I like Ledyssa. She seems straightforward." Marina said quietly and Garrett nodded. "I'd much rather have them as allies than enemies."

Curran turned back to the dragons. "We would be honored to join you."

Chapter Ninety-Five

STAR DATE: 20580.12.09

Dimension Five

Realm of the Forsaken

Aezorwyn

SHE FOUND CURRAN IN the castle garden, standing in the middle of the pretty stone folly that she loved. He was looking up at the night sky with a handheld telescope, a scowl on his handsome face. She walked over and set her hand on his back.

He lowered the telescope and looked at Willow. "I never told you that Rune Aezorwyn paid me a visit. Well, actually I've seen him a couple of times but," he paused, and his jaw tightened, "the first time was just after we had that fight. When I saw the wanted poster."

Willow nodded and moved closer. "Why did he come?"

Curran shrugged his shoulders and shook his head. "Because I was an idiot." He looked into the face of the woman he now knew was the other half of his soul. "I'm sorry, Willow. I should have trusted you. I should have been fucking smart enough to sit down and talk to you about that poster. Instead, I reacted. I behaved like a complete asshole. I'm pretty sure that I almost got my ass kicked by a Creator. Until that moment, I never believed they actually existed."

Willow smiled. "I sort of got that impression when I told you I had met him."

He shrugged again and ducked his head, a rueful expression on his face. "I admit he does exist." Lifting his head, he looked up at the dark expanse above them. "Doesn't mean that I'm going to forgive him."

Willow reached up and laid her hand against his jaw. "Rune is not against you Curran. He is not against the Dark Elves."

"I don't know what I believe in that regard Willow."

Willow nodded and slid her hand onto his. Looking up at the sky she pointed. "That's a really bright star."

Curran squeezed her hand gently, as he looked up at the star she was pointing too, remembering Rune's words to him. *"Only in darkness can you see the stars, Curran. And you are one of the brightest stars to ever light the heavens." He wasn't sure that he would ever believe that, but what he did know was that Willow was his bright star. His guiding light. In that, Rune was right. She shone for him.*

He tugged Willow around in front of him. He lifted his hand and stroked a strand of her bright hair back, his fingers lingering on the softness of her cheek. "You light the darkness for me, Willow. I don't think I could even see the stars if it was not for you. I love you. Will you marry me and become my Queen?"

Willow's eyes widened and she blinked. A smile lit up her face, and his heart stopped. Not because he was afraid, but because he could feel all her love pouring into him.

"Yes, Curran. I'll marry you. I love you. You think you are darkness, but I see you. I see your light."

"You forgot the Queen part."

Willow laughed. "I was hoping you wouldn't notice that."

"Ha. It's a package deal." He walked over to a small table she hadn't noticed in the shadows, and when he returned, he was carrying a delicate tiara that sparkled in the moonlight. Carefully, he placed it on her head. He knelt in front of her. "I, Curran Nadiir, King of the Dark Elves, pledge myself to you alone, Willow. You have my undying loyalty. I will stand by your side. I will protect you. I will fight for you and I will always love you. I need your light to guide me. I need your healing magic. I need your wisdom. I need you to show me the stars when I can't see them. You are my Queen."

Chapter Ninety-Six

STAR DATE: 20580.12.27
Dimension Five
Realm of the Forsaken
Aezorwyn

THE DAY DAWNED BRIGHT and beautiful, and Willow stood on the balcony watching the sun rise. The sky was awash in deep blues, oranges, yellows and soft pink. Curran had already been dragged off by Falcon, Garrett and Marina to get ready. A knock sounded at the door, and she went to answer it. Keanna, Maya, Kailene, Skylar, and Gracen stood on the other side. Some of them held trays of food and drink, and some had flowers freshly cut from the castle gardens. She stepped back and they came in.

"Have you eaten?" Kailene asked, and Willow shook her head.

"Too nervous."

Keanna laughed. "You have nothing to be nervous about, Willow. You have Curran wrapped securely around your heart, and you will be an amazing Queen."

Willow took a shaky breath and bit her lip. "The whole queen thing scares the shadows out of me."

Skylar nodded. "I can understand that, but how about we start with tea and something to eat."

The next couple hours were spent laughing, talking and changing into the beautiful ivory and gold gown that Keanna and her assistants had spent the last weeks working on. She felt like a princess from the ancient legends of King Author's court. The golden chain of the girdle wrapped around her hips and draped down the front of the long skirt. The sleeves were long and flowing, the top bared her shoulders, and the neckline was a vee that hinted of cleavage. Keanna set a wreath of flowers on her head and adjusted the gossamer thin veil that trailed down her back to the floor.

Willow took a deep breath when they asked if she was ready, and she nodded.

Curran was standing in the center of the stone folly, impatiently waiting for Willow. Falcon stood by his side, with Garrett and Marina standing to Falcon's right. Music began to play, and he turned to see his bride. He swallowed. Gods, she took his breath away. She made the walk to him followed by her ladies and he couldn't take his eyes off her the whole time. When she finally reached him, he took her hands and tugged her into his arms—kissing her until Falcon elbowed him hard in the ribs. Breaking the kiss, he scowled at his friend before looking back into Willow's bright blue eyes. "Ready?"

Willow nodded and smiled at him. They turned to face each other, and Anwen smiled as she took her place. She looked out over all the people of Aezorwyn. It was a good day. "Curran and Willow have asked me to unite them in marriage and to speak the promises and blessings of a new life together and the oaths of coronation. Do you bear witness to the King's chosen bride?"

The air filled with a resounding "Yes!" As the last of the Dark Elf people spoke in unity.

Curran smiled down into Willow's beautiful eyes. "The moment I laid eyes on you, I knew you were going to be trouble. I've always had a thing for trouble." He winked at her, and people laughed softly. "You changed everything, Willow. And though I am furious with the Creator, Rune, I thank him for bringing you to me."

"You're welcome" a deep voice filled with the mysteries of the universe spoke and Rune Aezorwyn appeared with his sister Eliana, beside Anwen. Eliana shook her head, her long hair shimmering with multiple colors in the sunlight.

Curran growled and Willow smiled. "When I first saw you, Curran, I knew you were dangerous. Yet I couldn't walk away. If I were in the same situation over again, knowing everything I know now, I would run to you."

Anwen smiled and looked at the two Creators standing beside her. "Do you wish to take over?"

Eliana smiled. "No. We are only here to observe. My brother just likes to make an entrance." They both disappeared and reappeared in the midst of the Dark Elf people.

"Curran, do you promise to love only Willow? Do you promise to protect her above all others? Do you promise to speak honestly with her and to hold no secrets from her?" Anwen spoke the promises seriously, her eyes intently watching Curran.

"I promise," Curran said.

"Willow, do you promise to love only Curran? Do you promise to protect him above all others? Do you promise to speak honestly with him and to hold no secrets from him?" Anwen watched Willow as she spoke.

"I promise," Willow said.

Anwen smiled and looked at Eliana and Rune. "Did they speak true?"

Eliana smiled and nodded. "They did."

"I witness the promises made and the truth of their words." Rune said with a wicked smile on his lips.

Anwen looked at Curran and Willow. "You are one. Remember your promises. They are the most important oaths you will ever make."

Curran pulled Willow into his embrace and kissed her. The Dark Elf people erupted into cheers and flower petals rained down.

When Curran ended the kiss, Willow turned and looked at everyone who had gathered to celebrate with them. It was overwhelming to see the joy on their faces. She smiled and looked at Curran.

Anwen spoke up. "Let us begin the coronation ceremony."

Curran turned and led Willow to a small table, where Anwen joined them. "Curran, King of the Dark Elves, you have brought before your people the woman you are mated to."

Curran nodded. "I ask that the Dark Elves recognize Willow Solar-Nadiir as their Queen."

Anwen looked over at the people. "Dark Elves, do you recognize Willow Solar-Nadiir as your Queen."

Another resounding "Yes!"

"Willow, the Dark Elf people recognize you as their Queen. Speak these oaths with the understanding that, if you fail in your oaths, the sentence is death."

"Willow, do you swear to do everything in your power to protect the Dark Elf people from their enemies?"

"I swear on my life to protect my people, the Dark Elves of Aezorwyn, from their enemies."

Do you swear that the enemies of the Dark Elf people are your enemies as well?

"I swear on my life that any enemy of the Dark Elves of Aezorwyn, is my enemy."

Do you swear to always look out for the good of the Dark Elf people?

"I swear on my life to do everything in my power to bring good to the Dark Elves of Aezorwyn."

"Curran, do you bear witness that your mate has spoken truth?"

Curran nodded. "I bear witness. Willow has spoken true."

Anwen smiled and looked at Eliana and Rune. "Did Willow speak true?"

Eliana nodded. "She did."

"I witness the promises made and the truth of Willow's words," Rune said an extremely satisfied look on his face.

Anwen opened a wooden box and took out a feminine version of Curran's crown and handed it to him. He took the crown and turned to Willow. "Before the Dark Elves of Aezorwyn, I crown you Queen Willow Soriya Solar-Nadi-ir." He eased the crown on her head, adjusting it so the deep green jewel rested against her forehead. "Gorgeous." He leaned down and kissed her.

Epilogue

DIMENSION FIVE

CAPTAIN ALEK TEMPEST stepped into the tavern, a slender woman in black leather, her blue eyes taking in the dimly lit interior in one glance. It was a busy night. The ale flowed and music played. Just what she'd hoped for. It was easy to be lost in a crowd. She walked over to the table she'd been told would be the meeting place in the transmission she'd been sent. The table was empty, and she didn't like that. Her hand went to the pistol strapped to her hip. Being first to arrive was a dangerous situation. She preferred to be able to watch the clientele's face as she approached. You could tell a lot about a person from their eyes. She looked around, noting the exits, before sitting down and tapping the tabletop. A menu appeared. She looked around again, glanced at the menu, and tapped her selection. The menu disappeared and she sat back, her eyes again traveling over the crowd.

The server brought a glass of teal colored ale and a basket of crisp salty bano quadrates. Captain Tempest raised an eyebrow. She hadn't ordered anything to eat. The server met her eyes before turning to attend another table. That was interesting. She eyed the basket of salty but nutritious snacks. Using a small palm sized scanner, she scanned the food. It was safe. She shrugged, helped herself to one, and took a sip of her ale. Several bano quadrates later she knew why the server had given her that look. Carefully she eased the message from the basket with another quadrate, being sure to keep it hidden.

Sitting back in the booth she took another sip of her ale and glanced down at the message. *Procure the services of the prostitute Lady Anaïs for the night.* She read. *Lady Anaïs is going to be in for a surprise.* She smirked and shrugged. *She could go either way, so it was no skin off her back. But for the night? Not for an hour? Fuck.* She wasn't made of credits. Well, actually, her credit accounts were full, but still, a whole night with a lady of the evening was expensive. And she'd bet there was no chance she was actually going to get to enjoy the services of this Lady Anaïs. The person she was meeting was a wily son of a bitch. Alek finished her ale and stood up, she walked over to the entrance to the pleasure rooms and winced as she paid out the required fee. There was a certain irony to paying for the pleasure of meeting a contact that could lead to her own capture or death. Wily son of a bitch.

Lady Anaïs was a beautiful blonde with large green eyes and a killer figure. Alek's clit throbbed, instantly reminding her that it had been a shadows eternity since anything had been snugged deep inside her pussy. She gave Lady Anaïs a crooked grin and thought maybe after she met that contact, she would put the rest of the night she'd paid for to good use. When the lovely Lady Anaïs turned and led her down the corridor to her room she gave a silent whistle. Now that was an ass.

Lady Anaïs put her hand to the scanner and Alek instantly became all business, her senses alert. She put her hand up to the scanner and smiled, the device would record that Jinn Starmen had entered, thanks to the micro thin layer of dermal enhancer she'd applied. From the moment she'd entered this establishment, every recording, every transaction showed her to be Jinn Starmen, a simple crew member of one of the hundreds of transport ships that frequented this planet.

They stepped into the room and the lights came on. Two men were waiting. Alek watched as Lady Anaïs went to the men and turned to introduce them. "This is the Hunter." Alek's eyes met the tall dark-haired man and nodded once. She'd done her research before coming to this meeting. She knew who both men were... well, she modified that thought... she knew of their reputations and exactly how dangerous they were. The Hunter and Jericho Solar. Two dangerous men and very unlikely allies. What the shadows was The Hunter doing in the company of a former Suzerain killing machine.

She wondered which one of these men would die after this meeting, and she had no doubt that one of them would. What the shadows kind of game was this? "Interesting company you're keeping."

The Hunter leaned against the wall and shrugged. "Did you bring the cargo?"

Alek nodded. "I've got what you asked for. Did you bring the credits?"

"We'll conduct our business after you're done with Solar."

Alek looked at the other man. "What can I do for you, Solar?"

Jericho silently handed Captain Tempest a holographic wanted poster and ignored the woman's low whistle of appreciation, as he pulled out his slim palm computer and transferred an astronomical sum of credits into the Space Pirate's accounts. "Find her. Betray me, and I'll kill you." Alek looked at him with cold eyes, and Jericho didn't care. He knew that Tempest wasn't someone to fuck with. Neither was he. If the space pirate was half as intelligent as it was rumored, she would have done her research before meeting him. Captain Alek Tempest knew exactly what Jericho was. Just as he knew exactly what Tempest was. If anyone could find Willow Solar, it was this space pirate. Jericho watched the woman, the only thing he didn't know was if he would have to kill her when he'd retrieved Willow. The less witnesses the better. There were already too many witnesses to this transaction. With an abrupt nod to the man who called himself The Hunter, he turned and walked out of the room.

Alek watched Solar leave and thought the man was pretty fucking presumptuous. She turned her gaze on The Hunter and Lady Anaïs. "You seem to be playing a dangerous game, Hunter. Solar is with the Suzerain."

The Hunter shrugged. "Solar is not your concern, Captain Tempest. Where is the cargo?"

"You know the deal, Hunter. The cargo is delivered when the credits hit my account, and not one second before. We've done this exchange often enough that you know the drill." Alek glanced over at the beautiful woman and back at The

Hunter. "You seem to have brought a lot of company to our meeting."

"Lady Anaïs, is one of mine."

"But not Solar?"

The Hunter snorted. "You are not listening, Captain Tempest. Solar is not your concern."

"The shadows he's not. He just put a million credits into my account to find a woman. A woman with the same last name as him. His wife? His sister? I'm not a bloody private detective. I'm a fucking... she paused and gave The Hunter a grim look. "Merchant... and I don't sell people."

The Hunter laughed. "You're a fucking pirate, Captain Tempest. What difference does it make if you deal in weapons or Solar's sister?"

Alek thrust the holographic wanted poster that Solar had given her into The Hunters face. "Because the Suzerain are looking for her too. This is no simple retrieval mission."

The Hunter took the wanted poster and looked at it. "The Suzerain, Jericho Solar and The Hunter, all looking for the same woman. Makes you think, doesn't it."

Alek stilled and looked at The Hunter. "What?"

"I've transferred 2 million credits into your account for the weapons, and another 2 million for the woman. We'll take care of Solar. You just bring the woman to me when you've found her."

Both of them touched their comm units in the same instant as a computer voice informed them that the deal had been completed. Payment had been received and the cargo delivered.

"Nice doing business with you, Captain Tempest." The Hunter nodded and walked out of the room.

Alek regarded the blonde woman who remained behind. She was furious. Fuck. She had been well and truly fucked over by those two men, and Lady Anaïs was somehow connected to it. She reached out and dragged the woman up against her. Lady Anaïs gave a breathy laugh and Alek's mouth was on hers. Her hands stripping Lady Anaïs' clothes away. Lady Anaïs' hands were just as busy tugging at Alek's shirt. She shrugged out of her shirt, backed Lady Anaïs to the bed and pushed her down on it. Lady Anaïs was glorious, with her long blonde hair and bare pussy. Her breasts were firm but a bit on the small side. She mentally shrugged. No one was perfect. She knelt one knee on the bed and grabbed her playmate's ankle and flipped her on her stomach. That ass was amazing. "On your knees." She growled as she walked over to the dispenser and punched in the requisite code for a big purple strap on dick.

SHE WAS WHISTLING WHEN she stepped into the airlock of her ship. The ship's computer reminded her that she was running late, and she laughed. Yeah, she was late. Worth it. Lady Anaïs was a hard core submissive and the things she'd let Alek do would linger in her memories for a shadow's eternity. Especially when she was weeks out into the middle of space with only her own fingers to relieve herself.

She sat down and began to tap the command screen as the engines fired up. Time for her to get back to work.

Her ship rocketed away from the planet and hit hyper warp speed, taking her thousands of parsecs away in a few seconds.

"Incoming message, Captain." The computer voice broke the silence. "It's heavily encrypted. Unknown origin."

Captain Tempest frowned. "Play it."

There was a brief silence then a woman's voice filled the airways. "Entering the Sol system. Target: Planet Earth. The nightmare continues. Assistance required. Vital that message reaches the highest level. Starforge out"

Alek's head came up, and the look in her eyes grew hard. "Acknowledged Starforge. Delivery highest priority. Darkstar out."

The End

The story continues...

Next Book

The Codes of Creation Multiverse: Mystic Havyn Dimensions Series: Book 1

The Ways Of Light

Coming Soon

You can find me at:
https://www.arliesheelin.com[1]
https://www.facebook.com/pursuingdreams.ca
https://www.instagram.com/arlie_sheelin/
https://twitter.com/ArlieSheelin
https://www.patreon.com/arliesheelin
I'm also on TikTok @arliesheelin_author

---

1. https://www.arliesheelin.com/

Glossary

CACHE: Hidden storage places

Creators: Beings who exist out of time and space. The last two surviving Creators, created the Multiverse

Com device: A communication device similar to a tablet or smartphone.

Com mail: Similar to Email with the added ability to have holographic or audio messages

The Dimension of Shadows: A place of near insanity, where nothing is real or what you thought it was. It's a place of torment and horror. It is a place of eternal punishment for those who have turned to a life of darkness and evil.

Various swear words are used in conjunction with this place of horror.

- Dimension of Shadows
- Shadows
- As hardy as the **shadow monsters** that inhabited the bowels of the Dimension of Shadows
- Shadow trap (Hellhole)
- Shadow archives/ Shadow warehouse/ shadows hoard (a helluva a lot)
- Exchanging one Dimension of Shadows for the next. (Exchanging one hell for the next)
- Shadow's eternity (helluva long time)

Elemental abilities: The ability to sense water, the ability to call a small flame to their hand, the strange ability to move the air into a slight breeze and terrakinesis (the ability to manipulate earth elements. Stone, dirt, sand, wood, metal etc.)

Energy Enchanter: A rare being who cycles the energy of a planet through themselves, creating a richer, more diverse, more resilient environment and people. They are soul healers

Energy Manipulator: A being who has the ability to drain a planet of its energy as long as he can channel that energy into something else

Godsdamned: A common swear word throughout the multiverse. There are two Creators, so this particular expression is plural

Ghost Universal Space Tracker: Also known as G.U.S.T. Created by the resistance, it is a tracking program that is not detectable to most computer systems. Curran had it secretly installed on all his ships as a backup system in case one of his ships went missing

Hologram Technology: Holograms are three-dimensional images generated by interfering beams of light that reflect real, physical objects

Holovid chips, Holo-cubes, holo-pyramids: Devices that record and store information in holographic form

Holo emitters: A tiny device (often an earring), designed by the resistance, that creates a nearly flawless holographic mask that changes a person's appearance

Hyper warp drive: Hyper warp drive combines the ideas of hyperdrive and warp drive

- **Hyperdrive** (Star Wars) is a fictional propulsion system that enables a starship to travel at lightspeed and cross the empty space between star systems using an alternate dimension of hyperspace
- **Warp drive** (Star Trek) is a fictional technology that enables space travel at faster-than-light speeds. The idea behind Warp drive is to create warp fields that form a subspace bubble surrounding a spaceship. The subspace bubble distorts the section of the spacetime continuum around the spaceship (rather like folding space), and results in the ship being able to travel at velocities that would exceed the speed of light. (Warp Drive is thought to be theoretically possible in the real world.)
- **Hyper warp drive** is the idea that a

spaceship could enter hyperspace and while in that dimensional highway they could generate a subspace bubble. The results being an even faster way to travel between star systems, and galaxies.

- **Hyper warp speed** is simply a variation of the name hyper warp drive.

Laser Pistol/Phase Pistol/Blaster:

Space age weaponry similar in appearance to a gun or rifle that uses a particle beam of intense plasma energy instead of bullets.

Laser Sword: Space age weaponry similar in appearance to a sword, often with a laser beam instead of a blade.

In-between: The in-between is the place where the creators existed. It is a place out of time and space, existing between nothingness and the Multiverse.

Invisibility Glamour or Invisibility Cloak: The ability to become invisible. A new magical skill that the Dark Elves acquired on the

planet Aezorwyn. They use it to protect themselves when they are on other planets. This skillset occasionally fails.

Millennia: The plural form of millennium. A period of a thousand years.

Multiverse: A multidimensional universe.

Spirit Warriors: A specialized unit of the Dark Elf Military. They undertook the riskiest missions.

The Sacred Stardust Chalice: A mystical healing chalice made from an ancient meteorite embedded with stardust.

Translator: A highly advanced device that translates foreign languages into the language of the person using it. It is normally an implant.

Acknowledgements

THE CREATION OF THIS book would not have been possible without these people. They have contributed a lot on this crazy journey. Thank you for your steadfastness, and your belief in me.

To my beta readers and my cover review team: Brandy, Andrea, Cara, Ann, Michaele, Johannes, and Dirk. Thank you for your patience and eagle eyes. My books are made better by your skills and the conversations we have had about this story. I cannot thank you enough for your time and willingness to help with this story.

A special thank you to Filip and Ann for the help with my blurb. I'm positive my writer's brain is not naturally geared towards summing up a whole book into two hundred words. Ann, you have a magic touch when it comes to clearly bringing out the important details.

To my editor Dennis Doty, who has had infinite patience with the delays involved with this story. Your mentorship, and friendship has been a light when I have been very discouraged with the twists and turns that kept showing up. Thank you for so clearly believing in me.

Don't miss out!

Visit the website below and you can sign up to receive emails whenever Arlie Sheelin publishes a new book. There's no charge and no obligation.

https://books2read.com/r/B-A-SLWO-XAPRB

BOOKS2READ

Connecting independent readers to independent writers.

Also by Arlie Sheelin

Codes of Creation - Realm of The Forsaken
Forsaken

Mystic Haven Dimensions
The Ways of Light

The Codes of Creation - The Zemyneah Experiment
The Way Maker

Watch for more at https://www.arliesheelin.com/.

About the Author

Writer, introvert, and a bit of a geek. **Favorite Authors:** Nalini Singh, Angela Knight, Sandra Hill, and Louis L'amour. I've raised my kids on a steady diet of **Star Trek** *and* **Star Wars,** which resulted in *them taking me* to sci-fi/cosplay conventions. Bonus points! I'm also an Indie RP writer - which means I write short story fiction online as some of my favorite characters. My drink of choice is tea, Earl Grey, or Chai. But on cold days, I go for Hot Chocolate with the odd venture into Peppermint Mocha. Caffeine is the magic elixir that helps fuel the imagination. I have a New Media Production and Design Diploma. - Which is a fancy way of saying I have creative skills with computers, mainly graphics.

Read more at https://www.arliesheelin.com/.